Stevie Smith

Stevie Smith

Between the Lines

Romana Huk

© Romana Huk 2005

All rights reserved. No reproduction, copy or transmission of this publication may be made without written permission.

No paragraph of this publication may be reproduced, copied or transmitted save with written permission or in accordance with the provisions of the Copyright, Designs and Patents Act 1988, or under the terms of any licence permitting limited copying issued by the Copyright Licensing Agency, 90 Tottenham Court Road, London W1T 4LP.

Any person who does any unauthorised act in relation to this publication may be liable to criminal prosecution and civil claims for damages.

The author has asserted her right to be identified as the author of this work in accordance with the Copyright, Designs and Patents Act 1988.

First published 2005 by
PALGRAVE MACMILLAN
Houndmills, Basingstoke, Hampshire RG21 6XS and
175 Fifth Avenue, New York, N.Y. 10010
Companies and representatives throughout the world

PALGRAVE MACMILLAN is the global academic imprint of the Palgrave Macmillan division of St. Martin's Press, LLC and of Palgrave Macmillan Ltd. Macmillan® is a registered trademark in the United States, United Kingdom and other countries. Palgrave is a registered trademark in the European Union and other countries.

ISBN 0-333-54997-X hardback

This book is printed on paper suitable for recycling and made from fully managed and sustained forest sources.

A catalogue record for this book is available from the British Library.

Library of Congress Cataloging-in-Publication Data
Huk, Romana, 1959–
  Stevie Smith : between the lines / by Romana Huk.
    p. cm.
  Includes bibliographical references and index.
  ISBN 0-333-54997-X (cloth)
  1. Smith, Stevie, 1902–1971—Criticism and interpretation. 2. Women and literature—England—History—20th century. I. Title.

PR6037.M43Z697 2005
828'.91209—dc22
                                              2004054896

10 9 8 7 6 5 4 3 2 1
14 13 12 11 10 09 08 07 06 05

Printed and bound in Great Britain by
Antony Rowe Ltd, Chippenham and Eastbourne

For Peter

Contents

Acknowledgements viii

List of Abbreviations ix

1 Between the Lines: Re-reading Stevie Smith and Literary Modernism 1

2 'The times are the times of a black split heart': Stevie Smith's Life and Work in Context 31

3 The Trilogy's Take-off in the Thirties: A Close-Cultural Reading of *Novel on Yellow Paper* 69

4 Framing the War: The Second Two Novels of the Trilogy 132

5 Between Waving and Drowning: Stevie Smith's Poems, Stories and Radio Play 215

Notes 296

Works Cited 318

Index 326

Acknowledgements

All drawings and poetry quoted are from *The Collected Poems of Stevie Smith*, copyright © 1972 by Stevie Smith. Used by kind permission of New Directions Publishing Corporation.

All prose quoted is from *Novel on Yellow Paper* (1980), *Over the Frontier* (1980), and *The Holiday* (1979) and from *Me Again: Uncollected Writings of Stevie Smith* (Jack Barbera and William McBrien, eds, 1981). All prose by Stevie Smith is reproduced by kind permission of the Estate of James MacGibbon.

'Rejoinder to a Critic' by Donald Davie is from *Selected Poems* by Donald Davie (1985). Used by permission of Carcanet Press Limited.

Every effort has been made by the author and publishers to secure permissions for all relevant works, and if any have been missed we will be happy to rectify the situation at the earliest opportunity.

I wish to thank the University of New Hampshire for the sabbatical that allowed me to begin this work. I also wish to thank Lynn McCormack, Administrative Assistant to the Chair of the Department of English, University of Notre Dame, for her help in reproducing the images of Smith's drawings, and Jessica Ritter-Holland for her help in translating German passages and lines in Smith's writings.

List of Abbreviations

The following abbreviations will be used for frequently cited books. References to primary works also appear in abbreviated form in the text. Please see *Works Cited* for details.

CP	*The Collected Poems of Stevie Smith*
ISOSS	*In Search of Stevie Smith*, Sanford Sternlicht, ed.
MA	*Me Again: Uncollected Writings of Stevie Smith*, Jack Barbera and William McBrien, eds
NOYP	*Novel on Yellow Paper*
OTF	*Over the Frontier*
S	*Stevie: A Biography of Stevie Smith*, Jack Barbera and William McBrien
SS	*Stevie Smith*, Sanford Sternlicht
SS: AB	*Stevie Smith: A Biography*, Frances Spalding
SS: AS	*Stevie Smith: A Selection*, Hermione Lee, ed.
TH	*The Holiday*

1
Introduction
Between the Lines: Re-reading Stevie Smith and Literary Modernism

Perhaps the only statement with which all of her critics would agree is that from 1934, when she first attempted to publish, to the present day, more than thirty years after her acceptance of the Queen's Gold Medal for Poetry and her death shortly thereafter, Stevie Smith has most often been classified as an enigma. Her tragicomic poems have dumbfounded her admirers as well as her detractors with their seemingly simple speaking voices infiltrated by the orientations of competing, incongruent discourses that interfere with her often quite traditional poetic forms. She 'writes so differently from everyone else', as Muriel Spark once put it, that influential contemporaries like Philip Larkin pronounced her 'almost unclassifiable', agreeing with others, like Seamus Heaney, that she finally must be called 'eccentric'.[1] '"Eccentric" and "quirky"', as Jeni Couzyn has noted, are the words 'most frequently applied to her poems by baffled reviewers', both male and female (37). Such labels have worked to isolate her, as well as inspire primarily biographical studies in search of the 'real' Smith – the one behind what Heaney referred to as the 'memorable voice', a voice that in her highly performative work seems to be constantly reciting or set upon a ventriloquist's knee. For many years this critical tradition, in its determination to read her writings as either pure or covert ('fausse-naive', in Larkin's review[2]) self-expression or revelation, caused critics to overlook the prescient critique of unmediated subjectivity which lies at the very heart of her work. Only by deconstructing a word like 'eccentric' with the tools of feminist theory did her readers become able to read it as *ex-centric*: a liminal position in society and language most famously described by Virginia Woolf and shared by other female modernists in England; such positions often produce fractured sightings of the self in the shadow of ascendant cultural forces even as both conspire in the construction of identity. Viewed from this angle, the works of a number of unread or misread writers were drawn into illuminating new relationships, which provided a starting-point for re-reading Stevie Smith. But it was only a starting-point – much remains to be done.

The tradition of re-reading

Such angles of approach demonstrated an unmistakably 'postmodern' perspective, and perhaps justifiably so, given that numerous key studies written in the last two decades of the twentieth century prompted our recognition that many female modernists – Smith among them – exhibited what would now be considered postmodern sensibilities. As feminist theorists like Janet Wolff and Patricia Waugh then began to argue, the same mainstream (meaning male) modernist critique of Victorian conventionalities that prompted the quest for new ways to capture the era's revised model of consciousness in writing ironically led many increasingly 'liberated' women to revelations of their own particular sort of *entrapment* within language – their construction, in other words, by dominating socio-literary discourses and representations of femininity. If the word 'modernism' summons, for most of us, images of radical, purgative, sweeping new visions of reality, new art forms to accommodate them, and crossed continental frontiers leading to heady cosmopolitan perspectives, it leaves out a critical range of female responses that rocked the assumption of such revolutionary freedoms by focussing on culturally constructed, internal barriers to vision, and the inherent limitations of their linguistic medium – responses we now characterise as '*post*modern'. Shari Benstock and the essayists in *Women's Writing in Exile* (1989) likened the female modernist's situation to that of the period's most paradigmatic one, expatriation; but they relocated it in her case across *internal* boundaries. In other words, they positioned her between 'patria's' rejected discursive positionings for her – spaces in language where she could speak only in the modes allowed by culture: that of wife, mother, supporter of the arts and similarly subordinate roles – and, on the other side of that internal divide, unmapped regions full of newly sensed but unarticulated, 'other' desires (Benstock 25). From her disempowered position both within and without, the leap into modernism looked more difficult, the steps towards it longer and over internal ground.

From such new perspectives it looked more and more as though the problem had to be, at its most fundamental level, one of language. As the tool through which identity is constructed, it is for the marginalised in culture both inescapable and inhospitable, promoting certain kinds of imaginings and expression while not providing for others. For the woman writer, literary tradition sets out additional delimitations by 'remembering' only those writings it erects, like Eliot's metaphorical monuments, as markers alongside or against which aspiring writers must define themselves.[3] But unlike many male modernists – Ezra Pound, James Joyce, D.H. Lawrence and T.S. Eliot, for example – who constructed their new art identities and epic versions of the history of consciousness by connecting themselves to selected precursors in classical Greek and (European) Renaissance literary traditions, female modernists, unable to locate themselves in any but the most fragmentary of golden age precedents, tended to question the universalising voices of that legacy, especially given the absences it left.[4] Their complicity as legatees of that tradition apparently created yet another kind of internal debate for many of them, as Rachel Blau DuPlessis wrote in 1985, 'between the critic and the inheritor, the outsider and the privileged, the oppositional and the dominant' (DuPlessis 41). Because they were never (and never can be) fully in control of the processes that dictate their positioning, DuPlessis went on to say, 'women's loyalties to dominance remain ambiguous'. Therefore, though they may have whole-heartedly embraced their new roles as what Virginia Woolf in *Three Guineas* famously described as radical 'outsiders', their 'use of language itself', Renate Voris wrote in 1986, 'may reinscribe the very structure by which woman is oppressed' (236–37).

It has now been variously argued that this kind of self-consciousness with regard to their medium and identity was altogether different from the self-reflexive (and ultimately self-empowering) foregrounding of device, and the artist's-eye-view, in canonical modern art. Its critique issues from a different position – not the transcendent one, whose detached vision, or 'impersonality' by Eliot's notorious definition, allows it to arrange and shape the untidy materials of life within new meaningful forms, but rather the position of entrapment, of rebellion from between the lines. Epitomised for some in the micro-linguistic deconstructions of Gertrude Stein, and for me in the more self-implicating deconstructions of English discourse as conducted by Smith, such revised perceptions of selfhood as being simultaneously constructed, complicitous and victimised permeate many women's texts to pluralise any ideological positioning for the speaking subjectivity, and thus produce writings marked by struggle. As Patricia Waugh has suggested, their modernist texts cannot, therefore, be read according to the era's dominating New Critical aesthetic, which called for visionary unity and autonomy – evidence of the 'transcendental ego' of the writer operant in its conception of the all-but-deified impersonality of art. Judged against the latter's standards, women's texts either went unpublished or were, in the end, found wanting. It has been the work of late-twentieth-century feminist criticism by both female and male scholars to re-read such texts for their *differences* rather than for their failings, as well as demonstrate that in many cases, as Elizabeth Hirsh argued in 1989, modernist women were engaged in a critique of 'the very standards which they have been held to epitomise' (15).

As the 'eccentric', Stevie Smith has never been characterised as the epitome of any trend or standard. She has, however, because she often wrote in discernible forms, or to ballad and hymn tunes, been considered an apologist for English/Anglican tradition; and she *has*, in her time and beyond it, been variously described as a Blakian Romantic, an Arnoldian Victorian, a royalist conservative, an Orwellian radical, an admirer of Eliotic 'impersonality', a confessional would-be suicide, a religious poet, an anti-Semitic writer, a popular balladeer, an anti-feminist, a proto-feminist.[5] But what her critics failed for years to consider is that the target of Smith's critique may be such positions and 'lines' themselves – or, more specifically, the collusion and contradictions they disclose when they encounter others inherent in her complex rhetorical environment. The 'peculiar', multi-vocal effects of her work, as Hermione Lee and others have called them (Lee 22), open up to new interpretation when we realise that *all* and *none* of these voices are her own. In other words, Smith's poems and novels were, quite early on in the century, taking part in what literary studies considers a postmodern project: deconstructing the traditional concept of a 'closed, fixed, rational and volitional self' by displaying her own composition by the many social, historical, philosophical, theological and literary discourses which, from her position of well-read 'ex-centricity' and partial (gendered, classed) exile, she perceives operating both within herself and at the heart of culture (Nussbaum 33). Postmodern theory has investigated the ways in which the very desire to believe in personal or individual integrity, self-determinative power and the 'agency to express and know and regulate oneself' enhances one's subjection to those economic and political pressures that limit expression; 'in order to preserve the existing subject positions', as Felicity Nussbaum wrote in 1989, 'individual subjects are discouraged from attending to the ways in which the discourses are incongruent' (34). Quite inadvertently, Smith's critics have for years participated in that discouragement by similarly not attending to what her work was actually doing. The wildly diverging readings of who she *really* was by social/political/aesthetic allegiance, as I referred to them above, are the product of her readers' picking out only one discursive strain to foreground from her mix of them in order to produce highly suspect sorts of critical judgements, usually in reflection of their own preferred ideological stances or critical prejudices. By foregrounding the *incongruence* of discourses in her work instead – a constant feature of what many critics have vaguely described as her uncomfortable, asymmetrical verse and shifty, narrational voice – Smith engages in the most potent political critique a writer can conduct: the exposition of covert ideologies struggling for dominance through language, and her own subjection to their influences despite her many strategies for resistance.

Therefore, for current women's studies critics to err now in the opposite extreme and claim that figures like Smith could *always* successfully resist incorporation through such 'antics' is, ironically, to effect a *modernist* reading in postmodernist clothing, casting the writing subject once again as fully unitary, transcendent and all-powerful.[6] It is, indeed, to misplace all we have learned about texts and ourselves as readers during these past thirty years of re-reading literary modernism – but this is a topic to which I will return very shortly.

To sum up the foregoing: The strategies Smith developed worked by splicing together, parodying, disrupting and distorting the various established voices that would shape her expression of self, or 'speak her'; critics only began to recognise and name such tactics following the advent of deconstructive as well as 'dialogic' or (largely Bakhtinian) socio-linguistic theory, both of which have been revised by feminists for the reading of muted feminine voices at unequal odds in the projects of language.[7] Indeed, Smith owes much – particularly in her novels, as we shall see – to earlier practitioners of such 'presciently postmodern' strategies such as Fyodor Dostoyevsky, one of Bakhtin's most celebrated contributors to the novelising-of-literature project. Yet Smith's strategies once (and not terribly long ago) prompted critics to read her work as simply being full of 'amusing shift[s] in point of view' (Thaddeus 91), or even to dismiss her, as did one respected critic of modernism, as a charlatan – as (once again) an 'infinitely-knowing' 'faux-naif' whose 'language, with its false simplicities of diction, insistently draws attention to itself in a coy, self-regarding fashion, and effectively undermines real communication'.[8] It was believing oneself to be 'infinitely-knowing' that Smith was, ironically enough, *critiquing* by drawing attention to her many incompatible, inculcated selves; but in the modernist-cum-Red Decade era of poet-prophets and revolutionaries, her damning suspicion of the possibility of 'real [unmediated] communication' would most probably have been unwelcome if perceived. As Mark Storey wrote in 1979, '[e]ccentrics are not dangerous, and their value fades with their passing'.[9]

Yet Smith's work has always been 'political' according to both postmodern *and* conventional definitions of that word. It not only commented on topical political issues and their spokespeople, particularly during the 1930s and 1940s, but it also conducted a far more broad critique of English culture than even her recent re-readers have given her credit for to date. This may in part be due to the fact that, as Elaine Millard argued in 1989,

> [i]n writing, and particularly in writing poetry, women are allotted personal, but not public, space, a private but not a political or rhetorical voice.... [T]hose women who have been read with any large-scale interest have tended to attract biographical speculation, rather than acknowledgement of their particularities of style or form.... [Such attention] sets the critic on a quest for personal relevance, rather than the play of intertextualities. (65, 67)

Millard went on to point out that T.S. Eliot's work, for example, was (or had been) much less likely to be read in the same way (76). As Alison Light pointed out in 1994, women writers have also tended to be referred to by first name in critical writings (249) – as Smith quite often is, even in the most recent readings.[10] But more to the point, criticism focussed on Smith has not only *been* dominated by what Millard calls 'quest[s] for personal relevance', many of them reprinted in the 1991 anthology entitled *In Search of Stevie Smith*, but it *continues to be* dominated by the same, even by those who set out to re-approach her work from postmodern perspectives.

Re-readings of readings of Smith's work indicate much about the history of re-reading literary modernism from feminist perspectives. As the most helpful of her critics in the Sternlicht anthology, Martin Pumphrey, concluded, 'Smith's "oddness" [or "eccentricity"] identifies her with other women writers whose poetic strategies have been directed not toward the construction of an authoritative and consistent poetic persona or self but toward disruption, discontinuity, and indirection' (101). Given that this is the case, we have still to discover why it is that less than a handful of feminist critics have discussed or even mentioned Stevie Smith in their recent accounts of female modernism. It has been typical, for example, that big, inclusive and ground-breaking anthologies like *The Gender of Modernism* offer only one indirect reference to Smith – often to acknowledge that celebrated modernist women (in this case, Jean Rhys) read Smith, though the critics themselves have not.[11] Each of the book-length studies written about her before the mid-nineties asserted that certain conservative elements in her work make it difficult to reclaim her for feminism. This seeming problem can in part be attributed to the kind of misperception described above, which has linked various traditionalist, anti-Semitic and misogynist utterances in her writings with *her* instead of with her speakers, whose stereotypical linguistic tendencies she presented to her reader for critique. These studies not only demonstrate contradictory literary analysis – by which modernist women are apprehended in double-consciousness but not allowed to reveal the temporally-determined faultlines of that struggle – but they also and iron-ically reinforce the gendered link between women's poetry and self-expression in the narrowest of terms. The subliminal messages of traditional literary criticism continue to seep in such ways into feminist re-readings of modern women writers. It seems that none of us easily escape the fate that Voris described for our forebears: that of inadvertently 'reinscrib[ing] the very structure by which woman is oppressed'.

In fact, the method that Smith's major critics have *continued* to adopt for reading even her most unmistakably satirical, rhetorically mixed passages (which concern a range of issues – British imperialism, literary socialistic thought in the Thirties, inter-cultural wartime prejudices, etc.) involves interpreting them all as expressions of Smith's *own* opinions, rather than attributing them to the speaker of the poem or novel and attempting to analyse the significant shifts and contradictions between speech, perspective and environment which construct the perceptual world of *English* subjectivity – not only *her* self. Yet Alison Light, in 'Outside History? Stevie Smith, Women Poets and the National Voice', began very helpfully to answer her own ques-tions about our reading habits in 1993 when she asked,

> How is it that Smith's poetry can be placed outside time and place and yet so clearly articulate, in Heaney's words, the registers of 'educated middle class English speech'? . . . [W]hy is Larkin's clearly a national voice

and Smith's not?... We might want to say that the kind of Englishness Smith speaks to and from – superannuated, parochial, often bored with itself and its conventions, but convinced of the virtues of ordinariness – is the kind of suburban Englishness more frequently vilified than recognised as one of the heartlands of national feeling and identity.... Indeed many of her poems expose the illusory nature of the authority, that of the parent or husband or religious dogma, the precariousness of commonsense, but in ways which do not let the reader settle into the luxury of superiority. We search in vain for that consistent and coherent ego in Smith's poetry, an authorial fiction which makes possible, however attenuated, however qualified, the bardic address from one representative man to another. ... Hers is a national literature at once enshrined and debunked as an unthinking part of consciousness; deromanticised and yet personalised; a central point of public reference and yet privatised.... If Smith's verse is, as Heaney says, more inward-looking, and more conservative in its social address, then it is also more radical in its modernism, in its refusal to offer a convenient attitude or summation; in its parody of the past, in its sending up of the very Englishness it evokes, and in its insistence upon drawing our attention to the psychic and emotional repertoires of an Englishness which begins at home, as equally played out in fantasy, as it is lived in 'the real world'.[12]

I quote at length because, although I disagree with several key aspects of Light's (now 12-year-old) argument, as well as her tendencies towards 'postfeminist' analysis from which I would especially wish to distance my own approach, I find these passages most helpful in constructing the kind of reading that would do full justice to Smith's work. But it is very important to first point out that Light falls back into the same problems outlined above when she pursues an argument about poetry's generic superiority to narrative, given its supposed license to explore 'psychic interiority' – or the as yet unlived, as Jacqueline Rose has proposed it.[13] With this tack she inadvertently relegates Smith once again to those realms of the 'so-called private life...remote from politics or public life'. As does Pumphrey when he suggests that Smith's speakers, like anarchical children, 'juxtapose the (private/secret) world of play and magical possibility with the (public) known world of the conventionally Real' in order to elevate the former as being 'radically detached from the surface of mainstream culture'; in his reading they draw easy 'division[s] between the stable authoritarian, restrictive world of adults and the linked, fluid worlds of play and fairy land that are inhabited by children, animals, supernatural characters, women, poets and the muse' (100, 102, 103). Drawing such divisions between worlds is something Light expressly wishes *not* to do, and tries to avert by 'insist[ing] on their interdependency', but ultimately does do because of the morphing power of traditional identity politics.

Ironically, it is Smith's *prose* that has been treated to the reading Light describes above. Her long-underrated work, the novel trilogy – *Novel on Yellow Paper* (1936), *Over the Frontier* (1938), and *The Holiday* (1949) – has suffered most at the hands of critics attempting to read it as being evocative solely of Smith's 'psychic interiority' or feminine angst. Its heroines, who to date have been read almost exclusively as autobiographical personae undergoing recognisable changes in female development, are more importantly part of a formal network of images and linguistic manoeuverings which connect and identify them with representations of the larger historical forces that shaped them: increasingly nationalistic and militaristic language (as well as alter-egoistic languages of disavowal and appeasement); politicised mid-century art movements and their visual as well as verbal vocabularies; rising documentary modes and journalistic discourse; the period's least as well as most familiar pitches of cultural (and gendered) propaganda; and even the suburban attitudes and most-quoted aphorisms that moulded Smith's own views. Although she did not, in her readings of Smith, expand upon her important introductory insights, Jan Montefiore was absolutely right when she suggested that Thirties women 'responded creatively to the social and political issues of the time in ways which are closely... related to the characteristic preoccupations of the male "Auden Generation", including both their left-wing politics and their *tendency to autobiography*' (23; my emphasis). Therefore we must begin to read Smith's often tongue-in-cheek, wickedly playful autobiographical insertions as having the same capability for expansive cultural and political commentary that we have allowed and *continue* to allow her male contemporaries' to have. What need to be mapped are Smith's experiments with the effects of collusion between discourses and ideologies upon such representative speakers – speakers who represent *much* more than gendered experience – as they travel, in revisionary epic/*bildungsroman* fashion, through the first part of this century into the Second World War. They are speakers who, like Dostoyevsky's from 'underground', have been 'listening [to culture] through a crack under the floor', registering its arguments about progress into the twentieth century in the midst of expanding theatres of violence, and who have 'invented [similar voices as characters in the writing because] there was nothing else [they] could invent' (Dostoyevsky 26). Smith acknowledges her deep sympathy with Dostoyevsky's proto-Beckettian project through her decision to quote *verbatim* from *Notes from the Underground* at the end of her trilogy. Therefore Chapters 3 and 4 of this book will be devoted to re-reading the trilogy as being something quite other than a 'portmanteau' full of odds and ends from Smith's life – a characteristic description which before the 1990s relegated its importance to some rung far below the poems.[14] These chapters will also raise questions as to whether the trilogy (or the poems, given their interrelations) *can* be read into the presciently postmodern feminist allegory that most of her current readers still create of the work.[15]

Rethinking the tradition of rethinking

But there are fine lines to tread and not tread, as well as other dangers here for me, too, as I attempt to lead readers into the necessarily messy because highly detailed and expansive 'close-cultural' reading, as I will call it, of Smith's works. The imperative not to concentrate on biographical recovery must be tempered by what I investigated earlier as a key insight in current reading practices: that culture inscribes us, language 'writes us', and (once again; it cannot be repeated enough) that women by their very use of it 'may reinscribe the very structure by which [they] are oppressed'. We must not therefore miss the extent to which Smith is herself a product and producer of the era she critiques *and* fails to critique. This fine line is blurred from the outset in Laura Severin's recent book-length study of Smith's writing, which on its first page suggests that I wish to dismiss 'historical and cultural readings' because, in my writings about Smith, I call for an end to the kind of retrogressive and falsely isolating *biographical* reading I describe above. Severin goes on in her book to conflate biographical and cultural reading in order to once again give us a conventionally heroic portrait of Smith as a fully-resistant, marginalised woman writer against a backdrop of solely women's issues and texts, reading her work in the light of her *life as a woman* and not in the light of the larger social and cultural text that informs the *writing*. If the strategies she uses to read Smith were actually *cultural* reading strategies, she would have found many other kinds of histories relevant to the reading in addition to the history of other women writing – which is where Smith is left at the end of Severin's book, quite ironically, given that its opening pages promised by way of quoting Light *not* to leave Smith once again in the position of being read as the 'ex-centric', working 'outside history'.

Less obviously and more intriguingly, valuable contextualisations like Gill Plain's of the second novel in the trilogy also depart from their own introductory insights into the historical moment of the Thirties in order to once again liberate Smith from them. Plain's reading, which intends to provide commentary on 'Smith and the Religion of Fascism', creates a context for the resurgence of interest in Roman Catholicism in post-Great War European culture, and thus for Smith's critique of it. But it manages to somehow miss Smith's own, at times, strangely orthodox thinking – even when Plain quotes from passages in which it is most uncomfortably present for us as readers. As a result, Smith's commentary on Milton's portraiture of Satan, for example, is blurred in the reading. Plain elides Smith's speaker's quasi-theological critique of art's romanticisation of evil so that it becomes solely a critique of secular language and codes, which makes little sense in this instance and avoids the very topic of her chapter: Smith's understanding of the relation between religious and political beliefs.[16] Even Smith's fully apparent, residual 'manifestation[s] of anti-German sentiment' (9) – a phenomenon which

Plain describes in her Introduction as having been evident in the textual culture of Britain before and during the Great War but diminished in the Thirties – is denied in this reading; Plain asserts, for example, that the frequent use of German language by Smith's increasingly bellicose and unsavoury speaker has to do with other things – 'secondary emphasis' of meaning and sound-value, for example – rather than the unmentionable cultural prejudice that is perhaps unfortunately but not surprisingly evident in her work. Like Severin and Civello, Plain ultimately resorts to a reductively gendered reading of *Over the Frontier*'s events. Even though she began by recognising that 'Smith is ultimately more concerned with exploring the individual's relation to power than with linking this relationship to essentialist categories of sexual difference' (69), *Frontier* ends up being about our speaker's 'triumphant multiplicity' (68) at the start of the novel having been 'denied' by the straitening forces of religion/fascism, or corrupted by 'belief' in 'a "masculine" ethos' (77).[17] Her reading, in other words, ultimately misses the novel's point about overall British/European 'subjectivity' in the Thirties altogether. Plain's focus on feminine selfhood – which departs from what she recognised as Smith's focus – leads her to remark, in oblique relation to her first insight above, that 'Smith's critique is focused not on society's implication in the process of war, but on the guilt of the individual' (71). But this of course bypasses much of what we actually find in the novels, and also and dismally returns us to the problematic isolation of women writers and their texts within a realm of issues dealing solely with their own 'psychic interiority' and 'private life' – something that Smith expressly parodies as a concept (in part through jokey references to Alexander Korda's 'private lives' films of the 1930s), as we shall see in Chapters 3 and 4.

Smith is also made to sound, in current criticism, as though she were writing in exactly the sorts of postmodern modes that we are now using to read her, but such anachronisms are obviously due to our failure to properly see the work – consequently, all we see is ourselves, looking. This happens in the course of very welcome but strangely dehistoricised readings like Richard Nemesvari's of *Novel on Yellow Paper*, in which he elegantly (and in part, I think, quite rightly) calls upon Jacques Derrida's poststructuralist ideas about the arbitrary nature of signifying relations in language, deploying them in order to understand the way that Smith fiercely interrogates the connotations of words by foregrounding the processes by which they come to be meaningful and confer authority. I will return to this helpful reading later, but *not* to come to the same conclusion that Nemesvari does: that Smith's 'new aesthetic... is based largely upon the perception that uncertainty of meaning and definition are not to be denied, but rather embraced', and that she desires, like the most extreme of postmodernists, unlimited linguistic free-play given her understanding that 'language is composed of arbitrary word sounds' (34, 30). A reading like this drains Smith's work of all of its contextual commentary, political relevance and historical angst, as Nemesvari's skeletal and ultimately unconvincing analyses of passages from the text make clear. As with Severin's reading of Smith's postmodern playfulness, we find here that Smith is not *subject* to the sorts of linguistic power-plays Derrida and others began to envision at mid-century but is already in control of them, able to manipulate them as she wishes. I too have been guilty, in my own initial work on Smith, of 'lioness-ising' her in this way, wanting to see her as just the sort of proto-poststructuralist feminist Severin and Nemesvari make of her. I also wrote myself into believing she was working before her time from a transcendent position of gendered difference, but I now understand this kind of reading as constituting excessive use of what predecessors in re-reading literary modernism provided by way of insight. Such misapplication of critical tools has come to illustrate one of the greatest contradictions in our re-reading of literary modernism as feminists: We call on theory that critiques 'infinite knowing[ness]', as Bergonzi referred to it, in order to set female modernist models of consciousness against male modernist suppositions about their own transcendental egos, but we manage only to recreate via the figures we re-read *exactly such knowingness*, setting them and ourselves right back in modernist as opposed to postmodernist discourse.

It seems time to acknowledge that Smith's views on feminism were messy and contradictory, and that her own gendered politics evolved primarily out of her broader critiques of – and infiltration by – culture, rather than *vice versa*. She remained stalwartly vulnerable to the era's stereotypical view of feminism, as Severin herself notes by quoting her well-known comment on Rebecca West's work in a review published as late as 1957: 'I would not call Miss West a feminist, because this suggests – and is meant to – an aggrieved and strident person. I would say, she is on the side of women.'[18] Her complicated attitude towards feminism is perhaps the best example of how interwoven she was by the crisscrossing threads of imagery and discursive mayhem that surrounded radical thought at mid-century. She quite often critiqued feminism to the extent that she critiqued all the many '-isms' established in both art and politics by the time she entered her formative years as a writer (in the 'Red' Thirties). Never must readers forget that the generative context for Smith's work was a home city through which organised marches by fascists affixing signs to buildings and walls (saying, among other things, 'Kill the dirty Jews') were followed by counter-marches or 'Crusades' by communists and other petitioners for world changes, whom Smith also distrusted for reasons that will be explored throughout the rest of this book.[19] It was a moment when one's own king, Edward VIII, was suspected (quite rightly, as was later revealed) of Nazi sympathies. It was an era of anxiety and escapism, of disavowal of developments in Europe and of pledging allegiance to political creeds at home. Her speakers call the latter '-ismuses' ('communismus', for example, among other 'idealismuses'). Smith's double-reference through these German endings extends beyond the obvious – that is, beyond the fascist shadow stretching over the decade; her sweeping use of the suffix for a variety of groups indicts all the other '-isms' darkened within it. Her calling up, more playfully, the ancient roots of English and the Latin superlative form of the suffix ('-issimus') perhaps parodies the supposition that revolutionary ideas are ever *sui generis*, or that they are, unlike other texts – her own novels and poems, for example – able to escape historical patterns of self-delusion and corruption which are facilitated by and embedded in language. 'There was nothing else I could invent', Smith's speakers seem to continually suggest, as if by way of subtextual homage to those like Dostoyevsky who foresaw their dilemma. Certainly the military/classical figures from whom her speakers take their names in the novel trilogy (such as her narrator for the first two books of it, 'Pompey Casmilus') suggest the same. And certainly many of the feminist figures Smith depicts are also 'strident' in their self-delusion – which would have made them doubly foolish in her eyes.

Smith could be cruel about women and their 'trappings', whether the latter have to do with conventional convictions or superficial new conventions that involve simple usurpation of male ones. Equally certainly she, like most quasi-liberal intellectuals of the time, held many feminist views – views concerning the need for full education and revised lifestyles for women, for example, and other views which, as shall be seen in Chapter 2, put her 'on the side of women'. It is also fairly clear that she demonstrated what we would now view from our angle of history as 'postmodern' reservations about romanticised or separatist re-constructions of womanhood, though I argue in this book that this was less due to her prophetic insight than to her very negative response to contextual stimuli, like the selling of glorified images of 'Englishness' and 'nationhood' amid oppositional idealisations of potential 'new world orders' in the mid-to-late Thirties. *All* such pitches could not have helped but resound with the propagandistic tones of either the Ministry of Information (for which many writers worked) or any of the revolutionary 'groupismuses' coming to form in the decade. It is for reasons like these that, though a professed admirer of Virginia Woolf, she seemed unconvinced by even the kinds of arguments about *dis*affiliation for women that Woolf began to formulate in the course of the lead-up to the Second World War. Smith wrote about such seemingly extremist stances as being poignantly swept up on the same tidal wave of mid-century history and rhetoric that all the rest, including herself, were in danger of drowning in. It seems that the philosophical position generated by her historical moment was postmodern to the extent that it was not unlike the one Janet Wolff describes for our own post-essentialist era, when 'objective' correctives as well as correlatives have receded into history and 'metacommentary' has taken their place:[20]

The feminist critique of knowledge and science should not make the mistake of claiming to substitute a new, 'correct' knowledge.... Arguing that there are 'no true stories', [Sandra Harding] recommends a feminist intervention which, in true post-modern terms, operates the destabilisation of thought, recognizing at the same time 'the permanent partiality of feminist inquiry'. (80)

It is in a very similarly self-conscious way that Smith's many poetic arguments and retellings of fairy tales and other cultural stories unfold. Her work often refuses to offer a 'right' way of seeing; its form of modernist irony differs from the more familiar, ultimately stable, classic sort, which indicates 'true' realities beneath 'false' appearances by grounding moral judgement in a speaker's 'most private and therefore most fundamental nature' (Glazener 121). It is the suspect genesis of what is perceived as one's 'most fundamental nature' that Smith and many of her female contemporaries explore; as Nancy Glazener explained in 1989, modernist women like Gertrude Stein depict 'interiority' as being constructed by 'exteriority', or discourses that mediate expression and social identity. And as Phyllis Lassner has argued more recently, in an article that delivers the most helpful reading of Smith's novels to date, '[Smith] imagines historic process as a debate which is knowledge-bearing in its confrontation not only with herself and her correspondents but with the consequences of discovering differences between a self-questioning rhetoric and that which is already persuaded of its truth' (144). In this context we can agree when Nemesvari argues that work like Smith's destabilises accepted ways of thinking *not* by offering alternative moralisations (even from a feminist standpoint), or alternative descriptions of fundamental nature, but by pluralising discourses and subtexts with all of their relative truths in order to demystify their illusionary construction of natural, shared reality. Her narratives, monologues and fairy tales usually 'disenchant' her readers from believing that anything but historically generated, socially constructed 'morals to the story' exist. 'Manners, morals, religion – all patterns' is what she wrote next to a line by Osbert Burdett copied into one of her reading journals: 'Man's desires are more complex than any pattern he can invent to lend them form and dignity.'[21] But the fact that some discourses receive differing values in her work, and that judgements – sometimes contradictory ones – do arise to situate Smith as an intellectual of her period must not be overlooked in our reading or we lose sight of the larger social and cultural project in which she took such relevant part. Smith's political opinions became quite available in her writings – and they are both like and unlike others' around her; this should not vitiate our developing understanding of differences in the thinking processes of female modernists. Recognising that all established patterns are invented, contingent, and not reflections of unchangeable truths or articulations of the 'whole story', Smith and a number of her contemporaries became able to 'envisage new possibilities in the interstices between discourses or to weave them together in new hybrid forms' (Nussbaum 37).

When, in Smith's work, such forms emerge hand-in-hand with the overwhelming desire to circumvent *all* available patterns, stories and discourses that surround or dominate her, the latter translates itself into the death drive for which her work, like Emily Dickinson's and Sylvia Plath's, is famous. But instead of reading such drives anachronistically, as being fully poststructuralist by motivation, we might use our new reading habits to re-interpret Smith's death imagery both a little less literally *and* a little less theoretically than we (including myself) have done to date. In other words, rather than solely linking Smith to other suicidal literary women, in order to discuss their gendered situation and psychology, we might also think about the abundance of suicidal imagery in other arts projects of the Thirties – projects that used it as political metaphor, or as evocative of the social rather than the gendered psyche. Equally well, rather than supposing that Smith's strategies were 'ahead of their time', we might pursue her relationship to the potent philosophical changes of thought of her own time and recognise her as a participant in those changes: in what, even then, was coming to form as the mid-century's 'linguistic turn' from modern meta-narratives of culture, and in the final stages of its digestion of early-century psychoanalytic ideas. Her era's seduction by Freud's theories produced not only Hitchcock's movies but politicised movements in the arts – such as surrealism, of course, which amply demonstrated such dual parentage. Smith quite openly invokes Freud by name along with several of his best-known constructs in her trilogy; therefore its central images – particularly riding hell-bent on horseback, or negotiating waves on flimsy crafts – not only can but *should* be read as figurations of the elemental death drive reined in or ridden out by language's 'talking cure'. And yet, though Smith's experimental use of Freud's ideas is quite overt, in the poems as well as the novels, she employs them as connectors of social psychology to patterns of disavowal in the 'body politic' – not, or at least not exclusively, as a means by which to probe her own developmental stages *as a woman*.[22] Smith's speakers in the novels – the 'talking voices' as she refers to them – ride and rein in a series of horses who become connected to unruly flights of both sexual desire and power-mongering as well as military excess unmistakably associated with the late Thirties. They are hobby-horses ridden straight out of Sterne through Browning and into Smith's present work, redefined by Freud but recognisable as having been active in a long line of specifically British if at times more broadly European subjectivities. Her speaker's is, in other words, an epic voice *as well as* and even more importantly than a private voice.

No matter how often we now assert as feminists (and postmodernists) that 'the private is political', there will yet be a difference between the two, particularly in terms of what, ultimately, becomes the primary object of readerly focus and critique in art. It is interesting that while as feminist critics we have asserted the need to see women as being the revisers as well as the subjects of analysis, in literary analysis we seem less able to see them using the same tools to psychoanalyse culture itself in the way that their contemporaries from Auden to J.F. Hendry most certainly did. Smith's analysand is both the public and the private world being spoken, quite unnervingly, in the same voice. And given that the 'talking cure' proves, for this voice, to be revelatory of only its own kind of living 'death', or entrapment in defining discourses, the death drive develops in Smith's work into another more complex desire to break through the circumference of language altogether – its 'tyranny of associations', as she will put it in *Novel on Yellow Paper* – and its available constructions of self. Such a drive might be seen to become, in other words, a 'rebellion... against the imaginary unity of the ego' (Boothby 39) and its farce of fortressed subjectivity as it was discussed earlier. Death becomes the alienated (or exiled) desire's referent for what is beyond available sign systems, beyond what Smith called the human 'pattern'. As Smith writes via playful political language and its idealisations in 'The Donkey' (a serious send-up of Yeats' visionary celebration of eternal patterns in 'Lapis Lazuli'),

> Oh in its eyes was such a gleam
> As is usually associated with youth
> But it was not a youthful gleam really,
> But full of mature truth.
>
> And of the hilarity that goes with age,
> As if to tell us sardonically
> No hedged track lay before this donkey longer
> But the sweet prairies of anarchy.
>
> But the sweet prairies of anarchy
> And the thought that keeps my heart up
> That at last, in Death's odder anarchy,
> Our pattern will be broken all up.
> Though precious we are momentarily, donkey,
> I aspire to be broken up. (*CP* 535)

Quite typically, Smith's alternative vision of 'mature truth' suggests no panoramic view of 'all the tragic scene', as Yeats imagined it, contemplating the 'ancient, glittering eyes' of his timeless, Far Eastern figures on their way up mountains of reincarnated, spiralling lives towards the poem's metaphorical summit.[23] Instead, she imagines all she *can* imagine: herself, like the 'asses' in Yeats' poem – whose lot it is to bear civilisation on its destructive, and ultimately self-destructive, cyclic path – finally let out of 'the shafts of regular employment' and set free from the patterns that have shaped experience.[24] As Marina Warner notes, the donkey and the goose (as in 'Mother Goose') are our 'proverbially foolish animals', yet 'the folly of such creatures is allied to simplicity, and simplicity can also be understood as wisdom' (36–37). Smith will always choose identification with not only the most familiar and over-written figures of English (and in this case French) lore, but also those that seem far more foolish than visionary – if foolish in the Shakespearean sense: as Lear's fool was foolish, playing the disruptive dramatic foil in 'all the tragic scene'.

Some of the problems in reading that I outline above demonstrate no more than the very old desire we inherit to receive from vatic writers word of some alternative, inviolate space in culture. They illustrate a powerful need to relate Smith's *truer* side of the story, or locate her 'solutions' to the discursive malpractice she exposes by tracking the subversive agency in her work down to some one or several privileged, 'detached' sources or states or pristine counter-worlds – of children or animals, most radically, claimed to have 'existed for her in a prelapsarian state' (*S* 26). Smith recedes even further into eccentricity as discoveries of her sojourns in such encapsulated spaces are made. But she was, as this first segment of my introduction has attempted to argue, actually only a rather alarmingly insightful fellow traveller.

Rethinking the non-canonical canon

A final series of thoughts that will surface throughout the course of this study question our general habits of constructing genealogies for literary innovation. As an American reader whose writing has concentrated far more often on postmodern or 'experimental' British poets and their precursors – the list of whom certainly does not include Smith – I have found myself constantly surprised by the radical philosophy of this work neglected by the avant-garde and 'mainstream' alike. We tend to recognise twentieth-century innovative writing by the degree to which it is disjunctive in form. I do not mean the degree of its metalinguistic play – which is a different thing altogether. Instead, I mean the almost quantitative measure of its formal departure from the norms of culture's speaking and writing habits – so much so that Smith's strategies of directly critiquing the same through defamiliarising *reproduction* of discursive structures and ventriloquistic techniques look too tame, given their general lack of formal and syntactical dislocation. (Perhaps they most nearly approach the techniques of Bertolt Brecht, 'performative' as they are, if shy of his ideological intent.) Such superficial judgement has been the cause of critics' inability to actually see what her novels are doing on the page or as wholes, or to note the intricate dissonance upon which the poems depend. Most do not realise, of course, given editorial interventions, that her first novel was originally written without much in the way of punctuation, though I will demonstrate in Chapter 3 that its radical nature depends in no real way upon that fact. And yet, I cannot help but wonder: were we to retrieve and focus upon those original manuscripts, would Smith, like her predecessor Emily Dickinson (whose recovered dashes and resultant disjunctiveness might be said to have helped launch her into 'precursor' status), find herself read alongside other groundbreaking modernists? Indeed, very recent studies have continued to assert that British poetry, thought less formally adventurous than American poetry, somehow missed modernism altogether, because it failed to produce an Ezra Pound or Gertrude Stein or even its own home-grown T.S. Eliot; that David Jones and Basil Bunting are the only figures who remotely fit the modernist bill. But what *is* the 'bill'? Can it be that radical forms should be assessed as universal – the same from culture to culture?

Antony Easthope, in an essay I published in 1996, blamed Donald Davie's and the Movement's retreat from the experiments of American modernism on his own culture's deep-set empiricism, what he controversially called 'the failure of Englishness'.[25] But American modernism, thought to be less tied to old European traditions, has taken its aesthetic cue from its *own* tradition of break-away and pioneering in every conceivable project – and its debts to nineteenth-century, romantic strains of transcendental thought remain evident in such departure, so that its forms of radicalism are, in that sense, deeply 'traditional' in the American grain. On the other hand, Smith's way out of what in her time George Steiner would cast as the impasse between corrupt *Language and Silence* that surrounded traumatic mid-century history and, subsequently, marked the 'linguistic turn' of pre-cultural-revolution philosophy was distinctly English. It could never have been the way of a William Carlos Williams, an H.D. or a Charles Olson, though it was similarly epic in proportion and avant-garde in its dismantling of the dimensions of identity. I would go further to argue that its lack of romantic/national or revisionist/spiritual pioneering aspirations causes it to feel, in retrospect, more in sync with what was to come in postmodern *re*-envisionings of vision itself than do the *oeuvres* of other modernists whose more familiar names we might list. Her culture's tradition of experimentalism has evolved out of British empiricism proper into a 'post-empiricism' that inflects its modern and postmodern practice; it involves a distinctly non-romantic, non-transcendental focus on social discourse and manners of speaking as being constitutive of a common if artificial linguistic reality. Writing that foregrounds the effects of such enculturation and its circumscription of individual agency will be very different from writing that assumes the possibility of Whitmanic formal departure – something Smith admired from afar, and called in an early poem 'far[ing] out...on a[n]...unexplored uncharted road', but could not honestly replicate as a strategy in her own work.[26] Smith and Stein meet in some instances – in the participial coming-into-being in language that Smith borrows from her in her prose, for example, many instances of which are discussed in the following chapters.

But instead of creating Cubist verbal artefacts that demonstrate the difference between language and its objects, or issuing disjointed propositions to foil reference and narrative progression – strategies Stein employed with the effect of locating the author somewhere beyond the constraints of linguistic codes, in a place of meaning otherwise – Smith always positioned herself and any emergent 'meaning' issuing from her writing firmly *within* the encircling discourses she set into motion in her work. Though her admissions and demonstrations of entrapment within certain ideas, like those of the Church and the conservative culture that bore her, certainly cause her to seem less radical than others who envisioned transcendence of such influences, we might argue that her honest self-analysis also took her some measure beyond her contemporaries when it came to revealing the discursive traffic in the speaking voice long before postmodern theory began to take apart notions of the unified 'self'.

I of course risk falling back into the trap that I just described – of believing in Smith's prescient postmodernism by projecting my own thoughts upon hers. I *must* still be doing that to some extent, unavoidable as such malpractice is. But my close-cultural reading practice *attempts* another kind of return, one that encourages thinking about writing subjects not in our terms but in their own, and as being situated – 'located', as we are too – in texts and time. Smith's was, as she put it in one poem and as Michael Horovitz remembers it from her 1960s readings, a 'worldly ear'; she was painfully open to the riot of contradictory discourses and 'structures of feeling' (as her contemporary Raymond Williams described them) shifting all around her. The study I have done is of course different from a conventional 'cultural studies' reading of literary work because it takes seriously this author's artistic intentions – the formal structures or fractures she produces, her generic devices and manipulation of literary codes – as well as her inevitable inscription by the more general thoughts, politics and words within the culture of her making. Rachel Blau DuPlessis describes such new forms of 'close-reading' as 'post-formalism' in her millennial book on reading gender, race and religious culture back into innovative American poetic texts in the twentieth century. Though my work differs from hers in many respects – particularly in that I find, as Smith did, that national boundaries deeply affect textual innovations of all kinds – I hope that the appearance of such new thought from leading critics and writers of the present moment suggests that my own comprehensive reading of Smith will be welcome at this point in time. The great irony is that we distort knowledge about *both* writers and time periods with any other kind of reading, rather than build clearer ideas about the complex workings of what we call 'history' and how subjects – including writing subjects, even 'radical' writing subjects – have operated both helplessly and hopefully within it.

The second section of this chapter is intended to provide another kind of introduction – this time to those of Smith's major themes and formal strategies that have to date received most attention. Their relationship to others' produced around her – and to strategies and prejudices embedded deep in her cultural context – will be more difficult to map, and will require the whole of my remaining space to be slowly unfolded in (forever only 'partial') explication.

II

A selection of central themes and strategies re-read

Both the allusive nature of Stevie Smith's work and her staggeringly prolific career as a reviewer provide us with evidence of the widely ranging reading habits and acquaintance with 'popular culture' that contributed to her repertoire of representative voices and views. Her interests ran international in scope and interdisciplinary in subject matter, encompassing tabloids and Hollywood 'talkies' as well as esoteric texts, though her *critique* remained primarily focussed on how those influential books, philosophical tracts, films, handbooks and textbooks that her contemporaries would have encountered in conversation, out on the town, at church services or in school impacted on her own culture as she knew it. Her work is, in other words, and as she once wrote, 'such an English mixture', explaining her reasons for doubting that it would be read in the United States.[27] She was quite wrong about her reception in America, but of course right about the fact that the heterogeneous nature of her writing indicates nothing akin to modernist 'cosmopolitanism' or transhistorical vision, but rather an interest in the variety of discursive influences crowding in, from the past as well as the present, upon the specifically English, twentieth-century mind.[28] Some of her favourite sources for allusions are, for example, Gibbon's histories, Shakespeare's plays, Grimms' fairy tales, the Bible, the *Book of Common Prayer*, classical tragedy and philosophy, contemporary theological tracts, military memoirs, German post-war painting, Hollywood westerns and the work of American humourists, continental and Russian novels, Romantic and Victorian British poetry, colonial 'blue books', handbooks on social dress and etiquette, *Hymns Ancient and Modern* and *Come Hither* (a book of traditional British ballads and rhymes). She attempted to deflect subsequent interpretations of her allusiveness as *allegiance* to such traditions by writing, in her blurb for the American version of her *Selected Poems*, that '[t]here may be echoes in her work of past poets – Lear, Poe, Byron, the gothic romantics, and *Hymns Ancient and Modern* – but these are deceitful echoes...' (*S* 244). Her echoes illustrate the haunted nature of consciousness, which she constantly exposes by collapsing lingering literary voices, contemporary idioms and influential dictions (a style that provoked an initial comparison with Joyce), allowing strange combinations, collusions and contradictions to appear in any single poem or paragraph. As she put it in one epigrammatic poem, 'Old Ghosts': 'I can call up old ghosts, and they will come,/But my art limps, – I cannot send them home' (*CP* 211). Such discursive events of course traumatise, to her purpose, the simple or traditional forms she chooses to write in – or rather, they shake them up to give a glimpse of the psychosocial trauma their conventional felicity covers. What critics in the past have identified as her 'unsure' or slightly skewed handling of metrics or lyrical lines must be re-read to quite different effect as the kind of splicing or collision of modes described above.[29] Her shattering of unified forms – whether it be through a trailing final line, an aberrant stanza or a sustained internal dialogue between aspects of a split 'linguistic consciousness', as Bakhtin would call it – bespeaks the complex, culturally mediated and constructed nature of even the most private of lyric utterances, and therefore the impossibility of speaking 'straight from the heart'.

Very often Smith's simple line-drawings, which accompany the majority of the poems, enhance these destabilising effects by serving as extra-discursive 'coda' of a supplementary, subversive or parodic nature. Not subversive *primarily* because 'doodles are personal', as Jack Barbera has suggested (236), and thus incompatible with New Critical aesthetics as the latter guarded the artwork's autonomy and the impersonality of the author, but rather because they usually maintain a relation of uneasy 'otherness' to the words of the speaker, often representing, in all their roughness, some other mute but alternative view struggling into expression. They are indeed 'half-wishful and half-skittish', as one *Times Literary Supplement* (*TLS*) reviewer wrote in deprecation, joining the chorus of disapproving voices which included everyone from her first reluctant publishers to her most well-known early critics and all but her most recent and strongest supporters. Such readers complained that the drawings are 'too cute', or that 'they are an irrelevance', or that they detract from the seriousness of the poems, or that, as Philip Larkin puts it, they 'have an amateurishness reminiscent of Lear, Waugh and Thurber without much compensating felicity' (77). But exhibiting 'felicity' is not the project of the drawings, while detracting from the words' definitive authority, as well as poetry's tendency to take itself seriously, *is*; the result is a kind of disturbance which is anything but irrelevant. Smith insisted that 'the drawings are so much a part of the verses that they must be published with them' (*MA* 298), and in the 1960s, as Barbera notes, she would introduce poems at readings with description of the drawings that should accompany them (224). Most critics have found it contradictory that she also said, 'Oh, I've got a boxful of drawings.... The drawings don't really have anything to do with the poems' (Dick 44). But though the sketches may not have been specifically made for the poems they accompany – indeed, may well undermine or contradict them – they do, as she also asserted, 'tie up with them' and 'must be published with them' because, it seems, their role is not to clarify but to destabilise with a slightly (or in some cases, very) different voice (*MA* 280, 298). As Kristin Bluemel has noted in a wonderful piece on Smith's 'doodles', it is '[p]recisely because the doodle itself is not an illustration of the figure... in [the] poem, [that] the visual object that is verbally represented must, in good ecphrastic fashion, be conjured up by the language that requires its absence' – with corollary conjuring enacted by the doodle, all of which 'keep[s] the motion between text and image in play' (118–19). While I have difficulty with the conclusion that her critique is thus one offered 'by a woman, [who] speaks with a female voice, and adopts feminine subjects and perspectives' exclusively, Bluemel certainly offers a fine starting-point for rethinking the inextricable place of the drawings in Smith's poetic project.

Laughter is one very important product of the drawings and indeed of all of her works, but Smith's laughter is quite different from that of Edward Lear or the American humourist James Thurber with whom she is often, as in Larkin's assessment above, categorised.[30] She would have particularly disliked her drawings' comparison with Thurber's, which she felt lack subtlety, 'seem almost on a schoolboy level of intelligence and scribble', and have the propensity to become downright misogynistic (*MA* 184). Her own sketches and variously absurd antics in her work at large seem rooted in a tradition that is distinctly British, as A. Alvarez has noted; his brief attempt to get at that difference is somewhat clumsy but has a point: 'In her way, Stevie Smith is as purely English as Dorothy Parker is pure New Yorker, and her best work is based on an English distrust of the emotions' (*Observer* 1975). Jean-Jacques Lecercle in *The Philosophy of Nonsense* might help us understand Smith's form of it slightly better; 'nonsense', he writes, 'is a true product of the venerable tradition of British empiricism' (200), operating importantly as its flip side and carnivalesque interference. That other Frenchman looking at the tradition from the outside, Jacques Derrida, also noted that 'English silly discourse recognises the norm of empiricist discourse by departing from it, through a departure that may easily carry it to a troubling extreme...' (1978, 85). Smith, I venture to think, would have heartily agreed; her insistence that her works 'are not *only* comical' (*MA* 298) seems to point us to the fact that they inspire laughter that is deeply submerged in complicity with the 'subject' and its laughable assumptions of objectivity as well as responsive to the funniness of the 'object' laughed at – a situation that is both doubly funny and disturbing, displacing. Laughter was, for Smith, as it has been for most theorists of resistance from Friedrich Nietzsche to Bakhtin and Julia Kristeva, the only way to destroy the illusion of absolute truth, self-righteousness and self-contained integrity, to open oneself to alterity or 'otherness', to scatter human patterns, and begin to 'seek knowledge not through assimilation but through interaction' or dialogue (David Patterson 299). 'When practice is not laughter, there is nothing new', writes Kristeva (225). Smith has similarly written that even the most revolutionary and idealistic of inspirations becomes 'distorted' when relegated to language and incarnated as 'ideologismus', but that 'where there is humour... there will be no Lenin, no Mussolini, and perhaps Christ will be crowded out' (*MA* 168; *S* 46). An historian like Eric Hobsbawm might help us to understand such a surprising statement when he writes, in a chapter entitled 'The Age of Catastrophe', that in the Thirties

> The force of the movements for world revolution lay in the communist form of organization, Lenin's 'party of a new type', a formidable innovation of twentieth-century social engineering, comparable to the invention of Christian monastic and other orders in the Middle Ages. It gave even small organizations disproportionate effectiveness, because the party could command extraordinary devotion and self-sacrifice from its members, more than military discipline and cohesiveness.... (76)

It helps to keep reading particularly Smith's earlier works against this kind of backdrop – one in which, as Hobsbawm suggests many times in his work, it looked as though the whole order of civilisation might well find itself reversed once again, and perhaps in a pendulum swing of unthinkable consequences for millennia to come. Like manners, morals and religion, political movements smacked for Smith of poor patterns by which complex human desires are badly (and sometimes violently) served; she was afraid of them all, and often made a joke by bringing names up as little packs of cards – Lenin, Mussolini, Christ – to signal the way that promiscuous power-mongering could almost interchangeably change hands. Laughter creates, in other words, and as Frances Spalding puts it, an 'anarchic freedom' in Smith's work which helps her to 'resist ideological terrorism' (139), if only for some of the time; as the somewhat unfully brainwashed central character in her second book of the trilogy – the surrealistic novel/nightmare, *Over the Frontier* – puts it, 'that innermost core of laughter within a secret heart... holds fierce and close within itself the power to dispel the dream' (200).

And yet, as we shall see in the first novel of the trilogy, the power of laughter is ambivalently as well as importantly imaged forth as Dionysus, who according to Nietzsche destroys the dream-like illusions Apollonian culture must create to define itself. Smith's choice of *The Bacchae*'s mythic story of derisive destruction for her novels' framework – as opposed, for example, to the Odyssean tale that informs Pound's and even Joyce's epics – tells us much about her alternative modernist vision's incompatibility with models that affirm the traditional building of selfhood in symmetry with the state. And yet as with so much of Smith's work, the deep countercurrents set moving against such radical forces are also strong, and seem to suggest that she feared, in her era's seeming 'collapse of culture', the loss of stability that flawed 'Englishness' in its highly suspect way offered to her generation.[31] Therefore her admiration for Europe's classical bedrock, Greek culture, long read as yet another indication of her deeply rooted traditionalism, *is*, at times, traditionalist, even if it is also and very importantly, at others, actually quite palpably *anti*-traditionalist. It applauds her classical forebears not only for their terrifying honesty about human limitations – about our smallness in an indifferent universe – but also for their deification of forces that are necessarily, periodically and radically destructive of all social constructions: forces of laughter and 'otherness' like Dionysus, much feared as well as welcomed.

The animals who appear so frequently in Smith's work are sometimes also celebrated for their otherness to human language and thought, if not domination. She never 'romanticises' them, however, as she puts it in one essay about cats; and as she once wrote to a friend (in her novels' breakneck style, without punctuation), 'to me an animal is an animal some nice some not but never anything that is not an animal' (*MA* 264). Her interest is rather in the ways humans invade and colonise such otherness, and in how animals both resist and succumb to their captors' constructions of them. In Smith's work we find that all of nature, because it is 'too dark for us to read' (*MA* 135), must inevitably be anthropomorphised or translated into images of ourselves – and into language, where they cannot be caught. She deals playfully with this idea in one less weighty review.

> And what in heaven's name is the cat-nature? Does it shine in the pretty eyes of our cat gathering in this sumptuous book [*Cats in Colour*], or is that a humanisation too?... We do not know, and as we do not like not to know, we make up stories about them, give our own feelings and thoughts to our poor pets, and then turn in disgust if they catch, as they do sometimes, something of our own fevers and unquietness.... But still they are not ours, to possess and know.... It is a thought that cheers one up. (*MA* 135, 136)

Knowing that we cannot *fully* dominate the world, cannot turn it into ourselves by channelling its forces through our own sign systems, is portrayed as being a comfort in Smith's poems. Therefore she often pictures that part of herself which attempts to resist, or remain 'other' to cultural constraints and coercions, as being 'animal'; like the 'mute exigence of the organic' and of all energies that remain foreign to language and to the acculturated psyche as Freud understood it, such forces run counter to 'the strictures of the imaginary ego and threaten to pull it apart' (Boothby 101, 102). Out of such associations, it seems, we get what I noted earlier: the death drive figured forth, in the novel trilogy, as the narrator mounted on running horses, as well as self-destructive tendencies made tigerish, as are the images of both our narrator and Dionysus in the first book. Such forces are only problematically domesticated, as is 'Flo', the zoo tiger (named after Smith's proper name, Florence), whose death at the end of *Novel on Yellow Paper* is foreshadowed *as our speaker*'s when the latter laments becoming trapped within the prison-house of language and her editor's conventions:

> Oh talking voice that is so sweet, how hold you alive in captivity, how point you with commas, semi-colons, dashes, pauses and paragraphs? (NOYP 39)

The animals in Smith's poems often become, to the extent that they are 'possessed' by their masters, metaphors for trained humanity, conditioned to respond to signs and signals, rewards and whips, all constructed by dominating forces in the cultural arena. Like the 'faithful dog-o' she often described herself as being in her own working life as a secretary (MA 293), or her 'Donkey', Smith's animal and human speakers alike frequently find themselves inscribed and therefore circumscribed by authority, as does the dog in one of Alexander Pope's poems selected for a collection of her favourite pieces from childhood, *The Poet's Garden*:

> Engraved on the Collar of a
> Dog, which I gave to His
> Royal Highness
>
> I am his Highness' dog at Kew;
> Pray tell me, sir, whose dog are you?[32]

It was Smith's sharp awareness of the social conditioning of human consciousness, with all of its needs and desires, which caused her to become highly sceptical about romantic love (or indeed anything romanticised). As we will see in Chapter 2, this differentiated her from a number of her female contemporaries. To some of them she seemed 'heartless', but in her work the heart*break* of her own philosophical convictions complicates any such simple analysis, or any attempt to read her deconstructive 'play' with such convictions as being simply and only that. Failure to believe in her love for Freddy – a figure who appears in the poems as well as the novels, and who is highly evocative of not only suburban middleclass-ness but also the dream of love and marriage – is one of the reasons for her narrator's breakdown in the trilogy. There, social pressure calls her to marry what she understands him to be: a 'chimeric' love, as she sees it, a consort constructed by her own suspect imaginings and not the real man for whom she feels something much less (NOYP 222 and *passim*). Smith's work demonstrates a constant fear of being caught up, with the help of propagated cultural fantasies, in the suburban values and encircling patriarchal narratives that constitute her setting; in it women 'have an idea, that if only they were married it would be all right' (NOYP 149). As her speaker in *Novel on Yellow Paper* says in an especially wry moment, connecting current literary/political fantasies about Stalin's emergent state with those of more conventional romance, 'it is like the refrain in *The Three Sisters*. It is the *leitmotiv* of all their lives. It is their Moscow.... [I]t will let them in to the Russia of their matrimonial ambition'

(149–50). 'Marriage I think/For women/Is the best of opiates', Smith wrote in one uncollected poem (*MA* 216). The obvious connection she makes between social and political discourse in these texts, written as they were at the zenith of British fascination with the communist Soviet Union, suggests her involvement in and suspicion of the 'intertextuality' of cultural propaganda, or its presence at every level of thought, writing and action (all of which begins to describe a latent politics that dovetails with her poetics, to be discussed at length in the chapters to come). Such suspicions cause the fracture of Smith's potential love poems, and even, at times, the rendering of love between friends, relatives and women suspect as well, if it involves role-modelling and the imbibing of social values.

Neither 'child-like' nor 'simple', then, nor the work of an 'ingenue', Smith's poems in particular carry and miscarry the rhythms of inculcating forces – nursery rhymes, ballads and fairy tales, for example – as testimony to their lasting influence and to the power of familiar sounds to produce conditioned, unexamined responses. But it is also important to connect Smith's use of such materials with the similar uses made by contemporaries like Louis MacNeice, a friend whose work she admired intensely and often alludes to in her own. Though untouched in criticism on Smith – which again, tends to relate her themes exclusively to other women writers – the links between Smith's innovations and MacNeice's more conventionally political but equally revisionary use of parable and an 'impure' poetic form help to explicate her similar involvement with political commentary, as well as her response to that powerful poetic force of the Thirties, the 'Auden generation' or 'MacSpaunday' group.[33] Smith's earlier critics often claimed that it was the *non*-political valence of such cultural materials as nursery rhymes that drew her to them, that she admired the 'straightforward[ness]' or 'free[dom] from moralising' that tales like those told by the brothers Grimm supposedly display (Montefiore 44). But there is far more to it than this; as Auden himself wrote, in introduction to the *Tales of Grimm and Andersen*, the brothers Grimm were the first to record folk tales 'exactly as they were told by the folk themselves without concessions to bourgeois prudery or cultured literary canon' (xix). Yet Auden's cultural politics as applied to the appreciation of folk tales suggests his vulnerability to making heroic stories himself, his tendency to create what Smith called 'schoolboy melodrama' (*OTF* 59) in tales like the 'Mortmere' stories invented with Christopher Isherwood. In his introduction to the *Tales*, he suggests that in such stories 'luck is not fortuitous but dependent on [the hero's] character and his actions' – and that 'the tales end with the establishment of justice', and appropriate rewards for good and evil (xvi). Smith's many and far more ambiguous remarks about such media carry dark indictments of what she sees as the insidious nature of that unqualified 'justice', and of judgement in general which comes masked as being non-judgemental because rooted in 'common' sense and sensibility: 'It is for their reasonableness the stories frighten and hold, for their matter-of fact, almost gay exploration of hazards, the easy cruelties being no more than is to be expected, if you do not behave yourself.'[34] A chilly illustration of Smith's almost Foucauldian view of 'crime and punishment', the complex tonality of such statements begs us to re-read the supposedly conservative 'fondness', as it was described, which she displays for using simple parables, rhymes, hymn tunes and their meters in her poems as her recognition and exploration of certain aspects of her own questionable cultural programming. And yet, we must also not shirk the recognition that certain traditional forces held her in a partly irresistible grip. For example, the force and authority of the Anglican Church (whose establishment marked the exchange of the old Canon Law for the new English Common Law and a distinctly English versus European Christian value system) remain visible at some level beneath the subversive facade of the same poems and the novels. The latter never manage a simple overturning of beliefs, but rather an uneasy, even tortured dialogue between speakers deployed by Smith who, jockeying internal positions at both the centre and margins of culture, much like the rider from whom she gained her nickname,[35] calls herself a 'religious-minded agnostic', 'a back-slider as a non-believer' (*MA* 202; Dick 45).

'Manners, morals, religion – all patterns.' Smith's relationship to Christianity, as played out in her poems and novels, may serve as the best example and summary of what has been said thus far about her main themes, philosophies and strategies. As Michael Tatham has suggested, Smith was 'one of the very few religious poets of our day' – one who 'speaks to our condition as modern piety can seldom hope to speak' because, though she longed to believe, she had no choice but to turn away from 'that appalling construction of human logic and perverse ingenuity, the God made with human hands – the father of the inferno and the church militant...' (133, 135). It is true that Smith understood Church doctrine to be a human construction – another unsatisfying, even catastrophic establishment of 'pattern'. It is also true that she repeatedly re-wrote its role in history by alluding to its credentials as *the* expert on persecution (having conducted the Inquisition 'for almost six hundred years', whereas the Nazis 'managed only thirteen' with their programme), and by speaking of it in the same breath as 'modern communism' under Stalin – both, according to Smith, were inaugurated by a 'handful of revolutionaries, with the highest aspirations for the good of mankind' (*MA* 168). She also objected to a number of the Church's operations on feminist grounds. She questioned the fact that only one woman was involved in the making of *The New English Bible*, for example; and when it came to issues of contraception in the 1960s, she laughed at 'the spectacle of a celibate priesthood discussing the intimate details of female anatomy' and conjugal relations (*MA* 199). Certainly Smith demonstrates a very British prejudice against *European* Christianity, or the 'Papism' of the continent, which social historians like Edwin Jones argue is at the root of the nation's specific history of xenophobia (234–35); we must also understand her as the inheritor of the nineteenth-century near-alliance between English and Prussian Protestant churches over and against Rome (most espoused by their blood relation in Prince Albert). Equally certainly, as Gill Plain argues, Smith was perturbed by the rush of post-war conversions to Roman Catholicism – such as that of her own sister, Molly Smith, or of the author of *The Spiritual Aeneid* (1919), Fr Ronald Knox, whom her characters discuss in *Novel on Yellow Paper* (179–80). Pompey's comments on its 'cliques and secret societies' effect, and its offering of what she tells us Queen Victoria and her own Aunt would call 'nonsense' – that is, ritual, smells and bells – seem connected to Smith's own suspicions about what Plain describes as 'the ascendancy of highly structured religious systems over more private forms of worship' (72) at the time or, perhaps more accurately, about Roman Catholicism's comforting and unquestionable solution of mystery to real historical difficulties. But Smith's speakers, like Pompey, overtly acknowledge the connection between their own history of Protestant, 'private forms of worship' and the fact that '[t]here's something of Mrs. Humphrey Ward in [her]' (*NOYP* 30): that nineteenth-century voice whose belief that the way beyond papist superstitions was through science and in expressly teutonic, even Aryan enlightenments in thought.[36] Perhaps Smith's work at its most 'moralistic' – an adjective which everyone from D.J. Enright to Michael Horovitz has used to describe it – would advocate nothing more than her controversial poem 'How Do You See?' does: no further 'enchantment[s]' (*CP* 518, 520) that sport dangerously absolute truths with mystifying morals, which in the Thirties too easily doubled for proliferating political beliefs as well.[37] As she puts it in a mock-epigrammatic piece from her equally controversial if unpublished essay, 'The Necessity of Not Believing':

> Know thy world, Man; through Art or Science, dote on it,
> But do not build a fairy tale upon it.[38]

And as Helen Carr puts it, in a short description that encapsulates beautifully the representative 'subject' *in*, as well as subject-matter *of*, almost all of Smith's work:

> Now in our post-Christian world the lack of guaranteed meaning is what most of us have to live with. For us, individual identity is what the nineteenth-century French poet Tristan Corbière called a 'mélange adultère de tout' – an adulterated/adulterous mixture of everything. We are each constantly changing, unstable, contradictory: formed, de-formed, re-formed by our personal histories, our social histories, our class and gender positions, our bodies, our hormones, our conscious beliefs and our unconscious drives. We are born into a maze of language through whose

contradictions and ambiguities we come to what sense we can of ourselves and our world. (140)

Understanding the resonance between such thoughts and Smith's allows us to see that what neither Tatham nor John L. Mahoney confront in their essays on her 'religiosity' is that it was jeopardised by much more than her trouble with the Christian doctrine of eternal damnation and hell – ideas she found contradictory to that of a loving God, and ones she suspected of having been made up to keep the Christian soldiery in line. Smith doubted the whole New Testament story, largely, it seems, because she believed that if there were such a thing as a 'true' story, it could never exist uncorrupted by intertextual power relations. She resisted the last century's updating of Biblical materials and prayerbooks for contradictory reasons: partly because they made clear to all, for arguably the first time, the highly debatable nature of scripture, but more importantly because she felt that the beauty of the materials' archaic sounds and poeticisations is the only sort of truth that is preservable. Religion was for her, as we shall see, a kind of art or fiction that *is* beautiful as long as it is acknowledged as such:

> My thoughts about Christianity are much confused by my feelings. My feelings fly up, my thoughts draw them down again, crying: Fairy stories. But how can one's heart *not* go out to the idea that a God of absolute love is in charge of the universe, and that in the end, All will be well? I do not think there is any harm in trying to behave as if this were the case. But if we say that positively we believe it is so, then at once the human creature is apt to do something that is dangerous and not very good; that is, to fall into definitions as to the nature of God and Goodness, and be angry with those who do not agree. (*MA* 153)

Smith redefines 'the Fall' above as being the propensity to establish absolute truths, and myths of infallibility; we shall see a political relative of this definition at work as a structural motif in *Over the Frontier*. Yet it is terribly important to note that her work constantly demonstrates self-reflexivity (or possibly 'back-sliding') about even this, her own anti-conviction. We see it in her characteristic splicing in of a distorted echo from tradition, from Shakespeare, as she makes her first point above; we are offered her own possible condemnation for divided thought and desire as we hear remnants of the regicide Claudius' tortured failure to pray for forgiveness in *Hamlet* (hence the capitalised 'All' recalling Claudius' fervent assertion that, according to Christian doctrine, 'All may be well' if he gets down on his knees). As in *Hamlet*, the conclusion may well be, if her echo above implies it, that

> My words fly up, my thoughts remain below:
> Words without thoughts never to heaven go. (Act III, scene iv. 72, 97–98)

'I daresay', she admitted in 'The Necessity of Not Believing', 'my own temperament, preferring this emptiness of an indifferent universe, is no more a pointer to absolute truth than the narrowest of orthodox religion' (31). If anything, it is dialogue between conflicting myopic visions that Smith's work promotes in an imperfect world because, as she elsewhere notes, everybody loves their own version of Jesus – though 'it is not the Beloved's features we see, but those of the Lover' (*MA* 203). In other words, and as with animals, that which is too darkly 'other' we tend to make up stories about, reading all we survey and imagine through or against ourselves. And our 'selves' in Smith's eyes too often read line for line in sync with an inherited cultural script. Thus Smith raged against poets she admired like Eliot who, in times that she felt called for courage and collaborative criticism, etched out only their own 'neuroses' and 'disgust' for humankind in 'terror-talk of cat-and-mouse damnation...', '"pacing for ever" (to use Mr Eliot's words with a different application) "in the hell of make-believe"' – in other words, passing off their internal hells and (often self-protectionist or racist) fears as modernist vision and prophecy, wrought through the transcendent possibilities of an 'impersonal' method of composition (*MA* 151). Smith's commentary on Eliot's work effectively deconstructs his poetics of impersonality to expose its *personal* agenda – one quite different in trajectory from that described by Carr. It was precisely this sort of self-*delusion* rather than self-investigation, couched in terror and nostalgia, that she most wished to avoid – or, failing that, to reveal in her own work.

Therefore if Smith did, in seeming contradiction, admire Eliot's essays and even, as some have claimed, his poetics of impersonality, it was from her very different modernist perspective which alters its power dynamic to direct its dissecting regard at *self* as well as the world. Such 'impersonality' works by abandoning the myth of separate subjectivity in order to speak from the interstices that in part compose its porous front, rather than from any position beyond it. In 'good faith', Smith could not speak of the beyond, or the origins of her desire for God (whose existence she never negated), given the suspect nature of the only means she had available to do so: the entangled discourses of history, power-politics, and social fictions of all kinds that have constructed her labyrinthine self. But she could resist by exposing the controlling force of religious and other kinds of rhetoric to which she knew she was most thoroughly trained to respond. Hers was, like that of Browning's (and later, MacNeice's) 'Childe Roland', in one of her favourite and most alluded-to poetic images, the kind of resistance which confronts the 'Dark Tower' to fight the impossible battle without an ivory alternate to believe in, to sustain her; she admired this romantic image because it was, ironically, 'so full of the feeling of courage without hope and resistance without belief'.[39] Her struggle within language – or from between the lines, as my subtitle has it – does therefore strike us as evidencing the early days of the 'linguistic turn' into postmodernism, with its multiplying versions of what it would mean to take courage in the light of culture's deconstruction as a Babel of falsities and even horrors. It is to her credit, it must be said, that at a time when many writers were caught up in spinning ideologically inflected manifestos or, later, 'new romantic' or 'apocalyptic' visions, she was engaged instead in taking a close look at those webs – what the Greeks would have called, in another era, the 'nets' that individuals and 'Fate' tend to weave in all-too-close coordination.

Ironically, it was only after T.S. Eliot suggested that 'it was time to re-assess non-modernist trends' (*SS* 210) that Stevie Smith's poems found their way into a major anthology, *The Faber Book of Twentieth Century Verse* (1953). Now that critics and theorists have begun to re-assess *modernist* trends, we begin to be able to *re*-read 'non-modernists' like Smith in order to re-think modernism itself. The following chapter briefly outlines Smith's life experience for the purpose of locating her position in her era's cultural text – both as the figure women's studies has discovered for us: a lower-middle-class working woman living in London's suburbs, a woman writer in a very masculine literary era and publishing world, *and* as an intellectual coming to adulthood in the bloodiest, most politically and philosophically unstable of historical moments spanning two world wars. If Smith was right in saying that her work changed little over the years, and if interiority must indeed be re-read as formed by the externalities and discourses that surround a writer's forming consciousness, then it is of utmost importance that something of that generative context be sketched out before beginning to 'close-culturally' read Smith's work.

2
'The times are the times of a black split heart': Stevie Smith's Life and Work in Context

In conversation with her friend Kay Dick, Stevie Smith once said: 'I love life. I adore it, but only because I keep myself well on the edge' (Dick 44). She seemed to gesture in that instance to the edge between life and death by suicide, the only unambiguous position of power she could imagine – and did imagine often, beginning at the early age of eight when, 'at the mercy of external forces', she lingered too long in a convalescent home after contracting tubercular peritonitis (*SS: AB* 15). 'The thought cheered me up wonderfully and quite saved my life', as she put it in one interview; 'For if one can remove oneself at any time from the world, why particularly now?'[1] Such imaginings, among her 'first steps...in heresy' (*S* 17), perhaps culminated and almost failed her in 1953, when she unsuccessfully slit her wrists while on the job as a secretary at Newnes Publishers. Critics who read suicidal tendencies back into all of a poet's work (as has often been done with one of Smith's greatest admirers, Sylvia Plath, as well as Smith herself) have made quite a lot of that single biographical fact. But her image of 'living close to the edge' also expanded into a figurative disposition towards *all* the many edges she occupied in her life between and after the wars – all the liminal positions she both chose and was forced into taking by 'external forces' too powerful to control.

Such positioning allowed her to momentarily and precariously resist that centre, that 'English mix', as she called it, of textual imagination and cultural prejudices that she so often acknowledged controlled all her thought. Long before W.H. Auden famously wrote in his poem 'September 1, 1939' that the Thirties had been 'a low dishonest decade' Smith believed it, viewing herself as damnably implicated by the many hypocritical modes of thinking that her speakers would describe as responsible for forging such times – 'the times of a black split heart' (143), as Celia describes them in *The Holiday*. Hers certainly was, as many have noted, a largely feminine world revolving at the edge of a very masculinist age (which to her chagrin found its reflection in the arts),[2] but her sense of exclusion *and* over-determination by the power-sharers of that age was generated by far more than gender difference. It is important to understand from her work that she neither felt at home in nor able to exit *any* of her spheres of existence; she viewed this as a condition of life in her 'times', writing that it is only at the brink of real or metaphorical death to the world that 'any... sensitive poet can say ["I am happy"] – or for that matter, any human being at all, conscious of exile' (*S* 297). She wrote of exile as a cultural and, given the exigencies of her times, all but ontological condition, not as one specific to her or even to her sex.

A childhood outside and inside text

Smith's own 'conscious[ness] of exile' began to develop early, for reasons that seem to have extended far beyond her banishment for medical treatment. Baptised Florence Margaret Smith on 11 October 1902, twenty-one days after tenuously surviving birth, one of her earliest memories would be her father's desertion of the family for a life at sea. Equipped with 'little sense of responsibility', according to her biographers (*SS: AB* 7), and a long-frustrated dream of joining the Navy, Charles Smith ran away from his wife and two small daughters, then aged five and three, to first join the White Star Line as a pantry boy, and finally become an Acting Interpreter in French in the Royal Naval Reserve. His method of keeping in touch – postcards sent, as Smith remembers, with messages as brief as 'Off to Valparaiso love Daddy' – left her all-female nucleus continually destabilised and uncertain, and herself as a little girl with 'a very profound impression of transiency' which would have endless repercussions in her life and work (*SS: AB* 8). Her father returned periodically to collect the Naval Wife's Allowance which Smith's increasingly frail mother received and unquestioningly turned over; for this Smith, it seems, unlike her older sister and her aunt, never forgave him, effectively casting him out of her circle of allegiances, refusing even to attend his funeral in 1949.

And yet her narrator's stagy rendition of her feelings about what appears to be an identical sort of father in *Novel on Yellow Paper* would give us pause in reading them autobiographically. There we are left in an indeterminate space between 'facts of [Smith's] life', if we as readers know them, and her 'life as text' in passages which perform, via ostensible autobiography, the complicating treatment she applied to even the most indisputable emotional facts, such as her feelings upon witnessing the slow death of her mother:

> You so much wish to alleviate. That is practical positive and desirable. You cannot. You imagine yourself in the sufferer's place. Already this begins to be dangerous. The livelier your imagination the greater your pity. And the greater your fear. This is already dangerous.
>
> When I saw the suffering of my much loved ma, I could not help her. I raged against necessity I raged against my absconding and very absent

pa, I raged and fumed and spat. My emotion I like to think was simple, pure and vigorous. But was there in it for all that an element of self-pity? I came in time to view my absconded pa without indignation. And if at first 'Revenge, Timotheus cried' I later shut up my old Timotheus. My mama had made an unsuitable marriage and no doubt my pa found it also very unsuitable. And unsuitable marriages breed the Pompeys of this world, and a lot of other troubles as well. (162)

Such a passage displays Smith's enduring interest in the ways in which a confusion of intentions and projections results in strong and seemingly 'pure' emotion. It leads above to what Smith seemed to despise: righteous-because-too-simple 'indignation', with a trajectory into the sort of (here specifically feminist) anger she regularly caricatured in her work. Merging personal and political landscapes, Smith constantly links the genesis of ideological 'vigorousness' with sympathies that are suspect, that reflect unexamined personal investments and psychological deprivation. It was a process she considered 'dangerous' at every level. And she would, as the last sentence of the quote above suggests, portray it as constituent within the larger political and historical processes that spawned the private and public 'Pompeys' of her era – most of the latter 'beginning to be dangerous' even as Smith was dubbing her novels' speakers with that name in the Thirties.

Her mother died by the time Smith was seventeen, leaving her in the war-exhausted London of 1919 with her sister and aunt to run their 'house of female habitation' (*CP* 410) and grow somewhat bitter about the male-centred ways of the world. Although she in part admired her mother's strong and forever uncomplaining loyalty to her father, Smith could not model herself after such dutiful, sacrificial, Victorian femininity; another part of her railed against patriarchy, and celebrated female companionship as does Celia, her narrator in *The Holiday*:

> [M]ost women, especially in the lower and lower-middle classes, are conditioned early to having 'father' the centre of the home-life, with father's dinner, and father's *Times* and father says, so that they are not brought up like me to be this wicked selfish creature, to have no boring-old father-talk, to have no papa at all that one attends to, to have a darling aunt that one admires, ... to have a darling sister that is working away from home, and to be for my aunt, for my sister, the one. (*TH* 28)

With strikingly Gertrude Stein-like movement, or syntactical evolution, this passage seems to build away from the male-at-centre, peripheral-female-self model to a female-surrounded 'oneness'; in the last three clauses above, 'the one' ambiguously describes both the speaker and the three women as brought together. As in Smith's oft-mentioned poem, 'A House of Mercy', feminine solidarity and autonomy *is* celebrated here; but like so much of

Smith's writing, this passage presents several contradictory lines of thought and cannot be recuperated for a straightforward feminist reading. And what distinguishes Smith from Stein is that her speaker's narrational control is much more insistently portrayed as being ephemeral – as encountering immediate competition from other internalised cultural viewpoints, each one with its own manner of speaking, so that self-definition (and speaking itself) is continually portrayed as struggle. Above, one hears such struggle beginning to surface between the redefinition of 'wicked selfish[ness]' as a positive thing, *and* the deprivation of a potentially positive thing in having 'no papa' (a loving word) to attend to. More dramatically, the tone abruptly changes as the passage continues, and bravado finds its place usurped by another kind of strong speaker: the voice of social conformity registering bewilderment at the difference from others – even female others – that exclusively female-centred existence can make:

> And what points the happiness of the home life to an almost unbearable sharp point, is the running around outside the home, this home of my Aunt, my sister and myself, and the getting by, and the social play-off, as a girl like any other girl, like any other girl brought up, that is not, when I look at these others [*sic*] girls, that is not, oh is not the truth. (*TH* 29)

The speaker's narrational trajectory founders here as it encounters the deeply inscribed need to be 'like other girls' – a social imperative that operates somewhat differently in its alternative form for male children, who are encouraged to be individuals, innovators. As the words constructing 'unbearable happiness' snarl around the recollection of 'other girls' and *her* difference, they are thus waylaid into expression of the unbearable pain that 'points the happiness' – the word 'point' being repeated here to signal the psychological blade and *counterpoint* of trauma that enables bravado by way of forcing denial.

These examples demonstrate the impossibility of offering any *one* of Smith's passages, however 'autobiographical', as proof of an opinion she held or emotion she felt. What they record are confrontations with internalised voices summoned into performance by the memory of a childhood experience – dramatising how it is, oftentimes, that a thinking subject will proliferate the discourses and contradictions of its environment, and then fool itself into thinking that it knows its own mind. Like Joyce's *A Portrait of the Artist*, Smith's work is much less a 'telling about herself' than it is a 'telling about telling', or the problems of narrating in words (and thus, we infer, forming in thought) a self. Gendered issues do arise, given that her subject is often female – though as often splayed between masculine terrains of the mind, and even given masculine names. Her use of autobiography therefore revises the concept of a 'self-centred' tale, or *selfhood* altogether. The traditional model of unified if 'limited omniscience', and *bildung*, in her novels is interrupted by the discursive forces that overlap and overwhelm the submerged, 'undomesticated' agent as Smith often depicts it, as though anticipating what feminists in the 1980s would refer to as the muted 'wild zone' (Showalter 471–72). Because language is built to accommodate such forces, the 'real' people who enter into her work from her life take form less recognisably as themselves than as discourses of one kind or another; as Smith herself warned, 'My characters start off by being themselves but are soon unrecognisable as real people' (*SS: AB* 174). Given that such lines infiltrate her own speaker's speech, perhaps all that we may learn about *Smith's* life and thoughts at the tenuous intersection of fact, fiction and entangled 'telling' is that many of her experiences, like the one related above, left emphatically divided impressions upon her as a result of her awareness of any speaker's ventriloquistic positioning in the relation of them. It registers an awareness, in other words, of being both the fabricator seemingly composing the lines *and* the dummy helplessly delivering them as they rise up from what is more truly a cultural repertoire. It seems hardly surprising that Smith would find the most compatible template for particularly her novels' speakers 'talk[ing] about [themselves]' (Dostoyevsky 3) in Dostoyevsky's 'underground' man, whose liability in having an 'acute consciousness' is such that he is aware 'every moment in myself of many, very many elements absolutely opposite' to one another – a phenomenon he dates to his own 'times' of Russian division and cultural angst 'in the nineteenth century' (2, 5). It would seem that this kind of awareness, updated, is the 'subject' of her work; and as with Dostoyevsky, whose *Notes from the Underground* she quotes *verbatim* at the end of her trilogy, it is not any *particular* subjectivity, not even her own, that interests her. It seems that it was her similar 'acute consciousness' within her times that, more than any other force, generated her Dostoyevskian sense of exile, of being apart from others – even female others – as well as her speakers' positionings at the margins of culture's inescapable conventional narrative.

It was in 1906 that the family – Smith's mother, Ethel Spear, her mother's sister, Madge Spear (always referred to as 'the Lion Aunt', the strong, commonsensical family manager), Smith's sister Molly, two years her senior, and Smith herself, known as 'Peggy' in those days – moved from Hull to the northern outskirts of London, to Palmers Green, selecting a house at 1 Avondale Road where Smith would live to the end of her life. Her biographers find the move difficult to explain; though supposedly effected for financial reasons, the new home presented a burden comparable to that of the one sold. Frances Spalding speculates that gossip about her father's leaving home may have driven the family south, and that desires to save face and protect the social future of the children may have caused them to relocate above their means in Palmers Green (7). In any case, there were noticeable discrepancies between the way this feminine household was able to sustain itself and the lifestyles of others in the suburb, reputed to be one of London's 'most snobbish' – where 'the straitened circumstances at 1 Avondale Road, where there was no maid or servant of any kind, would not have gone unremarked' (*SS: AB* 11). Enough money *had* been saved, however, from Smith's maternal grandfather's legacy to send the girls to fee-paying schools, where they found themselves 'among children on the whole better off than themselves' (*SS: AB* 11).

Though rarely discussed, the issue of Smith's class sympathies is of no small importance to her work. Her speakers often associate themselves (as in the first quoted passage of this chapter) with lower or lower-middle-class experience.[3] Her generation of writers, those who came to maturity *entre deux guerres*, was almost exclusively of the upper-middle-or-higher classes, as well as educated at Oxbridge. Smith might well have thus found herself in yet another sense on the outside, despite her sympathies with some aspects of the literary era's socialist agenda, for though she was descended from well-to-do grandfathers who found considerable success in their respective careers in the shipping industry, her own childhood experience was one of relative austerity, and her adult life was shaped by the necessity of working as a secretary in order to make ends meet. She and her sister retained, as well, something of the Yorkshire accent that their mother and aunt brought with them from Hull; Smith often retold the story of being weighed as a child on the scales of a local butcher, who remarked when she spoke that she was a 'foreign package'. Molly, more seriously, was forced to face the hard fact that her north country accent, 'unreceived' as it was in the radio and theatre worlds of the time, would complicate any attempt she might make to realise her dream of acting on stage. It is not difficult to understand why Smith, rather than 'extolling the virtues of Palmers Green' and southern England's 'middle-class virtues', as biographers of her life would have it, more often critiqued suburbia's snobberies and contradictions from her liminal perspective even as they worked to shape her, a child of the same world.[4]

Her essay, 'A London Suburb', often seen as a litany of its praise, subtly demonstrates this by moving in and out of bright, clear, almost wholly positive 'travelogue' discourse – 'There is much going on in the suburb for those who seek company' (*MA* 102) – and darker, uninterpellated imagery that mutely belies her proffered front of cheerfulness. For example, at the end of two paragraphs devoted to 'the high-*lying* life of a true suburban community' (my emphasis), and the beauty of its lake park which she indeed loved, she writes:

> At the corner by the woods the water by the lake is very dark, it is forty feet deep, and speaks again of the past, for here it was the old Lady Cattermole drowned herself. (*MA* 103)

Immediately following this submerged cry from between the lines of both the text and the context of 'life as usual' comes a new paragraph, initiated by an incongruent voice just beyond the surface of the lake: '"Mother," says the child, "is that a dog of good family?"' Such half-humorous juxtapositionings emphasise the suburban imagination's entrapment within, at its 'higher' levels (or 'surface' levels, as her joke goes), pedigree and proper behaviour to the exclusion of all whose experience might not conform – including a former 'Lady' who chose a way out which Smith often envisioned for herself. Inasmuch as such acculturation limits her/his ability to think or speak beyond limiting social discourse, the well-trained child demonstrates an ironic connection to doghood. In an equally self-deluded way, at the end of the essay, better-bred suburbanite adults strive to differentiate themselves from their neighbours by calling the *latter* 'suburban' – illustrating the very sort of snobbery and projection that in Smith's work epitomise suburbanity, and keep its hierarchy, at the expense of the poor and 'eccentric', in place and at peace:

> Life in the suburb is richer at the lower levels. At these levels the people are not self-conscious at all, they are at liberty to be as eccentric as they please, they do not know that they are eccentric. At the more expensive levels the people have bridge parties and say of their neighbors, 'They are rather suburban'. (*MA* 104)

Somewhere between these positions of unknowing eccentricity and identification with those who speak of suburban attitudes with disdain is the speaker of this essay. Smith intimates as much by having her draw it to conclusion from a position on the outside, yet looking through 'the fishnet curtains in the windows of the houses [at] the family life', with its father-centred scenes like the one I quoted earlier: 'father's chair, uproar, dogs, babies and radio' (*MA* 104). But a hall-of-mirrors effect here once again problematises any critique of this scene: If those at its heart critique *others* as being suburban, where do we locate our speaker's critique? Is she as suburban as they because she does the same? More about the coveting and distancing that keeps the suburbs intact will be said in my close-reading of *Novel on Yellow Paper* in Chapter 3; the novel's setting in 'Bottle Green' allows it to focus deeply on what studies of the suburbs during the decade reveal to be a politically-alienated as well as profoundly isolating context. The bright comment above about 'much going on in the suburb for those who seek company' will when further contextualised take on an especially empty sound. Here in this passage, it becomes impossible to know if those fishnet curtains divide a speaker drowning like Lady Cattermole from those in the family boat, or *vice versa*; which of these pictured, in other words, is actually lost? The question is a familiar one in Smith's work, surfacing, for example, in her best-known work, the poem 'Not Waving but Drowning'. Both there and here, as well as in the similar passage quoted much earlier, it would seem that resolving such issues is less the point than recognising the ways in which exile, desire and cultural programming split any speaker along a spectrum of responses and their attendant emotions.

Smith's descriptions of her 'happy' childhood in the suburbs must be re-read, then, as being made pointedly complicit in her world's shifting, often short-sighted, reality-constructing discourses that 'voice-over' the marginal or shut-out. And in doing so it is quite important to remember that Smith's work is always performative, is always built on the model of speech; even her prose is never straightforwardly descriptive or confessional. Her speaking voice is deeply *involved* in the struggle to win the voice-over competition between ascendant competitors and struggling losers – playing all parts 'herself', and sometimes even the silence that ensues in the text. In any case, it is a voice directly generated by her internalisation of suburban talk, though it modulates into parody and laughter at itself in moments critics have taken at face value, describing them as straightforward, even nostalgic, 'evocation[s] of... childhood' (*SS* 204). Another good example can be found in her send-up of Palmers Green, 'Syler's Green: a return journey', which was broadcast on BBC radio in 1947. It won praise in its post-war, conflicted moment of social reform, solidarity and desire for 'return' to the 'Little England' remembered (by suspect processes of nostalgia) as having existed at the turn of the century:

> Of course it wasn't always September or always sunny, but that is how one is apt to remember past times, it is always a sunny day. This sunny time of a happy childhood seems like a golden age, a time untouched by war, a dream of innocent quiet happenings, a dream in which people go quietly about their blameless business... believing in God, believing in peace, believing in Progress (which of course is always progress in the right direction)... believing also that the horrible things of life always happen abroad or to the undeserving poor and that no good comes from brooding upon them. (*MA* 84)

It becomes difficult *not* to hear this passage's gathering sarcasm, built out of snippets of familiar parlour philosophy. Although Smith's recollections of her rearing in the suburbs do often seem to evidence genuine nostalgia – what she in one of her many moments of self-implication calls her 'sniff of regional pride and smug self-righteousness' (*MA* 99) – she at the same time ridicules all of its usual referents, exposing their contradictions: professions of Christianity beside neglect for the poor; all-but-deified Victorian models of 'Progress' that led to two world wars; the celebration of a supposed 'innocence' that suppresses knowledge of the neglect, madness, suicide and even murder which find mention and burial in the course of these retrospective essays. Taken as a whole, their form mimics the linguistic process of repression by which culture produces memories of 'golden ages' (and Augustan diction, as the Movement poets were about to do[5]) by stoking conservative nostalgia as a remedy for unassimilated change. Britain at the turn of the 1940s was coping with not only the onset of war but also a growing onslaught of car-purchases demanding rapidly expanding road networks that were, in collaboration with other changes, forcing new models for housing, community, work, leisure and 'privacy' to come into being. Rather than offering simply a remembrance of things past, Smith's semi-autobiographical essays explicate the eerie connections between the *dis*connections and illusions informing 'private life' in the suburbs and those in broader social, national and international arenas.

Smith did well as a student through high school in Palmers Green, but began to do less well when, at her mother's prompting, she followed her scholarship-winning sister to North London Collegiate School. Many factors contributed to her poor performance there, not least among them her mother's final decline and passage in her last year – an event which so moved her that fifty years later, while being interviewed on television, she instantly burst into tears when asked if she had been present at the death. But Frances Spalding hypothesises that the repressive discipline at North London also contributed to her scholarly mediocrity by bringing out the worst in Smith, who was undeniably bright but 'who needed time to think her own thoughts' (27). To explicate the situation, Spalding offers a quote from Smith's speaker in *The Holiday*, who claims that it was at this stage that she

> first learnt to be bored and to be sick with boredom, and to resist both the good with the bad, and to resist and to be of low moral tone and non-co-operative, with the 'Could do better' forever on my report and the whole of the school-girl strength going into this business of resistance, this Noli-me-tangere, this Come near and I shoot. (118)

Because her distinctly American, 'wild west' expressions of warning represent the influence of another sort of discourse – that of 'rugged individualism', which became synonymous with American expansionism and capitalism in the mid-century golden age of cinema, with its John-Wayne-westerns – they should be read only very cautiously as autobiographical utterances. Yet it seems fair to say that the passage does contain some elements of Smith's own growing intolerance for educational structures and their collusion with social imperatives. Like Virginia Woolf, whose essays and novels she admired, Smith wrote against traditional sorts of education for women. These typically included, as she put it in one review of a book by Josephine Kamm on 'famous educating women', written for the *Spectator* in 1958, 'ornamental subjects ill-taught and unmastered', and 'intrusive smatterings of fashion' or social grooming at the expense of 'what the girls' brothers were having in their schools' (*MA* 179). One might even say that she moved beyond Woolf in that she approached the issue with slightly greater sensitivity to differences of class and race. She praised women educators who made 'advances against prejudice', and set 'democratic' examples by not distinguishing among their students on the basis of class and race as well as gender (*MA* 179). Focussing on the reported fact that 'the girls of the poor learnt better', she seems to have made the controversial suggestion that wealth and the different social training it demands only make unmediated thinking in the classroom all the harder. She even began to approach, in her novels, the difficult issue of women's sex-education. Her critique of joyless presentations that avoid facts, stress abstinence from alcohol to preclude loss of inhibitions and ultimately fill listeners as well as her speaker with 'profound aversion' (*NOYP* 138) is facilitated by the juxtaposed story, discussed in Chapter 3, of a school production of *The Bacchae*, whose Dionysian message warns against propagating such immoderate ignorance of human passion, and thus exposes at the same time the contradictions between what students learn from canonical art and from licensed agents of mainstream morality. Smith's various critiques of women's education bespoke her desire to see women taught to think for themselves, and to cast a suspicious glance at the motives of educators who seemed reluctant to facilitate such ends. She held a rigidified British social structure (supported by women as well as men) responsible for 'not fe[eding]' female students for fear they might 'become boys now, and boys, cast down' (*MA* 179) – a possibility she allows to stand in this particular review without comment.

On the job(s) and 'on holiday'

Smith's own possibilities, however, became limited by her rebellious response to schooling. She recalls for her friend Kay Dick that, what with '[m]oney being short and school report singularly unpropitious for a university whatjamacallit, I went to Mrs Hoster's Secretarial Training College, oh these colleges....' (*MA* 293). Her lament may have been due to the fact that Mrs Hoster's focussed even more relentlessly on social etiquette rather than skills: proper address for royalty, aristocracy, clergy and so on. She bore it out, however, because despite the interest she had expressed in journalism at school, and the encouragement she had received in her writing, she felt compelled to pursue what she knew would bring her a regular salary. Her job – her 'job job' as she often called it, to emphasise its monotony – at Newnes Publishers, working primarily for the baronet Sir Neville Pearson, bored her and at moments even drove her to despair. But it also provided her with enough free hours at her desk to produce typescripts of her own poems and even, when the time came, all of *Novel on Yellow Paper*, whose title reflects its genesis on the less expensive office paper used for carbon copies. Perhaps it was her ability to laugh at her situation – as this titular joke makes evident – that not only sustained her but also enabled her to satirise and transform the voices she heard around her into materials for her writing.

During the 1920s Smith did, in effect, and in addition to working at Newnes, put *herself* through the schooling she would have liked to have had. As her biographers have demonstrated, this was a period of 'prodigious mental activity' for her (*SS: AB* 52) during which she absorbed long, Catholic lists of literary, historical, philosophical and theological materials, all the while keeping meticulous reading journals from which many of her later works' allusions would be retrieved. She read Homer (in Greek, which she learned largely on her own), Shakespeare, Racine, Sterne, Johnson and Blake; she read, in unlikely groups, writers such as Spinoza, George Moore, Freud, Inge and numerous demonologists; she coupled her interest in Roman Catholic writers like Maurice Baring, Hillaire Belloc and G.K. Chesterton with an appetite for novels by D.H. Lawrence; she read the canonical moderns – James, Conrad, Ford, Eliot and others – with Kipling, Poe and all of modernism's hated Victorians also in hand. She was greatly impressed by continental writers like Dostoyevsky and Kafka, who provoked her emulation with their dark hilarity; and she was without question greatly influenced by the many women writers she read, from Frances Thompson, Dorothy Richardson and Woolf to Dorothy Parker, Anita Loos and even Agatha Christie. Begun as recompense for 'not having worked better at school' (*S* 44) and fuelled by her various intellectual struggles already underway, such as her epic one with Anglicanism and Catholicism (particularly after her sister's conversion to the latter), Smith's rigorous reading habits stood her in good stead later in the 1940s when, in order to supplement her income, she began moonlighting as a tireless, controversial but respected reviewer for publications like the *Tribune, Observer, Listener, Spectator, Encounter, New Statesman, John O'London's Weekly, World Review* and *Modern Woman*. Laura Severin's book, *Stevie Smith's Resistant Antics* (1997), carefully explains the conversation that Smith carried on with women about women's issues by reviewing for women's journals; in effect, all of Smith's reviews on a broad range of issues took their form as interventions, and together they might be seen to constitute her 'uncollected mini-essays' on mid-century culture.

In her time off – or 'loosed' from work, as she liked to put it in canine or equine terms – Smith could also become a very sociable being. She particularly enjoyed getting away from London, and had plenty of friends with seaside and country houses willing to indulge her fancy, in exchange for her good company and famously quick wit. This image of 'going on holiday' becomes an importantly ironic one in her writing, where it is used to portray the impossibility of ever fully 'getting away' or outside of one's own formative and imprisoning context; nowhere in her work does this become more clear than in the final novel of her trilogy, *The Holiday*. She often depicted attempts at such escape as tragicomic failures, ones in which inevitable misunderstandings duplicate the divisive prejudices, sexist attitudes, wartime fears and polarisations of the moment that, supposedly escaped, only reappear as chillingly inscribed within each vacationer. So it is that in her short story 'Beside the Seaside', for example, a *second* escape for the women characters becomes necessary – but it is, alas, only to 'Dungeness' where, as the place-name imagistically suggests, each remains unwittingly entrapped by her own learned responses, context and role.

Smith's role could apparently involve, according to her hosts and hostesses, that of the difficult guest at times – and even, at times, that of the difficult friend. Her biographers attribute this to what she herself calls, in the first quoted passage of this chapter, her 'wicked selfish[ness]' – her contradictory, demanding and even childish needs for both attention and independence. The appearance, as Frances Spalding describes it, of her 'tiny person' with her fringe-cut hair and school-girl dresses 'sustain[s] the myth of a slightly eccentric, childlike personality' (208); Jack Barbera and William McBrien in particular focus upon the strangeness of this child-like aspect, locating it at the core of the poet's psyche and as the voice that speaks in many of her poems. More recently, Laura Severin has fully reversed this reading, arguing that the dress was highly performative and enacted Smith's subversive suggestions in the work that the child is the mother of the woman in that she enjoys a stage of unfully enculturated response to the world.[6] This interpretation is encouraging insofar as it redirects foregoing critical processes by reading 'from her work to her life', rather than *vice versa*. But if we are to avoid simply inverting earlier biographical readings and ultimately repeating their mistakes – here, romanticising *the life* again by lioness-ising its presence behind the text in this way – the process needs to become a bit more complicated, and the life we need to locate if we are to understand the cultural locatedness of the text must be seen to be coterminous with it, in all its contradictions and tangled lines. In this instance, if we reconsider the same 'appearances' of contradictions as they take form in her work, we might see that though Smith actively deployed such disparate images and voices, it was not in order to discover any pre-pubescent feminine power. We must not paper over the fact that Smith *was* known to, at times, and quite problematically, interact like a child and compete with children for attention. She often dramatised exactly such internal and social conflicts: between those parts of self that long for inclusion, approval, caring and company, and those parts of self that are repelled by it, as she was obviously and often deeply repelled by her surrounding company, adults and children alike, as well as by her own susceptibility to immersion in their world. Taking full account of what happens in the texts – instead of theorising about whom we would *like* Smith to be from partial readings of them – leads us to understand that Smith portrayed adulthood itself as being continuingly juvenile, which of course complicates romanticised readings of her childlike speakers. She wrote that *all* are taught their needs and vulnerabilities, 'affections and passions, likes and dislikes, are "young"' (*MA* 124), and intimated in her work that like children, adults learn to mimic the discourses and opinions of their world in order to gain attention and acceptance – thereby gaining at the same time (and unthinkingly) its accumulated prejudices and corrupt practices.

Friends, relations and sex as translated into text

Smith incurred the anger of many of her friends and hosts by reproducing and often caricaturing, in her work, their employment of certain kinds of speech patterns and biases appropriate to their station or political stance; these are usually enfolded with her own mixed responses to and adaptations of their voices. Though such practice was essential to her art, which seems devoted to understanding English subjectivity as a struggle at the intersection of battling discourses, it did indeed alienate those who served as models, and jeopardised Smith's publication by houses leery of her reputation for producing 'libelous' writings. But she appears to have felt driven to make use of her materials despite her friends' feelings; her speaker at the outset of *Novel on Yellow Paper* even launches her narrative by saying 'Good-bye to all my friends, my beautiful and lovely friends' (9). As Spalding writes, 'it is surprising how few of her friends, even those she saw regularly, knew her intimately' (208); distance in friendship seemed to serve her work well. This of course makes it doubly difficult to piece their testimony as recorded in any biography into a 'true' picture of Smith – yet we might be tempted to hypothesise, given all the evidence, that she was at times rather inconsiderate, a Swiftian misanthrope. But *if* she was, her insertions of autobiographical materials into her work suggest that she critiqued herself as mercilessly as she did her friends; and indeed, as we shall see in Chapter 3, her speakers worry deeply that they are *composed of* their friends. Seemingly always desirous of, and even desperate for, their company, but also always a critic of it and of herself in it, one part of Smith was perhaps a bit like her speaker in the poem 'In My Dreams' who, after every longed-for visit, longs to be riding again into the night, back into 'exile', out towards the edge: 'I am glad I am going/I am glad, I am glad, that my friends don't know what I think' (*CP* 129).

Even Smith's lovers are found translated into her work as the vehicles of discursive forces with which her speakers must contend, a fact that makes her portrayals of them difficult to treat as being 'true to life'. 'Freddy', for example, her character based upon a neighbour named Eric Armitage to whom Smith was fleetingly engaged, all but incarnates suburbia, as I suggested in the last chapter – as well as perhaps film fantasies embodied in squeaky-clean footage of Fred Astaire and other 'moving pictures' of the Thirties. Even as a specifically British figure, Freddy represents an international phenomenon – a class-oriented 'meelyoo', as her speaker describes it in tried-on French – and one that Smith derides in her 'love poems'. In 'Freddy', for example, she explains with an indirect jab at 'Received

Pronounciation's' aspirated /h/'s, that '[she doesn't] anheimate mich in the ha-ha well-off suburban scene' (*CP* 65). Freddy upholds his social milieu's conventions proudly and unthinkingly – even 'huff[ily]' in the trilogy, announcing early on to newly intimate Pompey that he 'will have marriage now or nothing' (*NOYP* 107). Utterly non-dialogic, Freddy will not discuss Pompey's alternative vision of their relationship as being presently too 'delicate' to survive reshaping by such conventional plans. Her response is to voice a kind of moral outrage at his rigid conform-or-condemn mentality: 'How impious to destroy because not usual' (*NOYP* 207). She understands their growing love – which is 'light as gossamer... [and] strong as steel' (*NOYP* 207) but also 'unusual', largely because of her need for her freedom – to be the victim of the 'not growing at all but very entirely stunted' community. 'They' are not, in her view, 'of simple mind and kind heart' as Freddy avers, but are too 'narrow' to allow new possibilities to take unrecognisable forms:

> They... oppose every great idea that is at all difficult to understand, every great idea that is coming forth with blood and tears brought to birth they will beat it down and tread it into the ground. Yes they will do this if they can they will do this. (*NOYP* 219)

And yet, as will become clear in Chapter 3, these passages are couched in others that suggest that our speaker is herself very deeply indoctrinated by the same forces that ambush this love affair – that she, too, is the 'They' above, and an agent in the destruction at hand. Smith's portrayal of cultural forces dominating the formation of even the most intimate of bonds and barriers may tell us much about why she did not, as she later told Kay Dick, 'feel happy in love' (Dick 51). Or why she even felt 'frightened' of men (and perhaps of herself *with* men) at any stage of relationship beyond harmless flirtation, friendship or casual sexual encounter.

That she *was*, on occasion, a sexual being has not been questioned, nor has her sometime liaison with George Orwell (whose fiction in the 1930s greatly influenced her own), though her biographers disagree about the possibility of women lovers in her life. Smith almost never discussed her own sexuality, except in private conversations with friends whose accounts differ in fact and interpretation. Nor did she make as political an issue of lesbian or gay love in her writings as did many modernist women, Woolf and Stein best known among them, though she did mimic their detractors along with most other regiments of moral policemen.[7] And though her fictional personae do assert their enjoyment of sex, perhaps in order to fly in the face of lingering myths concerning 'nice women' and pleasure, Smith seems to have considered the mystification or fetishisation of any kind of sex to be as unnecessary as its censorship. For her, as for many mid-century women whose experience was limited by double standards and lack of education concerning female sexual needs and capabilities, sex seemed overrated; almost all of her remarks about 'the love-sex idea' characterise its effects as being both innocuous and fleeting – 'a desperate chance clutch upon a hen-coop in mid-Atlantic', as one character whom she liked to quote puts it in *The Holiday*, or a 'mirage [on] the desert of love' (49). The more worthwhile and difficult thing, as Smith's writings on related topics seem to intimate, was the sustaining of the precarious emotion itself, in the world and in any relationship. And 'love of any sort being held preferable to an absence of love',[8] she refused to dismiss any form of it for the sake of 'morality'.

Her own very fluid definitions of love, as well as her pained disavowals of any ability to understand 'the *à deux* fix' (MA 303) do reflect, perhaps, a confusion of desires; for though physically she seems to have been drawn to the heterosexual act, was even known to be quite flirtatious, she found herself unable to 'love men'.[9] On the other hand, although she apparently did not enter into any sustained lesbian relationship, and never, indeed, discussed the extent of her intimacies with women,[10] the close friendships she *was* able to form with them allowed her to understand and appreciate the female bond. This becomes most apparent in her attitude towards the lesbian love of Radclyffe Hall and Lady Troubridge, as expressed in her review of the latter's *The Life and Death of Radclyffe Hall*:

> If two human beings can live together in love and kindness, understanding and peace, they are to be felicitated and – if one can use the word stripped of all evil content – envied.... [T]here was this love between them, and no tyranny on the one side and no servility on the other.... In a desperate world, in the fearful business of being a human creature, they made a corner for themselves and were happy. (MA 191, 192)

At a time when heterosexual relationships might only rarely boast of having 'no tyranny on the one side and no servility on the other', it seems that Smith, apparently also not comfortable in the lesbian role, chose an independent lifestyle. Her choice certainly allowed her to avoid the selflessness demanded of women in conventional mid-century marriages, a part that she, never particularly robust after her childhood illnesses, simply felt, as she often put it, too 'tired' or 'selfish' to play (Dick 46).

After her sister's departure for a single life as a schoolteacher, Smith would live all of her life solely with her aunt, whom she cared for faithfully and would not institutionalise even when the latter was no longer mobile. 'Never let anyone say I never knew love', Smith once said with feeling. 'I loved my aunt' (Watts, Introduction to *NOYP* 7). She herself died only three years after the stalwart 'Lion', whose pet name connects her to the 'British Lion' – Smith's frequently and in this case affectionately used, traditional image for proud, no-nonsense England. 'But there are two English animals, you know', as her character Caz says in *The Holiday*, drawing upon both Santayana and George Orwell; 'always against the Lion of commonsense stands the Unicorn of fancy' (176). Her mother might have been the latter, the dreamer who painted sentimental pictures in the spirit of Landseer, won a local award for a piece of fiction when Smith was a little girl, and made 'an unsuitable marriage', as we saw Smith phrase it, to a handsome but irresponsible young man she might have refused if her own mother had survived long enough to advise her against it. Somewhere in between these figures – the proud lion who scorned men, marriage and her role within patriarchy, and the unguided dreamer who suffered at its hands – Florence Margaret Smith spliced another kind of self who, at the end of her teen years, would come to be called 'Stevie'. That nickname seems to have inaugurated for her a double life: first and always as her family's 'Peggy', and secondly as the emergent writer learning to enter into dialogue with all her many stewards of influence. The name was, quite appropriately, born of a misidentification, a joke – a shouted 'Come on Steve!' from a group of little boys when she, out riding rather aggressively and in 'unladylike' clothing, struck them as a caricature of Steve Donoghue, the famous jockey. Whether or not the name or the image generated Smith's later association of writing with riding, which she makes a highly complex sign in the novels, it heralded the first decade of her career as a poet, which she dates back to 1924. In 1934, when she began to send out her work, she introduced herself to the world as Stevie Smith. The sexual ambiguity of her name seems apt for a voice that emerged as such a complex refraction of that world's own inculcated voices, both female *and* dominating male.

II

Publication history and context: early reception

Smith's popularity as a writer came in two waves, one at the beginning of her career (1930s) and one near the end (1960s), first for her prose, and later on for her poetry, stoked by her remarkable success in the Sixties live reading circuits. Rarely, however, did she feel that her work was actually understood. Reviews from these periods indicate that it was largely her humour that was being appreciated, or the eccentricity of her later 'appearances' in performances. We can see now in hindsight that such reductive assessments were in part responsible for causing her first wave of positive response, and to some degree her second, to be short-lived. Most of the space given, in more intelligent reviews, to the larger implications of her form was spent on attempting to locate her through cross-breeding – her prose was 'Joyce out of Anita Loos', for example (S 88), her poetry a wedding of Blake and Lear: a pattern that insured her initial importance as a big-selling author in a line of big-selling authors, but also often made her seem to be simply derivative.

'One has to be à la nowadays', Smith wrote to L.P. Hartley (*MA* 300) – a state of literary affairs which of course masked the textual interplay and parody of views that have always constituted both the underlying humour as well as the deadly serious desperation communicated by her work.

Delighted as she was by the wide-spread attention (her first novel was even bought up by a New York publisher), it seems that her deeper disappointment in the actual readings of particularly the poetry prompted, in part, the resentment she felt throughout her career towards the control of successive, exclusively male literary guards encamped around figures like T.S. Eliot, W.H. Auden, Dylan Thomas and Philip Larkin – or André Breton just across the Channel. The Thirties in British poetry, at any rate, seems indeed to have been inaugurated by the publication of Auden's *Poems* in 1930; by 1933, Michael Roberts's two announcements of a 'new generation' of poets in his anthologies *New Signatures* (1932) and *New Country* (1933) had nearly eclipsed the possibility of media attention for any other sort of 'new' poetry. As Charles Madge's contribution to the latter book summed it up, however comically as it may seem to us now, 'There waited for me in the summer morning, / Auden, fiercely. I read, shuddered and knew' (Symons 21).

It may well have been in part because the 'Auden Group's' standards dictated both the publication and evaluation of all work produced that the manner in which Smith's formal strategies parodied them as well, pulling apart their constructions of revolutionary aesthetics, politics and spirituality, went unread and unremarked. Critics either considered her poems, in particular, as incompetent attempts at emulation, or depoliticised them by removing them from their literary/historical context – classifying them as 'wholly individual'.[11] Her friendships with select supporters and other women writers – Rosamond Lehmann, Inez Holden, Olivia Manning, Kay Dick, Sally Chilver, Helen Fowler, Naomi Mitchison and others, whose works also rarely appear in literary histories of the period – provided her with some sense of community, as we shall see. But Smith for most of her life and despite her initial success felt herself to exist on the literal and figurative outskirts of the literary world.

That world was especially reluctant to let women *poets* onto the scene; even recent studies (of particularly the Thirties) exclude them still, due to the infrequency with which their work was published and discussed in the major literary periodicals of the decade.[12] It is clearly impossible to speculate about the degree to which this situation affected Smith at the outset of her career, but we do know that the first publisher that Smith approached, Curtis Brown, Ltd, found her work to be far too 'idiosyncratic' to accept. Her reader further noted that her substantial batch of poems was 'imitative', 'blasphemous', and full of 'sexual ugliness'... 'the outpourings of a neurotic type of mind' (*S* 69, 71) – much of which echoes initial reviews of other female modernists, most notably Dorothy Richardson from whom Smith learned a good deal. Smith's bewilderment by the reader's report was matched only by her response to the suggestion she next received from Ian Parsons at Chatto & Windus who, apparently able to appreciate her ear for the interplay of discourse but not her strategies for the use of poetic form, told her to 'Go away and write a novel and we will then think about the poems' (SS: AB 111). Though it appears she balked at this assignment, she did go on to write *Novel on Yellow Paper* in a period of approximately two months, working in what she called a 'dream state' (SS: AB 112) and producing a text which, in its aqueous play of consciousness, invited from reviewers immediate and admiring comparisons with other modernist works, particularly the last chapter of Joyce's *Ulysses*.

Dialogue with other women writers

Those who also compared Smith's first novel to Richardson's *Pilgrimage*, which was serialised alongside *Ulysses* in the Little Review, or Woolf's fiction, or Anita Loos' *Gentlemen Prefer Blondes*, which Smith wrote about admiringly in her reading journal, may have been wrong in assuming single-gendered company for her but nonetheless made important connections. Smith was very keenly influenced by such female contemporaries who, with their explorations of subjectivity as dominated by cultural forces, and their portrayal of coercive patriarchal discourse at work in feminine consciousness, served as one set of mentors for her in her work. Smith's novel significantly forfeits the narrative control and mythic scaffolding of *Ulysses*, for example; claims such as Sternlicht's that it is 'formless' arise due to its lack of a familiar or classical frame. Which is not to say that it has no form, but rather that its imaginings of causality and 'ending' are a good deal different from even those modernists with whom we might most comfortably group her, for reasons that Phyllis Lassner has very helpfully begun to articulate and about which more will be said in Chapter 3. For unsympathetic readers her 'stream of consciousness' modes seemed more confusing than most, made as they were to incorporate a shifting array of contradictory rhetorical influences learnt from a modern, cosmopolitan and increasingly bellicose world. They allow willy-nilly entry, for example, for the likes of the 'Americanese', as she liked to call it, of not only Hollywood westerns but also of Loos' cinema-suckled speaker, whose perceptions of herself and her surroundings devolve from new and powerful paradigms on the silver screen – paradigms so powerful, in fact, that Smith's speakers will refer to their own narrating of their lives as 'this talkie'. Dorothy Parker – that other great American satirist, sometime Hollywood denizen and member of the Algonquin 'Round Table' group of writers centred in New York in the 1920s and 1930s – likewise influenced Smith with her work's focus on the pathology of conversational vernacular and other revealing modes of speech. What must have also attracted Smith was her 'theme [of] the pleasingness of death', and her continuous 'imagination of disaster' (Parker xiii, xxvii) – so much so that Smith later felt *Novel on Yellow Paper* was far too Parkeresque.

But important differences between Smith's work and that of Loos and Parker are pointed up by yet another comparison, this one made by a bright reviewer who suggested that *Novel*'s effect might best be imagined by uninitiated readers if they could picture Loos' book as rewritten by Gertrude Stein.[13] The Steinian connection is a significant one which alerts us to Smith's interest in, beyond recognisable voices like that of 'Lorelei Lee' (as Philip Larkin noted) or Parker's unwittingly bigoted party-goers, the actual morphology of language and its inscriptions of cultural power structures. Although Smith's reading journals make no mention of Stein, it is difficult to believe, as Spalding puts it (116), that she would not have at the very least read the best-selling *Autobiography of Alice B. Toklas* which appeared in 1933. Her speaker's mention of a letter she receives from Stein in *Novel on Yellow Paper* (64) is perhaps one hint of an imagined if not literal exchange and relationship. In any case, Smith's many repetitions and song-like riffs (the latter perhaps also influenced by Edith Sitwell, whose readings Smith was known to attend) often caricature or explore linguistic structures in such similar ways that reviewers immediately caught the connection, even if they missed the political dimension of Smith's Steinian dissection of idiomatic usages for their ideological import. And yet, by way of difference, Smith's combination of Stein's self-referentiality (or autobiographical elements) with less controlled, more fully self-undermining shifts and ventriloquistic contradictions also points up her distinctive focus on any speaker's/writer's inevitable *authorial* self-delusion by demonstrating her own proliferation amid social discourses. Smith's was a meaningful revision, then, or even critique of what the novelist Elizabeth Bowen called 'transformed autobiography' and Storm Jameson called 'disguised autobiography' – both of which imply a greater modicum of authorial control than Smith exhibits in their modernist quest for new variants of 'psychological realism'. Smith's work questions the location of even such new, modernist 'author-ity' as it was exercised in the writing of one's own life, which makes her strangely contemporary with present-day writers who struggle with postmodern, Barthesian ideas about 'the death of the author' and the inevitable slippage of one text into another. The reasons for her not becoming acknowledged, as Stein has been, as a precursor by current experimental or postmodern writers are complex and have to do, as I suggested in the Introduction to this book, with the culture-specific nature of her investigation of language and discourse. Her acknowledgement of entrapment in them made her 'modern' strategies seem *less* modern even though, ironically, they now make her look *more* presciently postmodern as a result.

It is therefore crucial that we discern, in those instances in which Smith *has* been compared to other female artists, but reductively, or simply on the basis of gender, how *different* her project was – how much it critiqued as well as responded to that of her peers. Perhaps the most frequent of such couplings have been with Virginia Woolf, whom Smith was compared to as a prose stylist, though the differences between them are more important than the similarities. Like Woolf, Smith indeed foregoes conventional plotting in order to 'reveal' human nature, but her method never involves what Woolf's famously did, particularly early on in her *oeuvre*: the creation of essential forces rather than characters, abstract narrative rhythms, and hypothetical 'feminine sentences' struggling free of the strictures of patriarchal grammar.[14] Smith's erratic and *un*natural rhythms reveal cultural rather than human nature – or perhaps the latter through the bars of its prison in language, where the struggle to express self is an unending opening of fitted boxes of responses programmed within rhetorical structures. Such a project constituted a challenge to even female modernism's utopian, aesthetic 'pilgrimage' towards re-envisioning consciousness in new and all but mystical 'significant forms' – a term coined by the Bloomsbury Group to whom Woolf (however tangentially) belonged.[15] Smith referred to such quests for the true self, discoverable by the artist in language, as 'that awful Bloomsbury self-righteousness and self-deception' (*S* 85). The realisation of such forms was incorporated into rather than dropped from the literary agenda of the Thirties; as Phyllis Lassner has very shrewdly argued, in her fine explication of Woolf's attitudes towards Jews, it became a way of envisioning the specific historical advent for racial atrocities evident in the Thirties as taking part in underlying and larger, mythologized cycles of human events which could be safely viewed from such modernist, transhistorical distances (139–40). Smith's views of evil, swayed by her love-hatred for the constructs of Christianity, do sometimes take large metaphysical sweeps, as we shall see in Chapter 4; but they are systematically overleaved with the ambiguities and specific historical atrocities of the moment of her writings. Despite the many differences in her work, Smith's prose fiction was initially welcomed only by those who saw it as fitting established modernist fashions – and by Bloomsbury's own aesthetician Clive Bell, for example, who in a private letter to Smith called it one of the best books he had read for some time.[16] The poet Robert Nichols even wrote to Virginia Woolf after *Novel on Yellow Paper* appeared in order to say 'You are Stevie Smith. No doubt of it. And *Yellow Paper* is far and away your best book' (*S* 98). Smith's first wave of popularity, in other words, came with her identification as a quintessential modernist of either the Joycean or the Woolfian persuasion; she was read into the lines of established literary frameworks.

That she *was* read, and widely, is a fact. Once published in 1936 (not by Ian Parsons, however, who even after bullying *Novel on Yellow Paper*'s originally punctuation-free-fall into somewhat more proper sentences and paragraphs, was unable to get it past his editorial board), Smith's work met with overnight success of the most unmistakable kind, becoming an instant best-seller. By 1938, reviewers were writing that 'with two books – *Novel on*

Yellow Paper and *A Good Time Was Had By All* [her first book of poems] – and some scattered poems in periodicals, she has managed to become one of the principal subjects of discussion at literary tea-parties' (*S* 86). By that point in the decade, as Kay Dick remembers, 'she was not merely fearfully fashionable, but revolutionary and daring to those of us in our twenties at the beginning of the war' (Dick 55).

Late-Thirties poetic politics and *Over the Frontier*

But from the point of view of many others, Smith had already begun to drop out of 'fashion' with the appearance of her second novel, *Over the Frontier* (1938). It managed to evade all conceivable limbs of the Joycean pedigree while, at the same time, shattering some of the less sophisticated if positive assumptions about her confessional nature that had governed the reading of her first novel. In response to *Novel on Yellow Paper*, David Garnett had written that 'Miss Stevie Smith isn't writing a novel at all' but 'saying just what she feels about herself, her employer, her aunt, her lovers, her friends and the good people, or not-so-good people, with whom she stayed in Germany'. Her prose seemed to him to be 'just a device for telling the truth which couldn't be told otherwise' (*S* 85) – a view made possible by combining fashionable stream-of-consciousness identification with the kind of misreading habitually conducted by a critical tradition that assumed women's compositions to be, at best, artless outpourings of their own 'honest' thoughts. In the case of Smith's second novel, however, any similar reduction of her narration to 'truth-telling', or her complex, only partly autobiographical, primarily discursively constructed speaking subject, 'Pompey Casmilus', to being 'indistinguishable from Stevie Smith', was forestalled by new formal strategies that demanded a different reading.[17]

Critical consternation ensued instead. Although *Over the Frontier* did indeed receive the attention of notable reviewers (many of whom again pronounced it 'not a novel'), her biographers report that '[n]early everyone had difficulty with the second half of the novel where the plot goes puzzlingly fantastical' (*S* 112). In this 'jarring shift mid-book from realism to surrealism' – to which even Barbera and McBrien attribute the fact, as they see it, that 'the novel is not finally a success' (112) – Smith calls both the concept of modernist 'realism' and the politicised projects of decade-old surrealism into question, investigating ways in which culture's fantasies and violence infiltrate not only contexts but artist's texts as well. As we have seen, Smith was always interested in the ways that seemingly separate discourses – like those in developing suburban life – are actually the producers as well as the products of larger and often deeply insidious changes in world culture. In her second novel, modernism's production of art-as-near-religion, as a separate and, in her view, escapist rather than political discourse, is called into play from its start – from its very first scene, which takes place in an art gallery. At its surreal heart, or the controversial middle of the novel, the separate spheres of 'private life', the arts and the darkening European stage come together quite dramatically when Smith suddenly sends her 'talking voice', who is obviously no longer simply *her*, into war-like mode and into situations that transform all of Pompey's former remarks about Jews, Germans and others into symptomatic constructions much larger than Smith's own personal opinions. Yet the metamorphosis is telling as well as chilling. Pompey's experiences convey the misery, danger and inevitability of *everyone*'s – including the artist's – riding on culture's tidal waves of coercive discourses and mediated prejudices; yet only a few, most notably the female novelist Storm Jameson, recognised its relevance to the historical moment.[18] Even Smith's most sympathetic readers and friends, like novelist Rosamond Lehmann, failed to discern her novels' project, and instead criticised what they saw to be mere slippage into self-indulgent weakness:

> I felt it has worried *you*, you hadn't been able quite to bring it off.... I know what it's like to be told one's second book has failed...Pompey is one of the most adult and enlightened women I have ever known. But sometimes I feel she lets herself be caught in her illness & weakness & little-girlness – then I am disappointed. (S 114)

Pompey's 'weakness' – her vulnerability to social/literary propaganda and dark, divisive undercurrents in the trilogy's contemporary setting – is the focus of not only the second novel, but the first as well. Yet to readers expecting what they had mistakenly taken *Novel on Yellow Paper* to be – 'amusing', plotless rambling revelatory of Smith – no such story was discernible.[19] If the novel's dramatic medial break had succeeded in shifting its readers' contradictory (i.e., modernist yet conventionally sexist) expectations away from autobiography, then perhaps Pompey's dark journey 'over the frontier' might have been perceived for what it is: a crossing of fine lines between illusions of independent selfhood and the surreal 'dream' of culture – or mass reality constructed through the very medium of her narration, of language. As Smith's speaker puts it at the end of the novel, she finds herself taken by surprise 'beyond the frontier of a separate life', but she is aware that it was due to the fact that there was something 'of [her] in it' – in the 'wretched event[s]' of the times (267).

The bewilderment of critics who 'did not understand what "frontier" it was' (S 112) or what the title of her second novel might mean ought to surprise us, given that the powerful enclave of writers surrounding W.H. Auden had turned just such phrases, available in the media as well as numerous leftist intellectual circles, into the mystical/political language for which Auden's early poems, 1930s poetry and the 1930s in general are now famous. Indeed, *On the Frontier*, a play by Auden and Christopher Isherwood, was staged in Cambridge in 1937, just as Smith was beginning to write *Over the*

Frontier; and Edward Upward's *Journey to the Border* was published by the Woolfs' Hogarth Press in 1938 when she published her novel, and so on – the list is long. The decade's events prompted a social conscience and political awareness such as might arguably be said to have never appeared with such overt force among British poets. Beginning perhaps with the Great Depression and proceeding with the era's Hunger Marches, Mass Observation projects, flirtations with communism and clamourings for social justice, swift developments in history allowed the new generation of artists, searching for a way to distinguish themselves from the ground-breaking high modernists before them, to respond with their own new forms of deepening and collective radicalism. Some of these forms began to take militant shape in poetry which, like that of other artists and writers around the world, increasingly anticipated and welcomed the first instance of cataclysm and socialist rebirth prophesied in the Spanish Civil War. It was the 'traditionally concerned group, the intelligent, professional-middle-class at the Universities [Oxford and Cambridge]' (Hoggart 13) – Auden, Isherwood, Stephen Spender, Louis MacNeice, C. Day Lewis and others – who invented a movement of their own which, though never openly affiliated with communism, became in some ways more dramatic; their vision was of their own class's demise, of a kind of social suicide in which they participated like religious prophets/martyrs working undercover against Britain's conservative political leadership. They themselves became, in other words, what Robin Skelton describes as 'the intellectual junta which saw itself as a kind of Revolutionary Council of the Intelligentsia' (23). Their works' imagery abounds with coded references to alternative leaders, frontiers and spy missions; it was avant-garde-become-vanguard, as Skelton goes on to explain in his well-known account of their writing of themselves into legends in their own time:

> This almost Messianic notion of The Leader runs through the poetry of the period, as it does through the politics. The Leader was not, however, a solitary, but a man accompanied by a select band of other explorers and adventurers.... There is, in point of fact, something curiously adolescent in the use of phrases like 'The Enemy', 'The Struggle', and 'The Country', and the deployment of such words as 'Leader', 'Conspiracy', 'Frontier', 'Maps', 'Guns', and 'Armies' in much of the writing of the period. The poets were, much to their embarrassment, and almost to a man, members of the bourgeoisie, and mostly products of public schools, and this may be one reason why almost all of their images of communal experience can be so easily translated onto terms of the undergraduate reading or climbing party. (18, 22)

Smith, on the outside of this group of 'men', as Skelton inadvertently but accurately identifies them, feared and critiqued their revolutionary practices for taking them 'over the frontier' of their own ambitions into regions where, as we shall see in Chapter 4, revolutionary language begins to sound quite like that of the oppressor, with disastrous results. As Skelton intimates in his final sentence above, the paradigmatic poetry of the Thirties transformed all that was admired in revolutionary communism into the metaphors, images and language of an exclusive group's experience. In Smith's view, theirs became just another 'party line' and/or tyranny, as she suggested by telling her friend, the Irish playwright Denis Johnston, after she had attended a leftist rally against fascism: 'Kingsley Martin only dislikes *other* dictators' (*MA* 270).[20] In order to engage the matter of supposedly autonomous discourses like those of the arts moving into unwitting collusion with cultural politics, Smith's speakers continuously enter into the latter's inflammatory rhetoric(s), deconstructing their encoded languages by acting them out, demonstrating their impact on the speech and deepest desires of her personae. She imagined those desires at work in culture in much the same way that her friend George Orwell did when he wrote, in his essay 'Inside the Whale', that even 'writers [were] attracted by a form of socialism that makes mental honesty impossible', because communism was 'something to believe in...a church, an army, an orthodoxy, a discipline...'. He went on to say:

> All the loyalties and superstitions that the intellect had seemingly banished had come rushing back under the thinnest of disguises. The "communism" of the English intellectual is something explicable enough. It is the patriotism of the deracinated. (2000, 122)

'My God', Smith wrote to Naomi Mitchison several years before the appearance of Orwell's essay, 'the hungry generations – ours appears to be famished.... Hungry for a nostrum, a Saviour, a Leader, anything but to face up to themselves and a suspension of belief' (*MA* 257).

Smith's own version of political writing

Smith's cultural politics, like her poetics, might be best understood as involving such 'fac[ing up]' to not only the loss of belief structures, but also the loss of the sense that new ones can be innocently remade; in other words, hers became a strategy of, as I began to describe it at the end of the last chapter, 'resistance without belief'. In this case, the phrase describes her resistance to existing social power structures – most of them promoted by conservative ideology – which she nonetheless refused to gird with belief in any messianic leader or salvific creed, particularly those of revolutionary radicalism as formulated in the Thirties. In this she is quite intriguingly also like a number of female artists who revolved outside the plots of their manifesto-making male contemporaries. Some of the most interesting among such women artists were those who were associated with that other influential group in Europe in the Thirties, the Surrealists. These loosely-affiliated members of the movement were less than reverent about André Breton's fiercely revolutionary manifestos, felt themselves outside his 'inner circle', eschewed visionary statements in their deeper focus on themselves as subjects, and found laughable and politically retrogressive many of the movement's reveries about female muses and sex as corporeal metamorphosis. 'Bullshit' was Leonora Carrington's summary response to those creeds (Chadwick 66).

And yet, although it was the apocalyptic violence advocated by her many 'rich communist friends'[21] that may have caused her once to write that the 'tale' of the 'Righties' might be 'safer...for mankind than the tale of the Lefties' (*S* 107), it seems that Smith's lack of trust for radical thinkers also exposes a deeply entrenched political correlative to her religious predicament of being a 'backslider as a non-believer'. And yet, again, she regularly pronounced *all* visions of political truth to be 'tales' – constructed narratives, such as her speakers produce, which are subject to the same 'distortions' that every impulse translated through culture into language, or 'revolution into government', inevitably undergoes (*MA* 168). In other words, though she was known to attend political rallies with her friends, and no doubt believed in the virtues of dialogue and criticism, it often seems that she had little faith in the possibility of any governmental 'story' or structure working uncorrupted for any length of time – a suggestion that her speaker Celia makes in a conflicted way at the beginning of *The Holiday* (9). This attitude colludes quite frequently and unhappily with the very sort of cynicism that she hated – cynicism that she understood as arrogant disavowal of complicity in the workings of culture. As we saw at the end of Chapter 1, she famously and sharply criticised T.S. Eliot, whom she identified as a representative of 'the arrogance of art and the arrogance of highmindedness divorced from power', for what she called his equally 'violent' belief in 'the sickness of states and the lies of statesmen' (*MA* 148) – a projection of blame that she felt assumes the critic's absolution from the same ills. She wrote with sarcasm that 'this does not seem like a constructive political opinion', that

> it seems rather childish, as if he thought men did not sometimes have to govern, as if he thought that by the act of governing they become at once not men but monsters. (*MA* 148)

Not to see them as 'monsters' is, of course, to be no less critical of the roles constructed for them to play. In her less idealistic vision, the romantic notion of the individual as self-determining and separate from the state simply undergoes a bit of inversion. In other words, in Smith's view, corrupt government for the most part only magnifies the corruption inherent in the very structure of – and at every level of – culture.

It is for reasons such as these that, though her critics and biographers have generally assumed she was clearly conservative in outlook, a 'fact' based upon such evidence as her interest in the Church of England, her allusiveness to Victorian authors and their poetic forms, and her refusal to become involved, as she wrote in one letter, with her literary friends' various forms of 'Communismus' (*MA* 259), we might begin to see that Stevie Smith's politics were, as Frances Spalding suggests, 'hard to pin down' (135) and no doubt highly representative of the confusions of the time. Certainly she sympathised with many of the radical left's ideas, given her own sensitivity to issues of class, and to the brainwashing of culture by social institutions (like the Church and marriage – two 'opiates', as she playfully refers to them via Marxist imagery) which exploit emotional needs in order to reproduce inscribed power structures. But as a voter, it is doubtful that she thought in terms of parties. In one of her less-often-quoted letters, after sharply criticising current political doubletalk and Chamberlain's 'appeasement' of the Germans in the Munich Pact, she looks presciently forward to the 'arrival' of Labour leader Atlee and, in the same breath, Conservative Winston Churchill, whom she appreciated for making the country aware of the danger in ignoring the Nazi threat (*MA* 271). Yet the point of revisiting accounts of Smith's supposed conservatism is not to turn her into an affiliate of any other 'groupismus'. As Malcolm Muggeridge incisively wrote in a review of *Over the Frontier*: 'Every variety of groupismus addict would be able to find something to object to in it, and therein lies its virtue' (*S* 112). Hers was also most emphatically *not* an 'outsider's' position – being more like an 'insider's' everywhere' one, and therefore one she continually indicted for its complicity in every movement she critiqued. Smith most often took in a view of both the revolutionary and entrenched groups that abounded as being produced by *similar* forces locked in hypocritical battle for dominance. She therefore at times felt that, because she had not written herself into any one political 'tale' but could see a role potentially written for her in all of them, she could understand slightly more clearly than her friend George Orwell 'what makes people tick, and the British people especially, with their long tragi-comic history of being tyrants on the one hand while blasting tyranny with the left...'.[22]

Literary politics and gender

Smith certainly also feared the *literary* tyrants of the period – the power brokers, many of them on the left, whose presences dominated the publishing world. She imagined herself at the mercy of a 'link-up' of forces that had little sympathy for her own work, Spender among them (*SS: AB* 224).[23] She called them 'The Choosers' in a poem by that name – referring at least in part, perhaps, to the Oxbridge coalition which she, like Skelton above, believed created an exclusive vanguard '...because it is like the school they never forget, / So-and-so must be the driven out one, this the pet' (*CP* 376). Among those 'driven out' by the dominant, with surprising efficiency, were the women poets of the period. Influential magazines generally published only two or three women during the decade; *New Verse* even conducted a sustained editorial defamation of that other well-known 'eccentric' modernist, Edith Sitwell, whom they called 'Old Jane' and judged to be politically incorrect in her upper-class orientation, behaviour and sympathies. Writers like Sylvia Townsend Warner, whose political orientation *was* correct – socialist if unorthodox – were similarly, if for different reasons, 'denied authority in the arena of politics and war' (Brothers 352). Warner was herself 'sarcastically dismissed' by Stephen Spender as a '*lady* communist', and thus, as Barbara Brothers describes it, both '[g]hettoized by the social text as *communist* and resegregated as *lady*' in order to be left finally 'unnamed', like Smith, 'in twentieth-century literary history as well' (352). During the war years, what Naomi Mitchison identified in a letter to Smith as the 'anti-woman pressure' in literary circles increased (*SS: AB* 190); as we have seen, it was then that Smith began to experience a decline in her own initial popularity, and though I have offered other reasons for this it would be foolish to discount the impact of sexual politics on literary careers at mid-century.

She certainly had much in common with other women writers who, in the 1930s and 1940s, when their views (whether hawkish or dove-like) on central issues like war were discounted, portrayed instead the ripple-effect of the times within personal lives. Images of profound helplessness, as well as Audenesque 'failed love' and rhythms of propulsion or acceleration into death/darkness pervade Smith's texts, as they do those of Olivia Manning, for example, one of Smith's closest friends during the pre-war years. An obsessive focus, too, on the fluctuations of particularly feminine subjectivity during the inter-war period and wartime mark both Smith's and Rosamond Lehmann's novels; moral questioning and guilt, passive dependencies and enervation of will compel and plague such speakers through contemporary landscapes. Smith's close friend Inez Holden, a novelist who found more success as a documentary journalist during the war, lamented what she saw as widespread critical misunderstanding of such women's works. In one review she quotes in exasperation a statement made on BBC television to the effect that 'some women writers had restless fidgety prose styles – like a woman searching desperately in an overcrowded handbag for a lipstick or a powder puff'.[24] Such disruptiveness, or 'speak[ing] with two voices' as Holden puts it (131) – or acknowledgement of one's predicament during 'the times of a black split heart' – was often disparaged as 'feminine writing', or weak form; Smith received such criticism herself from reviewers in the *TLS* and other highly visible vehicles.[25] She often counteracted the trend by reviewing other women's works with especial sympathy and, at times, high praise. She could also, however, and much like Stein, level surprisingly sharp criticism at some tendencies she disliked in 'feminine writing' – falling through it into the very trap of sexist language she abhorred, and demonstrating perhaps how it is that, as we have seen in Chapter 1, writers often helplessly re-inscribe the very structures that oppress them. Yet others of her criticisms seem consistent with her cultural politics, and can be read valuably in the process of coming to understand them.

For example, her sharpest criticism was reserved for overuse of 'the ding dong theme of love, love, love (if that's the word)' (*MA* 293) which she heard in too many of her women friends' work (in this particular case, Rosamond Lehmann's). Although her remarks about it certainly reveal her fear of her own possible limitations in understanding the phenomenon, and her susceptibility to culturally-induced anxiety on that score, they also illustrate her concern for the entrapment of women within long-playing imagery that represents them, even to *themselves*, as male culture's romanticised objects. For example, she described the process of female authors writing conventional romantic fiction as a 'falling in love with themselves when young' and not 'recognising [their recreation] for what it is – the waif as object of sexual desire' (*S* 63). By which of course she meant *male* desire, which she saw female authors allowing to usurp their own in their imagination of attractive feminine selves. Quite importantly and unusually, Smith was equally allergic to the somewhat opposite tendency to valourise rather than analyse feminine selfhood. Her own work does not portray women as being 'superior' – an observation Conrad Aikins once made when reviewing Dorothy Richardson's prose – but rather depicts them as being caught, often unwittingly, in the same constructions that victimise them.

She similarly mistrusted home-front work that glorified, romanticised, simplified or exaggerated wartime responses on the part of either soldiers or civilians – all of which indulged in what she saw as mythologising discourse. She reviewed Vera Brittain's *England's Hour* with an edge in her voice, recommending it but relating its effects with her tongue in cheek, and with a warning about misrepresenting history:

> A stranger reading Miss Brittain's observations of England's civilian population under fire might get the impression that not one stone was left standing upon another, that not one square foot of our island was left unbombed, that its heroic population... [was] in the throes of total death. (*MA* 176)

Smith had herself served, liked many women in London, in dangerous night fire-watches during the war, and therefore knew quite intimately the scene Brittain intended to 'document'. And in many ways she sympathised with Brittain's attempt to dramatise the violent consequences of reprehensible treaty-making at the end of the First World War. But Smith saw danger in perceiving war as a black-and-white political phenomenon, and thereby falling into nationalistic language. She understood it instead as a cultural event, given the manner in which all populaces define and maintain themselves in relation to 'others'. Nowhere does she make this more clear than in her novel trilogy. For example, as I will explain in some detail in Chapter 4, *Over the Frontier*'s narration depends on its speaker's repression of images of Germany's demoralised, ravaged condition following the Great War; this process becomes the unacknowledged engine that drives her articulation of mirroring fears, nationalistic sentiments and developing bellicosity.

Smith's choice to weave Germany's drama into her own speaker's narrative suggests her desire to understand the psychological mechanism of war interculturally, rather than from the perspective of her national space as Brittain had done. Therefore though she, like Woolf, 'loathed and feared all that the Nazis stood for' (Wilson 69), and knew, as Woolf in *Three Guineas* put it, that the key project needed was to 'attack Hitler in England', Smith also feared the heroicisation of her own culture (which Lassner at times hears happening in Woolf's work) and paid close attention to approximations of fascistic sentiments in her own tendencies towards nationalistic discourse. As Georg Grosz, the German artist she engages with in *Frontier* would explain, he felt assaulted by similar official stories of heroic ideals and future hopes in Germany even though all he saw there was 'misery, stupidity, hunger, cowardice and horror' put in uniform to exploit those ideals: 'The time I spent living under the bit of militarism was a continuous act of self-defence, – and I know that there was nothing I did which did not revolt me to the core' (Flavell 27). Feeling similarly, Smith turned her own stormy relationship with Karl Eckinger, a visiting German student of philosophy, into a situational *doppelgänger* in *Novel on Yellow Paper*, where her speaker's equally stormy affair with Eckinger's namesake becomes an allegory of Britain's potential confrontation with its mirror image should it interrogate its own cultural myths, myopia and blood hatreds. It becomes apparent that in a number of different ways, and throughout her career, Smith's advocacy of self-consciousness about the manipulation of perception by partisan culture and language – and thus her maverick propensity to dismantle even her own positions of criticism – set her at a radical remove from many of her contemporaries.

The middle period and publication miseries

After the appearance of her first two novels and three books of poems, *A Good Time Was Had By All* (1937), *Tender Only to One* (1938), and *Mother, What is Man?* (1942), all of which were published by Jonathan Cape, Smith began to encounter real difficulties with placing work done in either genre. Literary editors were rejecting her poems for 'not having the "right" tone or "voice"' (*SS: AB* 160); or, as she became more controversial in matters of religion, for being 'theologically unsound' (190). Some did offer to publish them without their accompanying sketches, which Smith would not allow.

It was also during these years that her third attempt at writing a novel, which she tentatively entitled *Married to Death*, was aborted after being sent to her long-standing supporter, David Garnett. He had written back in reply:

> I have done my best with *Married to Death*, but I can't read it, and what I have read leaves a confused impression in my mind. I cannot describe it better than I could describe the landscape of what I see when I have been swimming under water. (*SS: AB* 141)

It may be that Smith's intensified presentation of language as the medium through which her speakers struggle – and indeed in which they often drown – had produced the sensation Garnett lamented and could not read. I am tempted to infer from this, and from Smith's description of the lost manuscript's prose as being 'death death death lovely death' (*SS: AB* 140), that she had travelled even closer to what Samuel Beckett would later achieve in his death-driven prose works, which also foreground language as the foreign and inhospitable but indisposable medium in which his characters, like Smith's 'talking voices', find their questionable being in the world.[26] But Smith, apparently deeply affected by Garnett's criticism, came to explain her abandonment of the novel as her recognition that it 'display[ed] ... the very dregs of feminine talent' (*SS: AB* 148) – using against herself the very sort of discriminatory language she satirised in her work and, again, illustrating what she often attested to: her entrapment within it.

Smith's publication miseries extended right through the 1940s. Even her first version of *The Holiday*, finished in 1945, was rejected by Cape and Duckworth and not published until 1949, when she was inexplicably (or perhaps predictably, given its subversive nature) forced to alter it to accommodate historical changes. Possibly as a consequence of such discouragement, Smith devoted much of her time during the decade to reviewing books and writing short stories.[27] The latter, ten in all,[28] had better luck with editors; 'Sunday at Home' even placed in a radio short story competition in 1949, winning her a break into the BBC broadcasting that would prove so important in bringing her new readers. Performance of her work allowed Smith to communicate the shifting tones and off-key snags that occur intentionally at comic or uncomfortable crossroads between discursive lines and voices in it; her own voice was perfect for the job, with its strange mixture of north country, south cockney and north London accents. Her stories focus as much as her poems do upon speech; what Spalding calls their 'idiosyncra[sy]' and 'rawness', or 'spareness of storyline' (159) – to which she attributes their precarious publishability – are effects of this focus and, even more importantly, of their refractive relationship to narrative. Often they begin with familiar, reassuring, story-like gestures – 'It was a particularly fine day', for example (from 'Beside the Seaside') – which the reader swiftly comes to identify as being only part of a hodge-podge of discursive constructions collected within blurred frames of realistic-cum-fairy tale-cum-surreal-cum-absurdist narratives. Indeed, it might easily be argued that the dawning age of absurdism played a part in bringing Smith's work into new currency. But Smith's sudden shifts between viable-sounding voices and distorted quotations or poetic speech are often compelled by a black humour at once Kafkaesque and more disturbing, perhaps because her work remains in closer proximity to the mundane than to the fantastic, and leaves large gaps of pre-Plath imagistic muteness that suggest a lack of authorial control. It might be that Smith found such writing in prose, particularly in sustained form in the novel, to be far more immersing and troubling than writing poetry. Whatever the case may be, it is true that after receiving mixed and comparatively cool reviews for *The Holiday* – whose lyric intensity and discursive complexity marked, as she herself recognised, the high point of her prose writing career – she would publish only one or two more short stories before returning exclusively to her first love, the writing of poetry.[29]

It may well have been the hard fact that she could not place more than a few poems until the mid-1950s that ushered Smith deeper into the depression that compelled her to attempt suicide in 1953. As one questionable friend put it: 'Might not suicide after all have made sense? The unfashionable literary figure she had become...could hardly have foreseen any sudden burst of fame except posthumously.'[30] Yet for many reasons Smith might, to any other observer, have seemed to be on the rise again at the end of the decade: *The Holiday* had at last been published; Chapman and Hall agreed in 1950 to also bring out her first book of poems in eight years, *Harold's Leap* (which did, granted, sell quite poorly); Elizabeth Lutyens, the composer, had set a group of Smith's poems to music; and Anna Kallin at the BBC had championed her work, helping her to produce several programmes involving the reading of her poems and short stories. Smith was becoming a popular radio personality as well as a respected reviewer, and around her had appeared many strong and supportive friends, including James MacGibbon, her helpmate in finding a publisher for *The Holiday* and whom she would later name as her literary executor. Still, it seems not to have seemed enough. About the poems' failure to be published in either England or America, Smith is reported to have joked with Naomi Mitchison: 'Truly I need a shover, a nice honey-tongued worm, to belly around for me, some pretty young *man*, eh? with a "theory"?' (*SS: AB* 210; my emphasis). The same male coterie of critics and editors she had feared in the Thirties were still powerful presences on the literary scene; and the new, again virtually all-male 'Movement' in poetry, with its anti-modernist aesthetic, reverence for 'the purity of diction' and traditionalist values and forms, demonstrated very limited interest in Smith's 'eccentricity'.[31] The only magazine that would print her poems was *Punch*, and only 'sometimes', she lamented – 'if they're funny' (*SS: AB* 210). To Sally Chilver she expressed a wry bitterness because even those she had worked with for thirty years at Newnes Publishers appreciated only her comedy: 'They think I'm funny therefore I'm tempted to horse around' (*SS: AB* 213). She may have lost control over her own building frustration, as one account has it, and turned on her boss, Sir Neville Pearson, with her scissors before she, still in the office, slashed her own wrist.[32] However the story might actually go, Smith apparently hit, at the age of fifty-one, a deep rock-bottom of professional and personal despair – to which she responded by attempting to choose her own final option as she had first formulated it when a lonely child of eight, 'at the mercy of external forces'.

The final period and strange success

It was during her retirement, which immediately followed the suicide attempt, that Smith began to experience her second wave of popularity – and this time, due in good measure to a number of changes in her literary context, it was her poetry for which she gained fame. Her break seemed to come in 1955 when the poet David Wright (who, with John Heath-Stubbs, had edited the 1953 Faber anthology that included her poems[33]) became the editor of *Nimbus*, a magazine generally unsympathetic to the Movement; he promptly printed fourteen of the fifty poems that Smith had been unable to place. It seemed that suddenly her poems were appearing in more anthologies, and that she herself was appearing on more radio shows – 'Woman's Hour', 'World of Books', 'Brains Trust' and others, including 'The Living Poet' series produced by George MacBeth. She had even succeeded in writing a radio play, 'A Turn Outside', which was produced by the BBC in 1959. At the same time, a new book of poems, *Not Waving But Drowning* (whose title-poem would become her most famous of all) was published by Andre Deutsch; her *Selected Poems*, to appear in both the US and the UK, were also being shepherded into production with the help of one of Longmans' verse readers, the important poet Thomas Blackburn.

Blackburn's comments to the editors signalled his understanding that Smith's poetry had not been read properly during the era of New Criticism, which demanded that 'well-wrought', autonomous poems formally galvanise life's contradictions into new art unities. He reported that she 'is not a poet like Ransom or Yeats whose work will stand by a few poems because of it[s] sculptural formal quality. She needs room, makes an accumulative effect' (*SS: AB* 252). What he seems to have sensed is that Smith's poems, with their polyvocality and unending conflicts of desire, discourse and form, need to be read in plenty before readers begin to recognise their alternative project of expressing *disunity* and what that might mean. Certainly her critics have been right to assert that the slow demise of the New Critical aesthetic at last boosted Smith's popularity, but at the same time they are wrong in believing that the succeeding era of 'the personal voice' provided the 'right' context for reading her work. It is certainly true that mid-century poets of several aesthetic persuasions saw the beginning of a new era of 'personalism', as some called it, or of 'confessionalism', which understood the poem as being 'voiced' but, contrary to Smith's project, as being expressionistic, or revelatory of self. Although it is easy to see that Smith's poems would fare better in such a reading context, the consequence of viewing her through its framework, as most of her contemporaries and even her recent critics have done, is that our focus must be transferred from the conventions and 'lines' used by her speaking voices to *her* and what she felt while writing the poem, which as we have seen is a red herring in her case. On the other hand, and to be fair, Smith's poems are very much a *kind* of 'personal expression', though very different from most, in that they capture her (if also *our*) situation in language and culture as disseminated among an array of internal speakers. Present-day postmodern poets usually conflate such projects along with all others of the 'confessional' era when they construct their own literary histories, which should instead be seen to have been foreshadowed by new mid-century approaches like Smith's. In any case, whatever else might be true, it certainly does seem that Smith herself benefited in terms of popularity from each new framework that began to include her after 1955, however ill we might now see the fit.

Perhaps the most important of them all, and the one most apparently inclusive as a cultural phenomenon, was the 1960s cultural revolution. In the general atmosphere of dissent in England and America between events like the Suez crisis and the end of the Vietnam War, the rise of the Beatles, pop music and the 'hippie' generation, as well as the emergence of writers describing a New Left, caused a significant decentralisation of the arts to occur, during which places like Liverpool, Newcastle, Belfast and Birmingham challenged London and Oxbridge-centred 'movements' in poetry. Smith found herself, the so-called 'eccentric' ex-centric, suddenly in the midst of readers who embraced her for being exactly that. Its poets and audiences read yet another side of her work, adopting her as their beloved grandmother-gone-anarchist, an outrageously simple-sounding ingenue who packed a critical wallop into poems about the 'Establishment' – church, monarchy, aristocracy, patriarchy. Michael Horovitz, one of the poets who organised and became associated with the 'Live New Departures' movement – a radical, performance-based art experiment which often coupled poetry readings with jazz sessions in order to bring it all into their new public space – wrote after her death that 'Stevie took to the revivalist spirit of "Live New Departures" like a sainted duck to water – a cygnet – indeed, come to think of it, she was our Muse with a Worldly ear' (Horovitz 150). ('Worldly ear' is the title of a drawing by Smith of a black woman that Horovitz interprets as one depiction of her 'Muse'.) Like the American 'Beat' poets, part of their aim in art was 'to break through the high-brow game reserve', as Horovitz put it (*SS: AB* 268) – something that Smith's work, with all of its colloquialisms, heresies and irreverent scrutiny of culture, had aimed at for the full length of her career. A number of poets were influenced by her work: Libby Houston, Anselm Hollo, George MacBeth ('and even Robert Creeley', Horovitz claims) 'in their less obscurantist moods' (151). It was in great part the iconoclastic, Blakean echo in many of her poems (resonant in Allen Ginsberg's work as well) that such poets valued and reconstructed in his image; Brian Patten, a Liverpool poet, even honoured her in a poem entitled 'Blake's Purest Daughter', and idiosyncratic critical books like Arthur Rankin's *The Poetry of Stevie Smith: A Little Girl Lost* were no doubt inspired by such single-sided genealogies. Horovitz offers an example of her 'emphatic aphoristic edges', reminiscent of the 'English Blake', by quoting her short piece, 'To School':

> Let all the little poets be gathered together in classes
> And let prizes be given to them by the Prize Asses
> And let them be sure to call all the little poets young
> And worse follow what's bad begun
> But do not expect the Muse to attend this school
> Why look already how far off she has flown, she is no fool. (*CP* 269; Horovitz 150)

Though happily politicised at last, such a reading of Smith's work dangerously positioned her as the 'moral[ist]' of the movement (Horovitz 152), one who brought '[p]lain truths...home in intentionally spare no-nonsense terms' (151). She became, quite improbably, the poet who verified the *Children of Albion*'s conviction 'that anyone might look into his heart and write – and well, so he speak straight and true what's there' (162).[34] But as we have seen, being 'whole-heartedly' revolutionary, or verifying that 'the Muse' can speak from the poet's heart without getting tangled up in culture's discursive predilections, is not what Smith's art is actually about. Even in the above quoted, most seemingly straightforward of Smith's satirical poems, aimed at the same inbred 'schools' of poets we saw her treat in 'The Choosers', her speaker cannot escape complicity with those criticised and therefore ends up similarly lampooned. For example, its form of address – satirical couplets, straight out of the eighteenth as well as the nineteenth century, and Shakespeare's line distorted into her own fourth above – suggests an unavoidable steeping in the same traditional 'schooling' it parodies. Moreover, the position of the speaker appears to be *among* those left behind as the Muse withdraws in the last line – a line which itself trails off out of rhythm, leaving the reader of this ironically conventional poem-against-conventionality with a contradictory feeling of possible liberation from *and* entrapment within conventions. Blake's style of oracular prophecy and denouncement – his 'emphatic aphoristic edg[iness]' – became only one kind of tempting discursive mode in Smith's work, one at times capable of producing a romantic rhetoric of hieratic authority that she abhorred and undermined when aware of its takeover of her lines. For her, as for her predecessor Emily Dickinson – with whom she shared much, including strategies for speaking through off-rhymes/rhythms and colliding rhetorics – 'telling the truth' meant telling it not only 'slant' but deconstructed, to reveal the limitations, ideological partisanship or alternative authority constructed by any angle of critique.[35]

Such proto-deconstructive impulses indeed evidence something of a 'moralistic' as well as 'anarchic' bent in Smith's poetic practice. That may sound like a contradiction, but Smith's work *is* contradictory – and her own focus on exposing helpless contradictions even within a single speaker's speech should aid us in seeing it in her 'speech', too. Her work makes it quite clear that she understood that no critical approach comes free of moralising. It will become absolutely crucial to our reading of the novels in the next two chapters that we understand that Smith protested violently against the workings of her era's 'black split heart' *and* feared the violence of her own protest – both for what she could hear in it of alternative kinds of violence, and for what she dreaded might be there in her writing courtesy of forces 'beyond her control'. One of her images of 'Poetry' (or 'My Muse', as she puts it in a 1960 essay by that title) is, for example, strikingly violent in its figurative comparison of good art with 'civilisation's' potential atomic destruction – Dickinson's 'blown off head' analogy, perhaps, updated for a nuclear age:[36]

> [Poetry] makes a strong communication.... She makes a mushroom shape of terror and drops to the ground with a strong infection.... The human creature is alone in his carapace. Poetry is a strong way out. The passage out that she blasts is often in splinters, covered with blood. (*MA* 126)

These images are no doubt meant to shock us with their all but perverse allusion to the horrific events of 1945, which inspired fear throughout the Cold War and beyond. Certainly they do battle with those used in Donald Davie's famous poem, 'Rejoinder to a Critic' written three years earlier, in which he defends the Movement's Hardyesque, post-war 'neutral tones' for poetry:

> Donne could be daring, but he never knew,
> When he inquired, 'Who's injured by my love?'
> Love's radio-active fall-out on a large
> Expanse around the point it bursts above.
> 'Alas, alas, who's injured by my love?'
> And recent history answers: Half Japan!
> Not love, but hate? Well, both are versions of
> The 'feeling' that you dare me to... Be dumb!
> Appear concerned only to make it scan!
> How dare we now be anything but numb? (Davie 30)

Instead, Smith's almost gratuitous use of disturbing and indelible topical imagery – like Sylvia Plath's 'Nazi lampshade', her '...fine/Jew linen'[37] – illustrates the inexorable shaping of imagination and speech by history. Her novels certainly demonstrate her fear that the repression of 'feelings' that Davie's poem seems to advocate above results in what would be even graver consequences, as we shall see in the next chapter. On the one hand, then, she does seem to attempt to transform the influence of historical violence (which her generation saw more of than any other) into something that in her work constitutes a positive force: the dismantling of the very idea of 'the human creature...alone in his carapace' – that is, independent, sovereign selfhood – which results in an awareness that mushrooms out to explode, on a much larger scale, 'the human pattern' of thought and speech as discussed in Chapter 1. Therefore it becomes easy to understand why Smith's themes played well with the rhythms of the 1960s, even if such identification at times made them sound simpler than our re-readings find them to be.

On the other hand, such violent language is also recognisable as not only a new addition to the very alphabet of political theorising from the 1920s through to the 1940s, but as accepted rhetoric in European literary and artistic circles as well. For example, Mussolini's phraseology in the 1920s directly mirrors Smith's above when he suggests, while discussing the *squadristi*, that

> However much one might deplore violence, it is clear that, in order to impose our ideas on people's brains we had to use the cudgel to touch refractory skulls.... We do not make violence into a school, a system or, worse still, an aesthetic. Violence must be generous, chivalric and surgical.[38]

In Chapters 3 and 4 I will have more to say about the ways in which Smith probed the disturbing mid-century tendency to link discourses of health and the new medicine to discourses of violence. Here the latter's aesthetic 'laundering' is disavowed, but others did of course quite explicitly make violence into an aesthetic – Marinetti is one very noisy example. And in 1930s Britain, Wyndham Lewis continued suggesting in late-Vorticist manner that 'George [sic] Sorel is the key to all contemporary political thought' – referring to Sorel's book *Reflexions sur la violence* (1908; the first English edition was translated by the influential T.E. Hulme in 1916), in which he makes the claim that 'ethical life is inseparable from violence'.[39] Smith would very directly contemplate these issues as they pertain to art in her second novel of the trilogy – not in order to resolve them but rather to explicate all the problems involved in doing so. She seemed to have understood that the flip side to responsible portrayals of the era's violence often offered what appeared to be 'revel[ing] in the awesome power of unleashed aggression, recording it with something approaching sensual abandon, or at least a Nietzschean *amor fati*'.[40] But framing her own thoughts on poetry in the way that she does in the above quoted passage also *links* her to those 'fables of aggression', which Fredric Jameson suggests set the new model for social identity in the '-ism'-laden 1930s and 1940s. Certainly her speakers in her novels demonstrate the 'trickle-down' effect of their violent visions, as 'the necessary murder' committed by Smith's formerly suburban, uniform-donning narrator at the end of *Over the Frontier* suggests.[41] In other words, if she *was* the 'anarchist' that the decade's poets and audiences recognised and loved, she was of a sort that had no vision of any conventional kind of freedom from patterns of authority or oppression. All she seemed to have was a method of continually spotlighting them and thereby exposing them at various stages of their imagistic and linguistic internalisation, making the generation of such awareness her mode of resistance, her 'strong way out' – even if it blazed a trail that evidenced her own inscription by the very forces she longed to escape.

The success of her *Selected Poems* (1962) in both the UK and the US made Smith 'quite famous in [her] old age' (*MA* 313). She began receiving commissions for poems, and invitations from all over the country to read; she also began receiving letters and praise from top writers like Robert Lowell, whom she admired, and Sylvia Plath who wrote that she was 'an addict of [her] poetry, a desperate Smith-addict' (*S* 242). Even Philip Larkin, firmly positioned as the dominant figure in that still potent literary trend, the Movement, stalwartly braced as it was against 1960s 'departures' and experiments, wrote a largely favourable review that has been credited with 'chang[ing] people's attitudes towards Stevie' (*SS: AB* 257). He described her as a serious poet – a correction which earned Smith's gratitude, though she was dismayed by what he in his ambivalence famously called her: 'the *fausse-naive*, the "feminine" doodler or jotter who puts down everything as it strikes her, no matter how silly or tragic...' (Larkin 76). The jacket-blurb Smith wrote for the American edition of her *Selected Poems* might have constituted an attempt to curb the growth of such perceptions:

> ...Her metric, with its inner rhymes and assonances and the throwaway line that can seem mischievous, is very subtle. 'A daring and skilful technician' the *Times Literary Supplement* calls her. (*S* 244)

Nevertheless, 'skilful technician' was something she would only very rarely be called, while the contradictory labels of 'moralist', 'anarchist', and *'fausse-naive'* would dog her to the end of her life and beyond. She would go on to win a number of impressive titles and prizes, among them 'Poet of the Year' at the Stratford-upon-Avon Poetry Festival (1963), the first Cholmondeley Award for Poetry (1966), and even, in 1969, two years before her death, the coveted Queen's Gold Medal for Poetry. Yet still, many of her contemporaries, most of them male, who have gone on to write literary histories of the period, mention (*if* they mention her at all) only her 'oddness', 'quirky humour', or perhaps her 'endearing eccentric[ity]'.⁴² Perhaps only now, given our new focus on the workings of cultural forces in language, and our heightened awareness of women's alternative modernist projects, are we able to read Smith's poems for their 'subtle' and 'daring' technical skill and 'craftswomanship' – their transformation of discursive entrapment into art.

Stevie Smith died in March 1971 of a brain tumour which, with sad and strange appropriateness, made speaking and writing more and more of a struggle during the last year of her life. Her letters composed at that time suggest that she handled her condition with humour and courage. As she wrote to Anthony Thwaite, 'it is like the telephones scrambling their eggs' (*MA* 326), but she would continue to read her poems to large audiences until she could no longer pronounce the words. She appeared to be less troubled about her own fate than about the fate of her sister, who had suffered a stroke approximately one year before her own symptoms began. Her energies had, over the course of the decade, shifted not only into reading her poetry and negotiating the demands of popularity, but also into care-taking mode – first due to the debilitation of her aged aunt, and then, in her last three years following her aunt's death, due to her sister's failing health. These life-changes may have had something to do with the growing 'melancholy' that Smith said she sensed in her work after 1964 (*MA* 309). But then she was no stranger to illness or fatigue, and as she herself *also* said, with that wry twist that Glenda Jackson would later immortalise in Hugh Whitemore's acclaimed screenplay, *Stevie*, 'I'm probably a couple of sherries below par most of the time.'⁴³ Smith's work, like her humour and her lifestyle, altered little even when she found herself in hospital; there she continued to write from a position she had known intimately and all her life: balanced, as she had always been, 'well on the edge'.

3
The Trilogy's Take-off in the Thirties: A Close-Cultural Reading of *Novel on Yellow Paper*

All that I have argued to this point about Smith's writing becomes readily evident in the opening pages of her first major published work, *Novel on Yellow Paper* (1936). It is wholly aboveboard about its new procedures and even audacious in its announcement of what it will critique, as well as which topical discourses, attitudes, texts and thinkers it will snarl into its speaker's own complicit speech in scary demonstration of the highly 'overwritten' nature of her consciousness. These pages alone ought to have been enough to signal to its many contemporary readers – as well as to critics who attempted to analyse it over the next forty years – that Smith as a new writer was less interestingly 'a la', to use her derisory shorthand,[1] and more interestingly doing something risky and innovative. Certainly they should have been enough to signal that she was *not* an 'eccentric' using newly fashionable techniques to confess her own personal oddities in autobiography, but rather a sniper tucked into the very heart of contemporary culture, taking constant aim at herself as well.

Smith's speaker in the novel consequently occupies a kamikaze position that is very like – even as it parodies – that of Auden's stealthy time-bomb of a narrator in dozens of key Thirties poems, such as *The Orators*, or those of the more decadently declining, bourgeois inhabitants of MacNeice's edenic 'garden' of western cultural imaginings, aware of 'dying, Egypt, dying' from the very root.[2] Smith's 'yellow book', or 'novel on yellow paper' – a title that suggests not only her speaker's exploration of but also *copying* of the sensationalist discourses of her period, given its office denotation as copy paper[3] – must, in other words, be read back into the intrigues and anxieties that so potently informed both the popular journalism and politically-engaged writing of the Thirties. They could hardly be avoided at a time when ideological struggles like the one in Spain were, as Auden put it, 'x-ray[ing] the lies upon which our civilization is built',[4] prompting dramatic statements from writers like Smith's close friend, Naomi Mitchison, about the fact that during the decade 'one could not "go out of politics"' (Joannou 4). And yet it is precisely because her speaker is one who *cannot* fully understand or 'get inside', as she continually puts it, most of the old and new phenomena that define her politically – from classical-cum-Christian ideas (173) to new suburban values and prejudices (233) to '[her] country's successful delinquency' (*OTF* 272) – that her unmistakable formation by and complicity with the culture of her era becomes better illuminated in Smith's work than it does in more conventionally politicised writing. Though her speaker's commentary seems a 'personal' one, it is far more clearly exemplary of the way that public opinion was, in the Thirties, becoming redefined as interactive with widely held if internalised phobias and desires – as the Mass Observationists of the decade, for example, were engaged in documenting them.[5] Read from this angle, her only seemingly isolated voice, like that of the lost Kurtz in Conrad's wilderness, becomes far larger than herself, becomes that of her times – becomes even, at times, that of 'all Europe'.[6] Smith's version of its 'heart of darkness' gets an update to meet her own 'times of a black split heart', though she often, and particularly in *Over the Frontier*, chooses to simply confirm Conrad's turn-of-the-century prophecies through clear allusions to his famous novel published in the year of her birth.[7] Nonetheless, her speaker's very different sorts of skitterings from one discourse to another, through associative links that forestall any clear 'tale' or plot of her own from appearing, signal new developments in conceptions of individual consciousness in the Thirties. They also and at the same time point up Smith's alternative form of political critique, the latter generated by her sense of deepening *authorial* entrapment by the very context in which, as we saw at the outset of the last chapter, she believed we *all*, quite ironically, feel alien. Fredric Jameson has described it as a time when the new model for the formation of social identity was visibly shifting from cultural to political ones in the form of international movements, such as Communism and Fascism;[8] the impact of such seismic changes emerges in Smith's novels in defamiliarised images of national identity and spectres of English selfhood cast, along with many European counterparts, into a hall of mirrors. In other words, and in a move that links her to what will shortly emerge as 'absurdist' art tendencies, Smith seems to register the re-identifications and compulsions of that world of -isms (or 'ismuses', as we remember she dubbed them) through her speakers' sense of exile from themselves, and even from their own 'autobiographical' stories, as they become more and more aware of *being spoken* rather than speaking a non-ventriloquised speech.

A reverse 'coda': the opening of the novel

Smith's project of depicting her 'state' (pun intended) as it will be embodied by the novel's form of movement is introduced very quickly, on the very first page of the book, as it opens on her speaker: riding. This is almost certainly a private joke for those who know the origins of Smith's own nickname,[9] but it is also an important and complicated key to the project of the novel as a whole. Her speaker is not only riding here at the opening but also *remembering* a holiday spent riding, which scrolls out the centrality of, as well as the historical and cyclical dimensions of, this image that is about to become a rather elaborate metaphor as well. The horse she recalls riding here and elsewhere, periodically, throughout the novel, was not just any old horse but a rather fantastically destructive one called 'Kismet', whose name means 'Fate' – a red flag waved to readers, given that its Turkish origins and slippery connections with eastern invaders like the Huns call up empire's end for our main character, whose improbable name is a double-headed, historical/mythical, primarily Roman classical allusion: Pompey Casmilus. Indeed, the connection is made explicit at the very end of the trilogy when, in one of many eerie jokes exchanged between Smith's eviscerated and unhappy inhabitants of post-war Europe, the suggestion is made that the Germans will have been vilified through English propaganda as the 'bleeding huns' of the times (*TH* 197) – though the novels themselves suggest that their destructiveness was, like the fatal flaw that speeds unhappy fates in ancient tragedy, endemic in their context's pervasive and still-imperialist European discourse.

Much more will be said about this allegorical alignment of images in a moment, but it is important to note first that riding – an image that both initiates and drives the first two novels of the trilogy – describes what the writing is doing on an almost physical as well as figurative level. It links speech to movement, to being 'swept away' by language in a manner that obviously recalls the metaphorical 'hobby-horses' Sterne's speaker uses quite similarly in *Tristram Shandy* (1759–67). Yet it retools them along the Freudian lines of Smith's own time to begin her analysis of the psychopathology (and possibly looming 'fate') of English culture in the Thirties. I quote below the whole paragraph that dominates the fourth page of the novel, just to give my own readers a chance to see for themselves how Smith's speaker begins to 'move':

> The thought that comes to me now, that I am riding this horse, that puts his ears back and dances across the shadows, and glances with hatred and panic at the white gate posts, is the thought of all that I wish to say in this book, is the thought that works at me like a worm, like an intestinal worm that pulls and drags its alexandrine length along those five hundred yards of trouble. Mrs. *Haliburton's Troubles*, that is a book I read when I was a young child. Sometimes I think I have read too much. There were those titles of books I used to read-ride-ahobby-horse. Riding crops up and crops take me right back to Kismet [whom she just told us was a 'great eater' who 'crop[ped] the verdure' with a 'scythelike movement of his long head, his long snakelike neck']. Hobby-horse whoa-up. That book Mrs. *Haliburton's Troubles*. Not a thing I can remember about that book except that Mrs. Haliburton – or perhaps there were two ells – had

troubles enough which she bore up under and preserved a stiff upper lip, smiling to the end, when God stepped in and made all right. (12)

Riding could not be more explicitly linked to reading than it is above, as well as set on a course (or horse) whose name suggests that both the immediate and allegorical fate of this speaker will be determined by her degree of control over the cultural text that inscribes her. The way that speech is linked here to the mechanics of writing (or spelling) is extraordinary and, at first, seemingly absurd, but it accomplishes a good deal. Quite immediately it foregrounds the text *as* text, and the very thoughts of our narrator as generated *by* that text; in other words, it pre-empts our envisioning the text in Victorian terms, as our 'window on the world' of our narrator, and instead presents our narrator as someone who (like us) makes up her world out of a broader cultural text that literally 'letters' her supposedly spontaneous 'talk', her 'self-expression'. The introduction here of a misspelling for *Mrs. Halliburton's Troubles* (by Mrs Humphrey Ward, the Victorian novelist), which our speaker will continue to (mis)use, seems to signal both the erosion and perpetuated corruption of texts that may contribute to our loss of knowledge about sources but not to loss of the lingering effects of their influence; indeed, the misspelling of her mythical ancestor Casmilus in her very surname seems to signal this as well, as we shall see in a moment. Certainly we are swiftly jarred here as readers into awareness of the urgency of these kinds of revelatory projects in the novel whose very odd name, we suddenly realise, also reveals the materials for its own production like a theatre production exposing its properties backstage.

But for the moment, I want to focus on the way this paragraph moves. *And* the way it moves towards the *next* paragraph, which takes off in the direction of *another* vague memory of a Victorian book in which 'Providence tidies things up' (13) – that is, if one observes decorum and suppresses outward show of inner turmoil. This bit of cultural advice proves its power in the number of times it recurs in the novels; our speaker will come to analyse it at length as she contemplates the relations between national character and violence. Just here we see that this thought is ostensibly introduced in order to 'whoa-up' on the one cropping up – about destructive Kismet – and though the former would seem to focus on a happier version of fate as 'Providence', we later understand that such leaps of flight from one thought to its seeming opposite are actually connections by deeper association, as they would be in Freud's psychological models. In other words, 'Providence', or rather Victorian narratives of it, is paradoxically but pointedly linked to fate's devastations here at the outset of the novel in a way that we will remember as crucial later on in the text. Indeed, '[r]iding crops up' can also mean riding with one's whip, or 'crop', up and visible to the horse's peripheral vision; it signals a rider's threatening desire for either more speed or repressive control, though in this case the latter does not work because 'crop' takes up its other meaning – to emerge, as 'harvest' – and unruly associations 'take [our speaker] right back' to what she would avoid. Such runs of associative thought and the pulling up on them (as various 'hobby-horses') happens throughout the novel, reminding us of this paragraph at the start and its suggestion that riding (most often on horses somewhat beyond one's control) is analogous to reading and thinking as well as writing – or that reading/writing is like 'switching horses' as she does above, because each discursive line with its underbelly of repressed thought tends to 'take its own head' and propel our narrator off course. In other words, or in Gertrude Stein's words, as she might have put it, language writes *her* rather than she *it*. Or, in even older words, as Sterne's narrator put it nearly two hundred years before Smith, 'when [one's] HOBBY-HORSE grows headstrong, – farewell cool reason and fair discretion!' (113).

Smith's linkage of Sterne to Stein would indeed seem, as we know that at least some of her reviewers realised, to have produced one of the engines that powers the movement of this first book of the novel trilogy. She acknowledges the same quite playfully in her recycling of Sterne's devices as well as in, for example, her speaker's reference to a letter received from Stein, whom she must mention to readers because she 'think[s] the people must come in as they come' (64). Reading from another contextual angle, the seeming lack of control over what comes into range for her speaker might be interpreted as the novel's 'anarchic' drive – especially if readers remember the work of the Dadaists in the previous decade, and the fact that their very name was explained by Tristan Tzara as meaning, among other things, 'hobby horse'. But understanding how *all* such clues to the novel's form work together to deploy a kind of melange of current discursive possibilities allows instead, I would argue, for clearer vision of its *critique* of many of them – its position, as my own book's title has it, 'between their lines' – as well as her critique of Thirties political rhetoric and its sources in them. Certainly it allows for more satisfying understanding of the end of the second, far less anarchic novel, *Over the Frontier*, where as we shall see in the next chapter our narrator is literally raced off on horseback into German military territory as a result of becoming caught up too fully in just *one* line of her thought, one that borders dangerously on fascistic discourse.

Two broad options seem to be initially available to our speaker in terms of her movement vis-à-vis such thoughts – and only two. This may indeed be why, as her strategies for narrating her experiences from within her unfolding cultural text become slowly explicated, we begin to understand her reasons for calling herself, from the outset and without explanation, 'a desperate character' in it (16 and *passim*). To further understand this we need to complicate the kind of gendered reading that Laura Severin produces in her book on Smith's work, which includes one of the only extended treatments of the novels to date. There, in the interest of seeing the horse Kismet as a feminine force that 'transgresses rules', Severin reads the rider as a woman who can 'control both the flow of the conventional narrative and the radical digressions' (29). Yet the paragraph quoted above has already, on the fourth page of the novel, negated the possibility of this kind of reading in search of a postmodern feminist project. As the novel progresses it becomes clearer and clearer to us that the speaker's impulses to stop and go are controlled instead by something much less narrowly defined and far more sinister, and that both 'riding on' the talking voice with its discursive riffs *and* attempting to stop are alarmingly dangerous if unavoidable for this 'character' in the novel. Correlatively, she deems the horse that she begins the paragraph above by riding 'a good horse' (10) because it 'dances across the shadows' – horrified as it is by both the 'shadows' it so elides *and* the 'dead-end' or cessation to movement signalled by those white gate posts. The only alternative seems to be 'paus[ing]' and eating, as Kismet does, or 'la[ying] waste the Duchy of Cornwall' as she comically inflates it when describing the impact of such appetite on that part of the country. Although our narrator's judgement of good versus bad is as difficult to second here as it is throughout the novel – given that most of her opinions are delivered in the gallop of some one or other discourse/hobby-horse – it seems hardly right that we should disagree with her in this instance. Because to disagree is to value more highly this other creature, whose eating is likened to 'laying waste' the Duchy of Cornwall, a once-proudly separate cultural space with its own language that slowly eroded in the project of unifying the kingdom. Severin is forced to contradict her thesis concerning our narrator's control in order to celebrate this uncontrollable 'Kismet' as she does.

Yet rather than choosing between them, what should be important to us here is noting the very complex dynamic being set up: between stopping and destruction versus movement (if only laterally) and speech. In the course of our reading the historical depth of this double-edged image will become clearer, steeped as it is in Smith's reading of classical philosophy. It smacks of the Apollonian versus Dionysian forces frequently referred to in the novel, as well as her reading of Freud with his recasting of Eros and Thanatos and implementation of the 'talking cure' – the latter flagged here in her text three pages later by reference to emerging interests in psychoanalysts bought at 'a pound an hour' (15). But already in this early passage we can see the processes of repression and linguistic deferral at work: the 'all that I wish to say in this book', her seemingly singular thought, desirous drive or perhaps 'complex' of intellectual and emotional responses, as both Freud and the Imagists would have put it,[10] is deflected from exposition and displaced into multilevelled flights of speech.

Quite importantly, the 'all' she refers to in the quote above must, it seems, link back to what she began to bring up but then promptly dropped in the paragraph just before this one: her feeling of being 'janus-like' among her Jewish friends:

> Nobody knows but me what I think about that thing. But I get behaving as if they did know, and I had to pipe down and apologize, and not seem

to be taking credit for the happy accident of Nordic birth. There is nothing so superior as that false humility, and nothing that has made so much trouble, and nothing that will go on making so much trouble so long as things are. Oh, quiet, now, quiet. (11–12)

Though feminist readers refuse to acknowledge it, Smith could hardly have made it clearer at the outset of her novel that its very motor will be the ugly force it represses, that unspeakable 'thing' mentioned above which is both inside her and outside her – is, in other words, how 'things are'. That among the broad range of interconnected but unspeakable developments in her context was its veering into sympathy with Fascist anti-Semitism at the time of Smith's writing hardly needs evidencing. But pointing, say, to the creation of the BUF (British Union of Fascists) in 1932, or its leader Oswald Mosley's notorious speeches (particularly during the years 1934–38) promising the expulsion of Jews, as Eliot would also later advocate it (or at least the rescinding of their citizenship), is not enough, given that these phenomena were symptomatic of a much larger, older, and long-unspoken/unspeakable dynamic in both British and European culture at the time.[11] As Phyllis Lassner puts it, in deep agreement with my own reading of the larger picture of the Thirties as showcased in Smith's novel, 'Pompey's "janus-double-faced" feelings toward "Jewfriends" represent that occlusion in order to show how oppression of the other inheres dangerously in self-determination' (140). In the passage quoted above, the efficiency with which the repetition of the hazy word 'thing' suggests how that very specific but unnamed aggression underwrites, wordlessly, the equally unarticulated generality of how 'things are' is remarkable. Here at the novel's outset it sets us, paradoxically, a frame for her writing that pictures a very pregnant void, a chasm of the unsaid. Our speaker keeps reassuring us that she has a '60,000 word limit', which also suggests that hers will be a spontaneous flow of words to fill that space, to *say by not saying* 'how things are'. Therefore, while the chapterless nature of the text is reminiscent of other stream-of-consciousness ventures in its modernist sphere – such as *Mrs Dalloway* (1925), for example, which gave us Woolf's attempt to capture the ebb and flow of converging consciousnesses in post-war London – Smith's wields a sharply differing, *much* less gently politicised rendering of thought's movements because she depicts them not in fertile interweaving but rather in oppressive convergence of dominant discourses upon the racked space of a single mind. That this will happen through our speaker's giving in to what she calls, on the tenth page of the novel, 'the tyranny of the association of ideas' could not be made clearer here at its start. This, then, is how Smith will manage the psychoanalysis of her own culture: she will commit Pompey Casmilus as the patient undergoing Freud's talking cure, assuming that she, a seemingly insignificant secretary and thus-far unsuccessful poet, is (like Smith herself, through whose own experience the fiction often wends) as good a case in point as any other, given the overdetermination of everyday lives by the same intersection of discourses that underwrote the 'compositions' of Europe's more epically proportioned, tragically fallen Kurtz.[12]

Pompey Casmilus (and what's in a name)

And this then is why, as she invites us to four pages later, we must 'look this dangerous way [our speaker is] running on' (16) – to see what her 'not saying' reveals about other aspects of her context as well. At this moment in the text she is just beginning to reveal, however (and typically) abortively, what happens on *blue* paper, which is her boss's colour, as opposed to the yellow that she, his private secretary in the publishing business, uses for her own purposes (and to which we owe the title of the novel). Among the things that slip out onto the page about what happens on blue paper, before she 'pulls up' on the reins of her thought, is her writing 'to the stockbrokers for a couple of thou. in Tekka Taiping' – something that her powerful, popular-press-mogul boss obviously asks her to do for him. Pompey tells us his name is 'Sir Phoebus Ullwater', in keeping, perhaps, with the novel's other classical allusions, though this one seems more potently a joke on the tabloid industry, her workplace, as 'the source' of light in the Thirties, particularly as she first refers to her boss as 'that...black face Phoebus' (16). Thrown-in and unexplained references like this one to 'Tekka Taiping' most often become ones that we as readers are left to vaguely associate with unsavoury history – here, with either monies to be made out of trade in former colonies, or the suppression of the Taiping Rebellion against China in the nineteenth century, accomplished in part by British troops sent to protect their fellow-colonizer and trading partner from potential damage to its economy. Her 'sun's' (Phoebus's) continuing investment in that history, which funds him and trickles down to her, establishes the suspect lifeline that powers this civilisation on which 'the sun never sets' and in which she takes part, however small a cog she might be. Our speaker's 'running on' in this fashion – into other texts and subtexts that reveal dark shadows to her otherwise fairly mundane world – is referred to continually, as frequently as riding is mentioned, and suggests her inability to separate one textual plane from another, blue paper from yellow. Each bleeds into the other and informs the complex drives/ desires that power her own speech but that she cannot name.

Aside from Lassner, who treats it briefly, Smith's critics have been remarkably reluctant to consider the importance of her speaker's rather overwhelmingly odd – and very masculine – name in the first two novels (which extends by refraction into the third one, too, as we shall see). This may well be due to its discouragement of readers from seeing her speaker as an empowered and empowering heroine, hard as we might wish or try to do so. She takes the first name of a very questionable male historical figure – one of the anti-heroes of historical annals – and supplements it with a surname drawn from mythology: Hermes (or 'Casmilus' as she refers to him), whose activities as border-crossing messenger involve him in being 'double-facing,... riding through hell' (*NOYP* 212) – that is, engaged like our speaker in 'janus-faced' movements rather than in any mission of feminist social or self-development. Instead, even as she identifies herself, Smith's speaker makes clear that her character is far more than a semi-autobiographical actor in present time; she is, in startling relief, the product and representative of all that might be considered questionable in the long continuum of ancient European-cum-current-English culture. And she is, in other words, a conglomerate of both its historical and mythological (including Judeo-Christian) texts, and a mercenary informer about its separate and collective ills:

> Did I tell you my name was Pompey Casmilus? Patience I was christened, but later on when I got grown up and out and about in London, I got called Pompey. And it suits me. There's something meretricious and decayed and I'll say, I dare say, elegant about Pompey. A broken Roman statue. One of those old Roman boys that lost their investments and went round getting free meals on their dear old friends, that had them round to fill up the gaps, and keep things moving. (20)

Through a characteristic backsliding into bankruptcy rather than epic envisioning of modern progress, Pompey reveals herself as a microcosmic point on the palimpsest of western cultural imaginings: a baptised Christian who manifests her pagan rootedness in a text of commerce camouflaged as leadership and self-serving behaviour in the face of systemic collapse. Drawing that panoramic sweep into present mundane time and onto her own page, our narrator's taking on of association with Pompey the Great begs readers to draw a correlation between that other 'sponger's' machinations behind the scenes and our speaker's movements – reminiscent of Smith's own, as I noted in the previous chapter – between the houses of friends. Pompey the Great's betrayal of his rival Caesar, after both assumed their part in the First Triumvirate of Rome, took the form of colluding at home against him while the latter was abroad. This Pompey, like our Pompey at the beginning of Smith's novel, also 'said good-bye' to his friends and brother-in-law by making a colleague of one of the Metellus faction of senatorial extremists who were opposed to Caesar – thereby forcing the latter to 'cross the Rubicon' in order to plunge the Republic into civil war.

Pompey was a good soldier early in his career, but though the *Selected Letters of Cicero*, which we know Smith read (in Latin), describes him as a man of integrity and high moral character, such eulogistic accounts dovetail poorly with others that, aware of the degeneration of his activities once safe and housed amid the corrupt senators in Rome, recall him as being something less than a 'great' general, and as a statesman, weak and irresolute. Spalding tells us (117) that Smith copied into one of her reading notebooks these lines from Sacheverell Sitwell's poem, 'Doctor Donne and Gargantua' (the first two of which she quotes on page 43 of *Novel on Yellow Paper*, in a series of 'Favourite Quotations'):

> Pompey is an arrogant high hollow fateful rider
> In noisy triumph to the trumpet's mouth,
> Doomed to a clown's death, laughing into old age,
> Never pricked by Brutus in the statue's shade.

Pompey is not one of the 'tragic hero' cast, to be pricked by Brutus as Caesar must be. Edith Sitwell, as well as Sacheverell, seems to have been fascinated by this historical figure. Indeed, Smith, a Sitwell fan, may have also known the latter's poem 'Said King Pompey', which Sitwell summarised as being 'a poem about the triumphant dust' that sports its little life momentarily before being sent down in order to come up 'the Clown' – the 'Tyrant's ghost', brother to the 'Low-Man-Flea'.[13] Pompey is, in other words, the degenerate survivor of history, one of those who have 'lost [their] investments', as Smith's speaker describes him above, and have had to become 'meretricious', as she put it in the earlier quote – meaning insincere, even whore-like, to acquire power among rival factions and other unsavoury customers, however continuingly 'elegant' the outward presence might be.

When in the latter mode, Smith's allusion seems to shift from reference to Pompey the Great to Shakespeare's Pompey in *Measure for Measure* – that bawdy pimp and metaphorical mercenary who turns on his underground friends when given the chance for authority over them in prison. Smith returns again and again in the novels – and most conspicuously at the beginning of *Over the Frontier* (published in the year of the Munich Pact, which she reviled) – to the use of 'whoring' as a metaphor for the state of 'things' (meaning the arts as well) and of government in the Thirties. These doubling allusions to Pompey the Great work particularly well towards this end, as he represented 'an age' in addition to personal ambition, as Lucan made clear when he put these words into Cato's mouth as Pompey's eulogy: 'The citizen who died, though far from equalling/Our ancestors in knowing Law's restraints, yet served/An age which had no reverence for what is right.' (Greenhalgh 269; *Pharsalia* 9: 190–93). Much more will be said in Chapter 4 about Smith's depiction of her own Pompey as a representative of the decade's 'degenerate' or 'fateful riders', mounted on their own Kismets, continuing a long if long-disavowed tradition of leading the inflammable many into unrestrained destruction. In these first pages of *Novel on Yellow Paper*, she simply makes sure that her speaker brings up Max Nordau's work two paragraphs after she tells us her name, thereby juxtaposing revelation of herself with this Hungarian writer's well-known two-volume novel, *Degeneration* (on which she took extensive notes in her reading journals), in which he attempted to establish a link between genius (such as that of leaders, or of artists) and degeneracy.

Therefore while our first response to the image of Pompey the Great might be topical, relating his state of having 'lost investments' to that of the great number for whom it would have sounded familiar in the early Thirties, a second analysis might suggest even more. His state's 'state' – soon to be pushed over the brink from Republic to Holy Roman Empire – seems, in Smith's reconjuring of it, to reflect that of Europe as a whole in the Thirties, where empires under tyrants/geniuses like Hitler and Stalin were already discernibly coming to form to threaten 'degenerating' ones like Spain and Great Britain. From prose like Smith's it becomes easy to see that full-scale 'civil war' within Rome's inheritor, Europe, must have been felt in the offing, and between nations that had so recently conducted the bloodiest warfare in history due to largely economic and imperialistic interests. Smith's fears about German activity and ascendancy in Europe as enabled in part by English stagnation and decadence emerge in the novel as our encouragement to equate all 'Empires' with potential visions of the return of Dark Age history, poised as her own seemed to be to meet its subsequent fall or fate, *kismet*, from the 'barbarians' to the east. Though her speaker regularly equates German with English culture, as related in both genealogy and 'decadent' tendencies, her evident anxiety about the former as a developing actor in the Thirties is exposed in something like Smith's own tremulous prophesying:

Ah how decadent, how evil is Germany to-day.
 Now when a people has dictators, that is a symptom that they are running mad. They should then be watched. I think they should be watched very closely. And later they should be prevented. Now think it is not a nation but an individual, now see, this is like he had a disease.
 ... Well, there is nothing to be done about it, about the Jews and the atavism [of the Germans] and the decadence, no there's nothing to be done about it. So, help yourself to another helping of apple sauce, Pompey, I said: Help yourself to another helping of apple sauce. (104–45, 111)

So it is that in the meantime, Smith's Pompey represses her own evil thoughts about Jews, though she knows that all such thoughts 'swell the mass of cruelty working up against them' (107). The 'disease' of 'having dictators', as she will playfully go on discussing it, is something that overcomes individuals in ways synonymous with the overcoming of nations. She suggests in the word-play above that she/Britain is ripe for the overtaking by a tyrannical state, or for collusion in its decadent and self-serving appetites, just as she is prone, given her *repressed* 'state' of lassitude, to being overtaken or swept away by tyrannical discourse and its hobby-horses. This will indeed, as we know, happen by the end of *Over the Frontier*, when Pompey will be called 'Pompey die Grosse' by her dresser for war, Tom (228) – the German words producing that pleasing pun for English readers who see Pompey the Great's impending 'gross death' or assassination nestled within his very title 'the Great'.

Like her friend George Orwell (whose novel *Burmese Days* (1934) will figure in her own first book, as we shall see), Smith understood the formative *and* performative power of not only current propaganda but also textual traditions – particularly if one has, as she put it in the first passage quoted in this chapter, 'read too much'. She would agree with Orwell's suggestion, in *Homage to Catalonia* (1943), that even the kind of pacifism that Woolf promoted in the Thirties had its root in that tradition:

> Let Fascism, or possibly even a combination of several Fascisms, conquer the whole world.... We in England underrate the danger of this kind of thing, because our traditions and our past security have given us a sentimental belief that it all comes right in the end and the thing you most fear never really happens. Nourished for hundreds of years on a literature in which Right invariably triumphs in the last chapter, we believe half-instinctively that evil always defeats itself in the long run. Pacifism, for example, is founded largely on this belief.... But why should it? What evidence is there that it does?[14]

'Providence', in other words, 'tidies things up', as Smith's speaker suggested in the passage quoted earlier via thoughts on *Mrs. Halliburton's Troubles*, a text read in youth and never forgotten. Like Orwell, Smith seemed to understand in a way we might consider 'postmodern' that 'instincts' arise out of cultural inscription more often than intuitive wisdom. Like Orwell's main character, Flory, in *Burmese Days*, Smith's Pompey is all too unreliable or inconstant, ready to collude with domestic corruption and inadvertently become vulnerable to 'having dictators', just like her German counterparts. Pompey the Great's eventual fate of assassination in Egypt, where Antony too fell in his decadence,[15] may signal Smith's vision of Britain's fate as well within the larger theatre of Europe's fall – particularly given its and its allies' deeply suspect movements in the regions of Egypt and Palestine, as we shall see further on in this chapter and throughout the trilogy. Like her friend MacNeice, and Conrad before them, Smith saw in England the inherited stamp of Roman ambition, government and eventual degeneracy – signalling through such visions a dramatic revision of the Victorian view, which aligned its era of industrial 'progress' and imperialism with the gains of imperial Rome. Indeed, MacNeice's autobiography begun in 1939, and entitled *The Strings are False* after a line in Shakespeare's *The Tragedy of Julius Caesar*,[16] begins this way:

> So what? This modern equivalent of Pilate's 'What is truth?' comes often now to our lips and only too patly, we too being much of the time cynical and with as good reason as any old procurator, tired, bored with the details of Roman bureaucracy, and the graft of Greek officials, a vista of desert studded to the horizon with pyramids of privilege apart from

which there are only nomads who have little in their packs, next to nothing in their eyes.

Like MacNeice, Smith seemed to suggest that 'the strings are false': that everyone, including the string-strummers who play for embattled Brutuses – that is, the artists/writers of the Thirties – were too deeply asleep in the dreams of culture to ring a true note. Her novels cannot be read properly without situation in the same context as the above passage, dark as it is in its view of both the individual and the collective actors in its cultural backdrop.

The addition of 'Casmilus' as her surname helps us as readers to understand why Pompey the Great's social activities are related to our speaker's own, and how her supposedly innocuous visits to friends become enfolded in the dangerous stoppings and goings that structure both the novel's form and its ostensible narrative. It is identified by Smith's biographers as the misspelling of messenger-god Hermes's Phoenician name, which Smith would have had available in her copy of Lemprière's *Classical Dictionary* (where it is a misprint for 'Camilus'). As an image it not only reinforces the project we noted at the beginning of this chapter with regard to misspellings and corruptions of texts, but it also and once again returns us – via Hermes's godly responsibilities to travellers and roads – to the riding metaphor, just as the Sitwell quote above did earlier with its depiction of Pompey as the 'hollow fateful rider'. It very importantly extends that metaphor by aligning Hermes's mythical task of conducting souls to Hades – his free movement, in other words, in and out of the dark land of the dead, or 'hell' as Pompey pessimistically foreshortens it – with our speaker's movement from discourse to entrapping discourse in what she describes as her hellish visitations with contemporaries, 'all' of whom she said good-bye to at the beginning of this novel as it sets out to betray and convey them into the dark world of her book. These, then, and the discursive hobby-horses that move them and all around them, are what speed the novel's 'plot' *and* our speaker. 'You ride your friendships lightly, Pompey', as her chum William puts it near the novel's end (197), describing what we as readers by then also recognise but understand as another kind of dynamic. It seems to be one that allows our speaker the only sort of distance from those friendships that she can manage – and as such, seems akin to Smith's own practice of remaining 'between the lines' or even 'close to the edge', as she described it in the quote that I used at the start of Chapter 2:

> I have travelled and come and gone a great deal, I am a *toute entière* visitor. That is what I am being all the time. I visit and visit and visit, my darling friends, my less darling friends, my acquaintances.... [A]nd each least place where I visit I am so enchanted and so happy that it is another visit, and that at the end of the time I may say: Good-bye and thank you,

good-bye.... Under what tutelary deity shall I place myself? Under Mercury, double-facing, looking two ways, lord of the underworld, riding on the white horse, riding through hell, opener of doors; Hermes. (212)

The classical mythological rider she chooses is that 'shiftiest of namesakes, most treacherous lecherous and delinquent of Olympians' as she will call him in *Over the Frontier* (87). For she too is a 'two-faced' or 'double-faced' or 'janus-faced', as she called it, coming-and-going friend – one who is driven into company and knows that it defines her and yet cannot bear her friends and acquaintances for very long because, as we can see in the quote below, they mirror her own 'degenerate' identity. But like an updated J. Alfred Prufrock, who lacks something of that Dantesque capability to speak to inhabitants of hell and return to write about it,[17] Smith's speaker is also entertained by those who view her as a fellow inhabitant of their 'circle' and from whom she really cannot escape, even though she can be constantly caught 'straining' away from any one of them at any one time. In perpetual movement throughout the novel, then, we find her – or 'him' – the representative of culture itself, an updated version of earlier Pompeys:

> They are all so very different, from each other my friends, they are not at all alike, and cannot even be set down safely in front of each other. Show me a man's friends and I will show you the man. Then what sort of *man* is Pompey whose friends are 'all of different kinds'? Is there any Pompey at all? Is Pompey a chimera, a creature such as Lord Mellifont in *The Private Life*, whose existence depended on the presence of his friends? (196–97)

In almost every sense the character we have as our speaker is exactly this: the combination of all those satirised discourses heard in the book, all the conversations with friends who cannot be borne for long but who between them form her context for speaking, whose views invade her own. Her allusion here links up with the many references Smith makes to Sir Alexander Korda's 'private life' films of the period, from *The Private Life of Helen of Troy* (1927) to his most famous, *The Private Life of Henry VIII* (1933); at the end of *Over the Frontier*, Pompey's compatriot Tom will compare their military exploits with play-acting in Korda's films (269). The terrifyingly thin line that Smith saw collapsing between private and 'corporate' thought, 'real life' experience and performative ventriloquism is dramatised in these novels as her own only seemingly 'autobiographical' writing of her own 'private life'. That her speaker should define herself in the above quoted passage through the workings of an old adage, 'show me a man's friends...' – even to the extent of becoming the *man* in it (her emphasis) – is absolutely in keeping with the very ambiguous definition of selfhood that Smith's work sets out. In that definition, even specifics of gender are blurred in comparison with the contextual aphorisms, influences and scripted parts that dominate the existence or expression of identity. The fact that this is so and that Pompey knows it constitutes her 'little-ease', her Camusesque hell – one somewhat similar, perhaps, to the one that Pompey the Great experienced in his journey from being Caesar's brother-in-law and comrade-in-arms to his enemy ensconced in social rounds and back-stabbing discourse along senatorial dinner tables.

But our speaker's ability to 'whoa-up' on that ride towards her predecessor's 'high hollow fate' – which we might here associate with the loss of self altogether in a culture that is, as she put it earlier, 'running mad' – is accounted for by her nominal 'relation' to this other rider. This one is mythical but no less real, she suggests, in terms of powerful imaginative legacy, particularly in an era of atavistic re-creation of national/cultural identities. As Lassner has argued, Smith departs from modernist practice that 'reif[ied] mythological structures to envision historical process' in order to 'deploy them to expose their dangers to political discourse' (140)[18]. If Greek and Roman culture is our inheritance, if it defines a framework for our political as well as textual imaginations, then we make mean use of it, Smith suggests, perhaps by being 'degenerate riders' of its legacies. But then its own vagaries also encouraged imagination of some rather shifty characters – and Smith makes clear in a letter to the playwright Denis Johnston (who had congratulated her on *Novel on Yellow Paper*) that some of its deities offered fine templates for the self-serving and random bits of 'business' that she recognised as being constitutive of modern history as well:

> Casmilus is a dark name to fight under and he was a most awful twister he is the Phoenician Mercury-Hermes but the fact that he had the right of entrance to (and ahem exit from) hell has always fascinated me what a bore for instance he must have been for Pluto, Minos and Rhadamanthus, pursuing his frightful trivial quarrels into their country and doing a good deal of self-advantageous business on the side I make no bones to say. (*SS: AB* 118)

This speaker who takes this name becomes very dangerous in part because it describes a mercenary, 'fight[ing] under' a 'twister's' name and riding on towards one host and then another (as she does visiting friends). It is clear from the quote that Smith drew no line between Casmilus's interests or experience *outside* hell and the same when pursued into 'their country'. This is key to our understanding of her vision of the whole of European culture weltering inescapably in the continuum, as she saw it, between even the most 'trivial' quarrels of the Thirties and its newly developing forms of self-made and recurrent hell on the threshold of a renewed world war. And the fact that 'Casmilus' will be the name of her speaker's unattainable-because-blood-related love in *The Holiday*, finished *after* the war, redelivers the same imagistic landscape; the dissection of her speaker's sensibilities and her thwarted desire for wholeness dramatise the consequences of the era's internal divisions and duplicities.

The cat in the cradle

One further and crucial discursive riff that brings the movement of the novel into focus within its first ten pages involves a popular painting, many copies of which Pompey claims to have seen while on holiday in various parts of the country. Its image is one that will recur in the trilogy in several variations, continually offered to us as one that mutely registers something akin to what our speaker 'wish[es] to say' but suppresses; it has, she tells us, made on her the sort of 'childhood impression [that makes] a difference, as the psycho-analysts charge a pound an hour for saying' (15). The paragraph that describes it emerges very soon after the one I quoted first in this chapter, which diverted its flow from thoughts about (or aboard) Kismet the horse to *Mrs. Halliburton's Troubles* and other Victorian stories of hard times and Providential help. That 'ride' took her deeper and deeper into '[h]ow richly compostly loamishly sad were those Victorian days' (13), during which she began to incorporate in her own text lines from Tennyson's 'Tithonus', whose classical speaker has lived too long without rejuvenation, like the Sibyl of Eliot's epigraph to *The Waste Land*. It leads her to expand comically on all the decaying and dripping that goes on in nineteenth-century texts – 'always someone dies, someone weeps, in tune with the laurels dripping, and the tap dripping, and the spout dripping into the water-butt', and so on – until she suddenly links her present *'nostalgie'* for those 'open drain[s]' (14) of Victorian sentiment to this painting in a way that suggests that the dangerous floods of the times that she rides, just as she rides discursive hobby-horses and Kismet/Fate, are linked to that preceding textual tradition:

> And thinking of all this I have a great *nostalgie* for an open drain, like the flooded dykes they have there between the sodden fields. Like that picture when I was a child.... It turned up like the finger of God. In Lincs, where we were at Saltfleet. In Norfolk, where we were at Heacham. In Suffolk too, if my counties are right, where we were at Pakefield, there was that picture.
>
> There is a vast flooded prairie, a rushing mud-yellow foam-curded rain-lashed torrent, as if all the dams in the world were burst; swirling pushing leaping around, not hardly Christian, not Christian at all, but just the old element at its savagery, and no different from what it was before Anno Domini came that should daunt the flood. And riding – hick horse well met Kismet, whoa up, I say, whoa up – riding, now take it easy, on top of that brown flood was A little child shall ride it, in a cradle with a cat on top. (14)

Diverted mid-sentence, Smith's prose through her speaker's voice breaks its own syntax in order to shift from the dark energies signalled by address to Kismet into a new rhetorical tack – that is, from 'not hardly Christian' vision back into the ordering cadences of Biblical prophecy, even if the latter's interpretation of the picture seems no less dire: 'A little child shall ride it...' The capitalised preposition appearing suddenly mid-sentence is, like our speaker's mid-thought quandary about the spelling of 'Halliburton', and her adoption of an earlier misspelling of Camilus, a sign of the novel's foregrounding of her speaker's self-expression *as* text, and as text that demonstrates how culture's subconscious associations and re-contextualisations contribute to 'the word' for future generations. Certainly the new translations of the Bible that were being effected in the nineteenth century drew new attention to its unstable nature as a text, sifted as it had been through morphing versions of Christian thought. Attempts to divide largely Protestant, 'Indo-European Christianity' from 'Semitic Christianity' were then afoot, even in texts as mainstream as Matthew Arnold's *Culture and Anarchy* – therefore Smith may even be connecting what some saw as an 'Indo-European Melancholy' driving out a non-sentimental, rigid Semitism to her 'flood' of tears in this passage.[19] In any case, such shifts in her sentences again foreground the almost physical relationship of her speaker to the discursive materials she 'rides' so precariously. This one is symptomatic in that it arises, after a bit of weltering in mid-sentence, as something discrete, separate from the speaker's sentence, yet something that carries her on every bit as much as it does the child.

The complex significance of this image – which will reappear most significantly transformed near the very end of the trilogy (*TH* 169) – links up with the name that Smith's speaker will take in the third novel, 'Celia', given that both explicate Smith's fears about 'the return of the repressed' in mid-20th-century British culture. Because the 'dams' that burst above into the oft-reproduced picture appear in counterpoint to the equally oft-reproduced 'stuffy rooms' Pompey associates with childhood holidays, Smith seems to be suggesting that the repressive character of post-Victorian culture, with its fatalistic morality, close-latched natural instincts and deeply racist cultural 'ethnographies', bears this 'torrent' as its flip side: the dark undercurrent that it rides and denies articulation and that therefore 'carries it away'. We begin to understand the complex relation between this introductory set of images and our speaker's options for movement when, six pages later, just as Smith's speaker is beginning to explain how her vagrant thought-lines link up by the 'tyranny of the association of ideas', she suddenly wheels around for the first but not last time upon Jonathan Swift: 'And what do you know about that, Mr. Arch-Enemy-of-Elimination-Celia-Celia-Celia-Swift?' Swift's notorious 'excremental poems',[20] addressed to his mistress Celia, describe his speaker Strephon's horror that this object of his desire 'shits', among other things – that she cannot, in other words, maintain the porcelain perfection he seems to require of her. Yet the disillusion that Swift's speaker, named after the pastoral lovers of traditional eclogues, feels in this poem is highly ironic, since the facial pores he sees magnified in Celia's glass, used in her absence, are his *own*, and his *own* 'bowels' turn at his imaginations of her basin's uses. As in a later and clearer allusion to 'looking-glasses' that calls up Lewis Carroll's *Alice's Adventures in Wonderland*, during which Pompey tells us she often thinks of 'how for one dreadful moment Alice thought she was going to be Mabel' (63),[21] Smith here and constantly in her writings obscures demarcations between self and other as she thinks through projections of the repressed and the hypocritical disgust it stimulates. Her subversive joke in this quote highlights that irony, involving as it does an aural distortion and resultant re-rhyming of the most famous line of 'The Lady's Dressing Room' which finds Strephon 'Repeating in his amorous fits / Oh! Celia Celia Celia shits!', allowing Pompey's version to firmly lodge Celia via hyphens *within* Swift himself, and Swift within the slant-rhyme of his own 'shit'. Associated with uncontrollable 'flow' – that 'tyranny of the association of ideas' – that governs our speaker's own discursive 'movements' in the novel, Celia's eliminations become a figure for the text itself, its 'talking cure' that results in the exposition of darkness, the waste, that accumulates inside the body politic. And the 'morbidly body-conscious, body hating Swift', as she puts it later in the novel (213), becomes a figure of equally-internalised repression, disgust and, ultimately and importantly, hatred and violence against others for what must be denied within the self.

Pompey has it in her to play that figure as well. In the same way that her talk about her distant-cousin's wife 'Prunella' in this paragraph immediately led her, by that associative 'tyranny' of ideas, to thoughts of 'intestinal stasis', the illness that prunes may cure, Pompey continually demonstrates that her oral 'flow' reveals repressed elements in her own psyche, just as speech in Freudian psychology (and in Greek drama, as Smith well knew) reveals/conceals the unresolved complexes and cathexes of character that may lead to self-destruction. Given Pompey's representative status as our cultural analysand, the elements of her talk and of the childhood memories that enter in as both revelation and what begins to seem like collective dream are gleaned from well-known texts that underwrite the English imagination. Those include, as she makes clear here at the delayed end to her discussion of the ubiquitous picture in country houses, the more topical press as well as famous works of fiction (and her habitual 'Do you/Don't you see' address to her readers signals here, as it does elsewhere, her already-mentioned debt to Conrad):[22]

> Don't you see what I mean about this family and about the way people are good to me, and how lucky I am? And often I think I have a sword hanging over my head that must fall one day, because I am conscious of sin in my black heart and I think that God is saving up something special that will carry Pompey away. Like that flood that kid rode in its cradle

with that thar cunning cat sitting atop of it. And perhaps if the kid rode the flood o.k. that thar cat smothered it. For you can't escape your fate. And I've known cats overlay babies. It was in the newspapers. (28)

As experience becomes textual – she has 'known' what was in the papers – so does one's fate. And indeed, at the end of the novel, Pompey will be 'overlaid' by a cat, the tigress 'Flo', an account of whose death by drowning in her zoo cage is traded for our speaker's own end, given the latter's flagging will to continue. The fact that the cat's name is Smith's own – her given name being 'Florence' – marks not only the general self-reflexivity of the novel but also the *self*-destructiveness of culture as Smith depicts it. In Orwell's *Burmese Days*, his main character Flory shoots his own dog, also named Flo, before he in despair commits suicide; he is a figure whose hated facial birthmark represents all that he has helplessly inherited from imperial Britain and hates within himself. Similarly, 'cats in cradles' often represent, in cultural lore, the smothering of new life by parental and social programming. Much more will be said about this and the ending of the novel in due course; here, it is simply key to note that in these first ten to twenty pages of the novel, Smith has already set up her speaker as only precariously riding that torrent of cultural discourse that seems indeed destined to 'carry [her] away'. Through it she reveals both her pre-possession by the times that inscribe her *and* the directions in which she fears being swept through her own inclination towards repression of the self-knowledge that her 'talking voice' painfully allows.

Sick cats, anti-Semitism, and the British Lion

One of the most important keys to such self-knowledge that immediately arises for our speaker, in the wake of these first pages of the novel's exposition, is how the position of riding that 'mud-yellow foam-curded' torrent – a helpless subject-position, figured as the vulnerable baby in the picture – gives rise to a no-less-swept-away, but alternative, predatory position. It is a state she refers to four pages after the description of the holiday picture, while speaking again very directly to us as readers:

> Now Reader, don't go making trouble fixing up names to all this.... It's just all out of my head. And don't go looking like a sick cat for wicked envy, it's a thing you might come to yourself: if you'd got the sort of head I have. And don't get despairing either. Remember what they said in the thirteen hundreds: 'Accidie poisons the soul stream'. (19–20)

The 'sick cat' position is one that explains not only the possible threat to the baby from the cat in the picture but also the state of the realm itself. Because the other cat oft-mentioned in the novels is the old British Lion on all the standards, which in its relative wellness is figured in Smith's/Pompey's 'Lion

Aunt',[23] and in its sickness becomes 'the over-layer', the colonizer and self-destroyer, as we shall see later in the novel. The continuum of possibilities it represents are present in the individual Briton's 'soul stream' as well. Here, at the end of its expositional pages, in a 'moment of sadness' reminiscent of the river scene of *The Waste Land*, we find our speaker walking next to a similarly rat-infested river by her home (which is also 'curded yellow' like the flood in the picture) when suddenly we get a shocking glimpse of the 'sick cat', the 'accidie' within Pompey herself as she explains that 'By and by of course the seeping mud and those rat holes get into your soul and you get shot up again, as I was at that Jew party' (29). Eliot's poem bears complex relation to his later, smaller-minded, anti-Semitic and xenophobic prescriptions in his 1939 lectures, *Christianity and Culture* and *Notes Towards the Definition of Culture*,[24] a relation that deeply interested Smith. On a more subtle level, the fact that the sudden, uplifting recollection above is of another recollection is important; her 'shoring up' of memory through a refrain carrying this brand of poisonous cultural solidarity would have deep and sinister resonance with the Aryan project for Smith's readers. Such recollective retracking happens throughout the book, suggesting how fragile the feeling of being 'shot up' is and how addictive it can be. It also prompts us as readers to take up the opposing task of remembering earlier bits of the text that we, in our habitual project of building a coherent picture of our narrator that we can identify with, will have forgotten – bits that undermine our sense that this author has exerted the usual controls in the building of our 'character'. For example, here we are prompted to 'remember' the deep feelings of anti-Semitism and superiority that our speaker, whom we were just beginning at this point to associate with that vulnerable baby on the flood, startlingly recalled to defend herself against her riding partner's elegance on the second page of the novel:

> Leonie is a Jewess, but slim, and has a sense of *chic*. She is looking very elegant. She has a yellow pullover and fawn jodhpurs and a fawn felt hat. And who cares.
> Last week I was at a party at Leonie's. Suddenly I looked around. I thought: I am the only goy.... But then I had a moment of elation at that party. I got shot right up. Hurrah to be a goy! A clever goy is cleverer than a clever Jew. And I am a clever goy that knows everything on earth and in heaven....
> Do all goys among Jews get that way? Yes, perhaps.... It just comes with the birth. It's a world of unequal chances, not the way B. Franklin saw things. But perhaps he was piping down in public, and apologizing he was a goy. And there were Jews then too. So he put equality on paper and hoped it would do, and hoped nobody would take it seriously. And nobody did. (10–11)

It *is* hard to remember, once one has read more deeply into the book and come to enjoy the quirky frankness of this speaker, that she has been signalling to us that this sickness is there within her from the very outset of the novel – therefore Smith must continue to remind us of it. Like her character in her most famous poem, this speaker too is 'Not Waving But Drowning' in her own poisoned soul stream. And again like Woolf, Smith uses Jews in passages like the one above to represent not only a timely image of Europe's scapegoating and 'sick envy' of what it has long stereotyped as a suspiciously-well-to-do internal populace – brought to a head, perhaps, by the financial straits to be navigated post-First World War and out through the Great Depression – but also all victims of her culture's self-delusory and self-destructive dynamics. Such dynamics underwrite nation-building, too, as Pompey's quasi-comic reference to Benjamin Franklin (a 'Founding Father' of America) makes clear. The linkage to imperialising national attitudes becomes even clearer if readers pick up on the fact that in both of the passages describing the picture of the torrent she refers to 'that thar cat' in the language of the Hollywood cowboy films that infiltrated public imagination in the Thirties, summoning up heroicised images of American violence that 'won the West'. The rhetoric of democracy, she implies, like that of the fascistic state, is directly dependent upon the darker truth edited out but which, in her punning, 'lies' in all that goes unsaid.

One might argue that the dark fate of Europe's mid-century Jews, which Smith seemed to have had a prescient sense of, is in part universalised in the quote above in ways that Lassner rightly finds problematic in Woolf's work. It might be said, for example, that her use of the word 'goy', a pejorative term used by Jews to refer to Gentiles, suggests Smith's vision of reversible persecutions and large cycles of genocidal behaviour rather than those peculiar horrors that were slowly revealing themselves in the Thirties. Certainly Smith uses anti-Semitism almost as a trope above to refer to much more that goes 'undeclared' in American documents of equality and independence. Yet she also in her novels seems to historicise and particularise Jewish experience in the Thirties by prioritising it as *the* signal effect of those specific, emergent processes of repression in culture and discourse of the time. I would argue that in Smith's view, it spawned or illumined other effects she found various and apparent in everything down to the way one might look over at a companion presence like Leonie riding her own (hobby) horse. And yet in this instance, Leonie's very name seems to guard against our viewing her as essentially Jewish – or the inevitable victim – given that it suggests her ability to become leonine (or a British Lion) too, for good or ill. The complicated task of viewing social experience as historically specified and yet not *systematically* imprisoning each actor in its net was one Smith seemed to take on – and sometimes botched, like so many other mid-century writers, because the very dynamic she explored as inescapable and self-destructive was planted too deeply in her own cultural make-up.

The 'sick cat' response is related to what Pompey very importantly brings up as the 'forestalling principle' (33) that informs all manner of western cultural institutions, from established religions to national charters. A rhetoric of self-deception, built on an ironic principle by which disavowal becomes, as it does in Freudian psychology, 'the forestalling principle active and rampant', it is itself composed of a contradiction in terms. Meaning to delay, stop or repress the emergence of something, 'forestall' is also used in entrepreneurial language to describe the activity of buying up merchandise for profitable resale. It is, in other words, a 'principle' of activity that 'rides on' repression – the same principle that explains psychologically 'sick' behaviour due to repressed trauma, and the same principle that informs the 'whoa-up/talk on' form of this novel. Its broad applicability is key to both Smith's project of levelling institutional hierarchies and her modernist desire to chart out an essential mechanism – an all but 'gut instinct' – across the board in the workings of culture.[25]

It is, for example, no accident that she first brings up forestalling as a principle while discussing the long history of the Catholic Church in England (and its methods of recruiting):

> The early Christian catholic church was certainly puritan, like the catholics in Ireland. But the catholics in England nowadays trim their sails and walk oh so carefully-oh, and always set out to be so *simply healthy* and *patriotic*, according to the gospel of Fr. Martindale and Fr. Ronald Knox. You can follow up their line of approach. It is the forestalling principle active and rampant. Only sometimes, as forestallers are apt to do, they trip up. (33)

As usual, Smith's mixed metaphors are revealing; forestallers cannot 'trip up' unless they are indeed 'running on' some ulterior and/or mercantile level. Here, the references not only reveal the nationalistic cloak worn by such forces but also take us back to wartime rhetoric and begin to explicate how complex that ulterior level can be. Ronald Knox is a figure that Smith mentions in one of her poems as having been the topic of conversation in her own wartime household. His agonised conversion to Roman Catholicism in 1917, recounted in his autobiography, *A Spiritual Aeneid*, is compared quite unfavourably to what Wilfred Owen would have called the 'mirth' of the family's soldier friends[26] – their 'merry heart[s]' enlightened by the absurdity and hopelessness of rapidly 'modernising' culture as experienced from the trenches:

> Basil never spoke of the trenches, but I
> Saw them always, saw the mud, heard the guns, saw the duckboards,
> Saw the men and the horses slipping in the great mud, saw
> The rain falling and never stop, saw the gaunt

> Trees and rusty frame
> Of the abandoned gun carriages. Because it was the same
> As the poem 'Childe Roland to the Dark Tower Came'
> I was reading at school.
>
> Basil and Tommy and Joey Porteous who came to our house
> Were too brave even to ask themselves if there was any hope
> So I laughed as they laughed, as they laughed when Basil said:
> What will Ronny do now (it was Ronny Knox) will he pope?
>
> And later, when he had poped, Tommy gave me his book for a present,
> 'The Spiritual Aeneid' and I read of the great torment
> Ronny had had to decide, Which way, this or that?
> But I thought Basil and Tommy and Joey Porteous were more brave than
> that. ('A Soldier Dear to Us', *CP* 526)

The Ronny Knoxes of the world decide which of its existing dogmas to follow; the Basils understand the complicity and absurdity of all existing rhetorical stances and cavillings on pinheads. Smith's deep interest in the prevarications of theology, which I mentioned in Chapter 1, is combined here with her saturation by what Vincent Sherry has importantly described as the 'reasonable absurdity' of wartime rhetoric as it clung rather desperately, despite its many contradictions and empty moralisings, to practised models of English rationalism and Liberalism.[27] Both activities 'forestall' movement – like Kismet, the stopping horse – while the appetites they tacitly encourage by disavowing them 'lay waste the Duchy of Cornwall' or some other territory, be it material or spiritual.

Quite importantly, the particular sick cat envy involved in the latter is identified by Pompey as suppressed sexual longing 'run rampant'. She drives the undertow of this connection by beginning the passage quoted above with her account of a conversation with Karl, her German ex-lover, about Luther's identification with St Anthony:

> He was fond of Luther was Karl. And he told me how in bed one day Luther got thinking all sorts of thoughts about sex, and had visible temptations like St. Anthony.... But this St. Anthony he is thinking that sex is simply *horrid*, simply horrid, and just a cause of stumbling and vexation. But instead of saying: You boys want to play cricket and keep on going long walks, and getting healthily tired, like the Walk-it-off school of thought nowadays, he believed in prayer and starvation. He was a cenobite. (32–33)

Here she deliberately exchanges the familiar word describing the state of the abstinent – 'celibate' – for 'cenobite', a word that indeed means 'communal living among a religious order', but in this variant spelling (as opposed to 'coenobite') calls up 'empty bite' (from the Greek *kenos*, empty). The idea that one forestalls – in terms of denying for others as well as oneself – what one desires but cannot have (like, perhaps, Swift's Strephon as well? or Pompey beside the elegance of Leonie, or Pompey among 'clever Jews' at the 'Jew party'?) seems to undergird Smith's understanding of Catholic asceticism and its violent history, as her continuous references to the suppression of discussion of the Inquisition make clear. Its recruiting more 'carefully-oh' of converts in her own time also meant forestalling on the entrepreneurial principle: buying up 'prospect[s]' during the war with misleading rhetoric that denies its project while insinuating its effects. Underneath the forestalling talk is that 'active and rampant' principle of sickness that Pompey warned must be watched, goes 'running mad' – and is related, Smith very gently suggests, to what has already happened in Germany: 'Hitler cleared up the [decadent, hedonistic] vice that was so in Berlin... [a]nd now look how it runs with the uniforms and swastikas' (104). The purges of the Thirties – Stalin's, and Hitler's burgeoning one – were related in strategy to Torquemada's, in Smith's view, and born of variations on the same sick-cat envy. And yet we recall, once again, that Smith's speaker's anti-Catholicism takes both oblique and not-so-oblique part in the Protestant project of purging Indo-European Christianity of its papist *and* Semitic roots. It is essential that we as readers see that Smith's speaker demonstrates her own ability to get 'shot up' by such sick-cat processes – either out of envy, like Milton's Satan, or out of despair, like Eliot's wasteland wanderer, through the 'rat holes get[ting] into [her] soul'.

II
The place of 'romance' and gender issues in the novel

My haphazard introduction of Karl above, done in imitation of Smith's own strategies of storytelling, brings us back to the ostensible narrative that also runs through the novel: a very sketchy tale of failed love affairs and emotional turbulence that stretches on through *Over the Frontier* (1938) and modulates into a rather startling new version of itself a decade later in *The Holiday*, as we shall see in Chapter 4. But again, as in *Tristram Shandy*, or *Mrs Dalloway*, what 'happens' in the novels functions simply as a loose connector of other kinds of events. Given developments in her context, the latter are far more focussed on the dynamics of cultural discourse, and on the individual subject's resultant complicity within social turmoil, than those found in modernist work before the Thirties generally tended to be. I have therefore deliberately shaped this chapter in such a way that discussion of the novel's 'romantic' narrative, which tends to be foregrounded by critics in writings about the trilogy, happens *after* exposition of its far more crucial projects. Those projects have been obscured in readings like Severin's, as fine as it is with regard to certain aspects of the work, because she prioritises that narrative to the extent that she sees 'Smith's first two novels [as] romance stories literally cut with experimental sections or interruptions' (29), when the latter, as we have seen, *are* their content and dominate their movement. But it is, as Severin suggests, important to understand what sort of romantic narrative Smith's trilogy *is not* – as well as acknowledge the truly radical suggestions Smith makes with her interventions in the confused gender politics of what Alison Light has called the 'conservative modernity' of Thirties culture. It was a culture which, like Pompey herself, was 'Janus-faced, it could simultaneously look backwards and forwards' (Light, 1991, 10).

Her speaker introduces us to what her narrative will *not* be like on page 17 of the novel when, commenting on a ubiquitous image spotted in 'American paper[s]' – of 'Naughty standing in a mink coat, and the sugar dad...there with the cheque-book' – she cautions: 'There's no sugar dad in my life and those looking for sugar dads can shut up here and throw back at Miss-in-Boots cash chemists book-store.' This sentence/paragraph is frequently quoted by Smith's feminist critics, who take it as evidence of her novel's meta-fictional commentary on not only 'women in fiction' but 'fiction by women', as Woolf might have put it – which for ages perpetuated images of female identity existing solely 'in relation', or dependently on men. Certainly this updated figure of sexually liberated but financially leashed 'Naughty' in a mink perpetuates that tradition as it was being re-created in America in the guise of racy departure from the past. Smith's frequent and disparaging references to American money-making and spending as it was 'setting the screen' for the ascendancy of its example in the world are often spiked with the added suggestion that such newness was simply aspiring to take over the same old (European) story, *'mutatis mutandis'* (23) – as her interpolated narrative of her American cousin-of-a-cousin, Cyril, makes clear with a poetic ditty that reproduces Tennyson's portrait of nineteenth-century Napoleonic figures in 'The Eagle'. The above quoted passage seems to demonstrate that Smith reviled the collusion between (largely American) cinematic and tabloid images of women that were beginning to condition readers' desires and expectations. The constant abuse on this score levelled by Smith's speaker at her readers (male *and* female) seems to further evidence this, and indeed, near the end of the novel, Pompey lampoons their history and habits of reading (247) by returning to the cultural persuasions of *Mrs. Halliburton's Troubles* and ending with its linkage to current ladies' magazines.

Severin's work on this point is very fine and exemplary. She not only sketches in Smith's testy relationship with the women's magazines for which she wrote many reviews, but she makes fine use of Light's explications of the period while considering, for perhaps the first time, Smith's class affiliations and their possible impact on her projects:

As Rachel Blau DePlessis attests in *Writing Beyond the Ending*, Richardson and Woolf largely jettisoned the romance plot, using their fiction to explore communal rather than familial structures.... One has to wonder why Smith felt it necessary to return, at least partially, to the romance. The answer would seem to lie in Smith's class positioning. As Alison Light suggests, the interwar years were characterized by a downmarketing of the romance:

> The meanings of romance and of 'romantic' as terms of literary description become more narrowly specialized between the wars, coming to signify only those love-stories, aimed ostensibly at a wholly female readership, which deal primarily with the trials and tribulations of heterosexual desire, and end happily in marriage. At the same time, there is a sense in which, as part of the creation of this 'genre,' romance went downmarket as it was boosted by the growth in forms of 'mass entertainment' in the period and its commercialisation made it a bestselling form for a much larger group of readers. [1991, 160]

A secretary who had not attended university, Smith may have felt the need to dissociate herself from the genre's class implications through a direct attack, as well as to acknowledge the form's power over its women readers. (28)

It may well be that Pompey's seemingly non-ironised contempt for the majority of readers who bought Sir Phoebus's publications – 'these female half-wits [who] buy our publications and swell our dividends' (151) – suggests that our author's target is indeed (or at least in part) that growing mass of consumers that she served at Newnes' and that Severin describes. However, Pompey's barbed remarks about their taking quotations from her novel to '[their] high class parties' and other such places discourage us from seeing her 'direct attack' on romance readers as being focussed too narrowly in class terms.

And if we remember – with the help of the *Oxford English Dictionary* – that the verbal phrase 'to dumb down' dates back to 1933, Smith's in many ways deeply modernist Thirties critique begins to look as though it takes part far more clearly in growing anxieties about the whole of mass culture, not just that bit of it dedicated to reading romantic rubbish. As one commentator remembers it, '[e]verything was now aimed at mass markets and mass audiences.... Not all artists reacted positively to the democratization of modern life.'[28] The deep anxiety about these 'massive' changes in culture made their way into scores of journalistic texts and speeches – as well as introductions to commemorative books, such as *England Speaks*, published to celebrate the silver jubilee of George V in 1935. There Phillip Gibbs, respected former literary editor of papers like the *Daily Chronicle* and the *Tribune*, assures his readers that:

> We are still a nation of individualists, and I think that comes out in this book in which I have given a portrait gallery of people not yet standardised by the mass production of thought and character. (Giles and Middleton 33)

Nor were such fears simply elitist; as Emily Apter has noted, 'phobic visions of cultural standardization common in the 1930s' were deeply related to what figures like Erich Auerbach and Walter Benjamin envisioned as the potential and 'ominous marriage of technoculture and fascism' – a fear Benjamin articulated at the end of his famous essay, 'The Work of Art in the Age of Mechanical Reproduction'.[29] Pompey expresses such anxieties on a number of levels – for example, in *Over the Frontier*, she excuses her generation's fears even as she recognises that the earlier one 'lived through as many wars' by saying, uncertainly, 'But yes, no, all I can think to say is, Oh but the radio and oh but the electric bills, and oh but the underground railway and oh but the...' (108) – trailing off, but not before linking both the mentally deadening effects of her increasingly technical and mechanised, consumer-driven experience to what would come to be known as 'brainwashing'. The latter is easily accomplished, she often suggests, among not only those 'running on' the proliferating, specialist discourses surrounding big business and government but also among those becoming comfortable with the notion that, given the multiplying complexities of the world, sophisticated problems really ought to be made available through a variety of dumbing-down processes.

As usual, Pompey's favourite exemplar among the beneficiaries of such bifurcating cultural developments is the Church – that institution which, if any one of them might be, *should* be above all the other rats in the race. So it could be said that Smith demonstrates *both* her modernist elitism and her updated forms of Thirties politicking, for example, when her speaker suddenly begins discussing (with yet another Steinian as well as asyntactical gesture, this one evocative of empty repetitiveness) the new self-selling tendencies of the Church to 'cut out doctrine, and step down among the people... and just being kind and just being kind and' (176–77):

> Yes, partly it is our fault, because so often we are saying, we are crying down the intellect.... But we are clever enough when it comes to being clever in ways that it pays to be clever, we are not so stupid there.
>
> But now I think the Church should stand up, should get right up now and say: Stupidity is a sin. And then it should teach in very difficult to understand, very high-up language, not simple at all, but really very difficult, and it should teach the philosophy of Christianity in very high-up terms, and it should always speak high-up and well above people's heads, so they have trouble to understand. And then the Church might be empty. Very good, let it be empty. But by and by people would get sick at the way they missed the point, and they would get on their mettle, and be clever. Well think, the clever way they do the crossword puzzles, like the clever way they grapple with Torquemada, and the intricacies of the Stock Exchange, and the intricacies of, well say the intricacies of the law of libel, which certainly is not easy to get the hang of, and the intricacies

of, well say the intricacies of Somerset House, and the problems of taxation and economics. (178)

Pompey's attack is clearly levelled at a broad swath of cultural strata, all of which were developing corporate/legal literacies and modern ways of spin-doctoring current political developments (as well as Christian history, like the Spanish Inquisition's Torquemada). Yet we must always remember that even these unfully-ironised passages are not examples of Smith's voice *per se*, though the private joke here about the fact that Smith herself was constantly embroiled in threats of libel over her 'use' of her friends as artistic models for her work might suggest so. If we read it as such, we miss the crucial and latent cruelty in Pompey's condescending tone – its edge being the same one that cut at Leonie and that will, ultimately, cut down with her own gun an explicitly described member of 'the masses' who gets in the way of her vaulting military ambitions at the end of *Over the Frontier*. There *are* others of Pompey's own seemingly less-ironised comments that might be said to support Severin's class-oriented conclusions about Smith above; we encountered several in the foregoing chapters. But others *not* discussed by Severin give us a picture of her speaker, at any rate, that is unfortunately a good deal less flattering; for example, through the comments Pompey makes about northerners, like the unaccountably savaged Mancunian sat opposite her in a train whose intellectual powers fail him in the reading of *Lady Chatterley's Lover* (*NOYP* 109–10). It is often difficult to know whether such instances suggest that despite the fact that the immediate success of her first book would in some ways re-class her, Smith may not have wholly escaped violent responses to what she saw in 'the mirror' as her own northerner status (having issued from and partly retained the accents of Hull, as we saw in Chapter 2).

Severin's central argument breaks down far more noticeably with her actual reading of what she sees as Smith's 'romance plot' in the text itself, as well as her analysis of Smith's greater formal project in the trilogy. This is due in part to the fact that although Severin acknowledges, following the long passage she quoted and I re-quote above, that Pompey is 'susceptible' to the very social imperatives she deplores, her desire to make a heroine of our female speaker, and to read the lengthening 'intercuts', as she calls the speaker's digressions, as evidence that this is a narrative in which 'the heroine struggles more effectively [as the trilogy progresses] against the romance plot, despite higher odds' (30) causes her to misread – even miss altogether – the speaker's *main* conflicts given her decidedly non-heroic 'secret life that runs on' (64). The proportionally tiny bits of romantic involvement in the novels take on very different meanings and far more broadly political valences when the *majority* of its issues raised are paid proper attention. Ironically, Severin's treatment becomes a counter-productive reinforcement of all that critics have consistently done when attending to 'women's novels' (given that they are supposedly always and primarily about gendered experience). Such approaches to Smith's work have thus far distorted beyond recognition what goes on in the novels' digressions – which Severin reads as being composed of either gendered 'fantasies' or passages from her own reading journals offered as 'demonstration of [Pompey's] learning and her ability to use it against the culture that assigned her to the role of romance' (32). That this reading is untenable as well as reductive is difficult to see if, as I suggested in Chapter 1, one suppresses close reading and discursive/ cultural analysis of the whole of the text in favour of locating a predominantly feminist project within it.[30]

Returning to the short quote from the novel that began this section, it is, once again, of key importance to remember that Pompey is a *speaker* and not Smith herself – and a speaker who is highly suspect, as we have had ample opportunity to see by this point in the novel. Always 'running on', as she does, her outright denials like this are, however much we might wish to read them as evidence of her female resistance, often less important than her elisions and 'trip-ups' (which she as the product of a 'forestalling' culture makes) in maintaining the same. Throughout the novels Pompey repeatedly becomes that very sort of (female) figure she most fears and would reject.

Which is not to say that she *never* illuminates the peculiarly feminine aspect of her larger dilemmas in those digressions that involve her 'learning and ability', as Severin sees it. That aspect appears, for example, and quite dramatically, in the figure that haunts her after viewing Shakespeare's plays, which she tells us she cannot like (though they turn up regularly in unmarked quotes in the trilogy, evidencing Smith's indebtedness to them, akin to Woolf's). Pompey explains her repulsion by referring to them as those plays which she finds full of 'horrors and the bones and the charnel house', plays that conjure up 'Juliet's morbidity when she visualizes in such bludgeoning, strapping, head-smashing words all those things she would rather *not* do, but would rather not *not* do than lose her love': 'But here the echo from the future is so clear, the dead girl, no matter if she later rises, the dead girl and the two men at war upon her bier' (202).

Apart from being a truly innovative reading of Shakespeare – made long before feminist criticism had begun to remark upon the same sorts of recurrent images in the plays – this passage is of key importance to our reading of the trilogy's ostensible romance narrative. Pompey 'dies' twice – only ostensibly, like Juliet – in the course of the trilogy, and 'later rises' (to a kind of death-in-life state, culminating in ambiguous 'sleep', in *The Holiday*). It happens in figurative terms at the end of both of the first two novels, and both times because she is, on the surface, caught between what she would 'rather *not* do and what she would rather not *not* do than lose her love[s]' – Freddy and Tom, respectively. But Smith makes it clear – again, through the content and discursive nature of Pompey's long digressions, and through the highly topical, politicised and even nationalised language of the second novel – that Pompey is caught between much more than just amorous men, or potential marriages. In *Novel on Yellow Paper*, Karl embodies German discourse from Luther to Hitler (even that of Karl 'Marx', *OTF* 176) at one end of the novel, offering a timely comparative for what Freddy embodies at the other: the suburban Englishness of her own repressively civilised 'meelyoo'.[31] In *Over the Frontier*, remaining feelings for home-front Freddy are pitted against those for another Englishman, the very military Tom, who is responsible for her 'coming out' in soldierly uniform. And in *The Holiday*, where the same quote reappears in new form (31), she is, far more complexly, caught between two sets of brothers – abject Tiny and predatory Clem, prodigal Tom and military Caz – as well as the moral forces of life (St John at work; an obvious allusion to *Jane Eyre*) and death (as Rev. Heber, to whose peaceful 'home' she travels for her holiday). Far from resisting phallocentric coercion more effectively as the narratives progress, our speaker is wound more and more tightly in it. The 'two men at war on her bier' image above – an image that will be repeated *verbatim* but with a difference in *The Holiday* – represents, through changing relations in each novel, the contradictory and often very dangerous, dominating discursive forces of the time that through her speakers' very speech in the novels seek to 'kill' Pompey and Celia and thereby control them. It is true that Smith critiques patriarchy in deeply sophisticated ways through these figurations and their structuring of the trilogy, but it can only be through understanding Pompey's *complicity* in all that destroys her that we glimpse the real and exceedingly timely 'plot' Smith has on offer.

The binaries all these men represent blend in Pompey who, as our 'figure caught between', demonstrates their volatile overlappings with other seemingly opposed cultural discourses. By the end of the second novel, Pompey has graduated to being caught not only between lovers but, in war, between the orders of an allegorically-designated 'Archbishop' and a 'Generalissimo', having become 'too hopelessly involved, too set in and captive upon the will of these two men' (266). These representatives of powerful Thirties forces that ought to have been polar opposites, religion and political tyranny – forces that were, indeed at the very moment of Smith's writing, busily and publicly colluding with one another to fuel the far right under Franco in the Spanish Civil War – are certainly patriarchal figures. And Smith's gendered reading in the above quoted passage of the powerless states of Juliet, Hero, Imogen, Hermione and others in their respective plays by Shakespeare certainly begs us to think about the role of women set within conflicts between men. But the larger cultural forces that police far more than gender relations are what overwrite Pompey's relationships in the first two novels of the trilogy. Both of them end with pitiful invocations of a purer innocence in living and loving that *neither* Pompey/Celia nor her lovers can produce. When she says, in the final sentence of *Over the Frontier*, that '[p]ower and cruelty are the strength of our life, and in its weakness only is there the sweetness of love', she is speaking *from that position* of power and cruelty, having just presided in vaguely fascistic fashion over costly military manoeuvres, as well as having killed a man at close range herself. Certainly we will see that she has once again become 'the dead girl', one caught up in a world of men speaking, or warring, above her somnolence, forcing her to 'ride along' on the wave of historical bellicosity that informed the Thirties. However, and equally certainly, we note that the gender reversal that is also happening here rewrites sexual limitations *not* to celebrate feminine ascendancy but to broaden the epic tragedy unfolding before our eyes for all 'subjects' of her current realm. She does, in other words, finally meet her fate as Pompey the Great's namesake, explaining for us Smith's initial and strange dubbing of her speaker a whole novel ago. Having become like him too violently ambitious herself, 'too set in and captive [to these two men] upon [her] own pride' (266), she discovers that within her as well 'the very frightfulness of an unsatisfied personal lust for power, identifying itself with a national arrogance, [her] country's successful delinquency' (272), can split her heart in two and blacken it. The infiltration of what we *thought* we were reading – a monologue, a stream of consciousness – by forces that write our speaker into a larger, densely historical plot is, in effect, 'what happens' in the novels, dramatising what Pompey's life as a character is all about. We are charged, in other words, to consider the full complexity of these many levels of corruption and coercion, 'private' and public – and ask why Smith, like Auden, forecast for her times the comprehensive failure of love, and therefore what *larger* cultural significance the failure of romance might signify in her work.

Karl: Britain's German mirror image

Pompey's first romantic interest appears suddenly in our speaker's 'running on' and in a manner that begins to suggest how we might pursue the above questions. It happens just after Pompey's recollection of the walk by the blasted river, where she was 'shot up' again by the 'seeping mud' and 'those rat holes get[ting] into [her] soul', as we saw at the end of my first section to this chapter. The initial mention of his name appears out of the blue in what to me is one of the most enigmatic (if funny) and intriguing paragraphs of the book. It follows hard on Pompey's assertion that being 'shot up' by the river, as she 'was at that Jew party', has made her 'twice what I ever was before these days' (i.e., she is made bigger than life if she can, when feeling most low, re-envision herself as part of something larger and collective in its superiority). Then:

> And once I remember when I was walking along with Karl near Hertford on a wet day like this I am telling you about, there in the road was a dead vole sticking its paws upright – like a Christian it had been run over.
> Karl was a fine boy and we got on fine. (30)

This odd and abrupt introduction to Karl seems to suggest his association with a sickly-comic image connecting upright Christianity to a dead beast in *rigor mortis* with its paws stuck 'upright'. But whether the image is solely associated with him or with Pompey as well becomes unclear as, in the next few pages, we witness the beginning of Pompey's interrogation of (and *suppressions* of interrogation of) the 'goyhood' that 'shoots her up' too – that is, 'upright' – and makes her, like this German, into a dead Christian for participating in feelings of collective (and deadly) superiority over what she earlier dismissed as the 'clever Jew' (11). It all seems to begin with Karl who, as a figure our speaker tells us about only glancingly and without much but tongue-in-cheek feeling – one whom she says good-bye to on page 105 and whom we never hear of again, except in a short memory on page 191 – functions less importantly as a romantic interest in the novel than as a spur to Pompey's cultural conscience.

Thoughts about Karl summon up some of her longest digressions about xenophobia, religion, imperialism and violence, all of which turn on comparisons between the various 'righteous' poses of her England and Karl's 'beloved Germany' (49). The disturbing 'quarrels [that] must come' (46) between them preface Pompey's visiting of Germany (during which she only briefly sees ex-boyfriend Karl); her account of that trip and her consequent feelings about Germanness becomes one of the principal 'events' in this first novel in which, as I have noted, very little else actually 'happens'. Pompey's love/hate for this figure Karl, then, becomes far less importantly part of any 'plot' than a brush with German nationalist rhetoric, whose internal contradictions between 'black heartedness' and cultural refinement – as exemplified by Hitler himself, whom Thomas Mann in his 1938 essay 'Brother Hitler' identified as essentially an artist rather than a politician – reflect her own country's discursive double-dealings for political ends, and her own entrapment as a thinker/writer in those webs of identification and 'blackness'. This is swiftly flagged by her early account of seeing the statue of Shakespeare in Weimar (45), which suggests the overlap between the two cultures; Germany's notorious arguments claiming Shakespeare for its own are referenced here, instancing the ways in which culture and art are caught up in the aggrandising vision of nationalist projects.

Karl too seems a figure caught in variations on the same webs – as well as the only one in the novels whose autobiographical equivalent in Smith's own experience seems worth contemplating for a moment. Smith's association with a Swiss-cum-German man named Karl Eckinger in the late 1920s, just before her own unusual decision to travel to Germany (not being much of a traveller outside the British mainland), is described in detail by her biographer Frances Spalding. What interests me in Spalding's description of Karl is the deeply contradictory nature of his beliefs and allegiances in the Twenties and Thirties, and therefore his perfect modelling of the state of mind that Smith would construct for her characters in the novels. Apparently Eckinger's political/philosophical stances were so confusing to Smith's friends that they called him, 'wrongly' in Spalding's view, 'Stevie's Nazi boyfriend':

> As a student, Eckinger did occasional pieces of journalism, some for the *Basler Nachrichten*, and, according to his family, was sent to Germany [from Basle] to report on the Munich Putsch in 1923, after which Hitler was imprisoned for a year. Eckinger always claimed that this experience had forewarned him of what was to happen and that he was among the first in Switzerland to recognize the danger of the Nazi threat. He himself felt an antipathy towards the Jews and during the 1920s took steps to eradicate this by living among Jews when he moved to Berlin. Nevertheless, his profound admiration for German culture left him not untouched by the Herren-Denken attitude. He was, therefore, anti-Fascist, but tinged with some of the instincts and beliefs that helped bring Fascism to power.
>
> Culturally he was a child of the Enlightenment, an admirer of Lessing.... Though he professed a hatred for Wagner [who was most associated with German nationalism, and one of Hitler's favourites] and Romanticism, he had a romantic aspect to his nature which he kept carefully hidden. (75)

In this, we might say, he was not unlike Smith herself, whom he diagnosed (in a letter to his fiancée, whom he was deceiving with news of his 'friendship' with Smith) as having a secret life: '...the face she shows the world is not the right one' (*SS: AB* 78). I delve into autobiography here to speculate for a moment about the changing 'Germany' that Smith came directly into contact with and was depicting, and about why Karl, as an intelligent idealist who wished to think the 'right' things but could not control his leanings, might have been so easily transposed into her novel about inter-war discursive turmoil as Pompey's first major interlocutor and theatrical 'foil', her German mirror. Dozens of passages evidence Pompey's desperate attempts to differentiate German culture – its texts, its dreams – from her own. Inevitably, as in the comic but also chilling section on the 'deeply neurotic' (102) nature of German fairy tales, with their 'blood lust and ferocity' (formative as they are, or so the implication here suggests), we find that Pompey is describing her own reading, some of it customised from German roots. Here, 'Snowdrop' is obviously 'Snow White' with several other familiar stories like 'Little Red Riding Hood' folded into the mix (101). We also find Pompey exhibiting all the myopic, nationalistic and chilling traits that she accuses Karl of exhibiting – a strategy of cultural- and self-exposure that begins on the very first page of his mention, where he proves annoying to her for being chauvinistic and defensive of German culture even as she mirrors him with her appeal to us as readers: 'Do you know how it is with foreigners?' The question would have struck a chord of either sympathy or shame in a time when J.B. Priestley could write, in *English Journey* (1934), that he once sympathised with his small daughter's question: 'But French people *aren't true*, are they?' and 'knew exactly how she felt. It is incredible that all this foreignness should be true' (27). The next paragraphs go on to extol Englishness for giving the world Shakespeare, and so on. Such moments in Smith's text, particularly if read against this backdrop, make us sensitive to the xenophobic nature of many of Pompey's jokes about her 'foreign' friends – the ways they talk, look and think. They also make us aware of how easily and increasingly unravelled Pompey becomes when her own unquestioned beliefs are disturbed by this catalyst/Karl.

It is only after Karl comes into the book that Pompey begins to think longingly about sleep/death – or rather, more importantly, about falling forever asleep on the 'haystack' she imagines as her 'ivory tower' in the country (37), far away from the London that Karl finds so decadent and unsympathetic. (And it is important to keep this image in mind as we finish reading *The Holiday*, which ends with the decision not to go back to London after the holidays, but to fall asleep.) She does so just after Karl finishes his mini-dissertation on the visionary Luther, during which she went into the long digression on the 'forestallers' of both the Roman Catholic Church and Church of England that I discussed earlier. At the end of it we are back in the midst of their conversation, and Karl is describing Luther as being 'strong and single-minded, and not ashamed of his human frailties' (36), able to face his St Anthony-like temptations – such as jumping out of bed and exposing his genitals to the cold to defuse their influence – because he was 'not afraid of his enthusiasms like you English. And your Reformation.' Pompey is so 'vexed with this allusion to Elizabeth and the bishops', which in the somewhat bewilderingly truncated form of his last line above suggests a link between the English reformation and the '*un*exposed' agendas (sexual as well as political) of its monarchs, that she 'could not find a word to say' – a state that spells absolute confusion in a novel that 'runs on' many discursive hobby-horses. Turning abruptly upon us – her *Heart of Darkness* audience, or as she puts it elsewhere, her 'Wedding Guest reader' (174) – she then asks: 'Do you ever feel that way, you fool?' in order to suggest that her speechlessness before mention of the unexamined collusion of national/ rhetorical and doctrinal history should not belong to her alone. Her description of her automatic defence of that knee-jerk, righteous Christianity that became imaged for her and Karl by the 'paws upright' dead vole in the street is obviously meant to strike a chord with her English readers:

> Oh but first of all why did I come out like that, I wonder, about the Church of England? It is always like this; really I find myself perhaps a little hypocritical the way I will not have anybody say a word against that institution.... But actually I am not a Christian actively. I mean I am actively not a Christian. I have a lot against Christianity though I cannot at the moment remember what it is.

Oh I am so tired. There never was anyone so tired as poor Pompey at this moment at this page, at this very line, at this word. (38)

Directly after these thoughts Pompey experiences her first longings in the novel to stop, to sleep (perchance to dream – aye, there's the rub; we shall see how deeply Pompey's fears and desires are connected to Hamlet's similar wishes for escape from his own rotting state). Such stopping, as we know, is connected with Kismet's symbolic drive towards cessation and destruction; it is only *seeming* stopping, in which the repressed dreams and appetites 'run on', out of conscious control. In instances like these in the novels, the will to stop speaking, to sleep, is, as in Beckett's work, emblematic of the will to self-destruct in the face of exhausting visions of one's own inescapable script and *its* unstoppableness.

She goes on to deflect knowledge of her relation to the results of her country's imperialist violence as well as her own helpless defence of it in the ready rhetoric of 'pragmatics' and necessity, composed here of passive constructions that repress blame (or any closer analysis of it):

[*Karl speaking first, then Pompey, etc. As is usual for this novel, dialogue happens without quotation marks or obvious distinctions between speakers*]
The English, the cruel cynical flippant frivolous pragmatical English of the upper governing classes, the enemies of philosophy and music and of every high abstract idea. With greed and pride and arrogance they possess the earth.
   No no the English are not like this.
   You scattered the bones of the Mahdi.
   That must be done; it is something that has had to be done.
   Cruel and ferocious and cunning opportunists that grind the stupid fat faces of your own common people that sacrifice everything of the spirit to the preservation of your famous *status quo. You scattered the bones of the Mahdi.*
   ...Oh it was those classical scenes in *Faust* and the bones of the Mahdi that finally drove the rift between me and that sweet boy Karl the way I have said. (47, 48)

Pompey's earlier explanation was of her uneasiness about the 'false feeling of classicismus' in Goethe's *Faust*, which Karl gave her as a gift. Though as with so many of her feelings it goes only vaguely explained, it may well have indexed for readers of the time the prophetic fears that would of course accompany apprehension of the deeply romantic connection between Germany and Rome that informed Hitler's modelling of national pride and ambition.[32] But her corollary unease about German 'high abstract ideas', or idealisms – evidenced in her comic misuse of the German/classical suffix '-ismus' to denote ideological and often blind fervour, as in her versions of 'groupismus' or 'chimeraismus' (the latter referring to the chasing of romantic dreams, as we shall see) – is equalled in her reaction to the cruel pragmatism that Karl seems right in assigning to the 'English' (by the era's false synecdoche).[33] Certainly her responses to his repeated accusations about the 'scattering the bones of the Mahdi' (Islamic leaders) would suggest so to readers. Her defensive employment of the language of necessity here is contradicted in her next and desperate plea to remember the genius of the English poets, whose presence, she goes on to argue, proves that there is more to English culture than what she in effect agrees is its 'savage and...predatory' nature. Their references above to Britain's take-over, by post-First World War League of Nations 'mandate', of Islamic territories including Palestine and Iraq are, along with many more searching references to imperialistic subterfuge and its spin-doctoring in *Over the Frontier*, what cause Pompey to begin to admit that 'our so darling pet Lion of these British Isles' is a 'Colonising Animal' (105). Worse yet, she will herself, at the end of the second novel, seem to enact a scene very like the one Karl describes above, when she shoots the 'rat face[d]' old man who has taken hold of her boot as she tries to climb over a wartime stockade. He becomes a symbol of the 'stupid...common people' when she looks down at him and sees 'the backside of the world; the smug flat note of *that* vox humana' (249). In other words, she will herself, however shamefully and conflictedly, be illustration of that English 'opportunism' that succeeds hypocritically by 'grind[ing]' down the disempowered in a social system that depends on the latter's maintenance of the illusion of unchanging order, hierarchically preordained as good.

Lions are the select image of that order; and Pompey is, as the quote above makes clear, coming to finally admit the obvious: that it, like the animal, is predatory. The fact that lions are the predominant image for almost everyone British in the novels is key – and it disturbs feminist readings of Pompey's identification with her 'Lion Aunt' as being suggestive of the latent but suppressed power of Smith's feminine figures.[34] Pompey discovers that she is indeed a British lion like her Aunt, whose commonsensical 'foot on the ground', no-nonsense attitude towards life and politics and British colonies like India (as we find out later) is reflected in the above responses Pompey gives Karl about the effects of the mandates. Pompey is throughout the first two novels caught between her Lion Aunt's pragmatics and her own 'foot-off-the-ground' tendencies (38), which encompass her penchants for digressing and dreaming, or 'running with' any thoughts that come. Janet Watts, who introduced all three of Virago's reprints of the novels, uses the above foot-off-the-ground passage as a frame for her remarks on *Novel on Yellow Paper*, depicting through it Smith's own exuberance and wilfulness and loveable character which she reads as synonymous with the text itself. But we would do better to remember that to 'run with', as in 'run with the uniforms and the swastikas' (104), is a threatening as well as 'therapeutic' (or 'talking cure') image in the novels. Both the English and German, foot-on- and foot-off-the-ground modes can become tactics of evasion. Both can 'forestall', in the sense of repressing the connection between laundering discourse and actual desires/deeds, as well as the connection between what Pompey *says* in these pages and what she calls her 'life [that] runs on secretly all the time, as it must' (64). As I began to argue at the beginning of this chapter, the novels' multiplying allusions to Conrad's Heart of Darkness, particularly in Pompey's constant stopping to ask of us, 'Do you see?' in invocation of Marlow, that other revealing/concealing narrator – something which happens even more frequently in Over the Frontier (49, 72, 100, 106, 108, 177) – encourage us as readers to acknowledge that the British empire has also, with its 'civilizing missions' of predatory colonisation, engaged in forestalling gestures. Despite its very different and laconic discourse of 'efficiency', its 'secret life' of activity is very like that of the dreaming Germans with their romanticised rhetoric about the necessary expansion of what Karl calls their culture of 'true civilization', a culture he tells Pompey he would have fought for against the central powers. Her response below is a wake-up call to Karl, but we hear in it too her own desire for sleeping, as on her haystack, her 'ivory tower' (and even the phrase *ivory* tower might, given its associations with the exploitation of pre-colonisation Africans, have been chosen pointedly):

> Ah that beloved Germany and my darling Karl. I too can see that idea of sleeping, dreaming, happily dreaming Germany, her music, her philosophy, her wide fields and broad rivers, her gentle women. But the dream changes, and how is it to-day, how is it to-day in this year of 1936, how is it to-day? (49)

It becomes clear that the conflict Karl provokes in the first half of *Novel* glosses the continual dreaming that Pompey herself does, too, both here and in the second novels of the trilogy as well. Rather than being 'fantasies', her dreams demonstrate in Freudian fashion her endless re-routings of energies, her desperate diversions and deflections of what she is loathe to think through. She is indeed *ungründlich*, or un-thorough, as she says 'Karl knows' in her last, out-of-the-blue reference to him in the final pages of *Novel on Yellow Paper*: 'Karl said so. Karl knows. Watch Karl' (244). Karl must be watched, as she said '[Germany] should then be watched' (105); but she is also saying, by saying this, that *she* should be watched as well. 'Well look this dangerous way [she] is running on', Dear Reader.

Nietzschean destruction and Dionysus

Pompey's 'unthoroughness' – her repression of certain emotions, desires and avenues to self-knowledge, her 'running on' in order to skirt certain unspeakable discrepancies evident in the tumult of discourses she rides – is indeed capable of making her very dangerous, too. On the one hand, her unthorough thought-processes translate into inflammable complicity with 'a national ethos..., in our country's plundering' and with its bellicosity, as she puts it at the end of her military exploits on the last page of *Over the Frontier* (272); on the other hand, her sudden recognition of such manipulations and of her own part in them conjures up self-destructive loathing of all that is duplicitous in her and in others around her, in which case she becomes ferocious in yet another alarming way. Smith makes this clear by drawing still another plane of classical imagery beneath her 'plot' – this one investing her speaker with the logic-shattering compulsions of Dionysus over and against her own 'no nonsense', empirical, imperial (English) self as imaged in Pentheus, the repressed and repressive ruler of Euripides' play *The Bacchae*.

If we remember (and have read Nietzsche's *The Birth of Tragedy*), Dionysus signified to the ancients that anti-symbolic, anti-institutional, anti-illusionary force in civilisation: the force that deposes what Apollo composes, the latter representing that alternative force that creates out of the unspeakable multiplicity and primordial formlessness of natural impulses the 'veils' and figures of language, art and culture. The familiar image of Dionysus in winealtered states of ecstasy – as well as supervising savage power-reversals in culture – suggests his 'voluptuous compulsion' towards spring's unification of forces in nature, and their consequent and 'complete self-forgetfulness'. Conversely, Apollo is (in Nietzsche's quotes from Schopenhauer) the force that asserts self, the *principium individuationis*, and 'by this mirror of illusion, he is protected against becoming one and fused with his figures' (Nietzsche 50).[35] Smith's Pompey frets about 'being Mabel' in her Alice-in-Wonderlandish way just after her first demonstration of Dionysian anger precisely because she knows she *is* a reflection of not only the figures that appear in her looking-glass world but the 'figures' of language that shape her supposedly separate, 'individual' self. She is in herself the best exemplum in the novel of that classical struggle between individuating and dissolving, or building and destroying forces. Indeed, they form the two interlocking parts of her very odd name: first, self-aggrandising ruler, 'Pompey the Great', and second, a figure of underworldly power's undermining of territory in the person of double-facing Casmilus. Her 'Christian' name even recalls, for the homophonically-minded among us, the well-known destruction of the 'built' city of Pompeii by 'natural', volcanic disaster.

All of these things might suggest, in part, that internal as well as external imbalance between basic forces was the disorder of the day in Smith's view of the Thirties, full of as they were of Apollonian self-aggrandising leadership and post-1920s repressive conservatism. As Pompey tells us, it was a time during which 'Hitler cleared up the vice that was so in Berlin' so that it could then 'run with the uniforms and the swastikas' (104), breeding the two-faced, double-life thinking (i.e., 'sick cat envy') that results from a lack of Bacchic balance, self-reflexivity and integration (or 'integrity'). In other words, and in good classical fashion, we seem to have contemporary history as *psychomachia* in the novel. This is signalled by the fact that Pompey plays *both* roles – the role of Dionysus early on in *Novel*, when she revolts against being dressed to be more *'chic'* by her friends, and then the role of Pentheus in the pivotal moment of being 'dressed to kill' in *Over the Frontier*'s uniform-donning scene, which is spiked with imagery imported from the earlier *Bacchae* segment. Yet her long digression on *The Bacchae* that comes between these two scenes, about mid-way through *Novel on Yellow Paper*, begins with her recollection that she played the 'second messenger' in her school's production of the play. Therefore, the link between *this* role and the allusion of her surname to Hermes the messenger makes it clear to us that she is also a 'reporter' on and to the scene (classical *and* contemporary) as well as the subject of the drama. These personal and cultural interweavings are key to understanding not only Smith's social vision but her feminist and not-so-feminist ideas. They also explicate Pompey's longings for sleep, death – the end of being 'dressed' for these parts, of learning these 'lines', of playing these unsavoury roles ordered by her era's cultural script.

We see Pompey become Dionysian for the first time early on in the novel, when we cannot know that the same images will connect up with her long digression later in the book on the plot of *The Bacchae*. It is tempting to read this as delayed revelation of a transhistorical frame for experience, as I might be seen to suggest above and as often happens in modernist writing. Certainly Smith's apparent devotion to the alternate world of wisdom available in ancient philosophy and tragic drama might be said to link her to better-known contemporaries like T.S. Eliot, Ezra Pound and H.D., as well as to modernist psycho-social philosophers like Freud who found them paradigmatic of continuing human experience. But two slight differences in the way she employs classical themes give me pause in making those connections. In the novels, first of all, we have so much evidence that our speaker is a conglomerate of all she has read (indeed, we know that on the fourth page of the first novel she suspects '[she has] read a bit too much') that the classics become foregrounded as *reading* – even 'required reading', that is, set texts in school – rather than as indices of human experience. Like Woolf, Smith also seems deeply aware of the class and gender implications of such reading or not reading. And yet it *is* true that, unlike Woolf, she explores the ancients very thoroughly indeed in her works – and in her reading journals, where the effort she took to read the texts in Greek and Latin is evident. She does customise and update the 'stories' in comical fashion – 'So now Pentheus is living in the royal palace...' (131) – to make them one with her speaker's current associative train of thought. Given that the latter rules the novels' movement, and given all the references in the novels to memory and not remembering, I as a reader want to entertain the idea that Smith was adding another variant to the repertoire of modernist strategies in referencing the classics: she was exploring her own cultural 'programming' via texts that arise in close proximity to what her speaker delivers as her own thought. If this is the case, then the fact that texts are remembered without her speaker's awareness of their connection to her own actions and ideas gives us another way of reading the mentioned lapse in explicatory textual precedent: we are to understand that such 'information' is submerged beneath almost everything Pompey thinks and does – is part of the 'encoding' processes of culture that Pompey helplessly relates.

Secondly, it seems true that unlike other modernists who valorised the ancients – saw in them something 'numinous' and connected by origin to what had been obscured in the 'neo-Nietzschean clatter' of the modern era[36] – Smith draws in their thought as simply being generative of and continuous with the greater western cultural text that later collides with it. Certainly she, like Pound in 'A Retrospect' (67), found pre-Roman 'hardness' to be salutary in her post-Victorian period, flooded by the rhetorical sentimentalism that, as we saw earlier, she feared as the misplaced excess that her speakers ride like the baby on the wave. Yet in a passage like the central one involving Dionysus in *Novel on Yellow Paper*, *The Bacchae* arises not so much as a 'lesson' to us as readers (though it does appear as a set text for pubescent Pompey, recalled as one that had to be produced in Greek by all matriculating students at her school), but rather as a text summoned to do confusing battle with a series of other texts that arise as Pompey contemplates contemporary attitudes towards sex and other matters.

We find her caught, first off, between being told the 'facts of life' by authority figures at school and receiving the very different message communicated by items in the explosive 'canon' of literature set to be read. On the one hand, she remembers Miss Hogmanimy's repressive lectures about 'how babies are born', delivered with barely submerged subtexts concerning feminine social/sexual deportment, and on the other hand she recalls Euripides's carnivalesque morality in which women run free in Bacchanalian ecstasy, destroying men rather than procreating. The former come with 'all the weight of Education behind them' (136), as well as an injunction for the girls 'to sign a paper saying we would never drink anything but ginger beer and allied liquids' (126) – one of the innumerable moments in the novels when Smith plays with the connection between sexual and national politics, here with her pun on the 'Allies' of the Triple Entente. But the latter *also* comes as a weighty bit of classical education with a capital 'E', only with a plot deeply subversive of precisely that sort of conscriptive authority, cast as it is onto the hills of Bacchic drinking, sexual abandon and old alliances torn limb from limb. In fact, the associative engine that begins the intertwining of these two remembered texts twirls on the contradiction Pompey heard even *within* Miss Hogmanimy's injunctions against drinking, as our speaker tells us at the end of it all, twelve or so pages later:

But the part I was going to tell you just in the one particular speech I had to say, and how it was so incongruous, and yet how very funny, taken in line with Miss Hogmanimy and her opinions on the effect of alcohol on sexual behaviour, was just this. The last four lines of my speech [as second messenger], there were four of them in the Greek, and they went like this and meant just this, that I always wanted to get up and shout at Miss Hogmanimy because it was what she was saying, with all the weight of Education behind them. The words were, these were the words: Take away wine and there is no Cyprian, No other joy, nothing left to man.
Three cheers for Euripides and Miss Hogmanimy. (136)

Smith seems to show us, playfully, that English repression through cultural education comes with its own flip side and cure encoded in the 'can(n)on' taught in schools. Though they appear to be diametrically opposed, both texts offer destruction – if of opposed targets: Dionysus of man-made illusions, and Miss Hogmanimy of any reality beyond her cultural script: '[I]t was just impossible for her to get the medical side of the question across', 'being so tied up with love and religious sentiment'; her 'heart [was] in the right place but her wits...befuddled' (137, 138). She has so swallowed the codes of conduct (emotional as well as doctrinal) that any 'real' referent of her speech is lost even as she speaks of it, and any substance, like wine, which might blur those codes by unbinding bodily desire is made taboo – not only for herself, but for others whose lack of obeisance to her own 'gods' might present alternatives. But the fact that such alternatives insinuate themselves and rebel from within her own undeniable physicality – which is made apparent in her breathless way of speaking about sex, and her furious hiding of her own 'stout body' (137) – only stokes her envy of others' fulfilment and, consequently, her draconian attitudes towards others' 'joy': there shall be 'No other joy' if she may not have it too. Miss Hogmanimy is a reversed example, in other words, of a 'cenobite' as forestaller, because even as she carries out her task of teaching courses in sex education she fully destroys Pompey's initial interests in sex, creating in her a 'profound aversion from the subject' (138). As her name would suggest, she like Kismet 'eats up' what she has an appetite for and destroys it in the process.

Pompey retains 'a soft feeling' for Miss Hogmanimy, however, because 'she evinced every symptom of heart possession did Miss H' (137). It is key to realise that in Smith's view Dionysus, on the other hand, and despite his power to liberate the repressed from under its veils of illusion, has no heart at all:

[F]rom my study of the classics certainly I early got an idea of the Olympians as very beautiful, very lovely, cynical and always laughing.... Very cruel, very callous, we think the Olympians, but of course it is hardly their fault. They have no heart. They have no heart. (136–37)

Subversive laughter, as we saw in Chapter 1, is one of Pompey's *and* Smith's most powerful weapons as well – especially at this juncture, when Pompey is set to 'talk about' 'subjects about which there is most nonsense talked' (145): sex and child rearing. Her Dionysian laughter cuts straight through the 'sentiment' that befuddles Miss Hogmanimy and stokes her inadvertent maliciousness. But Dionysus is malicious too in this passage – and as 'lion-like' as Pentheus, that representative of monarchical authority whom we hear Dionysus will have torn apart by his maenads via Pompey's ever-ambiguous syntax that confuses killers and killed: '[T]hey will tear him apart like a lion' (133). Certainly Dionysus takes on a savage aspect in the final moments of the story when, after cajoling Pentheus into women's clothing as ostensible protection, he sends him out on the mountain of transported females while he waves and seems, to Pentheus's backward gaze, to be

> looking taller and bigger, and different. And laughing. Like it wasn't so much a laugh, as something he can't put a name to, not so much a laugh, but it is a laugh, but a grin, something like he'd seen before, with all those teeth.
> ... And Pentheus is never seen again alive. (135)

Dionysus's destructiveness is tigerish – and has for its 'decadent' descendant Pompey herself, who identified with Dionysus as a schoolgirl.[37]

This lingering identification emerges earlier in the novel in a passage that begins, ironically, with her mirroring of Pentheus instead of Dionysus, as she recounts being dressed in women's clothing herself during a 'make-over' by a friend-of-a-friend, Lottie. Told she should 'dress with more *chic*' by this ex-ballerina – another character Pompey derides for her foreignness (60), but tolerates for the sake of her friend Rosa who must protect what we suspect is a financial relationship between their two husbands – she submits to being festooned with fur and sequins and hat in front of 'a long glass' reflecting all three women. Suddenly beginning to 'laugh silently', like Dionysus, Pompey proposes her victim-status in this charade of gender-reinforcement by comparing their image in the mirror to 'Christ crucified between thieves' – that is, herself in the middle and innocent yet dying for *their* sins. But she also becomes unmistakably Dionysus the destroyer in the very next lines as she muses on the picture before her:

> Oh a green light shining through the dirty windows, on to a pink carpet, and the curtains were pink damask stamped with a floral dance of peonies, and the fringes were pink, and there was the dark face of Pompey with a long narrow head, and on top a hat like a turban wound round, and a fringe falling to the fur band round the neck, and one hand outstretched to hold the gloves of green velvet, and the other hand up to the shoulder to throw back the sapphire sequins. And there was something that I didn't

> like, that I couldn't think, and then I thought: It's the gloves are wrong. So I threw them down and took up the goblet, that was Fifi's [the dog's] drinking goblet, and there was a pot of stewed tea standing on the mantelpiece. So I poured some of that into the glass and I went back and stood up in front of the mirror again, and tipped up the glass away from me so that it slanted into the light, and the tea looked like wine, with the light slanting through it. And there was a fine picture again, and I laughed and looked to see the teeth showing through, and never shall I forget the fine picture that was. And my face was dark and brilliant and laughing, and Lottie's face was calculating, and then the calculations died, and the eyes were dead. And Rosa was frightened, and then the fright died and the eyes were dead. And I tiptilted the glass still further over, and I let the tea fall on to careful Lottie's carpet. I let the tea fall drop by drop till there was not any left in the glass at all, and I said: Blessed are they that shall not be offended. (61–63)

Performing the Christ-like miracle of turning tea into wine, 'dark' laughing Pompey, her 'teeth showing through' in something that is not quite a grin – that is more like Dionysus's terrifying expression in the earlier quote above – figuratively kills those who would bind her in the same code of feminine appearance that binds them.

My first impulse as a female reader is to congratulate her for her self-liberation, but then I remember that Pompey became similarly destructive, and with far less provocation, at the outset of the novel when she recalled riding with the '*chic*' Leonie – a word that draws these passages into relationship. If we remember from my treatment of that passage, Pompey's abrupt 'who cares' uttered to dismiss the memory of Leonie's *chic*ness was followed by her celebration of her superiority as a 'goy' over her 'Jewess' friend. Nothing is more important in our reading of the first two novels than coming to understand the complex mechanisms behind the full range of Pompey's violent responses – many of them prompted by the superficial successes of others, which would suggest her vulnerability to social critique and feelings of inadequacy. The response above comes just after her hateful comments about various of Rosa's party guests, among them the German emigrants Lottie and Horace (her husband), whose money, fatness, flamboyant coddling of their dog Fifi and mistaken usage of English expressions elicit Pompey's xenophobia and some of her most venomous barbs. It becomes apparent that in this culminating moment of many passages about party-goers and party-going Pompey is, in her 'turbaned' state above, clearly riding the 'high and hungry horse Kismet' (240), that Turk – whose movement, again, is not a 'running on' but a destructive cutting-dead, a devouring of the 'vegetable fields', of all that has been 'cultivated' in the heart and head.[38] Her destructive thought is at least in some part linked to Bacchus, seen as he is in that rejuvenating 'green light' streaming through the windows into the conventionally feminine construction of a pink interior in which they stand. And Pompey's 'long narrow head', surrounded by fur, creates a lion-like aspect for her as she makes ready to tear apart Lottie, the dominating figure in this situation. But she is also in an important way 'darker' than Dionysus – a fact signalled by her throwing away of the green gloves and her taking up of her destructive bent with a distortion of Christ's line 'Blessed are the meek' to justify her acts. The confusion of inherited but contradictory textual 'lines' evident in the passage showcases the process of thought-laundering that goes on throughout the novels, both outside and inside our speaker, where learned but repressed violence is 'made thinkable' in spurious Christian overlays. The very complex psychological path we watch Pompey take from victimisation to counter-victimisation becomes illustration of how the 'black heart' of the times perpetuates itself in everyday life – where 'sick-cat envy' between everything from nations to neighbours produces either domination or false pockets of 'cenobitic' thinking, 'shot-up' by despair and fury, whose repressed fears and desires emerge as violence.

Here, medially inserted into Pompey's speech, is the wilful *negation* of the process's clarification, a refusal to recognise what she sees herself becoming – a portrait of someone else – because '*that* [she] couldn't think' (my emphasis). And yet her fears in the next paragraph – the aforementioned one in which she 'think[s] of Alice' who 'thought she was going to be Mabel' – create of this a nightmare world of looking-glass self-incriminations because although she strongly denies that she could become like Lottie and Rosa, her very mention of that possibility and denial of Alice's fears in Lewis Carroll's text tells us more truthfully by association than any of her *assertions* might what motivates Pompey. She has what in *Over the Frontier* she will call her ex-military friend Ian's 'Alice in Wonderland Gefühl' (feeling), born of being on the warfront and wondering 'Where is the enemy' (64) given that all and none fit the bill. Her 'spiritual pride and intolerance' which she identifies late in *Over the Frontier* (220) but which are apparent from the first page of *Novel on Yellow Paper* cause her to repress what she knows: that she *is* indeed identified with these figures, as she makes clear in her earlier-quoted suggestion that she *is* her friends – that *all* she is emerges from her context. Her playing of Dionysus is apocalyptically shot-through with allusions to Pentheus as well – because Pompey has, herself, the disease of 'dictators' with all its nascent fascism. And we must remember that Pompey is dressed *not* to kill here but *to be killed*; she is, like Pentheus 75 pages later in the novel – and like, as I mentioned at the outset of this chapter, Auden's diseased orators – the very problem that she suffers from.

The fact that Miss Hogmanimy also has a smile that is not one – '[i]t came out like it was spontaneous, but somehow you knew it wasn't so-o-o spontaneous, but cleverly timed. Very cunning and clever was this smile' (126) – suggests that Miss Hogmanimy is also, like Dionysus/Pentheus/Pompey, 'always disguised' (132). But instead of destroying illusions with her 'facts of life' she uses the same sort of cover Pompey told us the cenobites use: the rhetoric of the *'simply healthy* and *patriotic'* (33). With it she spawns women that Pompey categorises and has contempt for: those with 'pop-eyed dreams' of what conventional life for them in marriage will bring, nourished by unmarried Hogmanimys in authority who assert 'how beautiful it all is' (126). These wives when such illusions are shattered will, 'instead of coming into line with reality', 'run mad at their husbands' in maenad fashion, 'but not so refreshingly mad as the women of Thebes' (150). This 'running mad' seems the opposite of the novel's oft-mentioned 'running mad' of 'people that have dictators' (105), yet it arises as a consequence of the same – of having been dictated to, or, in this case, socially-modelled. Yet in this mode it seems to have been taken one step on, into disillusionment; and though Smith's poems value this state of 'disenchantment', it can, when poorly met, look very similar to tyranny in its desperate destructiveness. Smith's complex social vision includes even victimised women in a chain of broader cultural depravity; that depravity encourages Pompey's 'degenerate' response above, too, which Smith portrays as being neither refreshingly Dionysian nor heroic but complicit in its contextual corruption. It is important for us as readers to acknowledge through this and scores of other examples in the novels that Smith's form of feminism was not automatically woman-centred; her near-to-misanthropic response to 'the negation of human intelligence' (154) in favour of cultural conformity extended to both sexes, and was especially bitter in her contempt 'for unmarried girls, the ones that are so cleverly and coyly oh.... [A]nd full of pretty ideas that are all the time leading up to washing up' (154). As Pompey says in one of *Novel*'s autobiographical passages, during which Smith's own life is invoked and her father's abandonment of the family is brought up, '[b]ut now I think that for the husband as well as for the wife, an unsuitable marriage must be a very dreadful thing indeed' (75) – suggesting with this that her indictment is of institutional discourse and those who either manufacture it or sell it to the young, rather than those who bear the brunt of the inevitable dissolution of its 'dream', or discursive illusion. Therefore, perhaps, we are offered the recurrent image of being dressed as a woman – as *both* a woman and a man, Pompey and Pentheus, are in the novel. Perhaps what finally gets sent out to destruction in the trilogy is the false image of conformity as empowerment: dressing to kill, whether in sequins or the star-studded collars of uniforms such as the one that will be buttoned onto our speaker in *Over the Frontier.*

III

Freddy and the suburban line

Nowhere are Pompey's own latent connections to conformity and 'suburbanity' more apparent than in the final sections of the novel, where – in between many other lines of returning thought – we hear snippets of her emotional responses to, rather than 'the story' of, her broken relationship with a neighbourhood man named Freddy. Though mentioned on page 71, Freddy is not properly 'introduced' to us until page 145, and then primarily as an apologist for the developing suburban worldview that Pompey brings into focus in these pages. Smith connects it, like everything else in the novel, to the decade's militarisations and self-delusions; in order to do so, and so demonstrate the deep interconnectedness between external and internal forms of propaganda, she must orchestrate almost all of the novel's earlier lines of discourse in a kind of crescendo that culminates, finally, in the implosion of her speech altogether at the end of the novel. Through such interconnections we as readers come to understand, first of all, how it is that a character – or a 'subject', in every sense of that word in English culture – can veer towards tyrannical opportunism like Pompey and yet have seemingly gentle, decentralising suburbanity as its flip side. In key passages like the one below, Pompey reveals/conceals much as she describes the real as well as figurative extension of her own suburb from another that is thriving in its business of small arms manufacturing. As she does so, she drifts into the very sort of suburban discourse that elsewhere in the novel she is capable of dismissing with considerable disgust:

> My fiancé and I, did I say that my fiancé Freddy and I both live at Bottle Green? This is a healthy residential district to the north of London. None of your Hampsteads or Highgates or Golders Greens, but just straight north in a line with Enfield, which is where they make small arms and have a market place and a residential district even superior to Bottle Green.
> The social round in England is very complicated, very intricate, but it is always the same in this way. Everybody is always trying to be the next step up, and that is all very hearty and makes for the survival of the *status quo*. Because, given a slight increase in income and ordinary luck, and a wife that is quick at noticing, there you are, you'll be one step up as soon as sneeze. And why destroy the social order when it affords you that fine opportunity? Why indeed? So we shall never get a revolution in *Eng.*, so long as people go on healthy envying and emulating the next step up, like I said. Oh how splendid this all is – no horrid gulf yawning between the proletariat and the next of rank.
> Now Freddy certainly knows a whole lot about the people of Bottle Green, and he is a very keen observer is Freddy, and tells me a lot that is so vivid, that I might have known it myself. (145–46)

Foreshadowing the chilling passages near the end of *Over the Frontier* in which, as we shall see, Pompey seems to know vital information about military plans and operations without remembering being told, this one suggests that her internal workings are 'always already' overwritten by her context. Here, as in the passage I quoted near the outset of this chapter, which conflated immediate knowledge/experience with what one reads 'in the newspapers' (28), she begins to collapse what Freddy reports to her and what she already knows. However relatively new the suburbs and their unstirred mix of conservative and liberal views were, Smith portrays their influence on Pompey as being all but insurmountable due to their having been distilled from the deeply contradictory ideological make-up of their wider context. Although deeply tongue-in-cheek, Pompey's virtual admission above that 'sacrific[ing] everything' to 'the preservation of your famous *status quo*', as Karl put it in the 'bones of the Mahdi' exchange quoted earlier, is the necessary counterpart to her peculiar form of opportunism. In the language of capitalist competition coupled uncomfortably with Marxism, she tries to explain how the social stability of the community is served by such 'healthy envying' of one's neighbour's goods – but we as readers remember, too, her prophecy concerning the baby in the holiday picture, and its probable fate on the flood with 'sick-cat envy'.

A number of earlier discursive strains in the novel haunt this passage. We begin, for example, to hear how the suspect rhetoric of 'simply healthy patriotism' that both the Church's forestallers and Miss Hogmanimy engaged in the course of their particular cultural projects comes into uneasy relation with competing economic theories. Especially worrying in this regard, of course, is the fact that Enfield's superior residential district seems to be annexed by unspoken (unspeakable) relation to its involvement in the making of small arms. And Pompey's momentary deployment of all of these discourses in a brave muddle seems prompted by her sudden adoption of an address of power (wrested suspiciously out of relation to a man) from within them: that of the fiancée. Given that this sudden introduction of us as readers to her fiancé and their suburb is actually an abrupt digression from what she had just proposed to talk about – 'how to bring up children' (145) – this passage might also be suggesting that such tasks are out of parents' hands; children become, inevitably, a product of their environment, and Pompey is no exception. It is worth noting one more time here that the digressions that happen in the novel are not usually, as Severin suggests, *away* from the romance narrative, but are as often as anything else digressions *into* it – particularly when it offers for a moment, as it does here, shelter from more disturbing collisions of thought that are far more crucially at issue for our speaker.

The 'run' of passages that follow the one above demonstrates this and, as per usual, has a complex trajectory. They begin with Pompey's sudden reversal, having just happily announced her own engagement, into a dissertation on the foolishness of girls who grow up dreaming about suburban marriage; she tells us scornfully and with high Chekhovian humour, 'it is like the refrain in *The Three Sisters*. It is the *leitmotiv* of all their lives. It is their *Moscow'* – their thinking being 'that if only they were married it would be all right' (149). In a foreshadowing of her next novel's title, Smith links Pompey's send-up of 'the Russia of [suburban women's] matrimonial ambition' with the decade's romance with Marxist revolution and the discursive codes of the Auden group when her speaker forecasts their (and her own) destination: 'Over the frontier at least, if not actually into the suburbs and citadel of *Moscow'* (150). As I began to explain in Chapter 2, the Auden group was renowned for their many encoded writings that depicted the transition from bourgeois pasts to 'to-day the struggle' (Auden, 'Spain') in phrases like *Journey to the Border* (Upward, 1938), and *On the Frontier* – the title of one of Auden's dramatic collaborations with Christopher Isherwood in the late Thirties for the Group Theatre in London. Although Smith's ventriloquised indictment of capitalistic self-promotion apparent in the long passage quoted above seems to depend for its irony on Marxist 'revolution' and identification of the 'proletariat', her texts make it clear that she was deeply suspicious of both – and the latter most particularly when explicated by the Auden generation's enchantment with communist ideals.

Her relationship to the ideological struggles of the Thirties is, as I began to explore it in the previous chapter, complex. We know that she refused to be 'rope[d] into the Haldane-Communismus gang' by her friend and fellow novelist, Naomi Mitchison (sister to J.B.S. Haldane, the great biometrics scientist well known for supporting the Spanish Republican cause and writing for the *Daily Worker*) (*MA* 259). And yet we recall as readers many sympathetic moments in the novels – such as the one in *Novel on Yellow Paper* after Pompey's trip to Germany, when she linked Communists to Jews as undeserving recipients of cruel torture at the hands of the Nazis (104). Her speaker's sudden eruptions into talk about the 'extremely class-conscious' nature of suburbia (208) would seem to suggest her ideological sympathy as well. And her Joycean depiction of 'the dead' of her neighbourhood – their *womblandisch* parks and houses[39] – might seem to some a version of 'Mortmere' (with its etymological play on dead spaces): a place that Isherwood and Upward invented as part of the founding mythology behind the Auden group's assault on the 'poshocracy' and its buttresses in culture. But it is also true that she most frequently labelled Marxism 'communismus', as she does above – another 'chimeraismus', a dangerous romance, as Pompey will label her own with Freddy (222). In any case, she seemed fully dissuaded that revolution could evade its engendering context by the time she wrote *The Holiday* during the war. On its fifth page her main speaker Celia is already worrying about the destination of all such ideological hobby-horses:

> Sentimental persons, I said [to Casmilus, her alter-ego], prefer always the revolutionary times.... But I like better the time that is more crucial than revolution, that is the time when revolution succeeds and must govern.

And I thought: Can resistance pass to government and not take to itself
the violence of its oppressors, the absolutism and the torture?

This passage might seem to some to catch Smith up (rather than Pompey)
in a proto-'Movement' sensibility, or as someone looking forward to the
politically-conservative backlash against the fervour of politicised movements in Thirties literature that would emerge in the early 1950s. Certainly
there is at least a hint of such in her speakers' 'pragmatism', as Karl had put
it to Pompey. But *Smith's* – rather than Pompey's – inability to participate in
any celebration of 'Little Englandism', and her lack of faith in any laundering
of language to arrive at 'the purity of English diction', will draw deep lines
between her and her contemporaries in the post-war era, as we shall see in
Chapter 4.[40] The above quoted passage could also be used to evidence *either*
a modernist view of the essentially cyclic nature of political violence *or* a
postmodern deconstruction of political rhetoric – but my project here must
become a bit more muddy as I find tracks of all these possibilities forming a
collision whose revelation as such is, I think, most clearly Smith's (at times
inadvertent) project.

The form of the novel's ending and the return of the repressed

Following this long riff on the allegorical politics of marriage, Pompey
returns to the originally proposed topic of child rearing in order to tell us
about her feelings of abandonment in childhood, accompanied by the
beginnings of her reliance on the option of suicide (all of which I detailed at
the outset of Chapter 2 as being elements of Smith's own experience). These
bleed into stories of her soldier-friend, William, who as I explained earlier
visited Pompey's home during the war years, when she was a teenager. It
becomes important that his friend's name, Tommy – a name taken out of
pre-existing mythologies of soldierly experience, 'the Myth of the Tommy at
the Front' (Calder 18), a fact that she underlines by later referring to him
as 'this *Tommy*' (226)[41] – links these sections to an earlier one in which
Pompey's fictional housewife, used to create a story of the 'bright little tight
little hell-box' (153) that is marriage, has a child by that name. These seemingly serendipitous but complex intertwinings work together to suggest
collaborations in the breeding of war – meaning all kinds of domestic
and military conflict; as Pompey says, 'unsuitable marriages breed the
Pompeys of this world, and a lot of other troubles as well' (162). It is indeed
all those troubles that suddenly emerge – or rather, *re*-emerge – in this 'run'
towards the end of the novel. Ostensibly Pompey is, by a certain point in it,
visiting William and 'telling him everything' about how she is, because
William has asked (189). This conversational convention – 'Oh, do tell me
everything' – is made comically literal in effect here, becoming the
'talking cure *within* the talking cure' (the 'play within the play') that highlights

Smith's ongoing narrative device. As such, it also points yet again to the 'hidden culprit', because Pompey digresses wildly once more all around the real issue, just as she has done for the whole of the novel. The real issue hardly seems to be the slow loss of suburban Freddy. It seems, more deeply, to be a matter of what on the final page of the novel she calls the 'the heart of pain' caused by a 'distraught mind' that is 'too little aloof, and yet upon no centre placed' (251) – buffeted by the discursive contradictions, hypocrisies and disenchantments of the times which undergird Pompey's loss of a fiancé and metaphoric death at the end of the novel. What we realise we have here in this last section of the book, then, is a formal 'resolution' – on the order of Eliot's symphonic one in *The Waste Land* – that includes nearly every foregoing theme/discursive mode used in the novel, from confusions about Christian doctrine and practice to even a memory of Karl, who reappears briefly and at an odd angle, eating with chopsticks in a Japanese café in Berlin (widening our focus, perhaps, to suggest pre-war Germany's gathering alliance with Japan). Even more noticeably we have reiterations of statements made at the beginning of the novel, like the one that informed us that our speaker has a 60,000-word limit. But the effect is vastly different from the final orchestrations of Eliot's poem; rather than vision, what we get is confusion, with the kind of dissonance that suggests no grail to be had for the proper asking, nor any set of directions for a return to sublunary control. Our speaker's increasing frenzy of changed scenes and topics culminates in her moment of fear, quoted earlier, that she may be nothing more than a composite of the friends she cannot bear but must visit – that she *is* Mabel. These are folded into thoughts that marriage as a cloak will never fit her compulsive rhythms of coming and going in and out of hell like her mythical ancestor who lives in her surname, 'in her blood' (198, 212).

Yet it is at the moment that she can no longer produce her inherited 'janus-faced' response to the world that all falls to ruin. In other words, it is when she can no longer face 'Sir Phoebus across the desk' (205) – that is, go on playing the part of the 'willing donkey' (204), 'forging' his letters while she conducts another life 'secretly all the time' (64) – that the flood comes back from page 14 to sweep away her decadent, 'scattered' self that had actually been composed (*and* affianced) by such duplicitousness:

> How can I face that face [of Sir Phoebus], no longer myself the limpid *animula*, no longer *vagula*, *blandula*, no longer *hospes comesque corporis*. But scattered, torn, shattered; born for this only, for this present disarray; through long first centuries accrued, through fire, through ice, through tropic mud and ice again, the sorrows of Pompey, the troubles of Mrs. Haliburton, the unappeasable, never to be appeased hunger of the ravishing Kismet, the Cornish diabetic, for ever eating and never nourished, never comfortable.

> Oh uncomfortable Kismet, what troubles of yours compare with mine? Oh cat on cradle, oh baby adventurer betwixt cat and flood. Oh flood of tears' flow. Oh sweetest scent of death. Oh disarray, dismay, and dudgeon. Oh *comble* of her dreams, her dreams' worst devising. Oh too prophetic dream. Oh night of Pompey.
> My sweet boy Freddy has left me. (206)

The break-up with Freddy is presented as only the latest in a disastrous flow of events that finally 'undo' Pompey, comprised helplessly as she is by name and discursive habits of the whole history of western culture's inner workings as they have forged our often violently-hewn *inter*connections – from male warriors/dictators to suffering 'Mrs. Haliburtons'. Instead of being climactic, this announcement – which follows her earlier assertion that she would herself like to break off the engagement for what she tells us would be the second time – is deeply anti-climactic, displaced as it is by the more important revelation of a far larger break-down happening before our eyes. No longer the *'animula, vagula, blandula* of the office' (204) (the 'little soul, wandering, pleasant' of Hadrian's famous address to his soul, which is 'guest and companion of the body'), Pompey ironically begins her own dispersal with these lines as she rebels against her two-facedness within the larger *status quo*. On the one hand, 'full of pride and *désespoir*, like the great angel Lucifer that fell from heaven' (216), she begins to try, once again, to 'get shot up', as she did during the first part of the novel, via memories of 'the Jew party' and her own superior goyhood. But just like Lucifer – and 'that great satanic Milton' who, she tells us, forged his attractiveness in *Paradise Lost* by getting 'shot up like [Pompey]', by having *'no middle flight'* (her italics) – she will assert her power only to fall back into that hell that she by surname must indeed visit and revisit, just as she does the friends she tried to say good-bye to at the novel's outset. She seems fated to return to them, her reviled generative matrix, she being another with 'no middle flight', 'no centre placed'. In other words, like Joyce's Stephen Dedalus in *A Portrait of the Artist as a Young Man*, Pompey as a character is unable to understand her 'foot off the ground' response to the world as being deeply conditioned by, and indeed entrapped within the parameters of, the 'foot *on* the ground' context that spawned her. Like Pompey, Stephen's defences against his contextual traumas as revealed in the opening pages of Joyce's novel are built on repression and therefore reproduction, in his emergent artist's code, of the same treatises and taboos that are present in the Irish Catholicism he hopes to evade. Had he woken to see this doubleness, and his redoublings upon his own path within the 'labyrinth' of his cultural text before the end of Joyce's novel, he might have, like Smith's Pompey/Flo at the end of her *Novel*, '[f]all[en] backwards into [his] pool' (251) – as indeed Joyce insinuates he must eventually do as he positions Stephen's final flight from the voice of the *son* of Daedelus, the ill-fated Icarus.

Like Joyce, Smith relates her context's continuing problems to ancient ones from which we have not learned – and in the case of both Stephen and Pompey, that problem is 'hubris', or the tendency to regard oneself as a god, to so 'out-god the gods'. In those moments during which she attempts transcendence of the suburban mindset she fell into above, Pompey takes up the position of superiority (assuming that she *can* separate herself from it) and condemns Freddy for his conformity to 'mediocrity' (219) in his demands of either 'marriage now or nothing' (207). But even here, her condemnation of him and 'them' intermixes with much of what she has said, in her runnings on, about *herself* – so that it becomes, very importantly, inclusive of both. Hers is, in other words, an attempt at convincing herself of her own ability to fly, keep her feet off the ground, that only demonstrates how deeply she is sunk in the mire. And of course, given the historical commentary at the heart of this novel, her own suburban mire that she describes below is connected to what she tells us 'all Germany was suffering from, the *männlicher Protest* [meaning "masculine protesting too much" about *"unser liebes Vaterland"* (our beloved fatherland) and "Our Happy Family"], that they invented themselves' (99):

> It is I think that in these people, wronged and insulted and rejected even in childhood there has grown up a desire for power and a self absorption a self-conceit turning mordant upon itself and in that self the seeds of intelligence uncared-for and neglected. Oh *männlicher protesting* mereness, oh inferiority lusting for power and by its own neglect of its own true happiness forced to live at what low level of intellect and spirit, taking pleasure in imagined insults and affronts, to brood upon them in the darkness and operating upon them to beget such knock-kneed down-at-heels wispish, waifish progeny.
> Oh my darling Freddy do not be so deeply dippy. You have nothing to do with these people, nothing at all, they are not your people. (220)

But Freddy is, indeed, the very embodiment of 'these people'. And every line of this description is true of Pompey herself, as we have just seen – from being 'rejected', as she suggested, in childhood, to being 'forced to live at [a] low level of intellect and spirit' at work and at play. She, too, therefore, takes pleasure in 'insults', as in the scene in which she as Dionysus drops the tea/wine on Lottie's carpet; she too operates upon such 'imagined affronts' to the point that she like a lion 'tears' even her lover, her Freddy (206 and *passim* – something she feels deeply guilty about. In the psychological economy of power-mongering violence that Smith envisions – and Freud documented – insult begets insult, and their 'progeny' inherit an earth that resonates here with Conrad's neo-biblical description of it at the beginning of *Heart of Darkness*, where 'mournful gloom' rather than the Holy Spirit 'broods' over the resolute darkness of western civilisation. Smith's vision of how nationalistic chauvinism bleeds into suburban regulation and repression of all but the same 'happy family' mentality becomes very clear in these final pages as the novel's various themes blend into sinister collages of shared rhetoric.

'Suburban neurosis'

And if that all seems somewhat over the top as a diagnosis of the suburban situation to us now, we must remember that it would not have been then. The range of writings about the suburbs, and the range of heated attitudes towards them, is hardly surprising given the profound changes that the building of the suburban perimeter caused between the wars (during which time, it has been estimated, 3,998,000 new homes were built). Whereas initial envisionings of suburban life – in, say, the writings of Ebenezer Howard at the turn of the century, about phenomena like Welwyn Garden City and Hampstead Garden Suburb – were seen to be inspired by socialist architectural reforms in the making of new millennial communities, however rooted those were in English pastoralism and the rural vernacular, later on, as Giles and Middelton argue, 'the cosy domesticity of suburbia was frequently attacked for its isolationism and cultural paucity' (195) as well as many other pernicious developments. In the fraught political arena of the Thirties, with all of its conservative/revolutionary flip sides, the rhetoric that surrounded the suburbs and their growth was highly divided between these two poles of opinion; and the issue was not simply whether or not the communities created were cosy or culturally deprived. One extreme in that array of opining might be represented in Dr Stephen Taylor's 1938 assessment, after a study of psychological disorders among the suburban community – and we recall here Pompey's snidely referring to all those going, in the Thirties, to the 'psycho-analysts [who] charge a pound an hour' (15) – that the 'suburban neurosis' he had discovered might well even undermine national security:

> The deep-seated aetiological factors of the suburban neurosis are... extremely complex. Existence in the suburbs is such that the self-preserving, race-preserving and herd instincts can be neither adequately satisfied nor sublimated.... [T]he symptoms... represent a sidetracking of frustrated emotional energy....
>
> Few who have not worked or lived in the suburbs can realise the intense loneliness of their unhappy inhabitants. There is no common meeting ground like the pub and the street of the slum-dwellers, and... [t]here is no community of interest as is found in the village.... It has been suggested that these new communities will only develop a true corporate sense with some revival of individual local leadership, analogous to the old village squirearchy. Perhaps the success of the totalitarian states with their lower middle classes is due to just such a reassertion of the 'Leader Principle'.

The prevention of the suburban neurosis, then, is in the hands of the social workers and politicians. And if they require a purely selfish stimulus, one would remind them that, in the latent feelings and strivings of the new mental slum-dwellers, there is waiting a most hopeful field for the teachers of new, and possibly dangerous, political ideologies. (759, 760, 761)

That was one (deeply Freudian) way of looking at potentially alienating effects of the new suburban phenomenon; another employed a valourising of the 'separate life', as Pompey will indirectly refer to it at the end of *Over the Frontier*, in order to construct a deeply reactionary and nationalistic inter-war response to current events. As Giles and Middleton describe it, '[t]he rhetoric of patriotism in 1939 drew heavily on the idea of protecting and saving a particular version of home and private life' (193) – the latter a going phrase in Thirties media and film which, as we have seen, Smith satirises as having been developed via the very instruments of propaganda that infiltrate and overwrite privacy. The 'ideal of England as "home" and the "English home" as signifying a specific set of domestic values' (193) was, quite interestingly, sold as a *traditional* ideal that needed protection, even though it in its new form had only recently been developed. In the second half of the Thirties, in an atmosphere of gathering national crisis, it found itself buoyed up by companion texts like J.B. Priestley's *Our Nation's Heritage* (1939) and Jan Struthers's 'Mrs. Miniver' column in the *Times*, where England was 'imaged as a national family who, having made mistakes, has been brought to its senses and given another chance to get things right' (114; autumn 1939, 'From Needing Danger'). The fact that 'Mrs. Miniver' would be made into a highly successful film in 1942 hardly surprises; it evidences what Light has called 'a patriotism of private life' (1991, 154) put hard to work in the background of Smith's novels – even by the Ministry of Information, in its 'secret' support for the 'most effective' films, as we shall see in a moment.[42] It also seems hardly surprising that Smith's own thoughts on the mobilisation of the suburbs are full of dark warnings – here, after all, in such oxymoronic rhetoric and situational ironies, are the potential fruits of the unexamined relation between privacy and militarism, essentialising discourse about 'Englishness' and construction of the 'foreigner', or the enemy. Unlike Light, whose concluding thoughts on those discourses of home and suburb are that '[p]erhaps inside every Mrs. Miniver was a national heroine, struggling to get out' (155), it seems Smith feared more than anything else the release of such forces (male *or* female) from the tensions and explosive contradictions of her own generative matrices.

Caught in the nets of fate – or words

And Smith's were generative matrices from which, as she portrayed them, she could not escape. Nor does her character, Pompey. Despite the fact that

Pompey is herself the very image of what she reviles, she more and more frequently, here at the end, images herself conducting a tigerish 'tear[ing] to shreds' of that very image, as well as a destruction of 'dishonourable *conseils*' (218) such as she gets on the subject of marriage and life in the suburbs. Pompey is like a figure 'riding her fate' (Kismet) out of ancient tragedy, then – like Racine's *Phèdre*, with whom she identifies herself in the quote above and elsewhere,[43] because she both destroys what she loves/hates as well as herself. Yet it is key that we remember that Phaedra's 'monstrous' desires are arranged by the gods and inherited from her mother, Pasiphaë. And she in turn was driven by Poseidon to beget the Minotaur with a bull because he wanted revenge against her husband, Minos, for his refusal of a white bull as a sacrifice. If we do, we not only collect the story as yet another akin to those of Shakespeare's women caught between men, but also think of its relation to Dionysus's driving mad of the women/mothers as revenge against Pentheus for his lack of reverence. These repeating structures of power tell us something about Pompey's unarticulated situation – caught in a net, as Oedipus puts it, of both victimisation by others and pathetic, hubristic suppositions of her own that she can 'fly by those nets', like Stephen Dedalus (Joyce 203). Indeed, she acknowledges her (textual) inheritance of classical *hubris* in a comic moment of self-reflexivity as she ponders how Venus, a god whose 'altars' she, a contradictory amalgam of pagan and Christian training, says she 'ha[s] never neglected' (199), might have upbraided her for falling in love with a 'chimera' of her own making rather than the very real (and 'tearable') Freddy:

> Very *farouche* and furious indeed was Venus: Well, Miss, you've brought it upon yourself, and now you'll please to suffer for it.... you proud prancing Pompey, you airy fairy piece of nonsense. You superior person, you *Hubris*. (222)

As with all of Pompey's seeming judgements, this one is both true and complicated by other texts competing for our attention. In this case, they include earlier passages, for example, in which Pompey avers that 'oh how sure [she is] that it is so much better to have love with all its pains and terrors and fanaticism than to live untouched the life of the vegetable. But how it tears one, and how *unruhig* it is' (201). Such contradictions help us to understand the confused lines of Pompey's thoughts and desires, as well as why she prefers Racine's remake of classical texts to Shakespeare's plays – discussion of which surrounds the above quoted passage as well. Watching Shakespeare's plays, she feels 'distraught and ill at ease' because the codes are mixed; the verse-art is coupled 'antithetically' with 'feeling [that] is so warm and so human and disturbing': 'the poetry is thwarted at every turn by the complications of this plot' (200, 201). 'But in Racine there is no feeling of antithesis, the verse and the emotion are perfectly one, they fuse perfectly and effect the purgation which is the essence of tragedy' (200). Struggling above life with its 'complications' is what Pompey continually wishes to do; her 'foot off the ground' reaction to her own text's being 'thwarted at every turn' by 'maladroitness', as are Shakespeare's, is to desire the 'noble elevating and loamishly-sad feeling' that Racine's texts afford. Yet such language takes us back to the retrogressive desire she expressed at the novel's outset for the 'loamishly sad...Victorian days' (13). And among the most important of the surrounding texts competing for our attention is a subtext that goes almost unmentioned – again, our recollection of the fact that it was Minos's transgression that led to Pasiphaë's downfall and Phèdre's misery. This cruelly powerful husband/father would then become the cornerstone of Minoan civilization and so respected for his fair-mindedness that he was made one of the three judges of Hades. But Smith seems to ask, with her juxtapositions of texts, questions about the intimate relations between the hotbeds of one sort of domestic violence and others in that other 'domestic' realm of legislation and state rule. What unspeakable hypocrisy and its ripple-effects buttress the great men who rise as 'fair-minded' figureheads of states? Like her contemporary, Walter Benjamin, her texts would suggest that every timeless monument to culture has its everyday victims. Pompey by name and lowly identity represents both, suggesting her entrapment in that long net of 'maladroitness' that makes seemingly private desires like those for love 'tearing' – for lover and beloved – given the reproduction of social violence at every level of culture.

Yet what is truly extraordinary about the novel's *dénouement* is the extent to which Smith suggests that Pompey's chimeric ideas about love *and* her inability to achieve it – as well as her violent responses to such failure – are all engendered by *words*. For a pre-postmodern novel, such clear focus on the specifically textual confines of a speaker's dilemma is extraordinary. Through Smith's orchestration here near its end, the whole flood of ancient texts that have haunted Pompey bleed into her best-known contemporary ones of all kinds, maintaining their contradictory directives and manipulations. Smith seems to play with the idea that those manipulations function as an update on the unfathomable 'gods' – derived in some ways directly from them, through the paradigms they have afforded for western thought. But, like many of her modernist contemporaries, she *also* – and not without creating contradictions of her own – gives us both the classics and the arts as 'descended' (in terms of inheritance) not into knowing hands but into decadence, having been co-opted for their 'use-value' by everything from education to politics to sales to adverts in a newly plugged-in age. 'Is not this advertisement-land full of easy rhymes?' (203) her speaker asks, decrying the siren-like sound of poetry deployed by commercial interests, and gesturing always at the proliferating slogans of her conflicted, hydra-headed political era whose effects on language were to encourage rhetorical abstraction and simultaneous simplification (another contradiction). Like her friend Orwell, whose famous and defining post-war essay 'Politics and the English Language' deals with exactly these kinds of contradictory developments, providing helpful background for what she too was theorising about words in her work, Smith found no seams between Thirties-style discursive corruption in the political sphere and the same within households, communities and the media. As Pompey approaches her 'end', it is her era's increasingly commodified and popularly pressed *words* that, like some ultimate divinity, most evoke her 'satanic' revolt. But like Satan caught up in God's created universe, or Fedja, the escapist but doomed character in Tolstoy's *The Living Corpse* (which Pompey is reading in German translation, importantly), Pompey has no way out of her textual environment, even though she knows it to be the real manipulator of all she despises about herself, including her engagement:

> I think I was too proud we must all have our womblands, mine is my ivory tower with Freddy open to the four winds of heaven, Fedja's is *'bei den Zigeunern'* [among the gipsies]. Freddy's is a little home. But oh it is only the words he uses that make me in my satanic mood, outcome of how many years of popular journalism, see instead of something you might like, just the something that is the something the advertisers are talking about, for their furniture, their radiogram, their washing-up machine, their home-mortgaging society.
> So Prince Abreskoff says: *'Wie können Sie sich so hinreissen lassen?'* ['How can one know that he is so enchanted/carried away?']
> Oh, my dear chap, that's easy enough, watch me. I can slip back, I can slip back through this crazy Russian-German play till I find what I am looking for. (242–43)

But this is of course what Pompey has been doing throughout her 'novel' – slipping through texts (in a proto-Barthesian sense, we *might* say) that both enable and entrap her imagination, carrying her away even as she searches for what she 'wants'. Her contradictory desires, for identification *and* death, as well as for 'all that [she wishes] to say in this book' (12), remain unnamed while displaced into the palimpsest of textual precedents that are their sources. 'Home' is nothing but a nest of 'words' above, and, never being found, it causes those who desire it to either 'run mad' or destroy themselves, as both Pompey and Freddy must do in their respective and figurative ways. The retelling of Tolstoy's play here at the end of the novel is both further demonstration of Pompey's dependence on existing texts for speech, particularly in her growing weariness as our narrator, and a last witty joke about her novel's form. Fedja is a suicidal figure whose death is aided by social manipulation behind the scenes, and whose time is stretched out by Tolstoy at the very end of the play in order to 'work off', as Pompey puts it, 'a lot of Russian nonsense on the subject of life and death'. That project can of course be playfully related to not only Pompey's 'talking cure' but our reading of it, reminded as we are here of the novel's subtitle: *Novel on Yellow*

Paper, or Work it out for Yourself.[44] The dissonance of the Russian Fedja's desire for his 'wombland' among the gipsies being delivered *in translation*, in her text's German terms, must not be missed (and indeed, Pompey draws our attention to the strangeness of this particular translation repeatedly, just as she did during her initial mention of the play on pp. 85–86). With it, she suggests that 'home' itself is a cultural and linguistic contrivance, the 'frothy Russian' desire sounding odd in 'precise German'. Fedja's and Freddy's similar human needs take very different shape in this paragraph despite their existence in it as sound-alikes by name; yet both sets of longings resonate with Pompey's earlier descriptions of women's hankering after marriage as their 'Moscow'. German/Russian struggles for supremacy during the decade – such as those in Spain – link these womblandish wishes and all such chimeras once again to political propaganda and nationalist aggrandisement. And yet, the last joke that arises in relation to this text, in a novel that has depended so heavily on *Heart of Darkness* for its subtextual references, is the potential intertextual *doppelgänger* afforded: the Russian play, like the text in supposed cipher in Conrad's novel, is simply a Russian reflection of German/English womblandish desires, as is the 'harlequin' figure Marlow encounters on his similar quest to find Kurtz.[45] Therefore, and instead of allowing us to read this revelation as a solely feminist one – one in which females exist in sacrificial as well as economically brainwashed relation to males – Smith identifies chimeric existence as, ironically, not only the one 'fact of life' true for her and all around her, but also as a range of discursive routes that are mutually supporting and even dangerously interchangeable. Freddy's longings to construct a suburban home, for example, are traditionally entwined with feminine goals. It is key to our reading of both this novel and *Over the Frontier* (where Pompey dons a male role) that we note that Smith consistently depicts those discursive routes as essentially 'unmanned' – as having movements of their own into which we slot like our ancient forebears, those helpless playthings of the gods, for whom, as Pompey says in an earlier, characteristically Sophoclean moment, 'it would have been better that they had never been born' (184).

Small wonder, then, that Smith chose the image of the chimera for Pompey's dreams of loving and being loved. A chimera is, in Greek myth, a fire-breathing 'monster' (cf. Pasiphaë's desire/progeny) headed up by a *lion*, with a goat's body and a serpent's tail. In other words, Pompey's wildly fanciful and damaging, 'chimeric' dreams of love with Freddy – figured as tigerish in its playfulness – tie us back to her own accumulations of national- and self-imagery, and therefore bear a darker etymological connection to *cultural* identificatory processes than we might have first thought. It seems that her desire for what she realises was an unrealistic image of Freddy/love – and for their lost times of 'prancing forth light and malicious as tiger on padded paw, to play, scratch, pat, prod, prink' in 'towers of several ivories' (206) – is linked by the image of the chimera to her desire for her own lion-like self, with its arch superiority over lesser-lights and 'foreigners', and its 'tearing' of them done in the image of England, that noble lion whose fair front is backed by a more foul behind. 'Pompey No Weakness, was my motto that I lived by, like I was Danton' (59), as she told us nearer the outset of *Novel* while describing her general social behaviour. Georges Jacques Danton of the French Revolution, like her forebear Pompey the Great, was another political opportunist whose 'high hollow fate' was to die 'a clown's death' (at the guillotine) in a violent time of change not unlike Smith's own in its revolutionary fervour. His slippery dealings have, like the Roman Pompey's, gathered conflicting reports through history due to their demonstrating no one direction or 'centre', blown about as he was, too, by dangerous changes. Smith insistently shows us, again and again, that the monumental powers in culture mirror the smallest, all of them occupying the same generative, cultural matrix of discourse/thought; our speaker is just the same sort of wind- and flood-swept figure, a many-sided chimera, an 'airy fairy piece of nonsense' dreaming dreams as dangerous as those Germany was dreaming, composed and buffeted by every discursive stream that surrounds her.

If we understand this, then we understand why her final 'recognition' or assertion of the novel must, quite perfectly, be of her *inability* to assert or put into language or writing the 'fact' she cares most about. She circles it – the *experience* beyond words that she seems at times to believe she and Freddy momentarily clasped: a Blakean 'innocence' in love. The latter was something Blake himself could not draw except as juxtaposed against the darker side of 'experience'; Smith, too, tries against the odds and her own admissions of corruption to write it, but stumbles due to discursive rather than metaphysical obstacles in the terrain:

> For me but one significant fact that stands out, and for which
> I would live or die. But this fact. That is this fact. That is.
> That is what I cannot bring myself to write. It has been written so many
> times and soiled with every falseness and base stupidity. Can you not see it?
>   Oh little creature form'd of joy and mirth,
>   Go, love without the help of anything on earth. (250)

Her Steinian introduction to such lyrical innocence – via repetitive deictic pointers ('this' and 'that') made to stand momentarily empty, signifying nothing, emphasising the symbolic rather than 'real' nature of her medium, language – makes it resound even more clearly within that realm of impossibility that Smith seems to intend for it at her novel's close. 'Fact', or innocent acquaintance with it, she suggests above, has been so overwritten that it has become inaccessible for our speaker. By this point, near the end, her claustrophobic response to that linguistic carapace out of which she can hardly see the 'real', the 'fact' – 'Can you not see it?' – is intriguingly like not only Conrad's but Samuel Beckett's, as a number of my earlier comparisons have been leading me to suggest. Four years her junior and another writer focused in a 'proto-postmodern' way on language, identity and death, Beckett's prose was also beginning to appear near this time (*Murphy*, 1938).[46] Smith's work often sounds like the *later* Beckett's, particularly in passages like these at the end of *Novel* that demonstrate fatigue in literally maintaining her existence through words, so that her Steinian repetitions and truncations become deadening: 'Oh there is so much about it and about. How many words, how many wretched words to be said, to be unsaid, to be said again, and gone over until you can no more. I can no more' (250). Smith returns us to the novel's central problem here at its end where, as at its beginning, Pompey shows us that 'the thought of all she wishes to say in this book' – meaning all the trauma and desire that motivates her talking – cannot, ironically, be put into words, given their 'falseness' and obscuring of such unspeakable revelations; hers exists 'between the lines', as my own subtitle has it, of all the set texts that form this novel. Its moment of conclusion is also impossible because the discursive lines that have spoken louder than words throughout the novel continue to come as a consequence of Pompey's lack of 'authorial' control.

Decoding the final image

The corollary dangerousness of the lion image – accompanied also and always in this novel by Germany's *männlicher Protest* above – works to obviate any possibility of seeing Flo, Pompey's tearing and self-tearing, tigerish alter-ego through which we exit the novel, as being simply the powerfully salutary, feminine force that Smith's critics have celebrated to date. Like the image of the cat riding on the baby's cradle borne by the wave of discourse/ history, Pompey's alter ego – opposed though it is to her swept-along self and her 'willing donkey' front – will in its 'sick-cat envy' destroy her and all in its attempt to gain the upper hand on the flimsy raft of power relations as Smith envisions them.[47] This is not to say that in some earlier, elemental, uncorrupted form it was a wholly negative aspect of her being. Indeed, we as readers sense some remnant of Romantic/modernist essentialism residing in that image wrenched from 'nature', and sympathise with its need for freedom when we hear, for example, very early in the novel, that her 'talking voice' has been '[held] in captivity,...point[ed]...with commas, semi-colons, dashes, pauses and paragraphs' (39). But Smith's study in this novel is of precisely how repression *alters* such forces, and of how language and cultural discourse condition and 'make ill' that cat, or the human animal, caught in captivity through them. Symbolised early on in the novel by this struggle with the Apollonian world of 'the publisher' who forces her into line with systems and signs, Pompey's deeper struggle to let her thoughts go free of 'harsh captivity' fails by the novel's end, as it must do for this 'desperate character', and is imaged in the death of the zoo-bound, mysteriously ill tigress Flo who appears suddenly, in the very last, short paragraph, only to die in 'pity and incongruity' by falling back into the pool in her cage and having to submit to 'the indignity of artificial respiration' simply to rise and fall again. A figure of Pompey's own metaphorical death here at the end of the novel, as well her rise again in the next by dint of her strong anti-depression drugs, Flo mirrors Pompey in being a 'mighty and unhappy creature, captured in what jungle darkness for what dishonourable destiny' (251).

The figure of Flo seems to also be a direct allusion to Orwell's *Burmese Days*, published two years beforehand, in which disillusioned and lovelorn Flory, our main character in a novel devoted to depicting racial and class prejudice at work in British India, kills his dog Flo before taking his own life. The animal, named after himself – just as Smith's tiger is covertly named after herself – cleverly extends his 'master's' identity as a white, superior citizen into the realm of those he is meant to leash, his binary opposites or 'black' colonials, and all but comically points up the Hegelian master/slave dialectic in the formation of British/Indian identity. Likewise, if with a kind of proto-Derridean twist on the Hegelian model, Smith's Flo is the captive identity in her speaker's seemingly 'free flow' of language. Pompey's despair and choice to end her form of discursive being in this text are very like Flory's, requiring the cessation of both her speech, her Freudian talking cure (the inner 'baby' being released on this flood of words) *and* her barely suppressed 'other' – in her case, that 'cat on the cradle' who is both what she has destroyed and herself as destroyer.

Stopping the 'Flo' of her work – this ending is both comic and coded. It seems crucial to end my long flow of a close-reading in this chapter, too, with a thought about codes and coding because they explain much about not only *Novel on Yellow Paper* but the whole of the trilogy and its context, commercial as well as cultural. As I suggested at the outset of the chapter, Smith depicts Pompey as a code-maker and -breaker within the very first segment of the novel; this activity will continue throughout *Over the Frontier*, and *The Holiday*. Obviously the centrality of the image's importance cannot be overplayed. But again, much is missed in assessments like Laura Severin's: 'Rebellious Pompey, expert coder, creates her own fantasy of desire in place of the one cultural convention has handed her' (34). Such a reading overlooks many things, among them the fact that her facility in using symbolic 'code' is, quite problematically, something Pompey later reveals is 'inherited' from her absconding father. Worse, he developed his version of the same talent in the military (the Navy):

> My papa was, among many other duties, in charge of the coding department. And very highly complicated it was, and I often think of him with very real sympathy when I am doing our own, by no means simple,

coding at the office. For as with me so with him, the people at the other end are simply not to be relied upon to decode the simplest words. (165)

The link between them could hardly be made more strongly; our task is to read this revelation, which comes as something of a surprise after so many pages with so little about her father's connection to her, as one that is both key and multiple in import. One could very easily take the route available into psychoanalytic theory, for example, given that her 'papa's' presence through his *absence* in her narrative of abandonment could give immediate rise to a Lacanian reading of her cultural encoding by patriarchal language itself. In such a reading, Pompey's escape from codes would be impossible, and to that extent it syncs interestingly with all I have thus far said about her character and speech. But the novel itself tells us this as well; its ways of connecting military to commercial and suburban 'codes' and discourses is at the root of what I have been trying to explicate with this long close-reading. We know, for example, that Pompey's coding is explained in connection with her cabling out from 'black face' Sir Phoebus's office for his various stock investments and returns (or at least, no other reason for coding is given in relation to her work). Depending on the business and his solvency as she does, she 'hopes Sir P. makes a lot of money' (18), and spends time as his secretary helping him monitor his money-making exploits. Like all the other discursive codes she allows herself to be hijacked by in the course of this writing's use of avoidance tactics, she tells us this kind of preoccupation is 'the only way [she] can lose herself'. Coding as covert business is certainly unavoidable, and connected to her *own* money-making exploits – the writing of this 'novel on yellow paper', for one thing, which she tells us is also done on the side, on company time, on company paper. Throughout the novel Pompey reminds us that she knows and obeys the rules of making money in the present literary climate. She issues a protective disclaimer, for example, just after suggesting that she will go 'a step further...and invent a code that doesn't need a codesheet' (19) – that is, this book – whose project is (like her author's, Smith's) to avoid libel at all costs, given her newly legalistic context, and not lose a publisher due to her 'use' of her friends: 'Now Reader, don't go making trouble fixing up names to all this. I say here there's not a person nor a thing in this book that ever stepped outside of this book' (19). Nevertheless, we know that she has said good-bye to all her friends on the first page in order to frame them in her picture of Thirties life; so she is, in effect, doing as the powerful do – breaking the codes and engaging in cover-up operations. Later, as she tells us her story about that wife in her 'bright little tight little hell-box' of married life, she again foregrounds the cover-up operations that mid-wife every text by telling us that she cannot mention certain things, like possible payments by cash instalments on the needed furniture, 'because, well, advertisers are so...There's just one word that covers that, and that is *delete*' (152). The fact that she is forced into codes in order to tell any narratives at all – and this one becomes aborted because it must have a certain kind of standard ending, which Pompey is too sick of to tell; as she puts it, '[y]ou can pay too much for a good dividend' (154) – is arguably the main point of this novel. As a user/abuser of codes she makes clear to readers that covert coding was increasingly the way of meaning and 'changing culture's mind' in the Thirties, both on the part of revolutionary *and* authoritative or nationalistic movements. We know that governmental authorities, for example, like the Ministry of Information, had its own programme for cultural propaganda, which depended on secrecy and under-the-table encouragement of certain codes to be played up in work such as films; as the programmers put it at the decade's close, in 1940,

> '...film propaganda will be most effective when it is least recognizable as such. Only in a few rare prestige films, reassurance films and documentaries should the Government's participation be announced. The influence brought to bear by the Ministry on the producers of feature films, and encouragement given to foreign distributors must be kept secret....'
> (Giles and Middleton 130)

Even films as seemingly innocuous as 'Goodbye Mr Chips' were deployed as good for underlining the 'English character' – and therefore the same constructions of Englishness and private life that were being woven into the war spirit as territories to protect from the foreigners. In this scenario, the codes and games being played in work by the Auden group – however similar it might have been to Smith's own, as I have suggested, in terms of its self-implicatory nature, its plans to self-destruct – must have looked to Smith and others outside it like inadvertent playing into the hands of all that it was revolting against. The same and more might be (and will be, in the next chapter) said of the 'occultation of Surrealism' that Breton called for in the Second Surrealist Manifesto, which claimed the movement as heir to ancient, secret hermetic doctrines through which it would transform human consciousness (Chadwick 190); again, the saviour rhetoric, the religion of politics, was something Smith saw overtaking the arts and dreaded as such. Certainly the playfully Audenesque title of her second novel, in which codes lead her speaker to 'surreal' ruin, suggests she was more than bored with the secretive, political, brainwashing/evangelising going on all about her in the Thirties. Its contradictions by other forces in culture were forking and reforking the path, any way you looked at it, creating an aporetic proliferation of ways; and Pompey, as we shall now see, was not fated to avoid any of them or take any road not yet taken.

4
Framing the War: The Second Two Novels of the Trilogy

Over the Frontier (1938) and *The Holiday* (1949) are best read as just-before and just-after pictures of Smith's wartime context (or rather its thought-world), with *Novel on Yellow Paper* having served the purpose of setting or 'framing' them from its damning angle. Her speaker in *The Holiday*, Celia Phoze – successor to the brainwashed and bellicose Pompey Casmilus (whose initials are reversed in hers, since she is given a name and nature that implies the 'freezing' of the runaway voice of the first two novels[1]) – gives us in one of her comments an overview of the movements of the final two thirds of the trilogy. Polarised as her speakers continue to be between deadly starting and equally deadly stopping, 'running on' *and* 'whoa-ing up' on the various hobby-horses that seem to be no more than extensions of the forces that dominated Pompey's civilian life, they seem once again to be offered no in-between, no respite from those discursive forces, no holiday or home-front. And both extremes of movement – running on into the fray *or* pulling up from the same – are, as we have seen, dangerous; but in the second two novels such dangers typically become explicated in military terms. Celia offers her summary of them near the end of *Holiday*, from her post-war vantage point and via, significantly, a line recalled from Kipling:

> An army, I said, in victory, full tongue across the desert 'For pleasure and profit together allow me the hunting of men'. It is exciting, is it not?... The victors, at war with the aftermath of war, grow tarnished, they are restless, they long for home, which way shall they look? The thoughts split up and the will slackens. (*TH* 184)

Which way shall they look, indeed? For 'home' is never anywhere to be *found* in the trilogy – it is only a chimera, a dream, as we saw in the first novel, although one that stirs the chauvinistic sentiments of war. And when war is over, and the heightened, jingoistic rhetoric of what one is fighting 'for' is on the wane, the conflict simply shifts to internal ground due to its even more deeply punctuated absence.

'A tide in the affairs of men' updated: nationalism, propaganda, economics, war and an introduction to both novels

Celia's quote above from Kipling's *Plain Tales*, set in India, suggests the confusion of stories that haunt Smith's English memory on the eve of imperial decline. Its use is especially effective, as it comes from one of Kipling's typical *fabrications* of a quote from an 'Old Shikarri', which showcases the displacement of origin and ownership upon which the text of empire depends.[2] And as we shall see in a moment, Pompey's earlier use of the French word for such longings for origins – *nostalgie* – to describe her feelings for the Victorian picture of the flood she often saw as a child in holiday accommodations foreshadowed very early on in the trilogy *Holiday*'s ironic depiction of 'home's' foreignness, of her characters' not knowing 'which way to look' for it. On a more complicated level, it suggests the word's wholly *symbolic* nature, as discursive cloak or mirage evocative of either romanticised images of a personal or national past (that upon further examination send characters 'running' away from the truth), or of images of ascendancy within the *telos* of classical Rome, that *ur*-empire, whose legacy retooled in the imaginations of the likes of Hitler would become the *collective* 'imaginary' over which all Europe was fated to collide.[3] As in *Novel*, Smith's speakers in the latter two parts of the trilogy are swept along in that same real/unreal flood of the picture – the tide, the 'tongues' (discourses, propaganda) of the times; as Pompey puts it in *Over the Frontier*, via a reference to *Julius Caesar*, '[t]here is a nervous irritation in this book and a tide in the affairs of Pompey which taken at the flood leads – God knows where' (106).[4] Like the Pompey of history and of Shakespeare's drama, Smith's Pompey will be revealed as both product and victim of the fatal vicissitudes of what Murellus calls with scorn the 'universal shout' of corruptible, unthinking public opinion; however, in Smith's novel, given her view of her own deeply unheroic age, those floods well-taken lead not on to 'fortune', as Brutus wrongly if optimistically puts it, but on to the unknowable, perhaps the unthinkable future. In other words, Smith, from her mid-twentieth-century view of European history, converts Shakespeare's possibly fortunate 'tides' into the ebb and flow of modern destruction – that is, the prophesying-cum-profiteering of war become its profligacy, which she always depicts as being the nadir of her European culture's pulse. Suddenly contracted, lost for orienting focus, insecure, directed back inward and repelled from itself, 'restless', self-destructive, it then requires deflection of those energies through being 'shot-up' again into superiority, into culturally enfranchising power, security and personal pay-back.[5] The latter drive from nadir to zenith powers *Over the Frontier*, although its ruling (and undermining) metaphor as we shall see is that of the 'fall'; and though Celia's name would suggest her rising in *The Holiday*, her struggle of the spirit ends on a benighted note.

The overt reference to 'profit' in the passage above and throughout the trilogy foregrounds the more practical cause for her era's bellicosity as Smith saw it: economics. It suggests her reading of the Great War's genesis, as well as her initial thoughts on the back-handed trading of contested lands in the Thirties – Abyssinia, Czechoslovakia – that she along with many others read *not* as appeasement but as the evident preamble to the next 'great war'. It would seem that like her friend Naomi Mitchison, and others in her circle, she too would have to be convinced that 'this was after all a war for survival, not an Imperialist war, as they had thought at first'.[6] Certainly we are reminded, as we read the above quoted passage from *The Holiday*, that Smith quite explicitly dubbed her ill-fated modern characters the legatees of profiteering men in history, literature and mythology. The dealings of Pompey the Great, and of the pimping Pompey of *Measure for Measure*, as well as of Casmilus/Hermes (who remains visible in the last novel as the ancestral namesake of Celia's alter-ego 'Caz', short for Casmilus), were those of self-serving men whose duplicity allowed 'doing a good deal of self-advantageous business on the side' of duty, as we remember from Smith's description of the latter (*SS: AB* 118; see p. 83 above). The full potential of this legacy unfolds, uncloaks itself, throughout the second novel, as we get references to other related 'dealings' concealed in the narration – like Pompey's own suspect stock-investing on the side, which we learn about through the surprising revelation, while soldiering, that she has all along carefully monitored her shares in things like nitrates, the chemical commonly used in explosives (169). Even more importantly, her many references in the latter two novels to not only topical issues but controversial figures like the very real Sir Samuel Hoare – whose unfortunate name and part taken in the Abyssinian crisis reinstate (pun intended) *Novel*'s motif of political 'whoring' within the pages of *Over the Frontier* – point up Smith's down-to-earth (rather than fashionably ideological) interests in just whose hands were getting greased in the run-up to war. Hoare, after all, found himself back in the Cabinet as First Lord of the Admiralty a year after his send-down and resignation for behind-the-scenes improprieties, effected with arch-fascist Peter Laval of France,[7] aimed at Italy's 'appeasement' through a plan that would have surrendered to the latter a large portion of Abyssinia/Ethiopia. Smith's condemnation in a letter to Denis Johnston in 1938 of Chamberlain's signing of the Munich Pact is followed by not only her interesting wish to become a presenter of the news on the BBC should 'this here war come off', but also by a rare expression of her fears and hopes for the future: 'Sam [Hoare] and John [Simon] are angling for the premiership and they are both of them plain rogues, something more I mean than just old so-and-so's....I hope Eden and Churchill and Atlee manage to arrive' (*MA* 271). Smith's politics evidence themselves in this statement as non-partisan and pragmatic. Eden the conservative resigned from the government in protest of the appeasement measures, and Atlee the moderate leftist would, as post-war

Labour prime minister, redirect domestic economic policies in favour of the working class (for whom he gained sympathy while employed as a social worker in London's East End). Smith's regard for the conservative Churchill, it seems, given her concerns in the trilogy, would have been similar to her friend Orwell's:

> The British ruling class are fighting against Hitler, whom they have always regarded and whom some of them still regard as their protector against Bolshevism. That does not mean that they will deliberately sell out; but it does mean that at every decisive moment they are likely to falter, pull their punches, do the wrong thing.
>
> Until the Churchill Government called some sort of halt to the process, they have done the wrong thing with an unerring instinct ever since 1931. (2000, 165)

Although Smith will caricature Orwell in *The Holiday* through her character Basil, a socialist who still reveres his deeply embedded Etonian values, her agreement with his sentiments above are fully evident in her texts. 'The ruling class are fighting for their own privileges', Orwell goes on; 'How can we drive the Italians out of Abyssinia without rousing echoes among the coloured peoples of our own Empire?... [So] long as the moneyed classes remain in control, we cannot develop any but a *defensive* strategy.' Smith's developing views on the quiet violence of inertia, and the necessity for war – so unlike Woolf's and other notorious female pacifists – had to do with her similarly keen distrust of her government's underlying reasons for their policies.

In addition, and more pressingly than in the first novel of the trilogy, Smith seems in these latter two to be exploring how states accommodate their financial need for a balance between security and aggression. They seem to do so, in her 'story', by prostituting their ethical and religious ideals to the material gains to be had via developing forms of economic-cum-political licence – whether they be brokered through the overt rhetoric of turn-of-the-century imperialism, or the newer and slyer tongue of burgeoning 'supply and demand' capitalism:

> But England is also a very cunning animal, very suave and astute indeed, and, *in only supplying a demand* that she sensed when first it came into the wind of modern humanitarianism, has thought up a lot of excuses for her âme intime de colonisateur. But these are to make you smile and turn away, they are not to be taken seriously except by smarty-clever babies like Professor Dryasdust who has on his mantelpiece, *pour épater* Pompey, Lord Mottistone and Sir Samuel Hoare, a picture postcard issued by the Italian bureau de propaganda to show a good Italian soldier striking

the slave-chains off the wrists of a kneeling Abyssinian. But is not this the very most harmless and elementary form of propaganda?

When England plays that game she can play it better than that, more thoroughly more vilely more unanswerably final. (*OTF* 99; first emphasis added)

The kind of propaganda Pompey refers to here is of the subtler sort, the kind that moulds her unwitting young professor friend and, we take it, other university intellectuals of his type in the Thirties. The frequent conflation Smith effects of economics, academics, politics and the arts suggests her vision of 'modern humanitarianism' as having been wrought out of collusion between only supposedly inappropriate bedfellows.

And indeed Dryasdust comes to us, ironically, straight out of Victorian literature. He is the fictitious figure to whom Sir Walter Scott pretended to dedicate his historical novels, and whose name became shorthand for others like Carlyle when referring to a pedantic sort of 'dry-as-dust' knowledge of antiquities, history or statistics. A joke updated by Smith, he becomes full of 'the derived heartiness of the Belloc and the Beachcomber and the oversimplification of life so dear to the rigid anglo-catholic intellectual' (89) – the latter type having increased in number after the Great War, adding further irony to Smith's use of the Dryasdust figure through its emphasis on mystery as spiritual fact.[8] This one's thought is positioned, in other words, somewhere between Roman Catholic and deeply anti-Semitic Belloc (with his most recent, 1922 writings being about *The Jews* and *Napoleon*, and his collaborations with Roman Catholic convert G.K. Chesterton producing the oddly torqued political newspaper, *New Witness*) and Wyndham Lewis (whose aesthetically modernist, proto-fascist views of the time were evident in numerous books and pamphlets as well as the 'Beachcomber' column of the *Daily Express*).[9] Seemingly deliberately here, as well as elsewhere, Smith conflates such a figure's sublimated right-wing leanings with his/her supposedly left-wing ones, supplying Dryasdust with socialist rhetoric for his attempt to '*épater le bourgeois*' in the persons of Pompey and this lord and sir with this postcard even though his sentiments issue from a similar imperialist positioning, given that he believes England's 'cunning excuses' for its own like misadventures (embodied here as a reminder in the figure of Hoare – who, as we must not miss, is suggestively grouped with our speaker). Once again, Orwell's views on such matters seemed to resemble Smith's at the time in that his assessment was that underlying chauvinism was making a muddle of ideological thought; as he wrote in 1945 in 'Notes on Nationalism', 'In continental Europe Fascist movements were largely recruited from among Communists, and the opposite process may well happen in the next few years. What remains constant in the nationalist is his own state of mind; the object of his feelings is changeable, and may be imaginary' (2000, 306).

On another level, the problem with Dryasdust's vision seems, in Smith's view, to be his merely 'academic' ability to study events, 'know' facts and see black and white lines as the indisputable text of history. If he *does* indeed understand the postcard's irony, Pompey sniffs, it is only because it employs the most 'elementary' of propagandistic practice. Smith's novel is concerned with teaching her readers to read more deeply, more self-reflexively, into the cultural intertext of such images, where even 'rigid' discourses like that of religion offer no sorting mechanism given their helpless entanglement in contemporary politics and nationalism. She has our speaker turn abruptly, just after the end of the quote set out above, to thoughts of not Italian but English propaganda during the Great War, and the fate of Sir Roger Casement, in order to underline the falseness of any avowed 'frontier' or border between good and bad states, or between ethics and expediency – then *or* now:

> My thoughts turn sadly to Casement and the astuteness of the at that moment of time necessary defamation of his character by the circulation of his diary. Ah ha, my little Professor [Dryasdust], there is propaganda in excelsis with the imprimatur of the British Government upon it. Must the Belgians be held to opprobrium at that fatal minute of history, with 1914 on the time sheet and the necessity of presenting to a public of military age the spectacle of la petite Belgique outraged and debauched by the advancing Pruss?... The men spring to arms. But if the sacrificial victim be not so pure, so immaculate, will that serve so well? It will not.... And fight? Oh no, we are not fighting to-day, thank you so much.
>
> Do you see? – How clever, how abominably necessary the discrediting of all that Casement, in his white heat of indignation, and a little stuff and nonsense too, had accomplished? Before the war, his name stood high, his word was taken, the opprobrium of the world fell upon Belgium, in her African misconduct. But alas, dear Casement, the times are against you, it is August 1914, it is later than that, already the sparks are set to a general conflagration, you must go. (99–100)

Turning to other kinds of 'African misconduct' via another of her many allusions to *Heart of Darkness* (made obvious again here by her reference to the Casement affair as yet another 'abomination' and her by-now familiar use of Marlow's narrative twitch, 'Do you see?'),[10] Smith not only re-reads Italian transgressions in the Thirties as exemplary of others, but also re-reads British policy as it was applied in the case of Casement. Knighted years before the war for his reporting on Belgium's conduct in the Congo, Casement's Irish nationalist activities led him to be hanged for treason in 1916. But that simple political story must, in Smith's view, be augmented by recalling the government's circulation of Casement's diaries (claimed by his Irish compatriots to be forged) which revealed the alleged homosexual activity that foiled any pleas for leniency in his punishment. His blemishing at just the right moment – the 'abominably necessary' one, in Pompey's account above – aided in the blanching of Belgium as well as good English recruitment to protect it as Britain entered the Great War between European imperialisms. Creating oversimplified 'spectacles' rather than reporting complex realities is what, Smith suggests, all sides were engaged in during the lead-up to *both* wars – the one she had already lived through and the one she, with her second novel, prophesied. The mire of deflection and defamation was such in Smith's assessment above that even figures like Casement were incapable of avoiding the 'stuff and nonsense' of equivocation (or projection) in his reportage on Belgium's activities in the Congo. It was newly flooding into even the privacy of homes through the radio – a device that Pompey often suggests is in good part responsible for the fatigues and enervation of her times.[11]

More conspicuously than in *Novel on Yellow Paper*, as a result, the thoughts that begin to control Smith's speakers in *Over the Frontier* come in a muddle, and even people become thought-lines, like 'Josephine's thought' or 'Tom-thought' (212). But most powerful are the 'unthoughts': repressed thoughts and desires that propel what Pompey calls the 'strong tearing movement with unthought of strength' that figures like 'Pouncer' (another 'sick cat' character) call up in her to send her off into that dreaded extension of sublimated discourse: destructive action. That these tacks develop from her speaker's unremarkable – even common – daily ones is key; it provides essential explication of not only the novels' form but of Smith's cultural philosophy as well. The exhaustion that results from her speakers' trilogy-long struggle with 'otherway thought [that] come[s] with wracking twisting and tormenting malice' (146) becomes so profound that by the end of the third novel, Celia's thoughts incline continually to sleep, or to some other kind of mental stupor. Yet never do these speakers actually manage except in body to go 'on holiday', as her last novel's title suggests, though dozens of wishful references throughout the trilogy express longings to get away, to be freed of not only the 'tyranny of ideas' (*OTF* 146) but consciousness itself – to be, in other words, in a state of 'actively forgetting' (17), 'unconscious happiness' (147). What we find over these final two novels, then, is that the Pavlovian-cum-Beckettian, 'bell-minded' (86) Pompey of *Over the Frontier*[12] – she who 'answer[s] too many bells', who is initially sent away to a sanatorium to get away from her thoughts, and who therefore begins the novel tranquilised by drugs, constantly wishing to sleep, but nevertheless producing hobby-horse-like responses every time something she or someone else says 'strikes a bell' (another metaphor for that 'tyranny of the association of ideas' that continues to haunt her from *Novel* (21), its prompts becoming more and more warlike, leading her as she says in this passage, 'to no good end') – suddenly wills herself, in the person of Celia, into the opposite state: an internally-divided torpor, her thoughts 'split up', as she puts it in the first passage I quoted above, her will to ride out 'full tongue' now replaced by the will to sleep, to not think about what has passed or is passing or is coming to be.

Like the manuscript Smith abandoned in 1939, 'Married to Death' (having begun writing it in 1937, even before *Frontier* was published), *The Holiday* is also, as Smith put it, 'death death death lovely death' (*SS: AB* 140).[13] All along, it seems, her envisioned end to the trilogy involved the stopping of all those discursive hobby-horses her speakers must helplessly ride, but as it turned out her first attempt at a draft of what such a state might look like was far too experimental for some. Her friend and erstwhile supporter David Garnett's fatal commentary on 'Married to Death', written in a letter to Smith in 1939, makes me all the sadder that it no longer survives: 'I cannot describe it better than I could describe the landscape of what I see when I have been swimming under water. One does not know who is who or what is what as you say yourself in one place' (*SS: AB* 141). Perhaps this lost work was Smith's *The Waves*, a Woolfian experiment, but one re-set to investigate not the essence of character – that modernist wild-goose – but the dissolution of it; we will never know. As it is, the trilogy still ends as it seems it ought to, with exactly that which we as readers have feared from its outset: the unhorsing of our precarious and degenerate speakers/riders with whom Smith has, quite against the odds, caused us to identify (thereby implicating us all). And it happens despite the ostensible victory over externalised 'evil forces' that 1945 was said to have brought.

I

Another reverse coda: *Over the Frontier*'s opening pages

Like *Novel on Yellow Paper*, Smith's second novel also begins with a 'reverse coda' – an indelible bit of 'writing on the wall' inscribed within the seemingly incidental or even parenthetical openings of her texts. Enactment of its 'script' or code follows, as we saw in her first novel; this chilling form of the inevitable repeats itself with even greater clarity, if also subtlety, in Smith's second instalment of the trilogy.

And again, like *Novel*, *Over the Frontier* begins with a picture of the 'degenerate rider' I refer to above. But this time it is indeed very important that it *is* a picture – a painting – that I speak of, because the novel continuously notes the complicity of high-cultural art in political discourse. Intriguingly, Smith constructs the novel in such a way that its language may take our speaker to the very front of war and yet be seen to never leave the picture gallery of its initial setting. Moreover and more accurately, as we will be told a little more than half-way through the book, our speaker has moved us in a 'great parabola', 'because this Painter Business' is crucial, generative, it 'circles in the widest outsweeping strong flight to the very first words that you have written' (163), demonstrating the interwoven nature of her cultural text. Its 'trajectory... [is] to attain such an encirclement, to hit back to the beginning' or, rather, become the unacknowledged matrix – the repressed 'dream' – behind a *new* beginning mid-novel, one that hurls our speaker out of thought and into action:

> For suddenly my sleeping dreaming eyes are open very wide, and my thoughts that left me on a wide high upreaching flight, to shoot so high and curve downwards on a long trajectory to the beginning of my thought, have come home to me to wait, very tensed, very alert and practical. (164)

Up to this point in the book all of Pompey's muddled thoughts, sparked by her initial ones in the picture gallery and others she has accumulated in her flight from them through parties and travels, have functioned to gather her up into the atmospheric fears and slogans and images of the times, the 'dream' of culture, out of which she emerges a suddenly different being – if only as different as we each of us are upon waking from the selves of our most illuminating-but-suppressed dreams.

The result here is that the 'foot off the ground' Pompey from *Novel* who only needed her periodic and problematic 'shooting up' has suddenly turned, after her 'high upreaching flight' over 156 pages of *Over the Frontier*, into a new and even more troubling figure. In the sentence preceding the above quoted passage her words were: 'Achtung, achtung! I hope that I am very practical' as she struggles to come to earth, to resolve her immersion in dreaming discourse through action. But she only manages it by problematically and unwittingly marshalling her thoughts to the rhythm she has told us she heard when riding in Halle behind pupils forced into moving their horses 'round and round... to the sound of Achtung, Achtung, shot at us like a canon ball' (84). Her chilling conclusion, as she thus 'wakes' from circulating in her culture's pre-war thought-world, is derived from one of the paintings she averted her eyes from in the gallery: George Grosz's 'The Old Men of 1922' from his famous *Post-War Museum* sequence. It evoked in Pompey unbearable feelings of relief/guilt and horror over such depictions of the fate of the Germans after the Great War (a common post-war sentiment in Britain). The language and imagery used in that passage on the eighth page of the novel reappears at this radical juncture as she decides that all the old men of war live in her memory, 'to come to us, to tell us, Es war einmal ein Krieg, Es war einmal ein Krieg we never knew.... Oh war war is all my thought' (163). The German in the latter quote translates into: 'Once upon a time there was war', which paradoxically enfolds Pompey's newly 'practical' and increasingly fascist conclusions in a life-long cultural text or dream that from childhood on, ever since her first brush with the art of (predominantly German) fairy tales, has worked to create of her, through a mixture of fear, desire and cultural atavism, the soldier she now becomes. As though illustrating Julia Kristeva's assumptions that war forms the 'underlying causality' of social organisation,[14] Pompey shows us that she always already knew this but repressed the knowledge, as is made clear when she is told by her one-time fiancé, Freddy, in a dream she has prior to her soldiering days, that she already *is* 'in uniform', long before the actual fact of putting it on. Even after she does at last don it to ride out 'over the frontier', we still have no change of figurative setting – on the final pages, she refers to the theatre of war she has joined as 'this galére' (267), this gallery, this picture gallery, this 'spectacle'. War, or repression of the thought of it, is imprinted on the very nerve centres of culture, she suggests; as Pompey puts it, 'we have in us the pulse of history and our times have been upon the rack of war' (94).[15] I must explore Smith's repeatedly underlined connection between art, journalistic and cinematic spectacles, politics and war at some length in what follows below given that this second book of the trilogy is the one dedicated most clearly to her cultural critique of contemporary art and artists/writers, and to the explication of what she saw as their often inadvertent complicity in the international tragedy whose prologue had already been audible for some years before this novel's publication in 1938.

As I began to explain in Chapter 2, even the most devoted of Smith's readers have missed the point of 'the jarring shift mid-book from realism to surrealism' (*S* 112) in *Over the Frontier* – and her biographers attribute its lack of success with readers to its strange fault-lines. But that shift lies at the very heart of Smith's formal experiment and innovation in this novel and is absolutely central to its meaning.[16] It of course involves the book's self-announced parabolic movement, and cannot be understood without further investigation of how Smith had been revising binary constructions of dream/reality since *Novel on Yellow Paper*. It should hardly surprise us that re-evaluation of such a binary would be at issue in the novel, given the fact that it was surrounded by an explosion of surrealist manifestos (brought most powerfully to London in 1936 with the International Surrealist Exhibition) and newly developed existentialist thought. It seems key to recall that Jean-Paul Sartre's first two novels, *Nausea* and *Intimacy*, were published in 1938 and 1939, respectively, with his monumental *Being and Nothingness* following only four years later to seal his opposition to the increasingly objective and determinist world view of the Communist International. Moreover, the seemingly indigestible form of Smith's novel, with its shift between real and surreal, links it to another similarly titled and similarly shifty one published in the same year, by the Woolfs at the Hogarth Press: *Journey to the Border* by Edward Upward. It is, however, important for us to note that Smith seems to have been parodying the sort of political use to which Upward put his protagonist's 'progress' through the terrain of dream/reality. As Stephen Spender describes it in his Introduction to the book's reprinted edition, Upward's persona, unlike Pompey, 'wakes' into *true* (communist) vision out of the surreal dream of bourgeois thought:

[Upward's] fiction tends to take the form of the journey or quest by a protagonist who, thinly disguised, and in altered circumstances, is, under various fictitious names, the author himself. He is an idiosyncratic observer who combines a caricaturist's vision of upper and middle-class English society with a developing belief in the workers and the oppressed. After an initial surrealistic phase, he is political in that he interprets the world as a struggle between those whose values are those of their own property, power and self-interest, and those who share the vision of a world which might be transformed in the interests of the whole community....

In being a writer with a social vision Upward fits into a category of novelists in this century... who reject the existing social order... to go in search of some achievable materialistic and social Utopia. (7)

We might say the exact opposite happens in Smith's novel. Surreal bounds become impossible to draw, and Pompey's moment of waking is, as we have seen, her moment of falling *back* into the submerged terrain of 'abominable' repressed thought and therefore into the most destructive of multilevel surreal landscapes. The noted 'shift' of her narrative form, in other words, takes our speaker nowhere new. Such strategies also have markedly different results from Auden and Isherwood's Brechtian ones in their play *On the Frontier* (1938), which similarly deconstructed the view of clear sides by placing an invisible 'frontier' centre-stage. Their desire to espouse very specific ideological solutions caused them to work into the play 'a significant shift of emphasis [when] the young lovers, who have been separated by the frontier throughout the play, affirm the supremacy of love, as they die', having abjured their earlier pacifism to become an insurgent and a nurse. In Raymond Williams's judgement, 'the effect of this ending is to eclipse the political impact of the popular rising' because the play ends on a 'lyric individual lament' (Williams 92). Smith's work also delivers its implicit critique of such sentimentalising of the heroic individual at the same time that she, unlike Williams, would extend such critique to the sentimentalising of 'popular risings', given that her novels relentlessly entwine all sentiment *and* revolutionary vision in the larger and less visible dynamics of their cultural text. Her engagement with the politicised tenets of surrealism, 'Audenesque parable'[17] and Brechtian defamiliarisation *is* an engagement, however, and not a disengagement. Her dialogue with those similarly engaged with such ideas, like Upward and other members of the Auden band in Britain, illuminates her own clear disillusionment with conservative British values and its social order at the same time that it emphasises her cynicism about the decade's too-simplistically radical ideological responses and dreams of 'world revolution' – or 'social utopia', as Spender puts it above.

Problematic readings of the novel also arise out of a lack of attention paid to its highly dense opening pages. None of Smith's critics takes the discreet section of thought these pages present into account when developing a reading of the novel as a whole. But Pompey's engagement here with the work of Grosz is key, as Smith seems to offer him up as an artist whose career is typical of those produced by social and aesthetic conflicts endemic to the period (and indeed, if she had only known it, Auden's trajectory of ideological engagement, exile and disengagement would soon conform to the same mould). As Pompey responds to Grosz's highly political and controversial responses to her era in art, she sets up Smith's critique of current movements in primarily painting, writing and film while all the while she inadvertently introduces much of the visual and discursive imagery that will determine her own fate in the novel.

It opens *in medias res*, with reference to Grosz – 'He certainly is the funny man' (9) – as her speaker walks into a picture gallery. She is talking to us, not only about Grosz's work but also about another gallery-goer whose story she had from a figure unknown to us, a 'Jack', whom she says she has told us about before. Comically, it at first seems to us that Smith's speaker Pompey has never stopped 'talking on'– that between the publishing of *Novel* and the publishing of *Frontier* she has simply kept on speaking, 'unrecorded'. But more significantly, Smith very quickly through this device unframes her new novel, allowing its narration to exceed its generic bounds as well as its expositional 'pretext' in order to allow it to recede back into an irretrievable moment, lost somewhere in the thought-world of this writing. I will return to 'Jack's' complementary and very short story in a moment, but first it is important to note what Pompey tells us her thoughts are as she enters the gallery: 'My mind was full of art and I had a nostalgie to be looking at these high-up and elevating canvases and there was especially the one that is called "Haute École"' which portrays a 'very classical...horse' (10), 'a ferocious and captive animal', and its 'degenerate rider' (12). Before I begin to dwell on this new incarnation of Smith's riding image from *Novel on Yellow Paper*, assessing the way it glosses our speaker's new movements, the word 'nostalgie' needs attention again – though this time in terms of its relation to the 'elevation', or 'shooting up', that the 'high art' and classical canvases seem to proffer for her. Art historian Frank Whitford gives us a sense of the immediate backdrop for the sentiment and this scene:

> The [International Exhibition] in Paris was not the only event of 1937 to reveal the dangerous fault line of European cultural thinking. Two other exhibitions, both staged in Munich, did the same more starkly. In one, painting and sculpture approved by Hitler was displayed. In the other, what the Nazis condemned as 'degenerate' was held up to ridicule.
>
> The 'Degenerate Art' exhibition consisted of works by the entire German avant-garde, all of them confiscated from public collections and later to be auctioned off abroad or destroyed.... In its distorted forms, unnatural colours and unsettling subject-matter it mirrored that violent disruption of established values which, during the Weimar Republic, had

demoralised a once-great nation and brought it to its knees.... The individualistic, divergent and critical clamour of the avant-garde was now finally to be silenced so that the single, harmonious voice of the Nation alone could be heard.

In the new German painting, images of healthy, handsome, confident and active people would replace those of the 'cripples, criminals and whores' which, according to the Nazis, infested Weimar art. In Germany, as in the Soviet Union, instantly legible and uplifting scenes would replace abstract arrangements of colours and forms 'devoid of meaning'.... From the art of one totalitarian state to that of another such images look, at first, to be virtually interchangeable. So, with the partial exception of Italy, do their cultural policies. All were oppressive and imposed by terror. All aimed to numb the critical faculties and satisfy the populist craving for comfort and reassurance....

In the democracies, too, the majority regarded modernism with alarm or puzzled amusement. This explains why an anti-Nazi exhibition of 'degenerate' German art in London in 1938 attracted much hostile criticism, some of it identifying Hitler's artistic prejudices as his one redeeming feature.... It was time for retrenchment, for a return, in politics as in art, to old, trustworthy certainties. (Becker and Caiger-Smith 4–5)

Pompey's 'nostalgie' for 'high up' (or 'uplifting', as Whitford puts it above), 'elevating' pictures – particularly one named 'Haute École', which refers to the classical or old-school art of riding – is immediately rendered suspect when contextualised. It becomes symptomatic of the 'retrenchment' Whitford describes above, with its attendant and delusory atavism associated with oppressive regimes. Again, if we remember, Pompey used the same word when recalling the ubiquitous Victorian picture seen on her childhood holidays in *Novel* – the one that evoked her 'great *nostalgie* for [the] open drain' (14) of Tennysonian nostalgia that might be said to have fuelled the kingdom's imperial aspirations. But as I suggested at the outset of this chapter, Pompey's continual use of the French term for it – a foreign word used, ironically, to evoke her own nostalgia or 'homesickness' – highlights the discursive rather than actual ownership of the past that is longed for. Here at the beginning of *Frontier*, this indexes the classical legacy that was being sold, 'virtually interchangeably', as Whitford has it above, in terms of aesthetic backlashings across Europe. The discursive dream of the ascendancy of one's own culture within Europe is, in other words, immediately flagged in the novel as something that draws Pompey too, has power for her. It will enfold her until she wakes into practical application of it, in her uniform, speaking in both English and German – seemingly 'interchangeably', we might say, to once again extend Whitford's comment on the ironies involved.

The 'degeneracy' she assigns to the horse's rider is somewhat more complex and difficult to read. We might be tempted, if we wish to see

Smith as covertly siding with the avant-garde, to read this rider as code for Smith herself. Certainly her own form of 'surreal' narration and use of 'unsettling subject matter' in these novels suggests her sympathy with the 'critical clamour' of avant-garde art of certain kinds; this becomes even clearer in her harsh judgement of what some saw as Grosz's abandonment of the same, as I demonstrate below.[18] But if that rider *is* actually an image of the modernist artist in the Thirties, it is one that Smith definitely complicates rather than unequivocally endorses. This rider's particular form of degeneracy is in Pompey's description less like that of the avant-garde as portrayed by Whitford above than a retrograde version of it, a kind of decadence that is 'fin de siècle', like the 'degenerate people you have in the drawings of Beardsley' at the end of the nineteenth century (11). His lips are 'pursed and pouting', he is seemingly 'very sly very supercilious', 'and his eyes beneath puffed eyelids are looking downwards'. Seemingly displaced and half-asleep, or 'dreaming', he is not only quite inappropriately riding in what our speaker describes as 'smoking' garb but is, further, desperately vulnerable, riding hatless, with a 'pink plump covering of soft flesh' over his bald head. Nothing in his pose would suggest his ability to control that 'ferocious and captive animal', his 'high-stepping horse that is so high up and arrogant' (17), offered here as a menacing, 'malicious' symbol of re-emergent classical styles of art.[19] Smith might be seen, in other words, to not only be sympathising with Grosz's intimations of an era ridden out of control, but also to be identifying the abstract forms 'devoid of meaning' described in Whitford's quote above with, in this image, the Pateresque, epicurean abandonments of having to 'mean' that her speaker comments on derisively elsewhere in the novel. Linking certain forms of modernist art with what became famously called art-for-art's-sake at the turn of the century may have been Smith's way of suggesting or prophesying that neither will have, in the end, offered much resistance to classical bellicosity within their respective pre-war contexts.[20]

Those solipsists who pursue their chimeric passions may even go 'falling falling... victim to a horrible whore' when thwarted, she implies – as does the figure in Jack's story as retold for us by Pompey on the very first page of the novel:

> [A]nd once there was a man that had got funny in his head with drinking a lot of Schnaps, and by-and-by he got up those steps and was stroking this Venus in a very deep-going and affectionate manner, he certainly had a strong natural affection for Venus and what was more like than he should go to stroking this classical plasteret to show how he was feeling this very deep-going affection that was so right and natural and at the same time so simply free and outpouring? But by-and-by the man that stood there in uniform, he was a very formal character, very hardened in the emotional arteries, well, see if he must not go and give him a great

push that sent him falling falling down that flight of stairs where at bottom he fell victim to a horrible whore. (9–10)

The last seven words above constitute the first of Pompey's own strangely fragmented 'Favourite Quotations' as she recited them for us in *Novel* (42). She seemed to enjoy there, via this unattributed snippet of a quote, the surprising phonetic symmetry between accusation – 'horrible' – and accused – 'whore'. Here at the start of *Frontier*, the same symmetry obtains between 'high' and 'low': desire – both decadent and emotional, perhaps even bourgeois – for the unrealisable ideal (incarnated as art, in this instance) demonstrates its flip side, 'degeneracy', when thwarted by culture's 'harder' imperatives as embodied by that military mirror-image in uniform. Smith's epigrammatic comment through this story on her era's art movements, their 'idealismuses', and their 'whoring' flip sides finds its socio-political equivalent, of course, in the prostituted dealings of government figures like the aptly-named Sir Samuel 'Hoare'. *Frontier*'s opening gallery scene, in a playful mirroring of this dynamic, shows us that Pompey when thwarted from 'possessing' the expensive 'Haute École' turns, just like the drinker of German spirits ('Schnaps') in the above quoted passage, to the lewd alternative – that is, to the all-but-pornographic and far less politically consequential of Grosz's drawings.

Just pages beforehand in the trilogy, at the end of *Novel on Yellow Paper*, Pompey imagined herself about to be punished by Venus for having 'fall[en] in love with a chimera' (*NOYP* 222) – that is, Freddy, whom we know functioned as a kind of distraction from the philosophical despair that our speaker, in those dangerous pauses that sometimes sneak into her digressive and obsessive talking, was hovering on the brink of. The need, at that brink, for 'shooting up' – something that in both *Novel* and *Frontier* has, at times, and in literal terms, been associated with drinking, as this man obviously does his Schnaps – can be seen as linked to the need for chimeric or heady distractions. The 'misuse' of Venus in this story, like the misuse of the arts that Smith seemed to critique in the Thirties, leads to the sort of end Pompey remembers Racine pictured for the excessive Pasiphaë and Phèdre: being thrown (*jeta*) or 'pushed', like our Schnaps drinker, to their sad fates (*NOYP* 223) – though by the time she wrote *Frontier*, her image has come to emphasise the military hand that will deliver the consequences.[21] At the very complex end of *Over the Frontier*, that hand will be Pompey's own, used against herself as well as her enemy, as we shall see; indeed, all of these images of chimeras and even of Freddy will return seemingly incongruously on the battlefront as Pompey confronts, at the end of her narrative *psychomachia*, what she has called 'the dream that slew the slayer and shall be slain' (200). Smith's entanglements of comments on art and culture and politics – intertwined as they were, too, in Hitler's portrayal of himself as classical art lover as well as military dictator – evidence her own political project in this novel of revealing what she saw as the intertextual dynamics of cultural disaster. Although she could not respect the stultifying, moralistic and self-involved despair she sensed in Eliot's writings, as I explained in Chapter 1, she does seem to cast her characters in *Frontier* into a messier version of the same – though perhaps in explication of the dangerous trajectory for such despair, as well as its potential for the 'active forgetting' that she will in a moment describe Grosz's rider, Grosz himself and her speaker as embodying.

Pompey moves from 'Haute École' to others of Grosz's works she likes – work that we as readers know represent this left-wing German painter's 'sell-out', his abandonment of his initial and shocking post-war social commentary (for which he was brought to trial three times for blasphemy and defaming public morals, for not 'show[ing] the growing proletariat as a "positive idea"'[22]) and, upon his move to America in 1933, his adoption of traditional, somewhat romantic modes. Pompey, who dislikes his 'cynical and malicious' caricatures of bourgeois society, is drawn instead to his 'funny', 'witty' caricatures of things like fleshy 'Girl Guides' and voyeuristic renderings of hanky-panky 'On the Beach'. The decadence/degeneracy of these drawings and of the rider in 'Haute École' entertains Pompey, who will focus on them in order to avert her art-going memory from a sudden flashback to Grosz's darker sequence, *A Post-War Museum*:

> And looking and laughing and thinking of all this my thoughts turn again to a darker memorial I have of Georg Grosz that is this dark memorial that is called A Post-War Museum where all of the ignobility and shameful pain of war suffering is set down with the precision of genius and the bitterness of a complete experience, oh here in this portfolio are such things as our security cannot conceive, cannot bear for one moment to contemplate. People say, Why, such things cannot be true, no it is a neurosis, why this George Grosz he is just a war neurotic, it is sad but he should certainly be shut up and prevented, why it is not at all a good thing that he should be let run round to infect with his neurosis his defeatism his anti-sozialismus the healthy unthinking happiness of our sheltered infant adults. (15–16)

National or social 'security' depends in this passage on 'unthinking happiness' and shutting up those who, with the 'precision of genius and bitterness of a complete experience', recreate unthinkable recent history – which seems to mean doing so without selective repression at work. Just after this paragraph we see the consequences of such release as Pompey helplessly overflows into recalling more of Grosz's 'portfolio' than she wishes to, including works like 'The Old Men of 1922': 'But oh the tearing searing suffering of Germany after the war... The Old Men of 1922, the old broken shamefully broken body of the shattered soldier drawn up lifted up crucified upon his crutches lifted up above the old-young child... and over it all and undertoning it all is shame and loss and flight into darkness' (16). The legacy of that repressed image is left to the 'old-young child', importantly – explaining to us how it is that later in the novel the images of these old men return, from deep within her memory, to summon Pompey to war. Far from suggesting that works like *A Post-War Museum* precipitate war (though she *will* launch Pompey into contemplation of the fine line between use and abuse of 'cruel' detail in art, as we shall see), Smith seems, given her speaker's 147-page repression of the pain its pictures caused in her thoughts of them, to suggest along with Freud that eliding trauma inevitably results in repeating or reliving it. Actively forgetting traumatic history, in other words, means donning a uniform.

The expatriate Grosz is compared to his degenerate rider in 'Haute École' in a way that will in a moment also illuminate Smith's speaker. Particularly her later war-like incarnation, whose powers of forgetting are such that she must be continually harangued to 'for once be a good girl and remember and remember all the time' bits and pieces of military intelligence (170–71). Or, as it seems, such disciplined encoding constitutes an aid to repression, substituting for a deeper-running vein of troubling and conflicted thoughts. Forgetting about *A Post-War Museum*, Pompey tells us that she and her contemporaries

> do not have to taste this cup of tea. No. For us there is this funny-ha-ha Georg Grosz.... So Georg Grosz is out of Germany now and he has made an escape to America and I am glad that he has done so. So now he can forget, or with the will not to remember he can... be still perhaps a little bitter and have his cynical laughter go echoing round the picture-galleries of London and New York, but it is only, Very funny, very clever, is it not? (17)

That last phrase will appear again later in the novel as Pompey is jolted out of her confused cultural dreaming and into her new military life. It operates at that point as a deflector, just as here it deflects Pompey from her disturbing thoughts about Grosz's earlier work. She next conflates the Americanised Grosz with the degenerate rider in his painting (through an initial, 'colourful' description that reflects what I hope is Pompey's familiar racism rather than Smith's own, impossible though as it is to tell):

> [W]hat is there still to say about the rider? He is perhaps rather a nigger in the woodpile, there is perhaps something a little enigmatical about this rider, after all what is he doing? I think he is doing this, with great application and concentration this is what he is doing, he is forgetting to remember the shame and dishonour the power of the cruelty the high soaring flight of that earlier éclaircissement, that was that pale éclair dans une nuit profonde, that rakehell of a beam of light that went showing up

the very sad bones of that earlier situation, that he is very actively forgetting and instead he will think of the easy generous light-running laughter of the English and Americans, and he is thinking of that American nationality that shall come dropping down dropping like a curtain to shut off from him for ever that sad sad situation, that perhaps he is already a little ashamed to have seen once and for all time so top to bottom,... to the very last outposts of the black heart of despair of the situation. (17–18)

And Pompey is, of course, also this same figure. Our problematic and ill-fated speaker will be deeply and repeatedly connected with this rider, whose bad posture on his classical mount makes him look 'long and slim' but with that 'feeling of plumpness that is a little feminine', slack in the saddle and bound to fall fatally, hatless as he is, were that 'malicious' horse to dance sideways (11) – just as Pompey's first mount did in *Novel on Yellow Paper*. It is not only that she also, as we hear 70 pages later, 'ride[s] so abominably not according to good horsemanship', 'so long in the stirrup, so slackly', so 'headlong over rough country' (i.e., with the desire to 'run mad', as we know 'people with dictators' do in *Novel*), but that she too, like Grosz himself as she described him above, can be 'malicious', she can 'out-Herod them all', as she did, when a child, all her riding instructors and detractors. In this complex syzygy, malicious horse and rider and artist and speaker merge; we have, once again, as in *Novel*, a centaur-figure of divided (European) late-Thirties propensities, haunted, decadent, volatile and primed for being carried away – in the end, to war. And indeed, her riding mistress foreshadows the same when she calls Pompey's poor style a 'pseudo-military style' of sitting flat (83–84). She is, in other words, already destined for a uniform even as a child, just as her prophetic dream will tell her she is. Smith seems to relate the poor government of one's 'seat' with poor government of thoughts – and to relate the riding 'headlong' 'that takes a girl out of herself' (84), and out of her traumatic memories, with falling once again into the same darkness that Grosz skims over with his new 'light-running laughter'. Therefore the very way in which Pompey's next move, or post-preamble narrative, begins – or dances sideways – should strike us as being ominous. Later we will understand that it was indeed that.

Remembering to forget: Smith's narrational dynamics

For she elects, after a break in the text following 'the black heart of despair of the situation' as she had painfully recalled it with the help of Grosz's work above, to launch into a 'good-bye to all that' – a farewell that echoes the beginning of *Novel on Yellow Paper*, though with a timely difference. We saw as readers of *Novel* that her good-bye to her friends at the outset was not and could not be successful, given that all her friends turn out to *be* her. Indeed, as we recall from Chapter 3, in *Novel* her greatest and most repressed fear is that she, like Alice in Wonderland, 'is becoming Mabel': a conglomerate of all the contemporary discourses and prejudices that she has been exposed to and cannot leave behind. Here, as Smith's world edges nearer to war, the implications of *Novel*'s model of consciousness for the making of history comes more closely and topically into view. Forgetting the violent and unresolved past is the first step to reliving it – and perhaps becoming something of an animal in order to do so, since Smith was, after all, known to quote Aristotle's distinction between man and beast: that only one can remember the past at will.[23] Perhaps she finishes or extends his criterion by adding that *forgetting* the past at will is even *more* human – or at least more common in her inter-war period, as the beginning of Robert Graves's well-known book *Good-bye to All That*, which I alluded to at the start of this paragraph, might be said to illustrate.[24] Smith clarifies her interest in this odd and potentially dangerous feature of human psychology by opening the third novel of her trilogy with Celia's paradoxical remark that she and her office-mate Tiny can keep their minds on their work, and *not* on their anxieties about sinister Clem's transfer to the office next door, only if they refrain from continual shock at being reminded of their new circumstances – only if, in other words, they consciously forget: 'Well, as long as we *remember*, we can think of something else' (5). This apt description of emotional fracture as dubious coping mechanism in what Auden and others have dubbed the 'age of anxiety' is essential to any understanding of *Holiday*'s narrational form – and Pompey does exactly such forgetting here, though with far less self-consciousness than Celia and therefore with more harmful results to follow by her story's end.

A couple of lines from what sounds like a bad Victorian ballad shoves Pompey off, away from her opening thoughts of the gallery and into the ostensible 'conflict' that gives rise to the 'story' of this novel. But the interruptive artificiality of this secondary start reminds us that the real conflict has already been exposed, and that Pompey *is* indeed, despite her disavowal, 'dropping the curtain' of romance narrative over it as a cover which functions every bit as effectively as Grosz's great escape:

> Even manly hearts may swell
> At the moment of farewell...

How true the poet's sentiment, benign, how *noble*. And if the manly heart, what of the heart feminine, may not that swell and fail and tear and burst for the sadness of a mismanaged love-situation, that is so much at this moment the situation between my departed Freddy and myself.

Yes, no. What of the heart of Pompey that lay down to die with the tigress Flo, to decline upon her paws, to give up a life that was so hateful. See my last book, Reader, where it says about Pompey and Flo.

And coming out of this picture gallery I must think of my own situation that is so heavy upon me. And I think: I will be so sad and, Nothing shall save me. For me there shall be no curtain, no curtain at all, to come dropping dropping down, to be in this way my America, my New-found-land, my sanctuary, my salvation and escape....

And enjoying and turning upon myself in my great disturbance, à l'égard de cet ineffable Freddy, I am thinking, Now my whole life is about to end, and everything is penultimate, and all these days are penultimate, and so now what is left of my life shall be a voyage autour de ma chambre.

Oh Pompey, think and count the flowers on your wallpaper, and remember to be sad, and remember and remember. (18–19)

In a narrational move that in its complexity rivals any other produced in the Thirties, Pompey does what she expressly says she does not do, and begins to remember to forget the engine of that action. Yet it is of course present in the very words she uses to describe her particular 'curtain' – a depiction of her heart 'tearing' and 'bursting' for a 'sad situation' – all of which are extracted and transposed from her description earlier of the 'tearing, seering suffering' of Germany and the 'sad sad situation' of the war that in the earlier quote she willed herself not to think about. Though she insists she will have no such blind dropping down on her memory, and sneers at the exodus of Thirties artists to America (utilising as she does so Donne's famous lines 'To His Mistress Going to Bed', thereby once again connecting escape or diversion with illicit desire), her very theatrical decision to draw down her own interior curtain is evident. Her sentences' internal capitalisations that signal the beginnings of fragments of bathetic lines above suggest the ready-made nature of the substitute script she chooses. '[C]oming out of the picture gallery' (18), and away from her fears that 'everything is penultimate' (19), or that the world is poised on yet another terrible brink, she vows to embark on a solipsistic 'voyage' that goes no further than her bedroom; yet, in a fascinating redefinition of the public effects of such escapist interior travel, the very word 'voyage' here foreshadows her imminent travels to the German sanatorium from which her military escapades will begin. She commences taking 'tablets' that three pages later make 'peace come dropping slowly, slowly' like a curtain, 'so slowly you would not notice' (22) – and it is 'enough to keep a tiger quiet' (23). This image of course takes us back yet again to the end of *Novel*, though in this second book of the trilogy, that potentially 'tearing' figure of the tigress Flo (or 'flow'; what Conrad refers to as lack of 'restraint' (57) in its darker forms) – represents another kind of threat, poised as she will be on the frontier of war. Pompey believes that 'turning' in this way 'upon [her]self', or wallowing in her constructed romantic sadness, will be her 'salvation' and 'escape'; and she indeed 'enjoys', as she says above, such partition from the thoughts that brought her anxieties on in the book's preamble. But just as she cannot elude the words of the latter she cannot, regardless of how far inward or outward she flies, escape the consequences of such forgetting. For the rest of the book Pompey will try 'to remember and remember' to focus on surrogate lines of thought, but they of course become entangled – while all the while beneath them the unacknowledged engine of the story roars.

A page-by-page reading of the novel would reveal that engine at work in every movement of the story, but a framing of the novel's major movements will have to suffice. The first two thirds, for example, might be outlined by three of them: the weekend visit with Josephine during which, Pompey tells us, 'the great idea came to Josephine that I should go with her... to Schloss Tilssen' in Germany (21); the costume party at Harriet's to which she goes dressed as 'the bounds... of Empire' (71); and finally, activities at the Kafkaesque castle that preface her 'waking' moment and take her to the book's surprising climax as she crosses 'over the frontier'.

Showcase: Smith's own style of 'the not quite funny enough'

The weekend at Josephine's swiftly follows on from the novel's opening pages and picks up a number of their suppressed motifs. In her description of it, Pompey primarily recalls sitting at the fire and listening to 'extremely bawdy' (24) stories from Uncle Ivor, an 'old man of war'. Ivor was stationed as a soldier on the Malay Peninsula, where Britain's activities as a 'colonising animal' reached its first peak in 1909 (and where the subjugation of these Islamic peoples might be seen as further justification of Karl's accusation in *Novel*: 'You [British] scattered the bones of the Mahdi'). The translation of Ivor's experience into endless, 'funny' tales, or into forgetting through decadence, mirrors Grosz's bawdy, 'very funny' alternatives to his own darker pictures from which Pompey earlier turned away. But Pompey finds Ivor's stories somehow 'not funny enough', and falls into a deeply disturbed state which is key to our understanding of Smith's narrative style in this novel:

> There is nothing worse than the not perhaps quite funny enough. For this, Reader, is what the young man said to me when I sent him a poem. And then I felt,... [i]ndeed it is better to be serious. And I thought, In future I will just write little delicate and sad pieces that are full of unshed tears, and at the same time *noble*, and not only thinking of the funeral paths, and of the dead man lying in the grave beneath, or of the church that stands out, a darker shadow against the dark shadows of the storm-swept midnight moonless sky, but that is waiting for the chords that will come, that are coming now, in Beethoven's funeral sonata, to bear up with them on their mighty wings the spirits of the redeemed.
> But what is Uncle Ivor saying, saying sitting there in the firelight. (25)

She next becomes even more deeply irritated by Uncle Ivor's method of storytelling, which is broken by the 'pauses in the flow of the raconteur':

Ah how nervously irritating are the imminences of these pauses.... Ah it is extremely unquiet this sort of talkie, that has these pauses coming on. It is a spiritual irritation, yes, it is very disturbing to me. Oh how bored I am when people will tell these funny stories, with the expectation of a something that is to come from you when the pause comes that is to be filled. (27)

Her momentary flight from Ivor's stories into very un-Pompey-like themes of redemption in the first passage above, delivered in predictably purple prose, echoes her departure several pages earlier into the similarly described (and italicised) *'noble'* poetic strains of farewell I discussed a moment ago. The inevitable failure of such a Beethovenesque line to actually project her into that hoped-for future state is signalled in its failure above, as a sentence, to exit the present-participle tense or bring its verbal sweep back to bear upon its subject. And, once again, the insertion of capitalised script into her own sentence suggests the ready-made artificiality of the alternative text she contemplates. Smith seems to be offering here yet another form of what, in her view, constitutes artistic decadence and deflection – this time via the time-honoured genre of 'lifting up' the dead into an envisioned future cleansed of their complicity in more messy history. The texture of Smith's poems, conversely, and in accord with what Pompey reveals here about hers, is disruptive and disturbing; as we shall see in Chapter 5, Smith's poems demand 'work' from their listeners and for many they are, no doubt, 'not funny enough'. In fact they and the novels, too, are rather *like* Ivor's stories, his 'talkie' (which again calls up film, that influential new art-form, about which Smith will have more to suggest before the end of the novel). *Novel on Yellow Paper*'s subtitle, if we remember, is 'Work it out for Yourself'; it too, like Ivor's tales, relies on 'the expectation of something that is to come from you' (us, in other words; her continually summoned and bated 'Reader'). As we have by now amply seen, the formal qualities of Smith's own prose are such that it succeeds in being neither escapist *nor* 'serious' in the way of Pompey's purple passage above. Instead – and again, like Beckett's – Smith's writing ironically foregrounds the silenced desperation that comes between words, in those systolic contractions of discourse when all that is unspeakable or repressed wells up, and 'shooting oneself up' with alternative rhetoric becomes one way of averting self-destruction. Being 'not funny enough', then, seems to refer to Smith's own formal choices in this Thirties gallery of potential writing styles. It seems to describe writing that is not escapist enough to escape being porous, being shot through (rather than shot up) with chinks that reveal a sadness that is too near the bone – 'the very sad bones of that earlier situation', as Pompey put it in reference to Grosz's early work. And the discrepancy between Ivor's seemingly mild, unwitting rendition of such storytelling and the extremity of Pompey's feelings in response suggests once again the subtle connection between our narrative's cover-up of disturbance and the real engine of this novel.

Josephine, too, tries to cover up the real reasons for Pompey's subsequently noticeable and monstrous, 'stormy' sadness by 'projecting...upon [Pompey's] vision' in her 'strong and forceful' way the suggestion that it is all really about Freddy (28). Although Pompey swiftly takes up this escape, as she did in the previous pages (and as she also will in agreeing to take recuperative time in the German sanatorium, or *schloss*), we hear quite readily now what is actually going on:

> It is not my life at all from the inside, but a Life of Pompey that we are for the moment looking at together. And it is for us both from the outside sad, in the way that the lives of Maurice Baring's ladies are often so sad, for the sake of making the pattern that will please and satisfy the desire of their creator – and to hell with the reader.
>
> But in the real sadness of désespoir there is a rushing tearing quality of unquietness that drives to death.... Each one [of my darling friends] has patched up for herself a peace and an integrity where they can be quiet. They have put up this tent in their wilderness. They are not altogether happy but only so much so as they have made for themselves this tent of quietness.... And for me it is still something that I must find, must come at or die. (27–29)

Smith suggests with her (not Pompey's) criticisms that much art and writing 'degenerates' into acts of forgetting real sadness in order to construct aesthetically pleasing substitutes, and in order to produce this salve for 'the creator' – 'to hell with the reader' or viewer. (She does so with a sideways swipe at Baring, one of G.K. Chesterton's crowd.) Josephine, whose time with our speaker is imaged in 'temperate hairbrushing confidences' which Pompey associates with '1910', or pre-war women, whose only thought was for love and its pleasures and pains (22), 'has created her picture of Pompey' that reduces her complex 'unquietness' to 'this pure element of sadness that is quiet and touching and in its quality eternal' (28). Pompey momentarily engages with her in this violence done to her own complicated self, as Josephine – representing yet another kind of artist in the gallery, or picture-maker – converts any disturbance she witnesses into an artwork that will comfortably fit in her own 'quiet tent' (an image that suggests both ephemerality and militancy). But Smith our author, as opposed to Pompey our narrator, will point up the traumatic origins of such painterly/writerly desire, and call it to account by making her own 'Life of Pompey' in this book one which exposes the latter's *real* unquietness, rather than the 'pure', pacific Victorian portrait of femininity that Josephine paints. In sum, these early passages explain by *not* explaining 'why this book is set to anger and disturbance' (29), at the same time that they critique certain simplistic, self-serving modes – nostalgic *or* avant-garde – in art.[25] Given Smith's apparent desire to explicate a very current and complex psycho-social, politico-cultural phenomenon that is suppressed but very much at work in the head of our narrator, the specific reasons for Pompey's 'sadness' or pain, which she refers to as a 'world pain' (113), can only be slowly and 'blurrily' exposed,[26] unspeakable as they are.

Pompey's pre-war thought-world: the costume party

Yet the reasons for Pompey's pain do become much more evident between pages 42 and 79 – the pages that encompass Harriet's party and, in microcosm, the cultural thought-world that surrounds Pompey before her sojourn at Schloss Tilssen. These 'thoughts that have so many behind them' are imaged at the start of this sequence as a tempestuous sea, its waves rolling in at her (perhaps in part as an allusion to the radio), 'crested and predatory', 'slithering up the beach of consciousness' (44). Still deeply involved in the problem of how to make art in her time, and having just contemplated, as the party starts, the idea that a writer must surely write by being receptive to her own thoughts, Pompey suddenly negates that notion by suggesting that one's thoughts are not one's own. If one pursues this 'clever idea' of opening the door to one's own thoughts, she suddenly thinks (weeping as she does so in order to demonstrate that her pain is *here*, and not in her 'sad' Freddy story),

> all these ideas that have by this time got so upstage and unruly, they will come rushing in at you from the outside-of. And heaven must help you in that last situation, for all else is up with you then, and you will have put yourself under a tyranny that will make Hitler look like the lady-companion that advertises in the Church Times for her keep, her bed-oh, with five shillings a week pocket-money, Catholic Privileges and Indoor Sanitation. (44)

Indeed, the figure who will give Pompey information and orders at the *schloss*, as she prepares for war, is by outward appearance an unassuming, pure and gentle, upright lady, just like this one. It would seem that for Smith, as for Woolf, Hitler is both an historical figure and, far worse, a state of mind. Hitler becomes the 'Hitler within' in this passage, the 'sick cat' poised on the cradle of our baby-on-the-flood narrator carried over from *Novel*. Much of what follows the above passage will comprise an attempt to avoid such predatory thoughts, as she does here – vowing to 'keep my thoughts from the thoughts' (43) – even though it seems an impossible task, as impossible as finding the 'right' form or line for writing and artwork to take in her times, as her critique of every alternative she knew suggests in the course of the novel.

Again like Woolf, and perhaps in homage to the latter's novel *Mrs Dalloway*, Smith stages a much larger and complex 'story' through her all-but comical focus on a seemingly frivolous event: a party. The effect is that the weight of that larger story bears heavily down upon our actors in the scene – so hard that once again, Pompey suppresses much of what is happening and what we need to know. This is perhaps why, in Smith's novel about forgetting, it takes nearly thirty pages or almost all of the party sequence's thoughts and events for Pompey to remember to tell us that it was a 'fancy-dress' party and that she came costumed to represent, quite significantly, the 'bounds of Empire':

> I am sitting on the floor fanning myself with my solar topee. Your *solar topee*, no really Pompey, this is the last straw. Neither the last nor the penultimate straw, Reader, did I not say that this party of Harriet's that went on and was and is this party in St John's Wood, is a fancy dress party and I am dressed in khaki shorts and shirt, solar topee and sandals and representing the bounds – limit to you, of Empire? If I did not say this it is because I forgot. O.K. – that is a fault.
> 'We have been looking for you everywhere,' screams Reggie.... (71)

Her jokey revelation – perhaps not funny enough? – is followed by another made via juxtaposition, a favourite strategy of Smith's. As Reggie comes 'looking for [her – i.e. Empire] everywhere', he inadvertently suggests, once again, that her idealised 'home' is only a nostalgic construction, a 'state' of mind, and nowhere to be found in the novel except in the 'representing' thoughts of our decadent narrator. Yet she cannot help but represent the national image whose captions formed her very thoughts, however much she may forget that she is 'in costume' – a corollary to her later suddenly discovering that she has always been 'in uniform'. It seems hardly surprising that this second novel in the trilogy abounds with *Heart of Darkness* imagery and language – far more than in *Novel*, as I suggested in Chapter 3; like Marlow and Kurtz, Pompey becomes more and more clearly a figure for the dream, the thought of Empire stretched to its very 'limit', as she confesses it to be – though she confesses it only 'to us', her Reader. As a figure of Empire, she will stretch her dreaming to the 'frontier' beyond which she like Kurtz gets a glimpse of her own flip side reality, beset as it has been all along 'by abominable terrors, by abominable satisfactions' (Conrad 88). The fact that she can be 'abominable', or even the 'abomination' itself that Marlow continually fears in Conrad's novel, is made plentifully evident in the ubiquitous appearance of that word in her self-descriptions and in thoughts that pertain to her. The above passage's revelations qualify the noticeable repetitions of the word's use in her many references to herself in preceding pages as being 'abominable' for her treatment of Freddy and other people (30, 32, 33, 41, 47); they also gloss her 'abominable' riding style about to be described (83), and other abominations such as the 'abominably necessary discrediting of Casement' which I reproduced in the earlier quote. The continued use of the word and its inflections constitutes nothing less than a poetic refrain, drawing us sonically back to Conrad endlessly and throughout the novel.

Here at this freakishly warm Christmas party – which seems to be a chain-like event travelling from one house to another, and indeed which seems to *still* be going on in present time, given the syntax of the above passage – everyone is, à la Auden, in their own ways symbolically ill. Moreover, all of them seem stuck in the same figurative space as her friend Stephen, who is unable 'to move away from the fire that is making him sick' (47). In other words, each is drawn like a moth to the deadly flame, the various 'diseases' – like 'dictators' – that Smith suggests will undo them in the end. The dance scene that follows recalls a story told to Pompey near the end of *Novel*, in which the 'awful' 'undirected energy' of 'Old Girls' over fifty seems to have an effect poetically analogous to that of the 'Old Men of 1922' from Grosz's *Post-War Museum* who continue to haunt Pompey's consciousness. These old women are also filled with an inner emptiness carved out by 'a canker eating away' at them, which forces them into likewise forcing the young – the 'old-young' as it was phrased by Pompey in the gallery – into 'febrile' dance with them that is 'so feverish... it has to be unhappy' (214). Such dancing, like its twin metaphor of riding, embodies impulses towards both violence and escapism, and the imperative to 'run away' from it all, to 'take [oneself] out of [one]self' and the entrapments of one's 'parental', cultural text. Here, Pompey prefaces the dreamlike dance that becomes the focal point of this long party segment by suggesting that the 'curiously hot and steamy atmosphere' is too much to bear, is

> so enervating to the body, so over-stimulating to the mind, and to the nerves and the thoughts, that keep such uneasy dance within the mind, the thoughts that go helter-pelter, shattering and scattering the peace of God that passeth all understanding, that never shall I come to know again, this outcast and abominable Pompey. (47)

Expanding on her only slightly tongue-in-cheek theme of biblical falling – initiated in the opening pages with the precarious rider in Grosz's picture and here extended by allusion to her postlapserian state – our speaker will next connect it with the bombs she fears will fall or drop into their eerie late-Thirties lull-before-the-storm. Links are also obviously made here between earlier references to the 'curtain' of forgetting and imminent destruction, the 'thunder stone to come dropping down' – 'dropping in silence and immensity from the sultry Christmas skies... where all is storm and confusion, disaster and malice and a false imagining' (48). Drawing the actual bombs-to-come into an imagistic continuum with pre-war discourse and its projections, appeasements and denials, Smith both historicises and demystifies mid-century violence, I would argue, despite the fact that the overlay of Christian mythology would seem to suggest her ahistorical apprehension of primordial human 'evil' afoot again, as some critics have contended.[27] Her interest is rather in '[t]his cruelty [that] is very much in the air now'; 'it is very dangerous, it is a powerful drug that deadens as it stimulates' the desire to view the effects of violence – whether it be 'photographs of atrocities' or of 'negro-baiting across the Atlantic' and more, as we shall see (58).

Though Harriet assures her that 'nothing' is the matter, and that she is at Pompey's side in this drug-induced, surreal scene, she suddenly 'vanish[es]', merging what our speaker thought of as her comforting substantiality with the 'false imagining' that incurs disaster. Such surprises in the narration allow Smith to equate, as she does in semi-surreal existentialist fashion throughout the novel, dream world and material history. Pompey, in her haze of liquor and drugs ('luminol and chloroform and valerian'), offers the flip side of the usual waking thought that 'life can be a nightmare' in a dream-recognition familiar to us all: 'It was a moment for a dream to think, We are all here, it is all right' (23). Such self-assurances are misleading in both waking and sleeping dreams, Smith seems to suggest. Indeed, the next scene of Pompey's dancing in a dream-state – as dream-incarnation of that 'uneasy dance within the mind' that all at the party are *really* experiencing – will recur in 'real life' at the end of the novel. There, in her last scene in her civvies, we will again find her dancing wildly and explicitly 'running mad' (210) with Josephine during an evening at the *schloss*; such dancing culminates in her being whisked away to war by Major Tom Satterthwaite, her alter-ego (and yet another Great War 'Tommie'), who has been waiting in the wings 'with so much an expression of violence hardly to be restrained' (213). In other words, this early scene with (or rather, without) Harriet hauntingly sets that later 'stage' or war theatre, Pompey's 'galere' – so that when we reach it we remember the falling that will, with deep irony, be interwoven with her later and only seeming *rise* to power:

> There is something of an acute pain of cruelty in this, to think for the moment it is certainly all very slap-up and o.k. There is no one there at all. I run through the immense, the enormous room, there is no one there at all. But there is the idea of laughter running after and before me. So there is music too....
>
> Oh now this is lovely, this is very swift and exhilarating. So I dance, faster and faster. And now faster again, with long wrenching outward movements, the long wrenching outward movements you have when you are under the anaesthetic, under the anaesthetic. And you dance and dance, with an intensity of concentration, an exaltation, an exhilaration of the spirit, and at centre a heart of darkness, of darkness and désespoir.

But the music grows faster, more slave-driving, more compelling. There is no rest, no pause. There are so many evolutions to be performed, evolutions, revolutions, and so little time. (49)

These rapid movements of evolving (in the Latin, to roll out) and *re*volving (to re-roll, circle) both imply a centre – though that centre in this novel is, as in *Heart of Darkness*, simply 'hollow[ness] at the core' (Conrad 74). In accord with Smith's political vision, the two seemingly opposed options of conservative evolving and radical revolution here are identified as movements that *both* merely circle round an always already informing (and unspeakable because unacknowledged) 'horror' at the centre; revolutions bring nothing new, in other words, just more dream repetitions of the repressed. Starring in them all is what Pompey continually describes as 'the raffish black and hateful demon that runs alongside' (28) – the force that is at the heart of both 'running mad' and this cruel running laughter (the same 'cynical laughter' that she heard echoing in the picture halls full of Grosz's American-phase drawings), the force that powers the unowned 'secret life' of both individuals and governments, the force that is always present because never exorcised. And yet to pause, to stop the runnings-on of language – whether it be Ivor's stories or the rhetoric of current incitements to revolution – is to suddenly and terminally see, as Kurtz saw it, the desirous, ravenous emptiness at the core of all that only-seeming, discursive reality: 'no one there at all'. That these dream-like passages will in a very real way inform the surreal but actual deeds of our speaker at the end of the novel is, in formal terms, the meaning of the narrative such as we have it. Smith's updated image of the volatility of Eliot's anaesthetised, Prufrockian generation, and her inversion of the usual poles of thought and action, suggest both her debt to current psychological models *and*, as I will suggest in a moment, her cynicism about the ways they were being deployed as revolutionary political tools in the Thirties by figures like Auden, Upward and Bréton.

The passages that follow the dance scene delve once again into artistic responses to violent times, and they take everyone to task – not just those Smith would consider the deluded visionaries. These passages seem to stem from Pompey's thoughts about the 'acute pain of cruelty' that she locates in Harriet's assurances above that all is 'very slap-up and o.k.'. This odd indictment seems to refer us not only to the obvious: to the cruelty of lies, to what Marlow called the 'taint of death', the 'flavour of mortality in lies' such as the one he will tell Kurtz's 'Intended': that her dreams of her fiancé's goodness and fidelity are real and true, following which Marlow fears, like Pompey, that 'the heavens would fall upon [his] head' (Conrad 42, 94). The indictment also references Pompey's ongoing contemplation of the effects of exposing as opposed to engaging in cruelty in art. She will tell us in this segment's long dissertation on various ways of 'lying' or evasion in writing that there are two extremes when it comes to the latter: (1) melodrama, examples of which include trends like Audenesque 'schoolboy melodrama' and 'the melodrama of the good white man bearing the white man's burden' (59), and (2) books like the one she sees a man surreptitiously reading in a railway carriage, *The Pleasures of the Torture Chamber* (55). The first 'cover[s] up and conceal[s] the bare bones that will not live again...and forget[s]' (60); the second, composed by a sensibility on the flip side, 'make[s] a lot of money writing about pain' (52) in a time when, as Pompey describes it (in what might double as an introduction to the Baudrillardian postmodern age),[28] many in an enervated populace have gone 'dumb-cluck on the sentient plane', their 'very high flash point' requiring those 'photographs of atrocities by Abyssinians' or 'negro-baiting across the Atlantic' (56). Pompey radically differentiates such cruel exploitation of an anaesthetised public from the cruelty of the 'éclaircissement' delivered through disturbing work like that of the early Grosz. The former sort is that sort that 'is very dangerous, it is a powerful drug that deadens as it stimulates' (58). It allows, in a very surreal sense, for the erection of the castle itself (erotic pun intended): an encasement that replaces sanity and tranquillity with full-scale illusion set in the heart of violence and darkness. Therefore her own stimulation into dancing by her drugs – 'under the anaesthetic' as she puts it above – not only reveals such propensities in her as well but suggests its *simultaneity* with her fate of running mad into war, where she has been all along, and where she will think how strange it is that she has 'no tears, no sadness and no joy' (245), is emotionally dead. Her dancing to the music of that 'idea of laughter running after and before [her]', which is presented as a conceptual choice that obviates pain, again reminds us of the 'cynical laughter' of Grosz's decadent sketches that went 'echoing round the picture galleries of London and New York' (17). It also recalls the cruel Dionysian laughter from *Novel*, which was similarly 'tearing' in its cynical, lion-like form, though here both substitute for the 'tearing, seering' recognitions made available in Grosz's earlier work and allow for worrying re-enactment, in newly destructive terms, of that repressed trauma. Such response becomes further linked to the dangerous release of inhibitions and need for stimulants that Smith suggests result in an appetite *not* for remembering, as one might with the aid of socially constructive 'cruelty that *is* art' (my emphasis) such as she finds in the earlier Grosz, and in Goya, but rather for forgetting by way of 'the cruelty that is *feelthy pictures*' (68) – a turn of phrase that collates voyeurism and violence, escapist desire and deadly pursuits.[29]

The choice of delinquency – and the lure of the *schloss*

It will not surprise us, then, that Pompey's lures into war will include sexual excitement and violence, both of them welcome distractions from the interrogating bare lights of the *schloss* in which she next finds herself. As we know, our speaker will do anything to avoid looking upon either 'the black heart of despair of the situation' (18) or 'this outcast and abominable Pompey'. Both she and her alter-ego, the mysterious and attractive Major Tom Satterthwaite, hate the light – they even 'fear' it (145) – and Pompey, in abandoning it to ride out into the darkness with him, returns again to the language she used to describe Grosz's 'enlightenment' in *A Post-War Museum*. She does so inadvertently and, ironically, through assertion of what she wishes *not* to do. When she claims that she hopes 'to resist all knowledge that might, however eventually, turn upon an explanation, and that again upon an *éclaircissement*, to... bring [her] back again to a life that is to [her] so profoundly so entirely unnecessary' (222), we inevitably recall and envision 'the power of the cruelty' as I quoted it earlier, in Grosz's 'éclaircissement' (17). She will elect, instead, to be *evasively* cruel in art, within her own text and through sudden suppression of her own knowledge. Therefore the break or awkward 'shift' in the novel that I described above must of course begin with her translation of the last seemingly desperate prayer she makes out 'of pain for the stain of the evil twined round the heart' into a funny picture, as well as with her mirroring quotation of the line repeated by the art dealer in the novel's first pages: 'Very witty this painter, is he not?' (12, 17 (with variations); 162, 163).[30] But the *dénouement* of this novel will be more cruel and violent than witty or funny; it will also be 'melodramatic' (175), as Pompey herself refers to it, as well as surreal and sexually charged and in accord with other Thirties strategies that were in Smith's view very dangerously accumulating an audience, be they never so beleaguered into self-awareness as her own.

We approach the period in Schloss Tilssen with the dawning realisation that, as the 'Tilssen-Germany idea that is already looming rather large' pervades Pompey's consciousness just after the party, 'already [she is] forgetting' (84) the life at work and at home that the next thirty pages or so will give us before she sets off. These are the pages that are full of references to Dryasdust and Belloc and Pater, Hoare and Casement and Kipling and others whose topical or subconscious influence on her thoughts I sketched out very briefly above. She also reintroduces us in this section to thoughts of her 'Auntie Lion', or 'Lion Aunt' from *Novel on Yellow Paper*, whom we remember as her emblematically British mother-substitute. In this second novel of the trilogy Pompey's personal Lion becomes more implicated in her cultural text, producing reading materials such as the *Blue Book on India* and military memoirs on 'Ethical imperialism' (95, 102) – reminiscent of Kurtz's 'report' for the society for the 'Suppression of Savage Customs'[31] – which Pompey borrows and quite symbolically 'loses', mentally burying them along with *The Relief of Chitral* which she tells us she once and forever left in a rabbit hole to protect it from the rain.[32] And yet she begins to mouth the platitudes of all these texts in alarming ways, illustrating how such burial or forgetting leads to subliminal incorporation. We watch the process happen, as readers, if we allow all of these bits of experiential and ruminative flotsam to settle and incubate in our minds (as they do in Pompey's) on our approach to the novel's turn.

Even the early, seemingly digressive passages on her Aunt Lion's loving rule over the garden's birds and 'marauding' cats will prove preparatory for interpreting Pompey's earliest cat-like movements in the *schloss*. When we find that she goes hunting, 'pad, pad' (139), in the middle of the night, the 'unchristian hour' (141), for a bit of 'nocturnal marauding' (139) in the form of a raid on the *schloss*'s pantry – 'nervous as a cat, as a young cat that is about to be sucked up the chimney by a puff of draught from under the door' (140) – and meets instead, for the first time, that feared 'draught' in the form of her corrupter-and-lover-to-be, Tom, it is difficult not to remember the earlier parable of her Aunt's well-policed garden whose biblical sparrows are shadowed by raiding relatives of her own 'Lion' species:

> But now the great black cat is upon the fence, tensed to spring, ... Away most unsympathetic of animals, away marauder.
> I run out into the garden, shouting as I run.... He can do nothing but slink away, landing with soft thud upon our neighbour's garden bed. There falling in with low company, his own companions of the midnight hour, he can for the moment absorb himself with their delinquent antics, birdless and breakfastless upon the call of love. (116)

With yet another of her inimitably obvious-and-yet-complexly poetic phrasal repetitions, Smith draws our attention through this passage all the way back to the opening of the novel, to the story of the man drunk on Schnaps 'falling victim to a horrible whore' after his attempt to fulfil his desires with the help of the wrong object – in his case, the plasteret Venus. Here at the *schloss*, in the midnight hour, Pompey also falls into low company due to her more complicated form of 'delinquency'. She has just confessed that she hates the bright light of the *schloss*, where she sees herself as some sort of 'monstrum horrendum informe ingens cui lumen ademptum' (138), associating herself through this famous Virgilian quote with that misshapen monster from the *Aeneid* 'whose only eye had been put out', given her own desire to 'resist all knowledge...and...*éclairecissement*' (222).[33] It seems that Pompey's progress through the first two novels of the trilogy takes her from being the baby on the flood of *Novel on Yellow Paper*'s prophetic dreams to becoming the predatory 'sick cat' balanced on its careering cradle, the 'black' threat to *herself* in edenic gardens.

Yet in the same way that the novel keeps sweeping back in wide 'parabolas' to its initial images, each time 'swooping back on a long homeward flight' (145) to collapse people and happenings in the *schloss* with those in London, such developments in Pompey prove to be no more than articulations of what was always already latent in her character from her story's outset. Therefore the greatest of Pompey's faults is shown to be her lack of self-knowledge; her forgetting of what she does know, it seems, is to blame for her fate. Nowhere is this made more clear than in the fact that Tom from the very outset is presented to us a product of her *own* consciousness – and indeed, in keeping with the project of rethinking the relations between dream and reality, Tom is first discovered as the usurper of *her* role in the dream that woke her just before the above nocturnal expedition. In this mid-novel dream, *she* is the figure 'sitting at night-time in a dark room...at the table... lighted by one candle...turning over papers, so many papers' (134). She tells us further that in the dream '[she] has a shade over her eyes' and is in uniform, though it is meant to be a secret, by order of 'some higher command', and in her mind the reasons for it are as yet 'not perfectly assimilated' (135). When, seven pages later, she discovers Tom sitting in the middle of the night in the light of a candle, she asks herself: 'But why do you sit in the light of a candle at this little table, writing, writing, my sweet Tom?', turning the cadence of her question into a balladic line as the text exceeds narrative and makes its poetic, dreamlike connections. The next lines are fascinating in their pronominal and syntactic ambiguity, for she then thinks:

> That thought must certainly have crossed my mind if not my lips, but then he says, I remember how at once it is something we have in common, how much he hates the hard light that shines down from the electric light bulbs. (141)

Such ambiguity is the only indication of what the half-thought following her question suggests she knows at a subterranean level but cannot acknowledge: that Tom is the alter-image of herself in her bad dream, and that he therefore is also (as we shall soon confirm) 'secretly in uniform'. The uncanny likeness of their thoughts, the fact that Tom refers to childhood memories that Pompey never told him about (of her parrot Joey, for example; 166), and a myriad other terrifying/comic details also confirm his identification with Pompey. In other words, our speaker is herself not only the drunken idealist reaching for his Venus *and* the 'horrible whore' of the earlier parable, but *also* 'the man that stood there in uniform' to throw the delinquent into the arms of his fate. In her all merge, the accuser and the accused, demonstrating that within mid-century selves as Smith viewed them the line between heroine and enemy was as unnoticeable as the 'ditch' that Tom will have to point out to her as the boundary crossed when they both ride, finally, 'over the frontier' (225).

'And on whose side are you?'

Tom is a British officer (169), which should be a straightforward identification, but he like Pompey and every character at the *schloss* has a flip side and a 'secret life', like the dark secret life Pompey confessed to harbouring while living with her Aunt in *Novel on Yellow Paper*. In this novel's expansion on the volatility of secret thoughts flowing in sanctioned and barely veiled ways beneath social 'codes', the difficulty becomes one of knowing the answer to what Freddy asks her in her dream: 'From whom is your commission?' (135). The question is asked of all the major players in the second half of the novel, even the 'very pretty old lady' Mrs Pouncer (another cat), a seemingly innocuous *schloss* sojourner who proves to be, under her dignified whiteness and delicate hands, with their mark of aristocracy in 'ancestral ruby upon ancestral setting', a main plotter and military organiser who will at a critical juncture give Pompey her orders. And yet upon finding her engaged in creating backwards-read code on the *schloss* desks' blotting paper, Tom admits to Pompey that he knows 'she's in it, my dear, she is very decidedly in it, but on which side, on which side?' (182). Pompey does not ask, as we do, what 'it' is; she seems to partly know, though we as readers feel much as we would in Kafka's *The Castle*: that an abstracted *They*, a figure of shadowy cultural hegemony, has cognisance and creates the constraints (*OTF* 143, 185–86) but only through the complicity of the individual. Here in *Over the Frontier*, it seems that the 'sides' to be taken are nearly and frighteningly interchangeable – or two sides of, once again, *Alice in Wonderland*'s looking glass. Thus Pompey, when deciphering the Pouncer's code, holds the blotting paper up to the mirror and tells us that her backwards writing – 'Issue of troops to blankets' – 'is now clearly to be read in my looking glass world' (181). The full extension of the potent fear Pompey felt in *Novel* – that she, like Alice, might *be* Mabel, another replicant cog in the wheel of her culture – is coming into sight here, since Pompey's revelation of herself as being not only *like* Tom but even more deeply enlisted than Tom is just around the corner. And although Pompey says she does not know (or cannot consciously acknowledge) whose ultimate, 'high command' she answers to until the very end of the novel, the final sections do offer clues as to which way she has been 'falling' all along.

This crucial moment that seems to give rise to Pompey's being tipped over the edge – the 'frontier' – of her own internal as well as external boundaries begins with her baiting of Josephine at a moment that, again, seems almost comically inconsequential: as they both take tea. In their company is the supposedly absent-minded old Colonel Peck, another fellow resident of the *schloss* who, like Pouncer, turns out to be an under-cover agent of war. Josephine, who has just been praising the running of Italian trains, newly improved under Mussolini, suddenly takes the more politically correct stance against the dictator's doings in Abyssinia. Pompey, irritated by this predictable attitudinal discrepancy of the British, sets out to 'be so annoying' to Josephine by turning her risibly typical focus on the efficiency of the rails into a Conradian trope for the rhetorical cover-up of cultural atrocities, and by speaking perhaps the most astonishing pro-fascist speech we will hear her make. Smith seems to present this speech as the logical extension of such dangerously unexamined discrepancies, as well as of (her own?) mixed nationalistic responses to the damning connections between British interests and those of Italy:

> But do not be so cross with Mussolini because certainly it is through him and through this African adventure of his that has for him had a successful outcome, it is through this that we without one stroke of war now have Egypt again within our hands... and no offence, no offence to anyone at all, that this grand piece of arrangement has made us again the master of Egypt and thrown into our hands all that convenient coast-line as well as the vast hinterland that runs up again, it is so convenient, to the ultimate last outpost of lower Egypt, with the Nile for our river and the whole vast darkness of middle Africa to link up maybe with our East African dependencies – oh so charming is this word dependency, how fascinating I find it. And by running ever southwards and downwards you will come to the Cape which was another oh so good arrangement though we are only so sorry that here we blundered a little to have something so crude as a war.... But there has been this Turkish arrangement and this Egyptian arrangement and if Mussolini in his Roman fury but little of Roman policy has accomplished this for us, and for himself but a patch of infertile and unquiet territory, have we so much to be annoyed about? Why, I think we should be very grateful to him, yes I think we should say Thankyou Mussolini. (155–56)

Immediately following this remarkable and blackly comic description of what, in sour keeping with Josephine's expression of admiration for an efficient train system, sounds like a travelogue through newly occupied territories in the 'vast darkness' (or heart of darkness) of Africa, Colonel Peck, who has uncharacteristically been 'listening with a quiet smile' and looking like 'the British Lion himself he is so sleek', suddenly asks Pompey: 'And on whose side are you?' (157). For the first time in the trilogy, Pompey finds herself, with this question, called to answer for her *only seeming* use of 'devil's advocacy'. And indeed, as we shall see, Smith deploys biblical language near the end of the novel to suggest that the devil is exactly what Pompey is capable of becoming. Quite uncomfortably here, Pompey begins to admit that she is on the side of her friends, her tribe, and not 'principle'; and that, for example, the Irish situation had her sympathy *in principle* but ultimately she could not side with 'them' in their supposed 'hysteria and malice'. 'And the Jews?' says Colonel Peck. Not wishing 'to be drawn' on that topic, Pompey at first recoils and then admits:

> I am in despair for the racial hatred that is running in me in a sudden swift current, in a swift tide of hatred, and Out out damned tooth, damned aching tooth, rotten to the root.
> Do we not always hate the persecuted? (158)

With the exhaustion of her delaying protestations that 'I have had some very dear Jewish friends', Pompey admits again that such answers are almost laughably stereotypical, the 'final treachery of the smug goy. Do not all our persecutions of Israel follow upon this smiling sentence?'[34] When the interrogation has cowed her, and all 'the virtue has gone out of her', she admits that she would not fight on the side of the Jews, no matter the extent to which she finds, as Tom puts it, 'in theory and mercy justifiable their cause'. As Phyllis Lassner quite exactly puts it in her similar reading of this passage, 'she sacrifices the anti-pathetic Other to the very history in which she colludes as writer and as actor' (143). Pompey's responses here ultimately mirror those of the race-loyal German, despite her Lady Macbeth-like attempt to cleanse herself of the blood her own teeth, British to 'the root', have tasted in celebration of her nation's aggrandisement. The 'no offence' above echoes from other passages in the novel where evasive conversational games facilitated graceful cover-ups for secret cultural prejudices 'running along' uncontrollably underneath; the latter become largely responsible, at every level, for building the flip side personalities that Smith explores with some urgency in this 1938 novel. In a sense, all of *Over the Frontier* might be seen as Smith's exploration of how individuals or whole nations could be so easily flipped over to reveal strong foundations for 'abominable' ways of thinking – ways that reflect the good of one's self and one's own, not the good of others which, she feared, however fine 'in principle', rarely serves as cause for war.

The exposure of her underlying allegiances casts Pompey into the dark night of the soul that precedes her getting 'shot up' again, awakening to her new/old incarnation as military player. Indeed, at her apotheosis as such, Tom will identify her as 'Pompey die Grosse', the emergence of all that has been latent in her very name from the outset of the trilogy (228). Until that moment, their wild rides away from the *schloss* together – the descendants of the rides on hobby-horses, or discursive riffs, that she took in *Novel on Yellow Paper*, the ones that 'took a girl out of herself'– have kept her from what we know are those chaotic, incoming waves of thoughts. But we as readers are aware that at the heart of what she flees is her general sense of 'world pain' and, far worse, her apprehension of *herself* as the very 'monstrum' (as we learned above) of her dreams:

> But these rides with Tom are a very great happiness for me and already I have not for a long time had one soppy thought of strain and turmoil and O Life, Life, and monster of my dreams, and Oh horror of fear and of thought coming upon thought from some far place that is not, is not heaven. (146)

With Tom on these rides she says she enjoys 'unconscious happiness' (147), but we are also told that 'beneath his rather inane talky-talk' – another reminder of inter-war film and its distracting and/or propagandistic uses – Tom has been slowly feeding into her mind 'something to do with gun emplacements' (149). Though her first response – 'this sort of thing...is rather Greek to me' – echoes Casca's in, again, *Julius Caesar*, she will upon awakening realise that she had indeed been assimilating it all.[35] She suddenly recalls, for example, the exact names upon the old guns at the fort (apparently a destination on some of their riding trips), as well as the trips to her 'un-Christian friend', 'old Aaronsen', a Jewish 'share-pusher', from whom she has purchased shares in nitrates both for the makers of those guns and for herself. All at once she and Tom think as one and seem to share such memories: 'He echoes my own thoughts' (167). And indeed, in the ensuing pages it becomes difficult for Pompey to know whether it was Tom who has been talking or whether it was *she* who has 'been talking for hours, for hours' (173).

At first it might seem that stereotypes are used or abused to depict the influences that sway Pompey. The old 'share-pusher' Aaronsen, for example, is made even more emblematic by being called 'Aaron' by Pompey (203) so that he as 'Aaron's son' becomes the namesake of Moses's brother and Judaism's first high priest, as though all of Jewish history were gathered up in his enterprising figure. He even tells Pompey that '[his] nose makes [him] have to admire [her]' for the hard bargains she drives (203). Certainly Smith was guilty of reproducing the same familiar and racist figures of avarice that she critiqued others for producing – Chesterton's 'Dr Gluck' comes to mind, for example, from the pages of *New Witness*.[36] But it is also true that Smith has been steadily deconstructing such stereotypes as well as 'good' v. 'bad' frontiers in the trilogy, so that by this point in the second novel even seemingly unequivocal condemnations of character – like the adjective 'un-Christian' for old Aaronsen – ring very thinly, and indeed lose their meaning altogether. For we as readers remember the equally enterprising behaviour of the 'Christian' church in *Novel*, and are only too aware of the genocidal Christian monsters at work in the background of *Frontier*, where Jews are to be sided with or, in Pompey's case, *not* sided with. As if to combat this simplistic view of how subjects function in culture, Smith's Pompey asserts that Aaronsen is the 'only really intelligent person' she has met since leaving London because he is 'many-sided' (203) – a fractured character gracefully surviving or surfing the dangerous waves of thoughts coming from within and without that Pompey also rides, if far less capably. Indeed, she depicts him more warmly than anyone else in the novel, perhaps because as a character he seems to understand almost intolerably well the edges of discourse that form and cut him at every turn. Such figures seem helplessly made-to-order by culture rather than essentialised. But Smith updates Conrad's revision of the archetypal in *Heart of Darkness* – his 'manager' of the Inner Station, for example, named 'Mephistopheles' by Marlow, who sees him as a 'papier-mâché' figure with no insides, just a place to fill within a coded system of power relations determined by corporate greed in cahoots with unspeakable histories of national enterprise – with comic, common awareness of what tragic Kurtz called 'the horror' and what Auden, like Smith, found only 'not quite funny enough': the growing appearance of the 'public face in private places', the movement 'beyond the frontier of a separate life' (267).[37]

Also like Auden *et al*. Smith seems to explain such phenomena through a *très*-Thirties indictment of conspiratorial 'capitalismus' (which her speaker would not, however, exchange for Marxist 'idealismus', as is made clear in the quote below as she dismisses 'Monsieur Karl', the pan-Europeanised Marx). In a passage that draws all of Pompey's experience, from her secretarial handling of stocks for her boss in *Novel* through to her training for underground war work in *Frontier*, our speaker demonstrates herself and every stratum of culture to be engaged in speeding the same disastrous ends as the result of being 'code-minded', or trained subliminally by the politico-economic language of the times that underwrites discourse in her everyday life in London. In the episode in which she and Tom linger in a stairway, listening as Pouncer scratches her backwards-writing across the blotting paper, Pompey very tellingly explains her sudden thrill at the idea that the old woman might be writing in code:

> But I am naturally code-minded, dear Reader, for all of that that I have to do with the dear and distant baronet, in my office in London.... For secrecy in many communications of financial importance is so necessary, and native clerks in mining areas are not above a price that is not above the worth-while sturdy consideration of an oh-so-practical fellow-magnate. When shares are to be held or sold or pooled or halved and when rumour is strong upon the wing, secrecy is of paramount importance, and when So-and-So will bring himself to be such an obstinate and unaccommodating idiot, oh there is no end to it all. For remember, my chicks, capitalism is not only wrong, it is also very difficult.
>
> Very difficult and exasperating indeed is this capitalismus toil that has in it all of the exasperating deviations and incalculabilities of the human factor, that goes to make it in its practical every-day application so much so very much more difficult and exasperating than the simple straightforwardness of the abstractions upon a theme that is all that there is of all that there is of Monsieur Karl.
>
> For in the *practique* of capitalismus indeed there is so very much of this exasperation and so-human incalculability that grates upon tempers and leads to the association of incongruous personalities with nothing to link them together but that famous Board Room table where baronet and lord, Empire-Blue-Eyes and Israel, come to have so much of agacement in the pursuit of dividends. (175–76)

In this early expression of fear about the rise of a complexly coded global economy, and of corporate/financial rather than 'inter-national' relations, Pompey makes clear why it is so hard to know 'whose side' one is on. The 'lion' sits down with 'the persecuted' in this newly-fabled, mock-apocalyptic Board Room scenario, all in the name of money; the toil of making accommodations on a day-to-day basis in capitalistic terms – meeting supply and demand pressures, as my earlier quote explained it – erodes differences and principles, although such dissolving lines must be kept 'secret'. Even old ladies like Pouncer enter the game, and are indeed central to it. As we find on the next page, their 'lack of previous business experience' and their 'so-naïve' thrill in 'supporting any venture provided it has to do with something that is *getting rather dangerous*' makes them the perfect investors/conspirators, particularly because they can be duped and divided from their dividends in the end. Following this line with 'Do you see?' (177), Smith connects them to Marlow's prompting aunt in the opening pages of *Heart of Darkness*. Yet whom exactly does one *now* serve? Or rather, how many? The share-pushing that Pompey engages in 'go[es] through Morgenbaum of New York, but the ultimate payees... are Birdie, Birdie, Strand and Dolland', the makers of the guns at the fort, at an address that she tells her readers 'is rather nearer our homes, yours and mine' (201). Pompey is indeed working for her country, we are assured later (255), but in a web of economic pay-offs that includes others working *for* others in this global network, and *us* as well as herself; we learn she turns a rather good profit in this venture that, with her last, updated Baudelairian/Eliotic aside above ('yours and mine'; 'mon semblable, mon frere'), implicates her readers in the same. Certainly Smith's own anxieties about the Jews as the world brokers of that business – Aaronsen in Germany, Morgenbaum in New York and so on – is evident in the novel, but they are not the 'ultimate payees' in her view; and, like Aaronsen, they are forgotten by dealers like Pompey who leave them to be taken by fascist forces.[38] As Aaronsen assures her, she has done 'splendid[ly]' by the set standards of such deals: 'the best soldiers', he remarks as they share a celebratory glass of *kirschwasser*, 'are mercenaries' (202). Pompey has, in other words, become the full inheritor of not only the historical legacy attached to her name but also the mythological one: she has flowered too as Casmilus, the mercenary, the comer and goer out of hell, crossing sides seamlessly and doing a bit of business on the side for her/himself (see p. 83). And yet Pompey is neither extraordinary nor a god, more disturbingly; she is simply, as Aaronsen notes, playing by 'the rules', or contemporary codes. This is the 'side' that Pompey is *really* on – this is the business from which she gets her 'commission', in both senses of that word, though the naming of her 'high command' is crucial to the story's conclusion.

'The end is where we start from': war as self-fulfilling prophecy

The full shape of the novel becomes stunningly clear in these final pages, as does the arc of relations that binds it to its forerunner in the trilogy. By the end of *Frontier*, Pompey has very tellingly *become* the degenerate rider in the painting by George Grosz that she wished to buy at its outset. Like the 'elegant' animal in that 'elegant' gallery, in the picture named 'Haute École' (10), her horse, she tells us, has 'something of that French elegance about him' (217). And he indeed 'dances sideways' (225; see also p. 11) just as Pompey fears the animal in the painting will, *and* he does so at the ditch that marks the frontier, so that Pompey indeed falls off as she worried the rider in the painting might (11). In other words, as soldier, Pompey is the incarnation of thoughts floating in front of a painting. In no other novel I know does such clear connection take form between art and war, imagination and reality, galleries and frontlines – or, even more deeply, between dynamics of cultural desire (meaning psycho-political trauma repressed as diverted expression) and later violence and acquisitiveness run loose under the standards of national security.

The revelation of 'Pompey die Grosse' as symbolic fulfilment of our speaker's own prophecy, the degenerate, monstrous product of her own unborn desires and ambition, is perhaps augmented by another set of allusions to *Macbeth* that her horse's odd name, 'Beau Minon', calls to mind for me as a reader. In Shakespeare's play, after Duncan's murder, as Rosse and the Old Man marvel at nature's strange heralds of disaster, and 'night's predominance' over the 'living light', Rosse reports:

> And Duncan's horses (a thing most strange and certain),
> Beauteous and swift, the minions of their race,
> Turn'd wild in nature, broke their stalls, flung out,
> Contending 'gainst obedience, as they would make
> War with mankind. (II. iv, lines 13–18)

Like these 'beauteous minions' (or 'darlings', by contextual *OED* definition), Pompey's mount Beau Minon is introduced to us twice as her 'darling' (217). Yet hers is one that is also wont to go 'adance', like the subject of 'Haute École' – and simply 'for the sake of a piece of white paper' (218), much like the horse Pompey was riding at the start of *Novel* who danced sideways at the sight of a white gate. In other words, these horses of the psyche, the thought-currents and hobby-horses of the times that Pompey has been riding all along thus far in the trilogy, are all a threat to the unwatchful rider. Like her soldier-incarnation riding Beau Minon, a horse who 'turns suddenly contrariwise' by habit (217), Pompey dangerously rides 'the swift-running, ever counter-running current of our human thought' (254) whose governance of fate tends to turn unnatural, making of animal nature a damning dramatic foil. It would seem that Smith felt her 'state' was in an equivalent moment of jeopardy, caught between governmental 'Hoares' on the one hand and artists calling for 'necessary murder'.[39] The other potent allusion in these passages further links Pompey and Beau Minon to Hamlet's situation of helpless imbrication in their respectively rotting states. For as we hear Pompey assert that no dark thoughts 'touch

[her] withers, however wrung and wrung again are the Beau Minon withers, to be set at late night upon such unfathomably motived departures' like the ones she is set upon nightly with Tom, we recall Hamlet's disingenuous reassurances to Claudius and Gertrude following the first acts of his accusatory and damning play-within-the-play, 'The Mousetrap', that though this is a 'knavish piece of work', 'it touches us not', because 'we that have free souls' are not implicated in it (III: 2, 237–38). Hamlet *will* be 'touched', as we know, by the poisoned sword at the end of the play, though here he asserts 'that our withers are unwrung' – a phrase Shakespeare coined from the familiar one concerning a horse's 'wrung withers' should it be tacked up with an ill-fitting saddle. Therefore this horse Beau Minon, with whom she comes to identify so intensely that she calls his wrung withers her own, and even changes his gender to match hers (251),[40] conveys her out of her world full of equally unnatural political atrocities over the frontier, to make 'war with mankind'. But once again, Pompey works out far too late exactly which side she is on. The series of further allusions in these pages to *Macbeth* – the trees that, like Birnam wood, come 'bending and lolling upon [them]' as they ride the 'blasted...heath' (218); the fact that Pompey overhears the prophecy from Colonel Peck that she will 'pinch' Tom's job, and recognises that in her 'secret heart of pride and ambition' that thought had already been stirring (220) – suggest, along with others from particularly Nathaniel Hawthorne's 'Young Goodman Brown', that Pompey's Macbethian 'daggers of the mind' will have actual and very surprising consequences, be the dark forest a dream or reality, be the witches real or no.

The uniform Pompey wears she calls, in the distinctly Christian discourse used to refer to the sacraments, the 'outward and visible sign of my inward and spiritual sensation, growing and growing with a strong swift growth to a full strength' (220). It will take her to the apex of her rise to power, at which point she recognises that her commission comes from the very top: the 'Generalissimo', whose foreign appellation playfully refers to both the French command as well as, given the mock-Italian ring to the word, Mussolini.[41] Even more surprisingly, she reveals the other source for her commission as the Archbishop. But in keeping with the other structural ironies that inform the novel, this arrival at being 'one with [the Archbishop]' (261) is imaged as Pompey's Satanic fall, veiled though it is in her culture's codes of divine heroism. By way of a deeply Freudian interpretation of 'evil', Smith equates her speaker's perverse pilgrim's progress with the directives of *thanatos*, the death drive – that alternative, resident instinct which Pompey recognises as among the motive forces behind her donning of this uniform and her 'awakening' into unquestioning and destructive action:

> [M]y unquestioning...is based upon a quick and too lively determination to resist all knowledge that might, however eventually, turn upon an

explanation, and that again upon an *éclairecissement*, to enfold me, and upon an *ordinary* wing bear me back again to a life that is to me so profoundly so entirely unnecessary. (222)

Her paradoxically active, 'quick' and 'lively' choice of unconsciousness, her 'active forgetting' of *ordinary* existence through military intrigue that is *getting rather dangerous*, showcases her flip-over to the opposing drive that Freud described in 1920 in his revision of the balance between mental forces.[42] Pompey becomes the updated, Thirties' version of Joyce's Stephen Dedalus in that she, conversely, *avoids* 'epiphany' or 'éclairecissement'. Seeing her choices in the light of understanding would force her to acknowledge her own 'pure righteous intolerance' (197) of others' 'idealismus barbarus' – whether it be the Germans' 'dotty idealismus' *or* 'Allemagne['s] barbare' that, *in company with its enemy*, detests the 'very essentially civilized, urbane and international...sweet cultured sentimental manner' of old Aaronsen, the archetypal Jew. She would, in other words, be forced to acknowledge herself eminently capable of 'this very barbarismus' she so 'ferociously' seeks to destroy; instead, she proceeds to unwittingly destroy herself. In a typical passage, one that begins with chauvinistic denials of being as bad as the enemy, Pompey veers very near 'them' and therefore up against precisely the sort of epiphany she wishes to avoid:

> In England there is no national ideology, or not one that is formed to be carried through, to be expressed in a word and impressed upon a people, as in Germany it is expressed and impressed, with what of an original pure intention we cannot know, with what of a calamity in event we know too well.
>
> And upon this side of the frontier it marches with the enemy, it informs their dotty heroism. But we shall win, we shall win. We have the arms and the money, the mercenaries and the riff-raff of many armies. Death to the dotty idealismus, death to all ideologies; death upon the flying bullet that has been paid for; death from the bent form of the hired soldier; death upon the wind from the north.
>
> And we are right, we are right; however riff-raff our armies, however base our honey-voiced Head-quarters....
>
> I grind my teeth to think of Germany and her infection of arrogance and weakness and cruelty that has spread to our own particular enemy, has set on foot this abominable war, has brought us all to this pass, and me to a hatred that is not without guilt, is not, is not a pure flame of altruism; ah, hatred is never this, is always rather to make use of this grand altruistic feeling, to bring to a head in ourselves all that there is in us of a hatred and fury upon a less convenient truth.
>
> How apt I was for this deceit, how splendid a material, that recognizing the deceit must take commission under it, forever following darkness.

How profoundly evil are our thoughts, and set upon a wilderness of lies, how come to an escape, how be free of our inventions, and the devil that is so skilful to be always within them. Yes, yes. Inside of the array of our most highest thoughts and seeming pure desires is his best good. (255–56)

Her commission is, in other words, from 'deceit' defined as the devil in this novel. The language of infection and disease – the disease of 'dictators', as she identified it in *Novel* – 'spreads' not only to the enemy but across the flimsy frontier that supposedly separates good and evil forces. Through the unfolding tiers of irony above, Smith suggests that the very supposition of such distinctions and pure intention is itself the cause of such contagion; one 'catches' the disease from the enemy in the process of righteous elimination of the other. In Smith's view, the language of religion *and* of the 'Republic' – whether it be launched against Caesar or caught in the mirror during the Spanish Civil War – covers as code for the 'secret life' of the unspeakable: that which, in all pursuits, accumulates a rhetoric of righteousness and thus, by the world's perverse rules, demonic and unnatural force. Therefore, when at this point in the trilogy Pompey says feels she is at last 'inside of', rather than outside of, all the influences that build her into their cultural 'material', as she puts it above, we know all is lost. She at last is 'pure', 'awake', and has a clear position in her culture's projects – and it is exactly this purity of intention that Smith aligns with vulnerability to the devil himself. We heard her complain in *Novel* that she has never felt 'inside-of' Christianity, for example (173); now, just before this passage's alarming revelations, she tells us it is 'so nice for a change to be inside-of, instead of perpetually and draughtily outside-of' (247). 'Outside-of' is where the thoughts came tumbling from in the terrifying passage describing the oceanic force of overwhelming influences that I quoted earlier. Being inside-of allows one the rhetoric, the code, to cover for the 'abominations' that all of Smith's insider characters perpetuate, from little old ladies like Pouncer to young Pompey – because all ideologies are, in Smith's mid-century view, only 'variations on a theme' (256), whether they be made manifest in Germany, Russia or Spain. And though not 'expressed in a word', England indeed exercises its own powerful manifestation of that theme in Smith's novel. She ingeniously suggests its manner of being 'impressed' upon her speaker through Pompey's description of how her coded messages arrive: they come from 'a *panjandrum* of a Chief of Staff' (237; my italics) – that is, an unseen figure, as defined in the fictional etymology for the word made up in the nineteenth century by Samuel Foote. The fact that these messages sound to Pompey as though they are delivered in the voice of a child effects an early image of cagey cultural hegemony – one that employs the front of innocence and the rhetoric of religion to promote ideals with dismantling flip sides: 'Thou shalt do no murder' the Archbishop exhorts, 'but if you must, let it be the enemy and not our own wretched troops, poor materials as they are and so hardly to be frightened and cajoled into enlistment' (248).

Travelling under the Archbishop's and Generalissimo's commission, still riding the same 'foam-curded...torrent' (14) from *Novel* that carried her as the baby in the cradle but that is now turning into 'the secret swift dark current of finance bearing upon it the curd and foam of the very essence of the movement of armies' (231), Pompey does indeed take over Tom's job, as she dreamed in her Macbethian way that she would. Like the hinder parts of a rocket jettisoned during take-off, Tom, though initially imaged as Pompey's militant alter-ego, grows weaker as Pompey grows stronger, becoming unwilling to take up operations, and even desirous of heading back to Tilssen (251, 269) in order to preserve what remains of their intimate happiness. But as Pompey is told by her general, 'he's not the man for [her]'; she has 'a sort of flair for all this', is 'quite remarkably strong' (266). Pompey is being groomed to 'short-circuit' him, as Tom knows (269) – she will emasculate him as well, leaving him weak in bed while usurping his role, one normally associated with the 'phallus' or 'Father' in psychoanalyses of culture. At the end of the novel, powerful people like the Generalissimo turn out to be, via Freudian symbolism, a 'parracide-in-posse' (264); they like our speaker are set up, by dreams of personal power and oedipal revenge cloaked in the rhetoric of righteousness, to be destroyers – they destroy, and will be destroyed by destroyers. The Generalissimo, whom we are told has a 'girlish lisp and frightful malice of intent upon his father', is the culmination of a series of images in the novel concerning those who, out of self-loathing, attempt to be what the dream of culture images as their opposite – the powerful – and end up having to both destroy what they fear they still are *and* those who have destroyed what they were. Thus this description of the Generalissimo takes us back to what sounded like a homophobic passage earlier in the novel, when Pompey asserted that

> the more feminine of the men will pretend to be so masculine it would surprise you, and they will prance around and dress up in coloured shirts and talk a lot about Jews and women for a dirge and a disturbance of all peace. And the women in their pants will prance around and they will also talk too,... and mostly it will be a pseudo-feminist talk to put you out of your mind with irritation. For by their clothes they would wish to approximate so closely to the masculine physique – and to whom for a good might that be? (151)

It might be difficult to escape the connections between the 'degeneracy' of Grosz's ill-prepared, effeminate rider at the start of the novel and the effeminate Generalissimo whose neuroses undergird his violent instincts. But the dynamics of censure and 'forestalling', as Smith had it in *Novel*, seem to be of far more interest to her than critique of any particular set of sexual tendencies – and no one is safe from engagement in such perverse and contradictory dynamics. Men who 'prance' and dress in 'coloured' (feminine) clothing decry the feminine in the above passage, as well as the victimised and the weak, while simultaneously threatening the established 'peace' or current cultural order that would indict them as effeminate. Women similarly dress in masculine clothing to decry masculine *and* feminine behaviour alike – further demonstrating that strange dynamic by which insufficiently processed reactions to familial and social oppression lead to the multiplication of violent and self-destructive (as well as conscriptable) responses.

The circularity and absurdity of the sexual drama as Smith paints it underwrites or mirrors the larger cultural one as she saw it; Pompey has herself demonstrated the connection between the two arenas. She has donned the most powerful of male costumes – a uniform – while decrying the 'will of these two men' at the top of the totem pole of power who commission her behaviour (266). Smith thereby enfolds her own vision of women's suppression as we encountered it in her commentary on female characters in Shakespeare into ever broadening frames of cultural oppression and backlash. Pompey – a figure risen to the very top – accordingly turns her back on all weakness, including her weakened former lover, Tom, as well as the weakness in herself that she fears will compromise her current feelings of being 'shot-up', impervious to self-critique, full of power. As evidence of this, she climactically shoots an old man who impedes her progress and whom we must see, given all the rhyming with earlier imagery that occurs in the passage, as a figure of the powerless (if equally cruel) common herd from which she arose and from which she has worked so hard and so fruitlessly to differentiate herself in the second part of the novel. He catches her foot as she tries to make her way over a high stockade after a bit of spying on the enemy. We are told he is a figure of incongruity here on the front: a 'rat-faced eld' (or elder) 'so wizened' and so full of cruelty and hostility couched not in ideals, she tells us, but in simple 'smugness' – a face she says she has seen often and everywhere in civilian life: London, Berlin, Paris, New York, the villages of Hertfordshire (249, 248). His is the face of 'smug insufferable conviction; the backside of the world; the smug flat note of *that* vox humana, *We are so many*' (249). In the next paragraph she repeats it again, this italicised quote she used earlier in the novel while contemplating Thomas Hardy's depiction of a poor boy's murder of his siblings because they 'Were Too Many' (53). At that point in her story, seated in the train across from the man reading *The Pleasures of the Torture Chamber* and feeling abject herself, she had identified with Hardy's abject boy – but now he seems to have become, in the face of this old man, the product of her own cruel projections. Tellingly, she refers to him as a representative of '*that* vox humana' in a novel overtly dedicated to understanding the psychological dynamics behind the deployment of 'us and them' rhetoric. To her 'liberalistic world-conscience, that is still persisting in Opposition', Pompey tells us she 'may say: He must not live to tell the tale, to put a something in jeopardy that must be secure' (250). But the fact that both she and we are not sure what that 'something' *is* that might be put in jeopardy is key to our understanding not only of what is happening here, but also our understanding of that vague 'world pain' she felt at the outset of the novel. It is precisely that which is *not* understood, which is not processed well enough for clear articulation, which is actively repressed – 'unspeakable', in other words, and therefore generative, in the Freudian sense – that drives not only every development in these novels, but every justification of cruel action. What 'must be secure' is the repression of painful knowledge itself.

With his 'long yellow teeth', the old man *also* becomes the ruling dream or 'Chimera' as she described it earlier – not only for the feminists she lampooned above, but for herself as well. 'He', as she referred to 'their' (the feminists') Chimera, also has 'long strong yellow teeth' which she said she hopes it will use to tear them up when it turns upon them pursuing it, as all chimeras must.[43] Here at the end of *Frontier* Smith finishes her two-novel picture of oppressed desire gone wrong – of transgressions against 'Venus', as we had it at the start, in the story of the man falling from the plasteret Venus to the 'horrible whore' whose damned features blend into the illusion of the desired. And Freddy, we recall, was identified as Pompey's chimera just before this, at the end of *Novel on Yellow Paper*; there, in a fairytale-like passage, he functioned as her dream-vision until 'the *chimeraismus* departed, and there stood a little monster' (*NOYP* 222) not unlike this 'monster' of an old man she shoots, '[f]or monster it is', she tells us (249). The part-comic if incapacitating deflation of her romantic dream at the end of *Novel* is far more tragically replayed here in the military arena, connecting levels of dream to dream; her figurative savagery of her relationship with Freddy as the tiger 'Flo' becomes her very real murder of this figure whose presence reveals the 'monstrous' in her own dream of power's fulfilment – and must therefore be slain. He isn't 'the enemy', then, as Severin argues (41), or cruelty itself, as Lassner more complexly reads him (143). To make these points doubly clear, Smith causes Pompey to sharply if fleetingly recognise that the old man she kills is connected to Freddy – something she apprehends in a moment's involuntary 'éclairecissement', we might say, when she 'flash[es her] torch' into his face (248) and sees, via a deep, 'impertinent' thought coming up from 'dark memory', 'something that did not at all belong to the essence . . . of Rat-face' but arrives through a 'surge-back to a voice' that 'questioned her commission' as Freddy did in her mid-novel, pre-awakening dream. Here she calls it her 'dream of weakness', of wavering in her quest for ascendancy, the memory of which must of course be suppressed like this poor old man because, as her last line of the novel will put it: 'Power and cruelty are the strength of our life, and in its weakness only is there the sweetness of love' (272). Pompey must purge such weakness in this scene, just as she has since the very beginning of the trilogy, though by such action she destroys her own chance for love and for the innocence we remember she so desperately wished humanity might regain at the end of *Novel on Yellow Paper*.

But of course she has been under the influence of what she has called, via a dreamily distorted quote from Thomas Babington Macaulay's *Lays of Ancient Rome*, 'the dream that slew the slayer and shall be slain' (200). More about the *Lays*, Macaulay's famously nostalgic attempt to recover a connection to triumphant ancient Rome, will accompany my reading of the next novel's opening pages. Here, the lines from the source poem, 'The Battle of the Lake Regillus', detail the arrival of the 'foredoomed' Thirty Cities who dared challenge the armies of Rome. Smith seems to have been most fascinated, as she writes elsewhere, in one of her essays about childhood,[44] with the 'heavy and haunting... secret meaning' of the bit from which she quotes; it describes a 'ghastly priest' of Aricia, who will shortly be destroyed with all the rest:

> From the white streets of Tusculum,
>   The proudest town of all;
> From where the Witch's Fortress
>   O'erhangs the dark-blue seas;
> From the still glassy lake that sleeps
>   Beneath Aricia's trees –
> Those trees in whose dim shadow
>   The ghastly priest doth reign,
> The priest who slew the slayer,
>   And shall himself be slain. (443)

Indeed the final rhyme above remains mysterious in Macaulay's lines, with no further explanation to couch it within the narrative. One suspects, given the preceding lines, that 'ghastly priests' and 'Witches' conspire in benighted cities not worthy of Rome's ascendancy to advise their leaders wrongly. However one reads these lines, the key here for us is that Smith interchanges 'priest' with 'dream' – the cultural dream of power that leads to the slaying of the slayer, the endless cycle perpetuated by the conjurings of illusions: (Macbethian) witches' prophesies that become real history. Rome and its legacy of Empire and violence – triumphantly destroying the Thirty Cities – become the dream of modern Europe. And most importantly, here in the trilogy, Archbishops and priests and keepers of the spiritual well are made complicit with the dream of power, which ironically requires a sense of 'righteous pure intolerance' to get its very dirty work done.

Pompey as she merges forces with the Archbishop and Generalissimo therefore becomes the chimera turning upon herself to slay and be slain. Her placement of her gun in the mouth of this figure (a classic choice for the suicidal act as well) amounts to her killing of not only this face of the commonest denominator of Thirties European culture but also her killing of her own humanity, sacrificed as it is to the dream of power. More complexly, it also amounts to her killing of the 'old men of 1922' in Grosz's painting, the memory of the suffering aftermath of war, the image in front of which she has metaphorically stood for the whole of the novel and which she suppressed in order to commence her own story. Both 'world pain' and its monstrous product of cruel new purpose are subject to circuitous cover-up in its densely complicated *dénouement*; Smith seems to predict that the acceleration of such processes were at her time leading to the evolution of a new species of human animal – one whose ability to 'forget the past at will' through violent suppression might be aided by the culture industry, as Tom's valedictory remarks to Pompey could suggest:[45]

> So run along and play with your Archbishop, your Generalissimo, your fur cloaks and brass bands... No, I don't think it is a piece of vulgarity, for them it is not, it is perhaps a survival. Korda, shall we say, and Cecil B. de Mille have not spoilt it for them. And yet – very ferocious and astute animals they are for all their playacting. (269)

Such filmic relief is also 'a survival' for our speaker, a heart-of-darkness business and an artistic enterprise that will not bear close scrutiny. In the final 'galère' (267) of the novel, we find Pompey precisely where she suppressed her imagination from going in the art gallery we entered with her at its outset; but of course she was always already there, as Smith has beautifully and elaborately made clear in this work. Pompey recognises that 'this cloak of *their* privilege, for *their* purpose' that she has taken on her own shoulders is remarkable for its 'overt slap in the eye to humanistic ideology', its 'childish delight in a daily use of colour and form' for parade, all of which has about it 'something of innocence' that is 'frightful' in its revelation of a Europe whose maturity differs in no way from its 'barbaric... youth' (271). But unlike William Golding and other famous mid-century commentators on the fundamentally barbaric nature of human instincts, Smith interprets such regressions as being the *result* of human development rather than eruptions of its unmediated origins.

It seems that the mediations of culture and the refinements of nation-states were for her at the heart of both personal and global twentieth-century tragedy, as she suggests in Pompey's summation of the state of modern civilisation:[46]

> Is the power and the very lust for power the very stuff of our existence, the prop of our survival, our hope of the future, our despair of the past? And if we cannot achieve in our individualities this power are we any less guilty if we pursue it, or again, abandoning the sweet chase, identify ourselves with a national ethos, take pride in our country, in our country's

plundering, or, if the mood takes us, in our country's victories upon other fields less barren, in science, art, jurisprudence, philosophy? Oh corruption, of uncertain mortality, how divide, without a national death, the springs of our being, brought forth in pain and set to its infliction? (272)

Smith's speaker Pompey finishes her two-novel dissertation on the relationship between 'personal lust for power' and nationalised ascendancy over 'others' with the startling suggestion that the personal – the 'private life', as Korda had been so busy documenting it in the Thirties among the rich and famous – cannot be separated or saved and, given its annexation by the state, cannot even be terminated 'without a national death'. Her long-running 'desires upon death' (272) throughout the trilogy are glossed here as nothing 'but a cipher, an ignis fatuus, a foolish gesture, a child's scream of pain': 'Not self-violence upon the flesh, not a natural death, has promise of release.' She asks herself, on this last page of the novel, whether in the 'smug entertainment [she] found... in the flattering incoherence of the Memoirs of Prince Von, so carefully excerpted, so many pages past, is there not this very frightfulness of an unsatisfied personal lust for power, identifying itself with a national arrogance, my country's successful delinquency?' – referring by this to the writings of the unidentified German prince whose admiration of British articulations of 'Ethical imperialism' she had, in a lengthy earlier 'digression', told us she and her Aunt were 'partial to', and had often read and internalised (101–02). The seeming confusion of German and English ideology is as purposeful here as it is throughout the trilogy, for through it Smith undoes the illusions of opposition upon which national power-mongering depends. Pompey's 'smugness' in reading about this Kurtz-like and oxymoronic celebration of the illusion of ethical imperialism links her to the 'smug insufferable conviction' (249) of the old man she has just killed – suggesting the fate, perhaps, of all 'the many' poised, like Smith herself, on the brink of new war in 1938. But Pompey Casmilus, a 'desperate character' forever caught 'inside' the cultural text, seems unkillable.

II

The Holiday's split subject and Smith's new experiments in narration

The Holiday's title might strike us as something of a joke after the end of *Over the Frontier*, though one offered with Smith's own inimitable brand of gallows humour – since, as we have been told above, there is 'no release', not even temporary exit, from the setting of her trilogy. We might even see her last novel, recalling the opening pages of this chapter and my description of its aborted predecessor in manuscript, 'Married to Death', as Smith's version of George Grosz's 1946 painting 'The Pit': a Heironymus Bosch-cum-David Jones-like depiction of the collapse of culture into Dantesque hell after the war, which M. Kay Flavell calls his 'most complex treatment of death pursuing humanity' (240). But in Smith's deepeningly Freudian analysis of the situation it is the other way round: humanity is stuck in the purgatory of mid-century angst and is, instead, pursuing death. As both Celia and the speaker in a short story Smith originally wrote as part of *The Holiday* put it, 'Freud said the German race had a stronger death wish than any other people. They ask for death, only on death can a new Europe be built' (*MA* 30; *TH* 88). Smith seems to suggest, in tragicomic mode during the war, that perhaps Germany suffers from the collective version of what Freud described in the final phase of his work as 'the compulsion to repeat', or the death drive, which in its case might mean either repetition of the *first* world war scenario, with its traumatic result depicted by Grosz in 'The Old Men of 1922', or perhaps worse when repeated in her newly atomic age: full enactment of 'the most universal endeavour of all living substance – namely to return to the quiescence of the inorganic world' (Freud 336).[47]

Flip side to the same coin is Britain, of course, as the trilogy's constant alignment of arch-enemies suggests is true. Smith's tongue-in-cheek entertainment of Freud's thought nonetheless seems to underwrite her reading of what she saw more generally as European culture's 'death drive', played out between conflicting forces relegated to what she continually pictures as the Hades of the 'holiday' post-war mode, where all are frozen in a twist of still-battling instincts. Her characters awkwardly articulate the situation with assertions that 'Always there is this war between Germany and England' and, more cryptically, that 'England is biological' – meaning, perhaps, that it still operates on instinctive 'hunting' drives, as 'colonising animal', playing active lion to Germany's passive 'ask[ing] for death on bended knee' to 'give them death to three times three' (88–89). Her speaker Celia – who is alternately identified with both England and Germany – is similarly riven internally, hopelessly bound in a love relationship with her supposed-cousin-but-secret-half-brother, Caz: a leonine, military figure whose tonal properties in the story continually rhyme with those of the hunt and ultimately with death itself. Often speaking in negative grammatical constructions, he says early on, 'I do not know...that we can bear not to be at war' (8). Yet by typical Smithian paradox we learn by the close of the novel to understand his peculiar form of negativity as conventional positivity – that is, that Caz in social terms is 'a very positive fellow, really' who would lead Celia out of Dostoyevskian consciousness of her spiritual corruption via 'observation, discipline and company' or 'purely scientific education' (194). Caz's energies lead to 'positive' action – war, and narration of the kind that sustained Pompey Casmilus – whereas Celia's, despite her name, lead her 'underground'. The complexity of the novel's form caused it to be rejected several times over before it appeared in print; and indeed, as Francis Spalding notes,

Smith 'expressed anxiety that she would never achieve a shape that the novel reader would accept' (*SS: AB* 191). As will become clear below, what we are offered in *The Holiday* is a complex parable of the same hunt-like forces operant in *Over the Frontier* now dangerously come to a pause, and possibly reversing, or reappearing in systolic post-war photo-negative. The constant references to desire, death and the *desire for death* in the trilogy culminate in this final novel as it waxes lyrical at the prospects of *not* running on, not hunting 'full tongue across the desert' anymore but rather, and in increasingly Beckettian fashion, impossibly finally ending.[48]

Yet Smith's critique is always directed towards her specific historical situation, despite her interest in such timeless psychological forces and her constant reliance on formative inter-texts such as Boethius's *The Consolation of Philosophy* to start this novel and Dostoyevsky's *Notes from the Underground* to close it. It is therefore somewhat bewildering that the short story I refer to above, 'In the Beginning of the War', was in large part edited out of *The Holiday* at the prompting of her publishers, who argued that though the novel was written during the war (by 1942 she had 25,000 words; *SS: AB* 174), its failure to find the light of day until 1949 meant that it must be 'updated to the post-war period' (*SS: AB* 175). It would take a rather poor reader of Smith's work to miss the delicate placing in time that each of her novels exhibits. Perhaps the real problem for her publishers involved the fact that, as the objectionable parts of this excerpted short story would have made clear were they included in the final text, Smith was sharply critical of the revered conservative government in power during the war, even though, as we have seen, she welcomed Churchill's appearance at the outset. Yet she was equally critical of the radical elements that opposed it, deciding that the war for all its necessary victories was evidence of Britain's and Europe's larger systemic corruption and decline. Recalling a meeting of the Inter-University Peace Aims Group during the war, Smith's speaker in the story, a girl whose memories merge with Celia's in *The Holiday*, damningly quotes a Communist party member who 'spoke about the unrightheousness of war, the bogey of nazi-ism, the bogey of atrocity stories, the bogey of war sacrifices' in a plea for withdrawal of support for Churchill's government. Her irritation is of course not with the idea of peace but with the cover-up of Nazi crimes to achieve it – that is, the processes by which 'other people's sufferings', like those of the Jews, and indeed truth itself has been made sacrifice to party politicking both before and during the war:

> I remember before the war none was more fertile and emphatic in atrocity stories than the political person with left wing inclinations. Then there was indeed revelations. But now because Government sings the sad song at once it becomes for them not true. For they no more than Government care for absolute truth but only for party expediency. (*MA* 30)

In this corollary to Smith's abhorrence of the conservatives' hypocrisy and criminal self-aggrandisement in appeasement in the Thirties, we get her disgust with the radical opposition's turnabouts in wartime. At the end of *Frontier*, Pompey had cried in despair, 'How base, despicable, how unutterably base' is the whole of the world situation – which led her to ask, 'And are there no tears?' (272). *The Holiday* delivers those tears – is perhaps 'marred by too many tears' in Inez Holden's view: 'Sometimes there are so many tears they seem to fall through the pages like a thin sad rain, and occasionally, I think, like angry rain working up towards a hailstorm' (Holden 132). In the short story, the tears belong to a young refugee doctor from Germany who, hearing the speaker's complaints above about the atrocities sanctioned by both right- and left-wing British parties, 'beg[ins] to weep silently.... He was thinking of the cruelties and that the times was set to death' (*MA* 30). These were, in Smith's view, 'the times of a black split heart', as my subtitle to Chapter 2 has it by way of a quote from *The Holiday* (143); it should hardly surprise us that in this final novel of the trilogy our speaker is consequently and quite literally split up as well – and thereby drawn to a halt, as the beginning quote of this chapter made clear.

She is Celia Phoze now, a figure who is always 'frozen' or cold in a climate of post-war arrest and fragmentation. As Smith put it in 'In the Beginning of the War', 'It will take England a long time to warm up, said [her speaker], feeling more wretched and like Sam Hoare than ever' (*MA* 30), which of course insures connection of this coldness to *Frontier*'s explication of English duplicity through the use of Hoare as exemplar. In a sense, all in the cast of *The Holiday* are even more deeply and dangerously self-conscious continuations of *Frontier*'s 'Hoare-like' thinkers and speakers. Each of them is now overtly engaged in cover-ups and codes, as Celia is in her work-place at the unnamed 'Ministry' (another echo of Kafka) where we find her decoding materials at the outset of the novel. There is an eerie connection between the Pompey of the first two novels and Celia; they share the same memories – even the same 'Lion Aunt' – but their obvious discontinuity demands our attention as well. It is tempting to read these figures as if they were moving along an historical continuum as one would Molloy, Malone and 'the unnameable' speaking presence to be found in Samuel Beckett's post-war trilogy begun in 1947.[49] In the latter, the disintegration rather than development of character is also at issue, as well as the fact that it cannot happen – that we all 'go on' recreating selves as characters through inherited cultural resources like language, following one another as do Beckett's shadowy figures, barely glimpsing someone ahead of them, someone behind. But Smith seems more interested than Beckett in how topical changes in history necessitate changes in the contours of character. Her duplicitous Thirties' figures change, become all 'split up' in this post-war novel, and even more 'desperate' than their predecessor Pompey. Left without the distracting focus that conflict provided, they find themselves turned inward and, ironically, thereby suddenly capable of seeing beyond the curtain to the backstage set-up for the theatre of war.

Such desperation is made most clearly manifest in Tom. By name he is, in part, Smith's character from the middle novel of the trilogy, though he is now transformed, has moved 'over [yet another] frontier'. Like Pompey in the previous novel, he has spent time in a sanatorium to re-emerge on an edge of a kind of madness that represents a facet of our new speaker, Celia, as well. He is a 'mad Tom' extracted from her own blood, her 'cousin' here, whose 'madness stretch[es] out and me[ets] in [Celia] something that was also mad' (25). Suddenly boasting academic credentials – he 'has for three years been a professor of English at Tokio University' – he becomes a figure of intellectual disintegration; his surname, 'Fox', further suggests his fable-like identification with 'cleverness' cleaved by trauma to leave as residue a largely predatory nature. Like an earl of Oxford (who might have written Shakespeare's plays)[50] he occupies a former De Vere family mansion used to house figures with 'nervous disorders' when he is 'shut away' for six months; but he always, we are told, had a 'Shakespeare-Bacon-De Vere sonnet-bug' biting at him, 'and in his madness the laughter would run from him as he made the brilliant cypher puns' (24). Smith's playful wit constitutes through Tom a glittering image of the disintegration of her own text's most English, traditional, and, as we have seen, centrally called upon muse – the 'incandescent Shakespeare', as Woolf famously referred to him in *A Room of One's Own* (58) – at the same time that she extends through him *Frontier*'s image of Grosz's 'running laughter' to its logical (or illogical) end. Indeed, Tom focusses the collective madness that each of her characters wittingly or unwittingly perpetuates – particularly our main speaker, whose work with codes and cyphers distracts her from her own despair. We also cannot ignore Smith's obvious references to a Lear-like family tragedy underpinning, by allegory, the whole of her country's complex mid-century decline. The fact that Caz's supposed father is Celia's 'cold...Uncle Edmund', who was in reality cuckolded by her 'not cold enough Aunt Eva, and [Celia's] own free-roving loving father' (30), sets up a family history – conducted, importantly, in India before arrival back in England – of incest and illegitimacy that Smith will use to poetically connect domestic and international history in the novel.[51] Tom is offered to us as blood-related to, or inextricable from, a dissolving and, Smith seems to suggest, illegitimate and 'mad' imperial family; in it, Caz is a figure of the disintegration of the military mythos and/or colonial rule (represented by 'Aunt Lion'), and Celia is, as her name suggests, a figure of the disintegration of spiritual life (represented by the clerical Uncle Heber). For as she shouts at Caz, having accused him of being contaminated by the spiritualism of the East given his duties there, she claims she is 'a child of Europe, Christianity is the religion of Europe' (165).[52] After which she turns violently away from him to 'pray in a gabble' and in some desperation. Fragmented and suddenly lost for purpose, or diversion from deeper traumas, all of Smith's characters in this final novel of the triogy 'split up', as my first quote of this chapter had it, into Celia/Caz/Tom, Tiny/Clem, and even Aunt Lion/Uncle Heber, as we shall see. Even the text is, for the first time in the trilogy, split up into chapters – suggesting perhaps the aftermath of the tidal wave of 'talkie' that powered the first two novels.

But to begin at the beginning: Celia is in love with Caz, an obvious extension of Casmilus, her former identity, whom she cannot marry because shady suggestion has it that they are brother and sister rather than cousins. And indeed, though we cannot be sure of it, Celia's Aunt Eva may well have been her *father*'s sister, and thus they may be the progeny of incest as well (30). They are, in other words, two deeply 'related' parts of one whole. Caz, short for Casmilus, is an inheritor of Pompey Casmilus's ability, as Casmilus/Hermes' namesake, to go in and out of hell; he too does his duty – in places like Germany, India, Palestine – and benefits from such commerce. Celia (with her name's root in the heavens, or sky) plays the part-time over-world Persephone to Caz's Hermes in this twentieth-century enactment of the legend that the two were illicit lovers (Lee 188). Caz is the one who, on holiday, 'will not let [her] pick' the flowers that speckle the 'absolutely classical' cliffs, rebuffing her with the question 'Do you want to raise the devil?' – or perhaps Pluto, that husband of our speaker who is 'married to death' (149). Though Celia knows she 'should fall in love with [Tom]' (29), her cousin to whom she is also drawn, and thereby reunite the family by bringing this 'prodigal son' home to his estranged Uncle Heber, she cannot get over her passion for Caz/Casmilus, that mercenary militant and conductor of souls to Hades. From one angle, we can read this post-Red Decade, post-war allegory or *psychomachia* as one in which spirit and intellect remain split by desires for delivery *and* self-destruction. Moreover, Celia represents a whole new 'Waste Land' generation who, like her, 'wish that [their] cousin Casmilus was here to fetch [them] away' (66); indeed, Smith in this rare instance in the novel spells Caz's name out fully, to make sure we recall his connection to Hermes/Casmilus. And in this instance, Smith's aborted novel's original name, 'Married to Death', also actually appears in the text to illuminate its underlying symbolism. Extending Celia's condition to the general realm, her friend Lopez (whom Smith's biographers identify as based upon Inez Holden) says to Celia, 'You are married to Death and Hades; all my friends are married to Death and Hades' (66).

We have in this, of course, yet another situation in the trilogy that, in Shakespeare-fashion, casts the 'dead girl on her bier between two men', though in this novel those patriarchal forces are by necessity even more wholly internalised than in the earlier books of the trilogy. Here, Celia gives her own blood, 'which is what they want for Palestine' (31), against her Lion Aunt's wishes; her self-destruction in recompense for colonial enterprise is such that she must 'come home in an ambulance... home on the bier; the dead girl'. There will be no more driving a 'false-simple road' towards realising desires, as Pompey managed it, with surprising ruthlessness, by adopting 'a side' to unquestioningly fight on. That game is up, as Uncle Heber makes clear, revealing as he does what was concealed by such pursuits:

> [T]he times are the times of a black split heart, with self-seeking driving a false-simple road for its own advantage through the bog and over the hearts. This was the false-simple way of the Nazis driving at the democracies, which are still too much split and dark, and on the defensive to preserve a way of life that shall encourage people to buy as many things as possible. (144)

Thus are Smith's characters, figures for 'the democracies', split in this novel – the most obvious instance observable in the twins Tiny and Clem. They between them constitute near abjection and hopelessness (Tiny) and 'malicious' avarice, the biological drive for survival in the animal form of Clem, that 'small sly fat beast', 'the worst type of rich person' who 'play[s] left wing politics but [is] looking out for himself'(44) and who endlessly pursues his brother and the whole cast of characters right through their 'holiday' and up to the last page of the novel. Celia recognises their inextricability from one another and the rest:

> oh, if only one could forget him, but he is always there, this rich cruel crafty man, wrapped in affability; where Tiny is, there also is Clem, he is the shadow upon hope, he makes one hopeless. (112)

Smith makes it hard to know whether Clem incarnates the life or the death drive – but '[h]e always comes, said Tiny, he has a sort of instinct. He is very powerful' (113). Celia is indeed caught between Tiny and Clem, as she is between Caz and Tom, but she herself demonstrates both 'dark' hopelessness *and* 'defensiveness', as Heber put it above.

Both she and Caz exhibit the tendencies of the 'democracies', as Uncle Heber describes them above, when they contemplate together (and indistinguishably) India's future, for example. Both are 'very pro-English', as Celia puts it: 'England has the seas, the islands, the continents and the straits, at each point she is vulnerable. She must fight and build up her credits, and fight upon a hundred fronts' (9). But while they think in British-speak that 'We are right to quit India', when they mull over the latter's fate when freed from its coloniser, they suddenly get side-tracked and switch into US-speak (which Smith always caricatures as being a jumble of political paranoia and market-madness): 'For if England quits India now, what about that base against their arch-enemy old J. Stalin, and what about India's lovely markets, eh? What about them, a fellow has to think realistically' (94).[53] Narrationally one with Caz at this moment, Celia becomes subsumed under masculine referents. And together they end up wondering, 'How can they work up the consumer mind in India's millions with no benevolent British Government in the saddle?' People must, as Heber mournfully suggests above, think about buying as much as possible. It is *consumption* that must be emphasised over memory of trauma and loss of faith, as the image of a 'green bronze [neglected] statue' in Clem's roof garden suggests. In it this 'rather good' statue is of 'the face of an old woman, it is full of doom. Underneath is written: Remember me' (112). But repressing it as Pompey did the painting of old men in *Frontier*, Celia immediately translates that injunction to mean 'Remember *Clem*', because as a symbol of the consuming world he is her nemesis and clearly part of her as well. All the characters of the novel are implicated in an irreconcilable assemblage of culture's incestuous relations: the tender and good allied to the bloody and mercantile, all quite stuck in a discursive quagmire. Cold, and even 'Phoze' or frozen, she is a reversal of Swift's unconstipated Celia, whose shitting we related in Chapter 3 to Pompey's 'running on' in discursive terms, her subjection of self to Freud's 'talking cure' and its insurance against psychic anal retention. Or more probably she is the product of that self-analysis, better aware now of the archipelago of parts that compose her and unconvinced that 'rebinding' herself in the service of living or 'fighting on' is what she really wishes to do. By the end of the novel, as we shall see, she also becomes by allusion Ben Jonson's Celia, his translation in turn of Catullus's Lesbia. Their *carpe diem* love songs both prophesy that '... if once wee lose this light/'Tis, with us, perpetual night' – and nothing is more clear in this novel than the fact that Celia, our child of European Christianity, is indeed on the very brink of 'los[ing her] light'.

The post-war setting and its crises of language and consciousness

Celia is speaker for a landscape that, as she and Caz describe it in the novel's opening pages, has left behind it 'the dreams and the scenery' (8). The 'false-simple', 'blurred film' of ideological-cum-personal dreams that relentlessly powered the late Thirties and Smith's *Frontier* has been cut short. 'Everybody feels that he is cold and lost', says Caz, holding Celia and 'rocking [her] gently backwards and forwards', while she confesses to feeling warmer in the subway where, like a near-dead figure, she can see others and be seen in the light but need not speak:

> They are alive alive-o, that before was wandering in a desert of night dreams and landscapes. Here on the underground train, I said (as we rocked more violently and the cold rainstorm beat from outside upon the window pane...) we are together, we are good humoured, we have good manners we have the excellent unconscious good manners of off-hand civil London. We do not talk to each other – my word that could be

a burden – but we smile, and perhaps a person may say something about the weather; that is nothing more than a smile. (7–8)

The encasement of these Londoners in the safe space of the 'underground' rail carriage is made synonymous with Celia's position in Caz's (or death's) arms above, as well as with their ride in the Dickinsonian 'locked carriage' which Caz will soon acquire to escort her to their holiday (83). In this last psychomachic novel of the trilogy, which has left off even offering quotation marks to display when speech, as opposed to thought, happens, we know to fold spaces, so that the 'violent rocking' Celia describes above is attributable to her group of passengers in the train and to herself and Caz, whom we know are 'rocking back and forth' as she speaks. These Londoners as she describes them have likewise 'awakened' from the violent dreams of Thirties culture in order to join together again in 'unconsciousness', as Celia longs to do – and will do in the end – with Caz.

In the meantime, their collective strategy involves eschewing words and discourse altogether – those words that 'could be a burden'. In *Frontier*, Pompey woke catastrophically once, to don the uniform of militarism, and then arguably woke once again at the end of the novel to despair of ever being free of it, moving as she had from one level of cultural dream to another. These characters in *The Holiday*, like so many figures in post-war Europe – Orwell, Steiner, Sartre, Beckett and so on – seem to have woken yet again to locate their difficulty or danger or inescapable clothing in language itself. For the duration of the novel, however, Celia (who like Pompey continually suggests she is a writer like her author) will rebel against the option of 'being dumb' in the face of the world as revealed after the excesses of ideologically driven action and discursive doubleness:

> One wishes to be admirable, to write something that is truly noble, but the times are wrong, they are certainly wrong, at least in the West they are wrong. And there are too many words, there is too much about it and about, one has this horror of words – 'I'll be dumb' – but no, one must not be dumb. Somebody should speak up. (53)

Yet, as Donald Davie put it in his now-famous post-war poem, 'Rejoinder to a Critic', the tide in poetry suggested the opposite: '... Be dumb! / Appear concerned only to make it scan! / How dare we now be anything but numb?' (*Selected Poems* 30).[54] And indeed, at least one key post-war thinker, Theodor Adorno, would seem to have sanctioned such a response with his far more famous suggestion that there should be no poetry after Auschwitz.[55] Smith's 'speech' through Celia here and through the writing of her poetic novel as a whole suggests her deep antipathy to the dawning of the 'Movement' in England with its advocacy of retreat into 'small clearances, small poems'.[56] Yet the above lines also mirror Pompey's similarly despairing thoughts about 'wretched' words at the end of *Novel on Yellow Paper* (250), and here they bleed into surrounding texts that communicate exactly what Celia does: that, 'at least in the West', the times have made words incapable of recalling any nobility onto her post-war scene.

Smith's characters seem to be plunged into what has been called 'the linguistic turn': that post-ideology-wars moment when fears of language itself as the coercive bearer of either violent forces or weakened consciousness in culture began to clearly emerge (paving the way for 'postmodern' social linguistics and poststructuralist theory as well). Such newly dawning fears resulted in, on the one hand, angry writings – her friend George Orwell's famous 'Politics and the English Language' (1946) comes immediately to mind; or, on the other hand, eerie silence – 'quietism', as E.P. Thompson would refer to it – on the parts of even the most radical or loquacious of writers and philosophers.[57] Sartre, we recall, in a recollective writing, lamented that in 1950 Merleau-Ponty succeeded in 'impos[ing] his silence upon [him]' – a silence sworn in response to disillusioning news about the Soviet labour camps and involvements in the Korean hostilities. It was a horrified sense of his own entanglement in the texts of political idealisms that had covered for inhumanities that shut Merleau-Ponty down during the years that followed; as Sartre observed it, speaking from his friend's point of view:

> History had definitely perverted its course. It would continue paralyzed, deflected by its own wastes, until the final fall. Thus, any reasonable words could only lie. Silence, the refusal of complicity, was all that remained. (*Situations* 276)

This intensification of the disillusionment that had already begun for many left-wing artists and thinkers with the Spanish Civil War – given its revelations concerning the hypocritical and self-serving nature of joiners in ideological battle – mirrored that of many other kinds of intellectuals at the moment of Smith's writing. Among the most visible of them were German philosopher and former Nazi-sympathiser Martin Heidegger who went silent about matters political after 1945, and the multi-lingual European Jewish thinker George Steiner, whose book *Language and Silence* (1962) is perhaps the most emotive and poignant account of what he refers to as 'The Retreat from the Word' after the war. In his essay by that name, he writes that '[i]n our time, the language of politics has become infected with obscurity and madness. No lie is too gross for strenuous expression, no cruelty too abject to find apologia in the verbiage of historicism' (1984, 304). Calling nonetheless, as Celia does, for some 'appeal against the strident muteness of the arts' (303), he still fears at the end of the essay that unless the language in newspapers and politics can recover itself on the slippery slope of recent history, '[t]here will come to pass a new dark age' (304). In many ways, *The Holiday* portrays

Smith's fear of the same, as her characters ride in their closed carriage closer along an edge that would seem to spill into an unspeakable abyss.

Another reverse coda: the opening dialogue of *Holiday*

Given her awareness of the 'burden' of words, yet her fear of silence, Celia tells us she is most 'happy when [she is] unconscious' (51) like the figures in the underground carriage. And she is most unconscious when she is busy decoding telegrams with her co-worker Tiny at the mysterious Ministry, forgetting the 'beastly unhappiness' that constitutes the corollary to *Frontier*'s 'world pain'. While 'the whole of the post-war h[angs] up on [Eleanor]' and Constance, their Ministry colleagues occupied with 'important' things (6, 32), Tiny and Celia open the novel like Didi and Gogo, trying mightily and comically in the emptiness that looms to *forget* important matters and carry on with very little. Or rather, as I suggested earlier, they labour to 'actively forget' such upsetting things – like the fact that Clem, representative of post-war greed and oppression, has been moved into the section next to them – by reminding themselves that 'as long as we *remember*, we can think of something else' (5). Again, theirs is simply a more overt articulation of the same psychological principle that powered Pompey's processes of repression in *Frontier*. Yet while she and Tiny (whose stammer is a foil to Celia's own difficulties with speech) try, quite symbolically, to decode the biblical number '7' in a telegram, Celia unconsciously sings a song to herself that articulates her own desperate spiritual situation while announcing a number of key themes in the novel as well. Once again, Smith offers us a complex intertext as poetic image to kick-start this third novel of the trilogy, and once again, we as readers are asked to 'decode' such materials – as the protagonists' fellow-travellers – in order to understand what culture cannot or will not state about itself.

Not surprisingly, given the role the 'Archbishop' played in *Over the Frontier*, Smith's vessel for her explication of post-war angst is the well-loved hymn 'From Greenland's Icy Mountains', which Celia sings at first absent-mindedly and then more and more loudly upon Tiny's protestations that she 'g[ets] the words mixed up' (6). Her half-remembered, half-forgotten, still-influential text here was written by the English clergyman Reginald Heber in 1819. And it is precisely *because* Celia does not make the connection between the Hebers that we as readers immediately suspect something key is being expressed about our speaker's initial subconscious desires and their end: her longed-for escape into 'the holiday' with her Uncle 'Heber', who is also a clergyman – *is*, perhaps, a figure for Reginald Heber himself. She describes her uncle as 'that blessed calm Heber' (56), whose rectory represents a heavenly alternative to Caz's less restful form of stopping, or death. His name, which means 'Hebrew', may even sound connection to a Judeo-Christian root recoverable from some pre-history prior to the violent anti-Semitism extensively showcased in the trilogy's first two novels, or prior to the further and fully decisive fall exhibited in the Holocaust during the writing of the last. But what happens here in this seemingly unimportant first moment of attempting to recall the hymn is what will also happen later in the novel, when Celia attempts once again to 'return' to Heber, this time her uncle, and his alternative source of spiritual calm. In both cases she finds it 'hobbled by past centuries' (194) – not only by Torquemada's legacy (191), but also by specifically English colonial history, never more exposed as embedded at the very heart of 'Englishness' and Anglicanism than at mid-twentieth century during the break-down of Empire. The hymn, its history and Smith's own mid-century history prove themselves inextricably intertwined in Celia's head, causing her to create gaps and jags in her cultural 'script', we might say, as she sings. Reginald Heber the clergyman became the Bishop of Calcutta by 1823, and his imperial views would fit the job; his hymn, the worst bits of which Celia 'forgets', is a missionary hymn about the take-over of 'vile' heathens:

> From Greenland's icy mountains, from India's coral strand;
> Where Afric's sunny fountains roll down their golden sand:
> From many an ancient river, from many a palmy plain,
> They call us to deliver their land from error's chain.
>
> What though the spicy breezes blow soft o'er Java's isle;
> Though every prospect pleases, and only man is vile?
> In vain with lavish kindness the gifts of God are strown;
> The heathen in his blindness bows down to wood and stone!
>
> Can we, whose souls are lighted with wisdom from on high,
> Can we to those benighted the lamp of life deny?
> Salvation! O salvation! The joyful sound proclaim,
> Till earth's remotest nation has learned Messiah's Name.
>
> Waft, waft, ye winds, his story, and you, ye waters, roll
> Till, like a sea of glory, it spreads from pole to pole:
> Till o'er our ransomed nature the Lamb for sinners slain,
> Redeemer, King, Creator, in bliss returns to reign.

Yet as we shall see in a moment, Celia's version replaces the colonised land, in need of delivery from 'error's chain', with the land of the colonisers, to suggest the *latter's* need of delivery from its own imperial barbarisms and their consequences. The fact that she gets her lines crossed mid-way through with one of those texts that haunted Pompey, Macaulay's *Lays of Ancient Rome* (1842), creates of this seemingly insignificant snippet of a song at the beginning of Smith's novel a textual complex that in many ways explicates the whole of the remaining narrative.

For Macaulay's celebrations of Roman might, so typical of Victorian imperialism, illustrate the hijacking of Christian ideals that powered the colonial project; the interplay of contradictory texts that best defines Smith's writing finds few better examples than this. When we remember that Macaulay was not only a poet and an historian but also instrumental in government – as a supreme member of the East India Company engaged in reforming Indian educational systems, and even as a secretary of war – the dynamic potential of these entangled intertexts becomes clearer. Her confused song pours Heber's missionary flood rolling over the yet uncolonised land right back into greater Europe, in a cycle of domination that, again, like Conrad's opening to *Heart of Darkness*, inverts Victorian progress and prophesies 'the empire striking back':[58]

> From Greenland's icy mountains
> From India's coral strand
> Where Afric's golden fountains
> Roll down the something land
> From many a lonely hamlet
> Which hid by beech and pine
> Like an eagle's nest hangs on the crest
> Of purple Apennine. (6)

The last four lines, which emerge after our speaker's memory comically falters, producing a 'something' as filler for forgotten words, are taken *verbatim* from Macaulay's second stanza of 'Horatius' in the *Lays* (420). Like so many of Smith's mis- or unattributed quotations, these lines are ones that most school children would have memorised at mid-century, particularly if they were products of the public school system (which itself receives a good deal of specific critique in this novel for creating the imperial mindset, as I will soon explain). Those 'hamlets', whether Italian or British – like the Hertfordshire villages that Pompey connects with her enemy's face just before she murders him at the end of *Frontier* – are deliberately used by Smith as sentimental images, which here are forced into complicity with the colonising project of Europe. The hunt for, ostensibly, souls, but far more obviously for world dominance – associated with the outriding phase of culture's dual directionality as was illustrated in the first passage quoted in this chapter – is repeatedly represented by the hawk and the eagle in the novel; the latter, the eagle, substitutes its story for Rev. Heber's missionary zeal in Celia's version of the hymn. But those Christian hamlets are made vulnerable in Celia's memory of its text when she tells us, in a long and pointed digression thirty pages later, that eagles are rapidly dwindling in number – that there are 'only twenty-four...in the whole of the British Isles' – however much an invincible image they once projected (35).[59] Hamlets and eagles and crests, a cosy/predatory image of ascendant Europe, are left 'hang[ing] on the crest' in Celia's poor memory – perhaps at the top of a wave, if one recalls the 'sea of glory' imaged in Heber's hymn. The Victorian flood as it was identified in the first novel of the trilogy is further explicated here as the self-inflicted judgement that Victorian sensibilities, 'rolling' over the colonised or dominated of the world, will bring back upon itself. And indeed, in Smith's eerily sado-masochistic model of cultural relations, built on religious impulses run amok, that return is actually *desired*, because 'people cannot bear not to be beaten' (43) – but much more will be said about this in a moment, particularly as we approach the novel's end.

The passage that houses the digression about eagles mentioned above is, like many in the novel, enormously complicated; as readers we must keep whole swathes of previous chapters in mind as we try to see the larger, and very frayed, situational fabric beneath the all-important, digressive words. Celia is here talking frantically in order to divert her cousin Tom; his hands have suddenly gone to her throat as they enter the studio in the Ministry where, as we were told earlier, Tom is meant to 'make a learned talk for the China Station' (25) – in, we take it, yet another British colony. This moment is the culmination of what Celia has been feeling all along is possible, each time this fragment of herself, 'mad Tom', comes like a prophet to the Ministry to seek her; it is that 'We are here to destroy each other' (34). It is precisely when Tom – whom as we have seen is a figure of English intellect – goes silent, or *stops*, that 'the madness [comes] back'; Celia's sudden, desperate attempt at *running on*, or filling that silence with words, any words, in order to divert what she acknowledges and sometimes even desires as her own inevitable destruction becomes an image of all the empty verbiage of the time engaged in the project of 'forestalling' that we saw in *Novel on Yellow Paper*. For her words that are meant to forestall endings *predict*, instead, the end of European culture as Smith seems to have envisioned it. Fate is depicted as immanent in and inextricable from the cultural text, in other words, because it is here, in her seemingly throw-away words about the end of eagles in the British Isles, that we recall the first song Celia sang in the novel, which was fashioned out of that cultural text, and which predicted the same end, as we saw above. With resounding significance, this section cuts itself off with an explication of the background noise that has, throughout the passage, framed their words in the studio; it is caused by what Tom sadly acknowledges as 'the African section' of the Ministry above them.

> The African section was still tearing heavily backwards and forwards over our heads. They appeared to be moving heavy articles of furniture about the room to try them in different positions in an indecisive mood. (36)

This portentous moment, with Britain's Chinese 'section' connected through the airwaves and its African one 'tearing heavily' above while its soul in the form of Celia all but implodes beneath and between them – 'I could not speak', she suddenly says, 'but was mad too' (36) – explicates what Celia cried out cryptically to Caz on the third page of the novel: 'England... is stretched out and thin. I feel...' (7). The fact that she cannot say what she feels – aside from 'frozen', as she explains at Caz's prompting – is, again, important; the novel's opaque veneer, its words, covers explosive materials erupting as a consequence of actual, 'real' history (unlike Macaulay's heroic ones), which none of the characters ever fully understands.

Just after the above section closes upon white space, the prose opens again with Celia's professed *attempt* to understand, to 'know about this sad deficiency feeling... that can produce suddenly the last strain, to break and destroy, that is the feeling of strain from the appearance that is one thing, and the reality that is certainly another' (36–37). Smith's mid-century sense of the chasm between language and reality splits open her own text at this juncture; we as readers confirm that her speakers' words and 'codes' and hymns cover over a world unrecognisable through them. And in the course of the conversation that ensues with her 'Lion Aunt' about her family, appearances duly fall away to reveal that her grandfather, Honorary Chief Engineer to the Royal Naval Reserve, was continually bribed by the military industrial complex for 'something', as she refers to it, that we cannot know, but which filled their cellar with champagne and prime venison and cigars, says the Lion. (39). ('[W]e had it enlarged' her aunt admits, 'and we used to keep the bath chair in front of the door, for really there were times when really if anyone had looked inside, it would have looked rather peculiar, oh rather peculiar – in his position.') Again, bits of Joycean-style autobiography enter into the mix here as they do throughout the trilogy, though Smith's grandfather was nothing so exalted (he was a shipping agent's clerk); for a moment, Celia's unspoken distress over her 'dreamy' mother's bullying by this patriarchal figure might be read and felt, very poignantly, as Smith's own lament. But at the end of this section's revelations about familial entanglements, Smith allows her speaker to answer her own question about the origin of her sadness with typical Smithian comedy and irony – so that we cannot be sure whether Celia is laughing as well, or whether we have another blossoming Pompey on our hands:

> I think, [Celia] said, that the reason I am often so sad is because I ought not to be in a Ministry at all, I ought to be a North Sea pirate, like my grandfather – a pirate, a pirate, a pirate.
> We are all seafaring men in our family, said my Aunt, with complacency, bustling me towards the door. (40)

In other words, the 'appearance' is that Celia works in a Ministry, but the 'reality' is that she like her ancestors is engaged in piracy, along with the rest of those with whom she works (and the ecclesiastical resonance of the word 'Ministry' should never be lost as one reads this novel). All of ancient sea-faring England and its modern descendants, secular and non-secular, rise up behind Celia and 'Aunt Lion', our representative of 'Great Britain', in this indictment.

Therefore even greater irony drives the opening of the next section of this chapter, in which Celia, arriving at work and reading the headlines about an 'Old Carthusian Mauled by Japs', thinks:

> When my Aunt shut the door it was another world and another century. As I step into the Ministry I think, I am now in the world of Carthusians-Etonians-Malburians-Wykehamists, with Japs upon the threshold and a hundred years set up against my noble elders, my noble Aunt, her noble brother my Uncle Heber. (41)

Celia's sudden desire to ennoble the century preceding her own must be seen as either residually atavistic or deeply disingenuous just after her connection of her bloodline to imperial piracy. And indeed, her office partner Tiny disrupts such ostensibly nostalgic response as he wryly suggests, upon being shown the headline, 'And how many Japs have been mauled by Old Carthusians, do you suppose?' (41). Smith's invocation of 'Old Carthusians' and other graduates of the most famous public schools for the privileged in England[60] sets up yet another of the novel's false dichotomies between the 'civilised' and the 'barbarians', like the one in Reginald Heber's hymn, though this one demonstrates the continuing hold of such habits of mind on mid-twentieth-century English thought. Japan's alliance with Great Britain in 1902, after the first war between China and Japan (1894–95) that marked the latter's emergence as an imperial power, suggested the identification between the two states; Japan had been more or less bullied into commerce with the West in the nineteenth century and gained most of its lessons in imperialism from Europe and America. After the outbreak of the Second World War, its desires to create a 'Greater East Asia Co-Prosperity Sphere' and its invasions in Indo-China could hardly be critiqued by the British, given their own struggles with Japan to keep hold of Hong Kong (gained during the Opium War (1839–42) and lost briefly to Japan from 1941–45). Indeed, Celia's 'coldness' towards Tiny for his critique of her sudden, patriotic sense of violation and for his satirical adoption of an American accent to effect it suggests that she understands this, yet that she wishes to forget what she feared at the outset of the novel: that England has lost its enabling belief in its own moral highground, has been revealed as 'stretched thin' in identification between west and east.

Her argument with Tiny is followed by Celia's stopping at Lopez's for morning coffee, over which she hears about the BBC interview Lopez had just done with a figure who, like Celia, 'never finishes a sentence, but says: "There must be a new, there must be, you see, it is not"' (41). This oblique reminder of her own state, and her inability to 'tell Lopez at all why I was so sad', gives way by rather violent juxtaposition in the next paragraph to her lying inexplicably prone 'upon the floor of the lavatory' in the Ministry, 'feel[ing] absolutely ghost-girl deficient', and 'star[ing] up at the ceiling where the plaster had been shaken off' (42). This critical, punning moment – one where 'Celia' meets 'ceiling', her heavens shaken by the war (a metaphor for the 'deficient' cultural architecture that limits Celia's quest for spiritual rebirth) – results in one of her most revealing laments in the novel:

> Shall I ever be rid of this misery, is it papa's legacy, or my mama's, or is it the war, or is it the guilt of our social situation that is so base bottom bad? This sneering situation that is built on money. (42)

But this 'base bottom bad' situation is not new; Smith has gone to some lengths to make clear that it exists on a long trajectory of situations lodged in the corrupted text of European-cum-American history. In Macaulay's famous introduction to the *Lays of Ancient Rome*, he writes that 'the author [of "Horatius", the first lay from which Celia inadvertently quotes above] seems to have been an honest citizen, proud of the military glory of his country, sick of the disputes of factions, and much given to pining after good old times which had never really existed' (419). Macaulay might have been accused of the same kind of self-congratulatory delusion Smith's Celia demonstrates in her weaker moments, though our speaker is caught in a contradictory struggle to both 'understand' her place in the unwritten history of her culture's corruption *and* be 'unconscious' – the latter being the only time she is 'happy' (51).

The British Lion, Raji, and postcolonial commentary in the novel

That fact that her Lion Aunt is said to have an 'eagle managing eye' (37), and that she includes herself, as we saw above, among the 'seafaring men' of the family is important to Celia's story. This loving surrogate mother for Celia is not only an 'honest' figure, one who like Uncle Heber is genuinely respected by Celia for demonstrating the 'integrity' that differs so radically from her own fragmented state (116), but she is also and simultaneously in the novel a *deconstruction* of such powerful illusions of integrity, and her views are a product of what Celia calls, when discussing the up-keep of 'too tidy' Christianity, 'the human wish for something finished off and tidy, something one can grasp lovingly and tight' (43). Despite the near-constant desire on the part of critics to celebrate her as a strong female character in the novels, she functions far more importantly as not only an emblem of England but the source of many of our speaker's most problematic views, particularly on issues such as freeing colonies like India (which achieved its independence in 1947, during Smith's revision of the manuscript). Frances

Spalding argues that Smith's real-life aunt, Madge Spear, changed her views about the British in India after meeting Smith's friend Mulk Raj Anand, an activist and writer on whom the *Holiday* character Raji is based (and whose book *Letters on India* Celia at one point summarises in the novel). Spalding also suggests that while in *Frontier* Pompey's Lion Aunt represented Smith's *own* middle of the road thinking on India, which was 'swayed neither "to the sentimentalism of the pseudo-Kipling tea planter," nor to those who cry "Abdicate, evacuate, India for the Indians"' but was inclined to think of independence as '"a something perhaps that must not come to pass yet for a long time"', in *Holiday* the assertion that 'We are right to quit India' proves that Smith's own views had also evolved through her friendship with both Anand and Orwell. Anand believed, Spalding goes on to argue, 'that his friendship with Stevie made her more able to understand why Orwell had resigned from the Imperial Police Service in Burma' (159). Although Smith did not accept Anand's communist views about the kind of revolution that ought to occur in India, it may well be that his influence upon her was indeed as great as Spalding suggests. But the views of 'Aunt Lion' are no gauge for such developments; she always was and remains in the trilogy a figure of dangerously influential and even appealing imperialist views that buffet the life of our fraying speaker. And as we know, the statement that Britain should 'quit India' is not made by her – and indeed, right after it we hear that the 'fine free song' about freeing India that, as we are told by our speakers, was sung before the war for the 'fine free hearts of America' constituted 'a fine sure twist for old Lion's tail' (94). In other words, the assertion about quitting India is deeply ironic at best, followed as it is by Caz and Celia's lament about the potential loss of India's lovely markets, as we saw above. And later in the novel our speaker contradicts entirely the line Spalding quotes above when she opposes Caz's reiteration that 'We should quit India' by protesting 'It is not so simple as that' (125). It would seem that Smith's presentation of her country's continuing mission in the figure of Aunt Lion – that 'colonising animal' – and her speaker's self-construction as a 'crowned child in a subject land' are simply offered as mutually untenable views in this novel whose 'subject' is the break-up of 'Englishness' itself.

Celia's Lion Aunt has 'a soft spot for Raji' (40) – and Smith's use of the name 'Raj' in her novel, however biographical the reference might be, nonetheless must be seen to make him a representative figure. He becomes a sign for British power in its colony, which is in large part what Aunt demonstrates affection for when she refers to him as a 'poor fellow': nicely weak and properly subjected. But this very affection, which Celia shares, makes it impossible for the latter to listen to Raji in any real way, as we hear when he delivers a talk at a meeting in London: 'Of course, as I had a friendly familiar feeling for old Raji, I could not listen closely to his talk' (95). This makes Celia no different from the rest of the audience to whom Raji was talking too softly and who could not, consequently, 'hear a word'.

They 'were too polite to say so', we are told, but the Indian audience member who hands up a note to urge Raji to speak louder does so with 'a spiteful look'. An argument follows the lecture, after comments from one 'young violent English person' (fashioned on Orwell) who suggests that 'no easy feeling of equality between intellectual Indians and English people was possible in India so long as this evil thing (the British Raj) was still in existence. Affection there might be, of a feudal variety, between the governing English and the simple people of India, but for the intellectual Indians, no' (96). This outburst glosses relations between Celia and her Aunt and Raji in the novel; we instantly recall upon hearing it that from the beginning Celia has been condescending towards her Indian friend, whom she tells us is 'the most intelligent Indian in London', and 'an honest person' which, she adds 'is rare, and rare indeed in an Indian' (13). Rather than 'affirming' the views of friends like Inez Holden, as Spalding suggests, Smith seems to be parodying here the typical sort of gentle racism that Holden immortalised in her diary:

> It is surprising to find a foreigner also coloured belonging to a dominated race so free, well at ease and without any kind of neurosis as Mulk, he is very good company, affectionate and witty.... (1941; SS: AB 158)

'It is wonderful that Raji can be so generous and free, for his upbringing was in an oppressed atmosphere', says Celia (14); he 'makes us laugh' with his stories of having 'been in an English prison-camp in India and... beaten up by the Indian police. He says that the Indians are abysmally childish' (13). Whether the latter is all that this former activist for independence suggests with these stories is not the point here – rather, the point is that this is what the English *wish* to hear and therefore *do* hear in his stories; this is what 'makes them laugh'. Caz's accusation that Raji would rather remain in London and be a 'party-pet' (93) than be martyred for his views in India helps to illustrate both India-stationed Caz's more violent disposition towards Raji and the reasons for the 'affection' the latter gains from both Aunt Lion and Celia. This Indian is controllable, a party phenomenon who elects to entertain the colonisers, and certainly no one to be listened to or taken too seriously. But as Celia says, in a flip side moment of recognition of all these dynamics of control, Raji's book 'that is so true about India, and so much the book that English people ought to read, and is so much the book that so many of them do not want to read',

> says that the English are practically invisible in India, by reason of the anger and the pride, and that all the cruelty there is, and the beastliness, is done by avaricious middlemen and Indian paid subordinates, and by the rich Muslim trading families, like the great mill-owning rich families of Bombay. And he says one of the most oppressive things the English have brought to India is that sense of secret opulence in a land of poverty,

and this opulence shows itself in close-curtained bungalows with plain outsides, and the luxury going on in a secret way, not sin, mind you, which anyone could understand, but just plain comfort, unindictable, untouchable, invisible and foreign. (97–98)

The line before this passage involves Celia in this 'secret' occupation, this hegemonic presence/absence by which Great Britain still rules India: 'I also was a crowned child in a subject land, I also was in India' she says 'hook[ing her] arm into dear Raji's' (97).

Celia's fond memories of an Indian childhood involve no Indians *but* Raji, and indeed involve him only tangentially. In every instance her memories take her back to visits to palaces by the seashore with Caz and to her uncle's 'fine cool stone house' (99) surrounded by jungle, and especially to moments when she and Caz are huddled together out of fear of 'the moonlight and the jungle that pushes up to the house' (30; see also 99). In these passages Celia suggests that 'the child Raji is watching us' (30), a witness to their 'secret opulence' and also to their developing incestuous relation; when he dares step in to take Celia's hand in one scenario he is beaten almost uncontrollably by Caz (99). In other words, what is remembered fondly is *not* so much the Indian setting, which frightens, and whose people remain foreign and necessarily subjected to British rule, but the illicit relationship with Caz that develops as a result of that fright and sense of displacement – and therefore, if we read this fact according to the novel's symbolic language, the illicit relations between spiritual and military might that obviate fear, construct 'home' everywhere, and inform Britain's imperial past. This is what underwrites her 'loving memories' (100). Her love for India, in other words, along with her Lion Aunt's, is incestuous – it is in the end love for self, for India as a sign of British power. And the old ape named 'Sinbad' who 'went with the house' and who frightened Caz and Celia by swinging outside it on warm southern nights was no one but themselves as well, a figure of old England – a pirate figure, straight out of Celia's pirating family, still primitive and 'so old and so sick, and yet alive, alive-o' (100; *CP* 252).

Celia as an image of shifting power relations in the post-war arena

This is the 'home' Smith's post-war characters encounter when they long for it and attempt to retrieve it, as I suggested at the outset of this chapter. Celia affirms as much when, having run back through these memories and having arrived at her Uncle Heber's home with Caz for her holiday, she says: 'So India with its fevers links with this cool Lincolnshire, where now we are, where now we are; and both again beneath an uncle's roof' (100). She means she and Caz by 'both' here, but we also know through Smith's typically ambiguous syntax that the point is that place, India or Lincolnshire, is irrelevant. 'England' or 'home' has always been an imposed state of mind and a mindset of imperial ownership, inherited from military Aunt Lions in cahoots with spiritual Uncle Hebers – though it is also one now set into disintegrative mode.

The idea that colonial rule functions without colonials is key to the novel. It illustrates, for one thing, what Pompey suggested in *Frontier* about England's modern adaptability – that is, that the strategies of colonisation have simply *shifted* from crude conquering to more sophisticated modes of global domination through deployment of developing capitalism's 'supply and demand' rhetoric (see p. 135). Even more importantly, it indicates Smith's interest in developing new views of how power structures work, which in turn suggests why Celia continually feels frightened by the 'secret' forces that have conspired to construct her. In a comical passage, during which he and Celia watch the Queen walk in below them on the first floor landing at the Ministry's Book Prints Exhibition – 'We could have poured sherry in her hat' – Raji deconstructs such sentimental images of power and assures her that alternative, secret forces operate in her homeland as well as in England's colonies:

> Raji said that throughout England there is this dummy-power idea. There is the King, but of course since a long time it is not the King who pulls the shower bath. And in the Civil Service, and in the City, and in the Ministries and in Publishing, it is the same, the power hides and works and pulls the shower bath. (56)

Celia's response is to abjure 'self-pity' and despair over this situation, in the same way that she earlier asserted the need to abjure 'dumb' silence and encourage 'someone to speak up': '... [I]n this idea of Raji's that we are treading a secret hell, and that we are weeping in the peasoup fog of a secret power... that we can do nothing but... so go out into the darkness, in this idea there is the poison of a beastly self-pity' (56). But this response is triangulated in the novel by her other two characteristic responses of either equivocating on the issues or seeking death, identified respectively (and partly playfully) in the novel with the propensities of England and Germany as Smith evaluates the broader dynamics of her European culture.

On the one hand, she is identified with England – not only overtly[61] but covertly, given that the descriptor 'shifty' is used for both Celia and her country throughout the novel in a kind of poetic weave. It grows darkest at that moment that argument about the worth of the British Raj erupts following Raji's lecture; during it Celia thinks to herself:

> We shall never budge, I thought, shift we may, on our own terms, but budge, never.
> And I thought again of Rome, that was taken captive, that had captured the world. And I thought: Happier the ancient world, with

Rome for an adversary, the Rome that could be broken and done with; but the British are like water that shifts to its own course. (96–97)

Merely shifting tactics of domination, England the 'biological', the 'colonising animal', adapts and survives. Celia, too, despite her despair and strong death drive, survives. She survives even her attempt to drown herself the day after Raji's lecture, when she swims out into the current thinking: 'I had a sleepy feeling I was floating away from the Ministry, and the London parties, and Lopez, and the Indian problems, and going to have a fine long sleep and no dreams' (103). She laments to her alter ego Caz who pulls her out of the lake that 'It is not that life is so awful, but that I am, there is no end to the pain and fear, and to the general shiftiness of my character...' (103). She had explained this suicidal bent in her shifty character to him several pages earlier, inadvertently, through her adoption of German while describing Germany's death wish: 'Listen Caz, *Achtung!* Please pay attention. Freud said that Germany had the greatest death wish in the world of any nation...' (88). In the pages following the suicide attempt, as they ride in the park near the lake, an escaped German prisoner falls from the sky in his troubled Hurricane and ends up in the same lake, provoking Caz's comment: 'You're the second person I've fished out of the lake this morning' (110). All of this tragicomically connects one side of Celia to that German propulsion towards death that, as we saw earlier, causes Europe to square off in the twentieth century: 'Always there is this war between Germany and England' (88).

But the other, British, 'surviving' side of Celia is the one that cagily shifts her ground in argument throughout the novel – demonstrating herself capable of turning her nation's leaving of India into a heroic act, for example, even one that proves 'The English law is above the world' (126). The rest of Europe would like 'to shift [England]' out of her colonies, in Smith's other use of the word. As Caz puts it, following Celia's remark that 'the rest of the world...with none too clean a forefinger, point out the path of sainthood for England to follow, while they go quite another way themselves': '[T]hey are so bored, really, just to go on seeing England there, it is getting boring for them, they think: That survival lump, it's about time we shifted her' (125). And indeed, Celia later tells Caz that in her dreams she – as both England *and* Germany? – *is* thus shifted, or will be in the end:

> Caz, I say, I once saw you, you were standing on the bank of a stream at the other side. There was a man with you, he had a plaster caste of a baroque face, with an elegant long nose, a little chipped. So there he stood, this plaster baroque person, and he twirled an hourglass at the end of a black moiré ribbon.
>
> I never stood with such a companion, said Caz.

> Oh, yes you did. I was walking by this stream and then standing still.
> It was a February filldyke ditch, flowing dirty below a factory town;
> very grim it was, this stream, and the factory town that could never be
> a city.
> So what happened? said Caz.
> Oh, I slipped, I fell; I fell into the stream.
> And I fished you out, I suppose?
> No, you did not move. And they said: 'That will shift her', for they
> were tired of my long death song. That will shift her, and I struck my
> head on an underwater snag. 'That will shift her', they said, and that
> indeed did.
> It was a dream, said Caz.
> No, no. (163–64)

Caz's remark strikes us as comical, given that most of what 'happens', particularly in this latter half of the novel after the cast's arrival on holiday, is dream-like – indeed often nightmarish, with dialogue as frenzied as that in a dark Pinter play. But here Celia/England is *finally* 'shifted', along with Germany and all else that falls into the stream or flood of the times that the trilogy has been surfing since the first pages of *Novel* – imaged, perhaps, in that 'moiré' or watered silk ribbon on which time swings above. Terminally polluted by industry and war, it swallows up our speaker so thoroughly that in her dreams even Casmilus no longer conducts her out from her post-war state of spiritual death back to the Hades of her holiday. It seems the fate of European culture itself has been predicted by this enigmatic image of juggled time: this plaster caste of a baroque face, an inversion of the usual Renaissance or baroque caste of a classical face. It may suggest a reproduction of the reproducers, indicating the playing-out of European history as a 'long death song' of reproduced violence, as Pompey's name in the first two novels similarly suggested.

The European Christian-cultural apparatus for self-destruction

Such cyclic violence is, as I suggested earlier, eerily sadomasochistic in the novel – a term Freud defined as dependent upon perversions of the death drive that occur when the instinct focusses outward to take another object or turns upon itself as said object. Smith develops her thoughts about the complex relationship between Europe's 'drives' run amok and its imbibed cultural text through an ongoing black comedy in the novel concerning its characters' schoolboy educations, all of which seem to have been built through not only punitive Christian formation but also on being 'flogged through Homer' and other classical epics. This particular comic riff culminates in the otherwise very dark moments of argument at the end of the novel when both strands of educational policy, secular and Christian, ironically intertwine in Uncle Heber's revelation that he, too, is a product of the system: 'I hold with discipline, control, sobriety and diligence. I was myself twice flogged through Homer' (196). This statement produces howls of laughter from Celia and Caz, as well as from us as readers due to the many repetitions this very same confession has had in the novel: '*Not you, too, Uncle?* we cry. Not you too? For first there was Basil [Smith's caricature of George Orwell], and then there was Tom, and then there was Tiny, and then there was Caz, and now there is Uncle. Not you, too!' Apparently no one in culture – not even the placid clergyman Uncle Heber whom Tiny described as 'happy and resolved and calm and loving' (188) – is exempt from the scars of such repression and 'control' in the novel; and of course, as readers of it, we are well aware of the potentially violent flip side to this kind of '*cultural suppression of the instincts*' (Freud 425) that results in Heber's mechanical announcement of his 'hold[ing]' with 'control' and 'discipline', and perhaps in his wielding of the same kinds of punishments in his role as teacher of the faith. This kind of education was connected early on and ironically by Smith to Christian formation, and thus to the very heart of European culture, when Celia exploded with her mini-dissertation on the 'too-tidy' – or oedipally repressive – nature of religion:

> [I]t too much bears the mark of our humanity, this Christian religious idea, it is too tidy, too tidy by far. In its extreme tidy logic is a diminution and a lie. These rewards and punishments, this grading, this father-son-teacher-pupil idea, it too much bears the human wish for something finished off and tidy, something one can grasp lovingly and tight, trusting to the Father, the Son and the Holy Ghost. It is the most tearing and moving thing, this wish to gain marks and approval, to plod on, with personal and loving chastisement, to infinity. This beating idea is also something that is always coming up. The truth is that people cannot bear not to be beaten. (43)

As Freud would explain it, 'Conscience and morality have arisen through the overcoming, the desexualization, of the Oedipus complex; but through moral masochism morality becomes sexualized once more, the Oedipus complex is revived' – as is new need for punishment at the hands of a parental power (424). Indeed, Smith makes clear that one of the greatest ironies inherent within such a system, extended into the secular schooling of children, is that girls are *not* beaten, though they too 'cannot bear not to be beaten' (118). Particularly given that, as Celia puts it, 'I do not see Christ in glory, but only upon the cross' (118) – an image perpetuated by Christian teaching as the dominant one, and one which encourages moral masochism by valourising the punished as the most worthy of love. Within this ironic and upside-down system of learning, Smith intriguingly suggests that girls may find themselves both 'fruitfully' exempt and yet condemned to fruitlessness as well, as this exchange between Celia and Tom, our broken figure of the intellect, makes poetically clear:

> And I said how girls were better off than boys in the way they came late to the Greek and ran quickly at it....
> And Tom said it was different with boys, this classical idea, and it was a burden and a misery and an outrage, and that twice was he flogged through Homer, and that the reason girls did not advance so far was that at girls' schools there was no corporal punishment and that it was only the fear of pain that would drive these bored and wretched children to their task.
> But I think there might be one good thing that would come out of it, and for that one good thing the years and tears of boredom must pay.... But that is a poor hang-dog argument, we should hurry up to find a better way....
> There is dead sea fruit in the schoolchild's mouth, and Africa and her deserts in the hair on her head. And there is the feeling of guilt in the schoolchild's mind, and she turns her head this way and that and cries: 'Now it is over, now it will soon be over'. (117–18)

Rather than celebrating feminine escape from the fate of cultural centrality, Smith quite typically has Celia recount that through her escape from patriarchal complexes she learned instead 'to be sick with boredom, and to resist both the good with the bad' and thus risk absolute extinction. In a fascinating later passage, the one following Celia's recounting of her dream of England's 'shifting', or its death, as her own, she remembers being in a cemetery and seeing epitaphs in which women are effectively erased from memory. Following her despair in recalling one fragment of a relational memorialisation on a stone – 'And of his wife Elizabeth', etched at the end of a long account of Thomas Krak's life and works – she 'wanted to pray' but could only recall 'Our father, our father' and nothing after that (164–65). The deeply ironic frustration and shame of the not-taught, not-flogged and thus not-valued (in the familial/instructive sense) links the female child to the 'others' of European colonisation – the 'deserts' of Africa – and those equally outside the brutal loop of inherited power. The desire for it to 'be over', for apocalypse and endings, the death drive towards extinction, seems juxtaposed here opposite the drives to either receive pleasurable punishment or to dominate and rule that grows out of the sadistic desire *to punish*, the inversion of the same.

Caz's 'I do not know that we can bear not to be at war' (8) resonates in the above passages, encouraging us to connect personal dramas with international ones. And indeed the more invidious results of what Tom called 'the fear of pain' that brings on male 'advancement' Smith documents in one of the novel's most central scenes involving yet another Dostoyevskian dialogue about leaving India. It happens very shortly after Celia, Caz and Tiny arrive for their holiday at Heber's, and it occurs over much drink, with repetitive transitions of 'That's the spirit, pass the whiskey' or 'That's the spirit, pass the beer'. In addition to comically underlining with such punning the gaping lack of 'spiritual' ease or steadfastness in either Celia (arguing *as* England here) or in the conversation itself, the scene reveals the economic ties between pagan Roman and Christian elements in the cultural legacy that our characters try (and fail) to discuss. It takes place in the Hades of Heber's 'dark and sulphurous' kitchen (124) – a description that will later be used to allude to the purgatory of Hamlet's father's ghost (190). All four characters are symbolically dark as well – 'dirty and muddy and tired' – as they begin to argue, and Celia moves the argument in a political direction with the comment I began to discuss earlier: that the rest of the world is 'none too clean' enough to point its finger at England for stalling in 'quitting India' (125). Calling up typical English images of India, Celia snidely implies that their rule of themselves deserves censure: 'Burn the widows, rape the kids, up the castes, and hurrah for Indian legal probity' (125–26). Shot up by this, she exclaims: 'The English law is above the world... it is not to be bought, it is strong, flexible and impartial' (126). Caz's snide response to this is to agree that it is not to be bought, 'at least by the poor' (130). Smith also comments on very recent legislation by having him immediately and coyly ask, 'And this new whipping law, this Emergency Whipping Act they have passed for India?' Celia 'wring[s her] hands in response, for indeed [she] felt it to be a shameful thing', but when she counters with the assertion that 'the inflammable student material' causing the problem is better dealt with through whipping than through shooting, Caz retorts with more agreement – a ploy Smith uses throughout the argument to suggest the ironic and horrifying simultaneity and reconcilability of all of these positions:

> Oh yes, much better... because you can do it several times. It is always such fun. I remember how I used to enjoy it so much at school, we always had this clean wholesome fun, we derived great pleasure from it, eh, Tiny? (126)

Tiny's uncomfortable and unconvincing response of denial is seconded by Celia's parodic description of the larger situation, which we as readers, however, understand is being offered without *Smith*'s irony: 'The British will always eventually pass flogging laws because the governing classes are flogged themselves so much through the public schools.'

Celia is just beginning to waver in her rhetorically familiar diatribe against India – her accusations that it was 'fighting for Hitler' with its refusals to support the British during the war, and so on – when Tiny chimes in with 'It was very much the situation that the Romans had with Christ' (127).

After which Caz brings up 'Mahatma' (or 'great souled') Gandhi and his infamous imprisonment by the British, as well as the 'very proper beating' his non-violent followers received after they themselves fell into 'violence and destruction'. Celia attempts to argue that the Indian Congress was crafty in its plans for all this to happen, so that it could escape 'the responsibility and the possibility – the certainty – of failing and being discredited', but 'all the time at the back of [her] mind is the thought of the expedient crucifixion' (127–28). This thought is the one that casts Celia into the mode of despair that sets the tone for the remainder of the novel. Like Dostoyevsky's famous 'Grand Inquisitor' section of *The Brothers Karamazov*, Smith's final pages of *The Holiday* contemplate the cultural imperative to once again 'crucify Christ' – or 'burn [him] at the stake' (Dostoyevsky 1981, 301) – should he return. The control of the Catholic-cum-many-headed-Christian Church – the 'expediency' of its methods of disciplining and punishing and rewarding itself – would be rocked by the reappearance of such a pure innocent, such an alternatively wise law-bender. As Celia says in despair to Uncle Heber, at a later moment of near break-down, '*Je ne peux pas le voir que sur la croix*' (135) – I do not see him but only upon the cross (translated from her earlier assertion (118) in order to, perhaps, ventriloquise all Europe). Celia also says at the end of the novel that Christianity has been 'hobbled by past centuries and torn by the sufferings of Christ that we deride' (191). And, by way of gloss, she told Tom that [heraldic, British] eagles are 'said...to eat young lambs' (35), like the very 'Lamb' of God referred to at the end of Reginald Heber's hymn. In other words, when the goals of imperial power are, as they were in *Over the Frontier* and the hymn, yoked to self-righteousness, they reproduce the same Romanesque ('Apennine') forces that expedite goals by slaughtering the innocent in the very name of the slaughtered innocent, Christ. The whole of this novel might be said to be an investigation by this 'child of Europe', this would-be heavenly Celia, of the emptied spiritual philosophy at the core of her history. It is a history which has *long* demonstrated, as Smith often suggested, quoting Gibbon, that 'it was not in this world that the Christians were desirous of being either useful or agreeable' (193).[62]

'It was a perfectly legal sentence', Caz asserts, referring to the crucifixion, 'and with the flogging sentence too, there is precedent and trial' (129, 130). 'Oh yes', Celia says, defeated, 'look[ing] at the tablecloth, the yellow pattern was faded in the wash. [She] said: The law allows it and the court awards' (130). This oft-quoted line from the courtroom scene in Shakespeare's *The Merchant of Venice* of course summons images of the allowable pound of human flesh taken for the payment of debts. But just in case her anti-Semitic readers of the time were still inclined to equate such bloody-mindedness with Jewish merchants, Smith has Caz remind Tiny and Celia that it is the Christian who deserves to claim connection to such classical legacies, for little has changed since the Romans crucified, along with Christ, many other Jews for the sake of expediency: 'The Romans said that Medicine Cross was the best remedy for Jewish obstinacy, we seem to have heard echoes of this in our own times' (129). Shakespeare's line, which Celia feels 'caught in a phrase the cruelty and the blindness of the world and history' (130), also takes us back as readers to the 'Judas pound' Celia obliquely referred to earlier in the novel when speaking about the survival tactics of her country amid inter-war and post-war rhetorics of change and 'new worlds':

> In Russia, we are told, there is this simplicity and single-mindedness that is so noble and so admirable, they have not been touched by the weakening and destroying civilisation of the West, they are not corrupt. And believing or half-believing this idea about Russia, we feel guilty and are irritable. It is that thought about a thought that nags at us, and we seem to do nothing but a lot of things that are nothing. For we are not prepared to give up our way of life, for we have no bloody revolution since three hundred years, for we have this disgusting temporising mind, we will give up a little but not everything, we will pare away a little here and there, we will make accommodations with conscience, but all the time, No, we will not give up our Western way, indeed we will not, why we cannot conceive of such a thing, not really to imagine it. And Government sees to it that the majority of the people shall have a stake in our civilisation, they shall have a qualifying Judas one-pound share. (54)

Capturing her characters' post-war in-betweenness – their 'devil of a middle situation' – this passage also suggests with its punning on 'pound' (as currency in sterling, and as flesh) the person-by-person, consumer-by-consumer selling-of-soul, and selling of *consciousness* as well as conscience, that in Smith's view made all of her compatriots culpable. As Celia says at the end of the argument I detail above, 'We are among corrupt people, how can we be innocent? How can we have a revolution and make a new world when we are so corrupt?' (131). And as we remember from the New Testament story, Judas was fated to hang *himself*.

Suggesting that western culture might do the same, Smith makes clear thirty pages later, via a poetic return to the initiating image from *Novel on Yellow Paper*, that the baby in the cradle on the curdling crest of hundred-year-old discursive hobby-horses, chauvinistic public opinion and imperial rhetoric has been killed or lost (see Chapter 3, pp. 84–85). All we have left is an 'animal without a heart' – the cat that had been teetering on the cradle's edge – now shivering on 'a piece of wreckage that was turning round and round in the current, hunting a beetle 'without a thought of its plight', decisively unconscious of its end-game moment in history (169). This rhythmically beautiful passage, during which Caz and Celia swim in melancholy fashion along a sandbar in 'earthquake weather', even over 'the core of the earthquake' as they leave the scene, is so dense that explication of it would require many more pages that I have available to me here. But it envisions an ending for European culture that continues to be violent; the cat 'pounces upon [Caz's] hand and t[ears] it straight across' when he tries to save it, though its teeth are chattering and it is as cold as our characters have been throughout the novel. As though recalling Sitwell's highly satirical first poem of *Façade*, 'Hornpipe' (which she was known to have heard in performance), Smith ends the passage with Caz dancing this emblematically British naval dance in an increasingly frenzied fashion, feeling chilled despite the hot air.[63] Celia thinks that he is like 'an abandoned shipwrecked British sailor', and as she claps in time he desperately dances '[q]uicker, quicker, quicker' (170), echoing the mad dances of Pompey in *Over the Frontier*. Like so many of the most important passages in particularly her last novel of the trilogy, this one requires the kind of reading one might do of one of her poems. It speaks mutely and in trans-trilogy fashion of the coming to an end of an era's movement, of its long trajectory, its 'long death song', while lamenting the bankruptcy of language to understand the same. Like her most famous poem, 'Not Waving But Drowning', this passage is evocative of such limitations in signage, though its meaning when translated into the national realm – with its military signals doubling as cultural emblems – is more sinister. Smith seems to prophesy her contemporaries' identification to the last with the aggressive repertoires of nations and their interests – their all-but-unconscious clothing, in other words, with the 'limits of Empire', as Pompey put it when she finally remembered her costume at the drug-suffused party in *Over the Frontier*.

Uncle Heber, post-war 'peace' and the end of the novel

Though the novel continues with further painful fights, it ends on a note of repentance and desire for impossible ending. We might understand Smith's choice to end the novel in this way by thinking back to one of her earliest published poems entitled 'Heber' (*CP* 20) – a short lyric about a mysterious figure of creaturely comfort in a household, but one whose inarticulate presence drives its speaker to despair. Like Uncle Heber, the figure in the poem is peaceful, in a calm state of equilibrium: 'And if I don't speak to him / He'll stay by my side', says the speaker; 'But oh in this silence / I find but suspense: / I must speak have spoken have driven him hence.' For seemingly similar reasons, Celia is on the attack as the novel draws to a close; she seems angry, she *must* rock Heber's unquestioning equilibrium, must get past the post-war 'suspense' of not knowing or not wondering what the fate of Europe's not-so-Christian Christian culture will be. After a further round of arguing, during which Celia subjects her interlocutors to quotes from her reading journal – Gibbon, Dostoyevsky and even Smith's own poem 'A Humane Materialist at the Burning of a Heretic' (192; *CP* 283), each evocative of the often bloody hypocrisy of western cultural beliefs – Celia bullies

Uncle Heber into acknowledging that as Christian children their fate will be 'always to be ruled by fear' (200–01). She does so by intercepting his initial response of 'storm[ing] and rav[ing] at [her]: You are blasphemous, spoilt and evasive' with one of her own that Smith would reuse in her poem 'Cool as a Cucumber': 'No, Uncle, I am nervy, bold and grim' (192; *CP* 240). She and Caz slowly overcome his look – 'the slant of a look of the Fairchild-père in [their] uncle's eyes' (196)[64] – by responding with cruel and destructive laughter to his admission that he too was flogged through the classics at school. Celia tortures him further by offering an impromptu text of her own for his next sermon – one that depicts death as the cold unknown; the kind of scenario Smith's poems often depict, as we shall see. She then upbraids him *and* the 'positive' Caz (194) with thoughts that sound much like Smith's theological ones: '[I]f men were not so positive they would be more kind.... I detest your Christianity that will be so positive. Unknown unknown, unknown, let that be the life to come and the world that lies beyond' (199). Celia's – and perhaps Smith's – only suggestion for salvation at the end of *The Holiday* is, ironically, one that advocates *not* believing in it. It seems that utter humility, or the Socratic recognition that one knows nothing, can predict nothing, is what Smith's Celia is drawn to, perhaps to curb the self-righteousness that conducts and covers up the 'business' of this novel. When Caz objects that Celia is 'mad' (like Tom), that 'Christianity is not the enemy, why nobody but the Archbishop thinks of it at all; it is the modern religions of Communism and Fascism, that is where we must look out' (199); Celia counters with a response that glosses the end of *Over the Frontier* for us as well: 'Ha, ha, ha, I say, so *you* say. But the Archbishop is in the right of it, he is a very strong man, very wise, very astute' (200). He knows how to harness the death drive to the need for such belief – for ends that Smith has connected throughout the novel to imperial or national gain. In what seems a quirky move, Smith suggests in these last pages that whereas other '-isms' which she found unsavoury would prove themselves so in time, the Church, like England, would simply shift its ground – always re-emerging in a form able to save itself by colluding with the worst in human desires. She seems therefore to bring up Confucius on the last page for what she considers salutary reasons – in order to attempt the move from Christian thinking about 'heaven or hell or the life to come' to concerns about the human world, exclusively (292).

Yet the ending to the novel is obviously and deliberately 'too tidy by far' in its final prayer and sharing of Confucian wisdom (which cannot arise without reminder of the part that China has played in this novel). It is not *only* that her sudden resorting to Eastern wisdom in a novel that has focussed so resolutely on the indestructible and imprisoning text of western culture is fairly suspect. Far more importantly, this ending is simply not adequate – it happens too quickly, as is often true in Smith's most uncomfortable poems. In the space of less than half a page, Heber, Caz and

Celia – who have been fighting – quite improbably bless one another, as well as the absent Tom, and lie down to sleep: a split subject/family recomposed in unconsciousness. But Smith has made it impossible to believe this recomposure will last, whatever its worth. Although Clem, that very figure of expediency and the literal nemesis of all those heading off for their 'holiday', has, just after his violent arrival, departed in pursuit of Tiny – who has made the symbolic choice to return to life as opposed to remaining in the suspended state of the others 'on holiday' – we are told on the penultimate page of the novel that 'He looks like he would say: I will come back for you another time' (201). And most importantly, we know that this decision to collectively fall asleep – from which Tiny with a shudder roused her earlier, beseeching her to 'wake up, wake up... come back' (187–88) – is the wrong one; such unconsciousness has been highly problematised in the trilogy as an 'active choice':

> God bless you Celia, Celia, said our uncle, and you too Caz, and my son Tom, God bless him.
> God bless us all, sir, said Caz, and took my hand in his.
> Amen, I said, and fell asleep. (202)

Though we *wish* to believe our characters have at last some measure of peace, these final words of the novel are, again, too tidy. In the back of our minds we recall that lying down with Caz is synonymous with riding in the train of history into unconsciousness, as she did when rocking in his arms at the start of the novel, and as she did when riding in the locked carriage with him on their way to this suspended space, this 'holiday'. Caz's response, so like *A Christmas Carol*'s 'God bless us every one', is too innocent – and we know these characters are *not* innocent; we have been told so too many times in Celia's desperate lines. And, less than five pages ago, Celia and Caz, while cruelly making fun of their weltering uncle, inadvertently connected Celia to this sleep as her fate in the 'perpetual night' to come. For in their mocking of educational imperatives they had hilariously decided that it was 'a shame that little boys should get smacked for such dreary and second-hand cheap thoughts as Nox est peretua [*sic*; should be 'perpetua'] una dormienda... Et cetera' (197). This is of course a reference to Catullus's fifth song to his love Lesbia – translated in part, significantly, in Ben Jonson's song 'To Celia', in which his speaker says: 'Suns may set and rise again; when the brief light once (and for all) goes out for us, an eternal night must be slept.' With exquisite irony, Smith makes sure that what her characters will enact is quite precisely those 'dreary and second-hand cheap thoughts' that infiltrate them and even name them as products of their cultural text.

But is this the eternal night come? We also recall that less than twenty pages prior to this Caz had said 'Men pray for peace,... but when it comes

they are like rabbits that foul their pasture, like dogs they lift their legs
upon it and say: "Peace hath her victories no less than war, but no one
quite remembers what they are"' (183). Celia 'love[s]' this perversion of
John Milton's perversion of Cicero in his sonnet 'To the Lord General
Cromwell' (with the title continuing 'May 1652./On the proposals of certain
ministers "at the Committee" for the Propagation of the Gospels'). In the
sonnet, these particular lines suggest the need for more peacetime evangelism
to ward off the 'secular chains' being proffered by mercenary heathen, and
the octet regales Christian conquest even more brutally than does Reginald
Heber's hymn:

>   Cromwell, our chief of men, who through a cloud
>   Not of war only, but detractions rude,
>   Guided by faith and matchless fortitude
>   To peace and truth thy glorious way hast ploughed,
>   And on the neck of crowned fortune proud
>   Hast reared God's trophies and his work pursued,
>   While Darwen stream with blood of Scots imbrued,
>   And Dunbar field resounds thy praises loud,
>   And Worcester's laureate wreath; yet much remains
>   To conquer still; peace hath her victories
>   No less renowned than war, new foes arise
>   Threatening to bind our souls with secular chains:
>   Help us to save free conscience from the paw
>   Of hireling wolves whose gospel is their maw. (Milton 324–25)

Caz's perversion of the heart of the sestet takes the idea back to Cicero's in
De Officiis (I, xxii, line 74) (and indeed, earlier (151), Celia had lamented
that she had 'become a Cicero of the grievance and the vulgar phrase'),
because both Caz's and Cicero's versions not only warn that 'most' do not
understand the worth of peace but suggest that peaceful accomplishments
should be 'more important' than warlike ones. Milton's use of a warlike
metaphor to advocate the 'Propagation of the Gospel' contributes to *The
Holiday*'s warnings in general about Christianity's increasingly incestuous
couplings of militancy and religion for the sake of expediency. The most
central theme of her post-war novel, as my first quote of this chapter
suggested, might be heard in Cicero's *Defensio Secunda*: 'If, after putting an
end to war, you neglect the arts of peace; if war be your peace and liberty,
war alone your virtue, your highest glory, you will find, believe me, that
your greatest enemy is peace itself; peace itself will be by far your hardest
warfare' (Milton 325, n. lines 10–11). Although Celia laughingly counters
Caz at this point – 'but men are noble animals, they are not dogs and
rabbits' – a page away from the end of the novel she will assent, recalling
her own and her country's long history of 'shiftiness'. Her only answer will

be to wish without hope, as she has done many times in imitation of Hamlet, that her death might be a sleep without dreams:

> I have a long sad pause for a moment while I am thinking that I hope so much that death is the death of the mind, and I think: Oh, beastly mind that shifts so much, that is a tyrant, that runs every way and every way at once; that will be one thing never, that will be no one thing that is not laughter, contempt and war. (200)

But at Heber's they are, as we saw above, in Hamlet's father's purgatory, merely shifted but not at peace. In Smith's *post-war* novel there is, ironically, no peace. Thus as we come to the end of her speakers' 'running on' along shifting and often militant discursive terrains we realise, paradoxically, that what we have come to is impossible: the end cannot come. And therefore the novel closes as it does, on a wished-for but tenuous sleep that is far less genuinely peaceful than Beckettian: another balancing act upon their 'cradle' (European history) careering on the flood.

Added understanding of why Smith may have ended the novel this way is provoked, perhaps, by the 'prophetic' quote, as Celia calls it, from Dostoyevsky's *Notes from the Underground*. Celia raises it as [Smith's] extraordinarily self-reflexive final commentary on the *writer* in such times, and on the act of writing. Celia has been writing throughout, we are told; and Caz has repeatedly if enigmatically commented that 'it is this writing business that makes you so sad: Oh, it is that, on top of the war and after-the-war and being in the middle of things without the turning point yet come, that makes you cry. Oh, the writing business is very corrupting' (156). She admits as much as well, for as she tries in a kind of frenzy to 'confess' her ills and fears to her uncle, she is again stopped by the consciousness of how she is sounding, and how impossible is her desire to 'speak up', as she put it near the start of the novel (53). Thus she suddenly switches to quotation, and carries on with Dostoyevsky's thoughts, *verbatim*:

> Oh, I think, this is something that must prick home to every writer that has sensibility and a desire, to establish himself. I look maliciously at Heber, I am reading it (I say) through my tears. 'And how persistent are your sallies, and at the same time what a scare you are in. You talk nonsense and are pleased with it; you say impudent things and are in continual alarm and apologising for them. You declare that you are fond of nothing, and at the same time try to ingratiate yourself in our good opinion.... You may perhaps have really suffered, but you have no respect for your own suffering.... You doubtless mean to say something, but hide your last word through fear, because you have not the resolution to utter it, and only a cowardly impudence. You boast of consciousness, but you are not sure of your own ground, for though your mind works,

yet your heart is darkened and corrupt, and you cannot have a full genuine consciousness without a pure heart. And how intrusive you are, how you insist and grimace. Lies, lies, lies. (192–93; Dostoyevsky 26)

The quote functions as a framing device in the novel as a whole; it balances – or rather, unbalances – the earlier long digression about another 'prison' writing, Boethius's *The Consolation of Philosophy*. Smith quotes from her own review of Helen Barrett's edition of the latter, in which she critiques Boethius for not being terribly philosophical about certain things – like his anger at his accusers, whom he describes in ways she found 'unlikely' (52) – but then pronounces 'heroic' because despite his despair he was able to 'g[et] the better of his feelings' (53) and hand on to others his own form of consolation. However, Smith makes it clear within the whole of her own book's trajectory that his project – to explain 'good and evil, and justify the ways of God to man' – can no longer be undertaken by the likes of her characters; Celia calls Caz and herself in these final dialogues of *The Holiday* '[a] pair of hangdogs, a survival from the fearful thirties, no good at all' (190). The world as she saw it in the 1940s had 'shifted' to some place where any attempt to depict 'dignity in suffering', as Tennyson also did, quite sincerely, in works like *Maud*, can only look 'very absurd indeed' to post-war eyes:

> for the life that we know does not, oh does not give dignity in suffering, indeed the life that we know seems like the Nazis to give always the maximum of pain with the maximum of indignity. So we cannot believe a word of the *Maud* situation. (181)

Though she longs for 'the simple noble way of going wrong' that was possible for earlier literature, with its clear lessons and morals, Celia cannot offer any. She must 'hide [her] last word through fear', as Dostoyevsky's underground writer put it, because she has not 'full genuine consciousness' with a 'pure heart' that, as he tells us, is necessary to be 'sure of one's ground'. Smith portrays Celia in her last 'sallies' towards 'speaking up' as being forced back to her 'script' – her written notes on and quotes from texts she has read – as though she has little generative articulacy outside them, or agency to move beyond the givens of her own inscription by culture, by all the texts she has imbibed. She 'drop[s her] head upon [her] book' (193) at the end of this tirade and weeps; every motion of these last pages, excluding her last one of exhaustion, details an ironic struggle to be conscious of her own overwritten 'unconsciousness' – or rather her purportedly victorious, post-war state of mind.

Stevie Smith's novel trilogy is an extraordinary, fourteen-year exercise in self/cultural analysis that merges condemnation with comedy and much poignancy as well. It contributes in radical fashion to mid-century expressions of concern about the complicity of all as partakers in the language of power relations, due simply to helpless inscription as everyday 'speakers' in the immensely complex and coded structures of culture. It succeeds against the feared impossibility of writing, at the same time that it demonstrates a necessary change of countenance that Smith seemed to have decided texts must take. Never 'at home' on their rafts of discourse, Smith's characters – multiple personae or 'rafts' for her own fractured thought – exist 'discomfited' in her novels, as we shall next see they also do in her poems. And they do so by virtue of Smith's extraordinarily dialogic strategies which, as many have noted them in Dostoyevsky's prose, cast irreconcilable argument against irreconcilable argument in despairing attempts to analyse her own English programming, her own imprisonment in the deeply unresolved *and thus repeating* deceptions of her cultural text. Unlike her contemporaries she had only wavering faith that she could be 'less deceived' (Larkin 1955), however – unless she 'broke herself up', subjected herself to the most brutal kind of analysis. And yet even about this fact she has a sense of humour, and a caveat, as her poem 'Analysand' makes clear:

> He chases his tail
> Like a puppy-fool
> And wonders it tastes stale
> The puppy-fool.
>
> All thoughts that are turned inward to their source
> Bring one to self-hatred and remorse
> The punishment is suicide of course.
> . . . .
> For fuss and fret
> His tears fall down
> His brow is set
> In savage frown.
>
> But is it surprising Reader do you think?
> Would you expect to find him in the pink
> Who's solely occupied with his own mental stink? (*CP* 54)

And yet thus, with 'tears fall[ing] down', we know, Smith's Celia writes:

> At night time when one has a fever one thinks of the grief and the grievances. One will write a book then; ah, ah, ah, how thick the tears fall down. Page after page of the new novel unfolds itself. In the night hours, in the midnight hours of the flowers of revenge and memory, the novel is finished. It is called, My Humiliations. It needs but to add the title as the tears fall thick upon the burning flesh. Ah, ah, ah, My Humiliations. (151)

Both the burned and the burning, analyst and analysand, Smith's speakers like Smith herself and others whom she implicates in her trilogy's hall of mirrors perpetuate and explicate the violence that enables culture and writing, too. My long analysis of the novels has changed the way I read the poems. So to the project of the next and final chapter of this book.

5
Between Waving and Drowning: Stevie Smith's Poems, Stories and Radio Play

> The Failed Spirit
>
> To those who are isolate
> War comes, promising respite,
> Making what seems to be up to the moment the most
>   successful endeavour
> Against the fort of the failed spirit that is alone for ever.
> Spurious failed spirit, adamantine wasture,
> Crop, spirit, crop thy stony pasture!
>   – *Mother, What is Man?* (1942)

By way of opening example, a poem like 'The Failed Spirit' from Smith's wartime collection – remarkably never discussed as such[1] – is newly illuminated by careful explication of the trilogy at the same time that it illuminates aspects of the novels as well. Upon reading the above poem we find ourselves instantly back at the start of *Novel on Yellow Paper*, where Pompey began her monologue with a description of the 'Kismet', or fate, of her times. If we remember, it was presented to us as the recalcitrant and deeply destructive (hobby)horse she had been riding, whose sole desire was to 'crop a wall of its plant life', 'crop the verdure', 'la[y] waste' all pastures with the 'scythelike movement' of his grazing head stolen, it would seem, from time itself (9, 10).[2] War offers, as we have seen, terrible and ultimately self-destructive distraction from the isolation of the spirit that has been failed by, and *is* failed as a result of, Europe's religious and philosophical soul being 'sold out', made cost-effective in 'successful endeavour' translated into the languages of commerce and war.

    In effect, *all* of Smith's poems – from her first collection including work written in the 1920s, *A Good Time Was Had By All* (1937), to her last which was published posthumously, *Scorpion and Other Poems* (1972) – were conditioned by or set in this landscape of never-ending 'post-war', as Celia phrases it. Indeed, at least in some respects, it would not be wrong to think of Smith as being, broadly defined, a 'war poet', given the continual and desperate attention she paid to her culture's endgame expressed in the extraordinary violence of her 'times'. Others of her more thoughtful contemporaries like Geoffrey Hill were conducting similar interrogations of English history, religion, commerce and warfare, and were arriving at roughly the same conclusions about the present at roughly the same time as Smith but with less interest in allowing poetry to lose its gravity, both in the rhetorical and moral sense.[3] Though like Hill, with whom Penguin Modern Poets anthologised her in 1966, Smith 'exposes the muddle of Europe's dreaming', as Jeremy Hooker once beautifully phrased it,[4] and, more problematically at times, moralises about her 'state', she far more often abandons all dignified poses and poetic registers in the interest of conducting the same kind of messy self/cultural analysis in the poems that she does in the novels.[5] As the suddenly extended and prosaic, 'business-speak' third line of the above poem demonstrates, colliding as it does with the project of this otherwise high-mindedly moralising lyric Sally, Smith explores the ways in which every kind of recognisable rhetorical strategy and mundane speech-habit is complicit, takes part in that 'muddled dreaming'. The failure that is read as victory, the drowning that succeeds in looking like waving, the war on others that offers 'promising respite' – all guard against the more terrible realisation of one's paradoxical 'isolation' without the boon of independence from complicity: one's culturally induced 'spuriousness', politically, spiritually *and* artistically speaking.

A brief introduction to reading the poems

The result of having close-culturally read Smith's trilogy before approaching the more famous poems is that the latter far more clearly demonstrate their embeddedness in the same context – the fact that they are anything but 'eccentric', in other words, explicatory as they are of specifically English/European, early to mid-century cultural, military, spiritual, economic and philosophical crises. Many other kinds of insights into her manipulation of so-called 'voice', intertextual reference and form in the poems arise following such readings of the trilogy, but this first realisation is one we come to quite quickly, particularly given Smith's frequent importation of her poems and short stories into the highly topical novels and *vice versa*. I have tried not to discuss the busy traffic between novels and poems and stories in the course of my readings of the trilogy, not least because the length of my chapters on it would have stretched even further beyond the limits allowed by publishing conventions. But it is quite clear that the work Smith was doing in the Thirties and Forties involved both genres almost seamlessly, as though the 'speech-acts', the 'talkies', that constitute the action of the novels partake of the same repertoire of responses to the 'times of a black split heart' that the poems do, if in another generically coded register. Both *perform* the inability to speak or write in any simple, singular or clear fashion. In effect, all of Smith's works are performative works, and the addition of drawings – her extradiscursive coda – to the poems underlines this fact, as does her work's active demonstration of its inability to use any one 'line' to ward off the influences of other spoken and written discourses in either the public or private realm. Much more will be said about Smith's drawings in the second section of this chapter, after a close look at the workings of her language in the first collection of poems as it interacts with the prose. Her desire to foreground her contextualised inability to write 'purely', as Celia described it at the end of *The Holiday*, may account for what looks like Smith's deliberate awkwardness when she inserts poems and stories into the novels, or prose into the poems. Moreover, it seems certain that, given her far more risky and experimental conception of what Louis MacNeice famously referred to as 'impure poetry', Smith's mixing of genres was intended to serve us as a guide for reading her poems in general. The latter are, in other words, as deeply shot through with the inconsistencies and dangerous currents of thought and public speech of their time as the novels prove themselves to be upon thorough reading.

Therefore it is hardly surprising that, as we have seen, many readings of Smith's poems in the last dozen years have taken a partially or fully devoted Bakhtinian approach, given her remarkable 'novelisation', as such readers call it, of the poetic text. That poetry (which Bakhtin described as a genre largely confined to 'monologic' utterance) can provide the medium for dialogic encounters between contradictory internal as well external discourses has by now been asserted many times, and has at least in part underwritten the approaches to Smith's work recently made by critics such as Martin Pumphrey, Sheryl Stevenson and Laura Severin. Smith's poems and prose truly must be read dialogically as novelised forms because they do indeed *represent* utterance – particularly the 'internal stratification of language' (Bakhtin 1981, 264) – rather than attempt unified self-expression in narrative *or* lyric mode. Indeed, her work was doing so decades before our newly evolving definitions of subjectivity made Bakhtin's theories popular and taught critics to be unable to read *any* genre or speech act as the vehicle for unified utterance – as 'a voice...completely alone with its own discourse' (Bakhtin 1981, 328). Were Bakhtin aware of her work, we might say with some confidence following our close-reading of the trilogy, he would have found it as potently dialogic as Dostoyevsky's, which we know Smith admired and found sympathetic to her own project. This assertion alone should force more re-readings as well as re-categorisations of Smith's contributions to twentieth-century writing.

But thus far, attempts – including my own in the past – to faithfully execute a Bakhtinian reading of Smith's prose and poems have failed, largely due to their reluctance to allow Smith to become 'all broken up', as close-reading of the trilogy makes clear she tried to be, in order to reveal the 'internal stratification' of the languages that composed her. Instead, as I suggested in Chapter 1, even Bakhtinian critics have ironically *marshalled* the work into 'unified utterance' by choosing one thematic thread out of many, like 'childhood' or 'death', as being valourised in it or central to it; or by choosing one concern, such as her concern about the condition of femininity in her time, as being separable and 'primary' (Severin 52) – that is, the author's 'voice' making the one meaning we should hear emerging from the work as a whole. Most of these readings have a gendered project in mind. As I argued at the outset of this book, Smith's positioning as female within that social space that she plumbed as the heart of her own inner darkness *was* no doubt crucial, given what it perhaps enabled: the self-divisive, 'outsider' perspective, as Woolf famously described it, upon internal realms of *heteroglossia* reflective of and effectively controlled by dominating (male) discourses in her historical context. But Smith's 'feminiz[ing of] her models', for example, as both the traditional reading of her work by Christopher Ricks and the Bakhtinian ones by Stevenson and Severin describe it, leads to nothing remotely like a celebration of female power; unless one decided that her refusal to discriminate between men and women when it comes to levels of cultural corruption adds up to such a project (and in one sense, that may seem quite right). As she puts it in one poem, 'Dear Female Heart', which is difficult to assimilate within feminist readings of the poetry in general:

> Dear Female Heart, I am sorry for you,
> Your must suffer; that is all you can do.
> But if you like, in common with the rest of the human race,
> You may also look most absurd with a miserable face. (130)

The poem is accompanied by a drawing of a disoriented young woman between her narrow (single) bed and her looking-glass, attempting thus far unsuccessfully to comb her unruly hair and keep her straps from falling off her shoulders. We might think only of Smith's reprehensible essentialisation of the capitalised 'Female Heart' as one that remains miserable in its attempt to win a man and a double, married bed by primping – and indeed, an element of this *is* there, as we begin to realise after looking at *all* of Smith's poems about women, not just the ones that seem to offer a revolutionary take on their situation. But like all of Smith's poems, this too-tiny and too-seemingly-simple one begins to fray as its speaker, speech and underlying assumptions are dismantled. It actually becomes quite a large poem in import as the suggestion is made that this speaker's agonies connect her to 'the rest of the human race', all of which looks, whether prettified or not, out through masks that hide what, in another poem (depicting a male in its drawing), is called a 'monkey soul' ('The Face', 175). The image of a monkey – which as we know produces what looks to humans like a smile when it is feeling fear – is a perfect one for Smith's poetic repertoire. As an image, it reduces both empty vanity *and* its seeming opposite, the Dryasdust intellectualism she often targets, to cloaks for souls so desirous of what they can never obtain through such reproduced, learned behaviours that their only recourse is to maintain faces 'So vain... so eloquent / Of all futility' as they find ways to 'bang about' for attention, usually by 'utter[ing] social lies', as she puts it in this brutal poem:

> So wretched is this face, so vain,
> So empty and forlorn,
> You may well say that better far
> This face had not been born.

The speakers in these poems are not rescued from the Sophoclean nets of their all-but-classical fates, as this last line, reminiscent of the Chorus's last speech in *Oedipus Rex*, would suggest. The wretched state of humanity is reduced in her modern portrait of the same to being a product of social lies and greed rather than pride and the vagaries of the gods (and indeed, our man in the drawing for this poem is walking by a door that reads in tiny letters, 'GOLD'). These seem to substitute for 'civilisation' in Smith's vision of her context full of 'monkey souls', though she never idealised, in Victorian fashion, 'golden age' humanity either. Nor did she idealise, in modern/postmodern fashion, femininity. Nobody flies by the nets of cultural ventriloquism in these poems, though the poems often add a dimension of extra-discursive desire – never *solution* – to the mix.

To date, famous and seemingly simple Smithian quotables have most often been created by lifting them out of their context in the text as well as in history – again, something that neither the sociolinguist Bakhtin nor the close-reader nor the cultural studies theorist could ever advocate. In effect, critics have done just as Hugh Whitemore did when, at the very start of his 1977 play, *Stevie* (later televised), he spliced in lines from Caz and Celia's dialogue in *The Holiday* so that Glenda Jackson could forever immortalise Smith as someone who said 'Life is like a railway station... The train of birth brings us in, the train of death will carry us away' – as someone, in other words, riveted solely on the business of mortality (Whitemore 13).[6] But those lines – spoken by Caz, *not* our main speaker – are crucially sandwiched between the lines in a dialogue that contemplates much more than that – including the reasons, as he puts it, that 'we cry so much' in the 1940s. His question about the latter receives Celia's answer:

> It is the war, I say, and the war won, and the peace so far away. Some of our friends, I say, seek refuge in a high-pitched nervous giggle, very girlish. This goes on for a long time, it is no good, it is very facetious; very fatiguing for all of us, no good at all. (*TH* 155)

This in-betweenness (as my book's subtitle has it) and inarticulacy, which Caz also associates with being 'on top of the war and after-the-war and being in the middle of things without the turning point yet come' (156), best explicates these now famous lines about being between the trains of life and death, for his lines that follow hard on them are: '[W]e are cooling our heels upon the platform and waiting for the connection, and stamping up and down the platform, and passing the time of day with the other people who are also waiting' (155). Until her readers begin to realise that the subject imaged on the platform is English culture itself at mid-century – 'when will we shift her?' – and not specifically Smith, no access to her poems' real 'subject' will be gained. And until we read all the lines, as well as between them, to understand that a specific historical situation, imaged in a tangle of 'say[ing]', gives rise in her poems to the sense of being at a loss for words – and as a consequence 'nervously giggling' in a high-pitched and inadequate, 'no good', 'facetious' way – we will not be able to fully read the complex 'not waving but drowning' that happens in her often facetious-seeming poems. 'I say...I say', says Celia, repeatedly and awkwardly and self-consciously in the passage above. Smith does so, too, always. She is always aware of writing as a speech act, its self-protective bravado or evasive practices literally infiltrated by 'Voices Against England in the Night', the title of the poem she inserted into the central fight about India between Caz, Celia and Tiny in *The Holiday*. In a moment I will turn to that war-time poem, and its layering of the novel's text at the point that it awkwardly arises: in the midst of an argument that Celia is making from an angle seemingly antithetical to its suggestions. First, however, it would be useful to return to the pre-Second World War collections of poetry to consider in detail the development of Smith's 'impure' poetic practice.

I

The pre-war poems: *A Good Time Was Had By All* (1937)

Taken as a whole, Smith's first collection, published at the latter end of the Thirties and inclusive of poems produced in the 1920s, is focussed on the post-First World War landscape: on its various forms of fall-out violence and on the mad willingness of its people to perpetuate self-destruction. Send-ups of the situation as she saw it abound here, most clearly in poems like 'The Suburban Classes' which offers a mousetrap for their good riddance because 'There is far too much of them...Spiritually not geographically speaking' and they 'Menac[e] the greatness of our beloved England' as 'they lie/Propagating their kind in an eightroomed stye' (*CP* 26).[7]

> Now I have a plan which I will enfold
> (There's this to be said for them, they do as they're told)

> Then tell them their country's in mortal peril
> They believed it before and again will not cavil
> Put it in caption form firm and slick
> If they see it in print it is bound to stick:
> 'Your King and your Country need you Dead'
> You see the idea? Well, let it spread.
> Have a suitable drug under string and label
> Free for every registered Reader's table.
> For the rest of the gang who are not patriotic
> I've another appeal they'll discover hypnotic:
> Tell them it's smart to be dead and won't hurt
> And they'll gobble up drug as they gobble up dirt.

The voice offering this limerick-like satire, whose unexplained disdain seems based on the ease with which such satellite communities may be remotely controlled, is equally implicated through its similarly unexplained patriotism with regard to 'the greatness of our beloved England'. Perhaps there is no mistake by the typesetter, as one might have assumed: 'enfold' put down for 'unfold'. As it is it seems *all* (including 'readers' in libraries – and those of us reading these poems?) are 'enfolded' in this plan to dupe those in thrall to the power of print and/or fashion, including its maker.

'Private Means is Dead' throughout the collection, as one punningly playful central poem has it; in the place of such independence and volition, 'Captive Good [is] attending Captain Ill' (*CP* 74). In these first poems one can see the beginnings of what, in the novels, will become a black comedy about the spuriousness of 'private lives' – the idea that anyone has escaped being herded 'beyond the frontier of a separate life' (*OTF* 267). Captive Good, as we are told in this poem, could 'tell us quite a lot about Captain Ill, if he will'; but in this collection, we have foreshadowings of what Smith would elaborate so chillingly in the trilogy: the maturation of coded cover-up, propaganda and spin-doctoring in the ever more popular press. Christopher Ricks very beautifully suggests that 'this early poem [is] partly about the language's being eager to doff its civilian clothes and don its uniform' (1984, 245; *ISOSS* 197); however, he then abandons that suggestion to explicate the above line as a Shakespearean allusion (Sonnet 66) to, yet again, Smith's own desire for death. But this short poem has little to do with her own death, as the remainder of the lines, following the announcement of the death of 'Private Means' and the captivity of goodness, make quite clear:

> Major Portion
> Is a disingenuous person
> And as for Major Operation well I guess
> We all know what his reputation is.

> The crux and Colonel
> Of the whole matter
> (As you may read in the Journal
> If it's not tattered)
>
> Lies in the Generals Collapse Debility Panic and Uproar
> Who are too old in any case to go to the War.

Smith's linguistic joke is on the graduating failure of leadership, and *its* (as well as language's) 'disingenuousness', its popular-press 'lies' – *not* her own fate. It concludes with another suggestion that occurs often in this collection, and even more often in the next: that the success of 'Captain Ill' depends on the conversion and deployment of the young.

Therefore, perhaps, we might explain the presence in this first collection of two poems about, surprisingly enough, paedophilia. It seems less a matter of Smith's 'fixation about sexual perversion', as a reader for the publisher Curtis Brown suggested when he read 'Lord Barrenstock' (*S* 69), than a matter of Smith's interest in the relation between psycho-sexual perversion, power and the processes of enculturation. Both poems are, like another called 'What is the Time? Or St Hugh of Lincoln' (71), about boys being trapped and led away by 'old and blind/And weak' men, as this poem and its accompanying drawing makes very clear. While the seemingly simple ballad for 'St Hugh' (formerly known as the boy 'Hughie' in the poem, before his abduction up a 'crooked stair') might be read as a particularly disturbing example of Smith's theoretical collation of psycho-sexual trauma and religious fervour as we often saw it in the novels, 'Lord Barrenstock' is more topical and complex. Its subject – 'Lord Barrenstock and Epicene' who are 'yet not two lords but one' (70) – is obviously a kind of unisexual entity whose 'stock', or bloodline, is barren, sterile; it is also one that deals clandestinely in stocks, the 'futures' of which are thus condemned in this poem. Like Eliot in 'The Waste Land', Smith seems to deploy an image of 'deviant' sexuality in evocation of mercantilism embedded in cultural sterility, but her 'epicene' image is paedophilic rather than homosexual. Her questionable speaker's critique of this figure begins with the query: 'What's it to me that you have been/In your pursuit of interdicted joys/ Seducer of a hundred little boys?' (69). In typical Smithian fashion, the list of wrongs rushes out of iambic tetrameter and pentameter into extended lines of finance-speak that, in this case, turn on a couple of dactyls to comic, near-Gilbert-and-Sullivan-like rhythms:

> You trod the widow in the mire
> Wronged the son, deceived the sire.
>
> You put a fence about the land
> And made the people's cattle graze on sand.

Ratted from many a pool and forced amalgamation
And dealt in shares which never had a stock exchange quotation.

In their latter-day 'enclosure' of the people's land for themselves, such figures perform a violence – our speaker calls them 'unsocial acts' – that would seem to promote 'privatising' but, in Smith's repertoire of interesting reversals and paradoxes, instead promotes the death of private means for the many once again. The 'forced amalgamation' seems to proceed in kind from the rape of the little boys: a secretive 'sharing' that, like the shadily described share dealing above, is private not public, not socially regulated. Such are his/their 'interdicted joys', Smith suggests, using a term of (sexual) pleasure to describe what is obtained by forcefully annexing another. And yet once again, the poem's speaker is suspect. We learn that the answer to her/his original question, 'What's it to me?' is, disturbingly if comically, not that these acts are 'unsocial' – but that Lord Barrenstock's/Epicene's 'tie is crooked and [our speaker] see[s] / Too plain [he/they] had an éclair for [his/their] tea'. In other words, this speaker is as deeply under the spell of superficialities as our suburban class was in their rage for fashionableness. What is really the matter in his/her eyes is that the Lord(s) are 'too fat'; their 'shape is painful to the polished gaze' – they are 'too ugly to be such a sinner'. The advice 'Be good, my Lord, since you can not be pretty' suggests as Smith often does with that last word's unisexual descriptive: that in her hollowing culture, pleasing veneers like pleasing language cover acceptably for a host of sins.

Like *The Picture of Dorian Gray* ratcheted down to apply to more mundane subjects and situations, Smith's poems in this collection have ugly, revealing backsides covered over by seemingly innocent fronts. Take, for example, the 'merr[y]...puppy shops' from whose 'cold shadows at the back' children need to be led

> For the Hound of Ulster lies tethered there
> Cuchulain tethered by his golden hair
> His eyes are closed and his lips are pale
> Hurry little boy he is not for sale. ('The Hound of Ulster', 15)

Everywhere in these poems it is the enslavement of others, and of freedom itself, which allows for the only seemingly innocent buying up of pleasures.[8] This poem composed not long after the bloody fight for Irish independence in the Republic would seem to comment on the successful retainer of the North in the Kingdom's puppy shop of captives, though this surreal apparition of legendary Irish warrior Cuchulain still threatens and requires suppression. Here once again a child is led away, this time by the adult, 'courteous stranger' whose happy description of the shop has 'beguiled' him from what he then asks for: knowledge – that is, the real backstage to the unreal illusion of sanguine ownership that he would be taught.

As Smith's critics have long recognised, Blake's *Songs of Innocence and Experience* are often hovering in the background of Smith's work; she worried that '[h]is are very easy echoes to catch' (J. Williams, *ISOSS* 43). The above poem might have been illustrated by Blake, the bound tragic hero Cuchulain with his 'golden hair' enchained by the mind-forged manacles of the shop-goers. But Smith's visions involve none of Blake's fervent sense of divine immanence within the human, and no retrievable Albion; they reflect the lemming-like accommodation and unthinking control that she and others like Orwell feared were slowly taking over twentieth-century language and desire. For example, her own 'Little Boy Lost', once he has followed his father into the Dantesque 'dark wood', is not so much made a victim of dark *experience*'s flip side to *innocence* as chillingly rendered 'suburban', or 'normal', settling for being 'happy enough' and reconciled to purgatory:

> The wood was rather old and dark
> The witch was very ugly
> And if it hadn't been for father
> Walking there so smugly
> I never should have followed
> The beckoning of her finger.
> Ah me how long ago it was
> And still I linger
>
> . . . .
>
> The sun never comes here.
> Round about and round I go
> Up and down and to and fro
> The woodlouse hops upon the tree
> Or should do but I really cannot see.
>
> . . . .
>
> The wood grows darker every day
> It's not a bad place in a way
>
> . . . .
>
> Did I love father, mother, home?
> Not very much; but now they're gone
> I think of them with kindly toleration
> Bred inevitably of separation
> Really if I could find some food
> I should be happy enough in this wood
> But darker days and hungrier I must spend
> Till hunger and darkness make an end. (61)

In tone and attitude as well as genre – unravelling 'fairytale', one might call it: far more lax in its merged, uneven and finally broken quatrains giving way to couplets than Blake's tightly heroic quatrains were in the original 'song' – this poem more than any other in the first collection foreshadows Smith's famous 'The Frog Prince' and others of her inimitably 'disenchanted', mock-fairytale mode. Smith continually – and in some ways like Eliot – compares the dramatic wrongs depicted by great writers of the past with their accommodation in her present. She folds the suffering *dramatis personae* of former works, like Blake's heroic boy, into the non-heroic, anonymous, representative speakers of her fairytales penned for her own times, employing a mode that traditionally teaches children about common or feared fates in the 'real world'. In the backdrop of this poem are the growing suburbs of England, with *their* (unacknowledged) backdrop of the Hunger Marches – the latter the material result of, ironically, the materialism of the people led by the powers-that-be that fill these poems: the 'Lord Barrenstocks' whose criminal selfishness (backed in his case by blue blood) caused the stock markets to crash, go 'barren', given their 'forced amalgamations' and rape of the economy. Her 'little boy' growing up in this scenario does not heroically object, like Blake's, that his lot is circumscribed to 'pick[ing] up crumbs around the door'. Smith's just 'follows' his father into the bewitched space of the woods, while Blake's boy suffers for rejecting such bewitching, handed-down 'mystery'. Like Shakespeare's Cordelia in *King Lear*, he suffers for rejecting, with the voice of good 'reason' before a Church 'Father', the rhetorical gestures of love-pledging required of subjects – whether of the Church or of the King – in exchange for power-sharing:

> 'Nought loves another as itself
> Nor venerates another so,
> Nor is it possible to thought
> A greater than itself to know.
>
> 'And father, how can I love you
> Or any of my brothers more?
> I love you like the little bird
> That picks up crumbs around the door'.
>
> The priest sat by and heard the child;
> In trembling zeal he seized his hair;
> He led him by his little coat,
> And all admired the priestly care.
>
> And standing on the altar high,
> 'Lo what a fiend is here!' said he.
> 'One who sets reason up for judge

> Of our most holy mystery'.
>
> The weeping child could not be heard;
> The weeping parents wept in vain –
> They stripped him to his little shirt
> And bound him in an iron chain,
>
> And burned him in a holy place,
> Where many had been burned before.
> The weeping parents wept in vain –
> Are such things done on Albion's shore? (Blake 217–18)

The last unanswered question above resounds in Smith's poem, too, but only in our ears, not our speaker's. For her likewise unchampioned little boy who must speak for himself exercises no such powers of reason. Smith would have had more sympathy with the limiting 'reason' of the boy in Blake's poem than Blake himself might have had, believing mightily as he did in the transcendent powers of Imagination. Neither limiting reason nor corrupt 'priesthood' would have, for Blake, provided the liberation of the soul. Smith's own philosophy was too painfully sure of what the first stanza above suggests: thought is imprisoned by its own genealogy and context. And indeed the 'priest's' actions exemplify this, as they are bound by the same 'iron chains' that bind the boy since they harness the Church to ancient forms of barbaric violence rather than any judgement that might be seen as other-worldly. The mental violence, too, of the inaccessible keepers of 'our most holy mystery' – like that of the evil priest Smith extracts from Macaulay's *Lays of Ancient Rome* in *Over the Frontier*[9] – is a theme that as we know Smith was particularly keen to unfold in the trilogy. The use of such secretive privilege is in part what keeps the boy subservient and supplicant, a bird longing for the crumbs left around the door through which 'priests' in all their mystery disappear. Smith's decision to draw our attention to this poem by entitling her own the same suggests that a like background drama – centuries old yet infinitely reproducible in Europe – surrounds her own little boy; though his vision is blurrier, he 'really cannot see'. The increasingly complex cultural forces that control him – the 'ever interlacing beeches / Over a carpet of moss' that disallow him access, though he 'reaches', to where 'the breezes toss' – have become even more 'slick' in their use of 'captions' and 'print', as 'The Suburban Classes' puts it, so that 'the wood grows darker every day'.

Smith's emphasis on the impotence of language conscripted by cultural propaganda is very strong in this first collection, foreshadowing the same emphasis in her works to come. It in part explains her choice to depict as such the 'nonsense' she heard all around her, revealing the incongruent and often painful relation between what *is* and what is said, or representations of what experience is *supposed* to be. Her poem 'Breughel', for example, which Hermione Lee quite aptly suggests is built on a rhythm akin to Blake's 'Mad Song' (Lee 190), transfers the latter's isolated despair in order to produce the same sort of 'frantic pain' when looking upon what should be a warm village scene. As in *The Holiday*, when in Celia's final 'sermon' that she ghost-writes for Heber she pictures the future as a 'winter landscape... by Breughel out of Hecate' (198), Smith here converts what we familiarly think of as Breughel's loving touch in his paintings of dancing peasants into a rollicking emptiness, 'a dream' in which they 'evilly speak':

> Their words in a clatter
> Of meaningless sound
> Without form or matter
> Echo around. (84)
>
> . . . .
>
> Must thy lambs to the slaughter
> Delivered be
> With each son and daughter
> Irrevocably?
>
> From tower and steeple
> Ring out funeral bells
> Oh Lord save thy people
> They have no help else. (84)

Despite the metrical fun that Smith always indulges in – the gully formed in each line by interpolated anapests to create a sound more rolling and dancing than Blake's (and more like William Carlos Williams' 'The Dance'); the alternating unstressed endings of lines emphasising the half-funny, half-sad, trochaic trajectory of the content; the contrived (if not marked) delivery of 'de-li-ver-èd' by metrical imperative, which reduces the urgency of the speaker's plea to archaic gesturing – the poem is nonetheless as anguished as Blake's. Its speaker foresees 'the slaughter' – the next world war, perhaps, in madly revolving repetition of the last – that meaningless words and evil speech will bring on; thus this speaker might also tell us, as Blake's does, that 'to the vault/Of paved heaven/With sorrow fraught/My notes are driven' (Blake 12). Though it seems an overly dramatic suggestion it is, quite markedly and repeatedly in this collection, the death of *all*, not simply *herself*, that looms and, given the ambiguity of the prescription in the last stanza above, may even prove necessary to save people from themselves. When we recall the suicidal and murderous solutions suggested by Auden in his writing, as well as the genocidal ones being worked out in a very real way across the continent even as she wrote these poems, her only partly tongue-in-cheek, Sophoclean suggestion that 'it were better for man had he not been born' (as we just saw it in 'The Face' and throughout the novels) seems less surprising and comparatively mild.

And yet like Blake's speaker, whose words seem repelled by heaven's 'vault' to fall on 'night's ear', and who swears himself back to darkness rather than light – 'After night I do crowd/And with night will go' – hers is also left undone in this poem. It happens not only through the contrapuntal effects of its uneasily comic rhythms, and her speaker's too-righteous, outdated, rhetorically conventional language of condemnation – 'The ages blaspheme'; 'The people oh Lord are sinful', and so on – but also through the dialogue it bears with the poems that surround it in the collection. For example, the same 'clatter' of words in 'Breughel' is located *within* the next voice we hear speaking in the poem that immediately follows this one in the collection, 'The Blood Flows Back':

> The blood flows back behind my eyes
> For fears I cannot recognise.
>
> I stood upon the brink
> And heard the clink
> And clatter of my own thoughts.
> Fear drove them on, the craven crew,
> My soul was sick,
> I knew it knew
> For the first time
> And saw
> The thoughts that thronged its house
> All fears and lies
> All fears and craven subterfuge.
> My soul was sick and wished to die.
> Weeping its immortality
> My soul stood there.
>
> Ah me, ah me,
> What use contempt and hate?
> My self is welded to a whole
> And hidden thoughts must have their place
> With Will and Soul. (85)

Describing the same systolic/diastolic rhythms of cultural aggression and regression that we saw in the trilogy – the near-Nietzschean 'Will and Soul' as she puts it above – this poem diagrams both the revelation and suppression of those 'thoughts' that Pompey 'saw', at times, but more often 'hid' from herself. Their hiding, as we know, allowed her to *act* without the self-contempt and hate that otherwise would have 'stopped' her on her ride. Turning around the familiar expression that depicts 'life renewed' as 'blood flowing back', this poem suggests that such flowing back behind the eyes, so that the thoughts and fears revealed in the second stanza cannot be seen or recognised, allows for *the integration of self* – something that Smith always complicates as a good, given the repression of self-knowledge it must also deploy in order to act unthinkingly. And though this speaker surely means on one level that 'Myself is welded to a whole', which represents her self-integrity – her thoughts, Will and Soul working together in seeming unison – the line also suggests that no speaker can separate themselves from the cultural whole that convenes those thoughts that occupy one's 'house', 'that come rushing in at you from the outside-of', as Pompey despairingly put it (*OTF* 44).

We wonder about the speaker of 'Breughel', therefore, whose position seems judgemental, and somehow *above* all that 'clatter'. We wonder even more about this speaker's potential decision to call down divine as opposed to human slaughter, particularly when we recall the advice given in one of the earlier and most haunting poems of the collection, 'Es war einmal' ('Once Upon A Time'): 'Pray not to heaven' (36) for the death of your prey. The latter's title is linked to what will become Smith's crucial passage in *Over the Frontier*, when Pompey 'wakes' to understand that 'war, war is all my thought'; as we recall, she comes to that realisation after hearing in her mind the 'Old Men of 1922', from George Grosz's series, *A Post-War Museum*, coming back to tell her 'Es war einmal ein Krieg, Es war einmal ein Krieg' (163): 'once upon a time there was war'. This poem, written in fable mode and in Dickinsonian meter (not unlike 'My life had stood – a Loaded Gun'; Dickinson 369), seems to obliquely explicate those lines in the novel. For though its story is about hunting, not about war – and those two activities are intimately linked in the trilogy, as have seen – its predatory subject connects excessive success to a divine will, and assumes the right to call upon 'Heaven' for service in the selfish cause. From the outset our speaker desires nothing but to shoot and kill one bird after another, finally praying to be sent 'the best/That ever took/Lead to its breast'; the prayer *is* answered, but with a phoenix against whom the bullet ricochets, killing the killer instead:

> The phoenix bled
> My heart can not
> But heavy sits
> Neath leaden shot.
>
> . . . .
>
> Pray not to Heaven
> He stock your bag

> Or you may feel
> Your vitals sag.
>
> Pray not to Heaven
> For heavenly bird
> Or Heaven may take you
> At your word. (36)

This very pleasing and witty ballad – with its playful suggestion that you 'watch out, you may get what you ask for' – extends such bits of common wisdom to the enlistment of divine right in killing. The latter echoes what the trilogy reviles as 'righteousness' in the desire of dictators, which must strip out the lives of the supplicants – their very humanity which has been overreached. Here, by illustration, the desired 'stocking of the bag' with superlative destruction causes one's own 'vitals to sag' – the rhyme equating the booty bag with the supplicant's sagging body, and therefore precisely the superseding of self desired. Our *speaker* and not the prey takes the 'lead to its breast'; she/he becomes her/his own 'best bird'. We saw the process work in *Over the Frontier*; Pompey in her supersession of character at last shoots herself in the form of the 'rat-faced eld', who mirrors her and Freddy as well as all the 'old men' in her head whose desires have become her own. Even more topically, the poem's German title implies we must extend the parable to, specifically, Germany in its Freudian 'death drive', as Celia will describe it in *The Holiday*.

The more familiar poems in Smith's first collection require re-reading against the backdrop that these others, in tandem with the novels, provide. Even 'The River Deben' (48–49), which lends itself to being read as yet another about longings for death – imaged here as rowing into Styx-like forgetfulness – is spliced in at a provocative point in *Over the Frontier* that deepens its representative nature and temporal references. There, Pompey is at the very climax of her expression of 'disturbance' due to the many inescapable thoughts that will, in two pages, finally send her off for rest at the *schloss* in Germany. Her monologue has just accelerated, following 'a long long extract' from a 'military memoir to which Auntie Lion and I are so partial', the German one written in admiration of England's 'Ethical Imperialism' (101–02) which I discussed in the previous chapter. The memory of it and the mutual admiration she felt for it so haunts her she will return to it, as we saw, at the very end of the novel. Here, following what sounds like a panic attack while going about her tasks in the office, such as her somewhat shady secretarial one of handling stock-buying (an image which as we know will be fully-blown into her own dealings in war materials after the novel's surrealistic 'shift'), she suddenly announces that she was 'sick at heart with a great world pain', and that as a writer, too, she has 'so many many thoughts' that make it even more impossible to 'keep that peace and integrity of the inner life of the soul' (113). It is only at moments like this that she 'become[s] quite set to death', and prone to recalling experiences like the one of rowing at night on the 'dark and phosphorescent waters' of the River Deben – after which we get the whole of the poem, and her wondering whether 'peace... is only to be found perhaps in death' (113).

Opposed to this beautiful reversed *aubade* (whose final lines plead with day to 'tarry' *not* so that our speaker might linger in the love-bed, but rather so that she/he might remain with 'Death in darkness blessed') are poems about violently *riding on* rather than *stopping* – the rhythms of the trilogy – such as we see in the wartime landscape of 'The Fugitive's Ride' (79–80). And though Frances Spalding is right to suggest that the riding image in Smith's work signals 'the compulsive and the inescapable' (*SS: AB* 146), it is not simply a psychological cocktail involving her own death that such rhythms describe in Smith's work. In her war story, 'A Very Pleasant Evening', Smith's character 'Roland' described the poem which loosely inspired this one and a number of her others, Robert Browning's 'Childe Roland to the Dark Tower Came', as 'an exact spiritual description of the detail of the Flanders battlefield' (*MA* 33–34). In 'The Fugitive's Ride', the ironic 'wetness' of the field which is obsessively and wildly referred to (though it has not and 'does not rain') is, obviously, and though the speaker would not name it, blood. We have the riding imagery of *Over the Frontier* in particular evoked here, as the speaker 'pick[s his/her] way' over plains and ditches. Moreover, the frantic imperative to ride on for this speaker who, though inexplicably 'fugitive', has *not* 'done a dreadful deed of blood' however much she/he seems to identify with such criminality, more broadly illustrates the 'talking voice running on' both in the trilogy and the poems. Its vague complicity with and yet denial of what it is riding through, its involuntary part in the 'blurry film sequence' of the times, its movement towards the dark tower, perhaps, which Smith described as a 'symbol of loss in a lost land' – all describe the plight of a speaker who 'dares not stop' or she/he will be lost as well, caught by all that must be avoided and denied in order to maintain, however fraudulently, that 'peace and integrity of the inner soul'. The 'whoa-ing up' in the trilogy is explained here, too, parenthetically:

> (Now hold up horse a moment pray,
> Don't sidestep in that foolish way,
> If you fall down upon the ground
> There is a chance you will be drowned.) (80)

Sidestepping – as we saw Smith's speakers fear it in the trilogy – gets one 'tripped up', particularly if one is in the game of 'forestalling' fate by going with the flow, buying into the market, speaking the speak that covers for the vague but pervasive crimes with which one is always complicit and from which one is always running. As Pompey put it, just before she gave us the extract from 'Ethical Imperialism' I note above – and just *after* her chilling, heart-of-darkness-laden 'justification' of what happened to Casement –

> I understand the motives of my country.... That she has conquered in greed, held in tenacity, explained in casuistry, I agree. But fools asking foolish questions have nothing to expect but folly or casuistry. And here for folly is the Commission from Heaven, and here for casuistry is the Sole Good of the Resident Population. And beneath both, there is a modicum of mishandled truth. Such, as I have shown, is the âme intime de colonisateur, and such again is the good of the native population, that is not the whole and sole consideration but a substantial part consideration, resting, again at basest, upon the convenience of the army of occupation, upon the ease and economy of public services. No empire has ever survived a too savage oppression of subject peoples. 'One must be friendly', as a certain great actress of my acquaintance said, confronted at Frinton by children of divorce on both sides of her family, and by their coresponding papas and mamas. One must be friendly.
>
> (*OTF* 100–01)

Smith's critics may have made the mistake of reading such explosively contextualised passages as evidence of her 'conservatism', but Smith's uncommitted political eye was clearly viewing what we might now think of as the unutterably complex mechanism of hegemonic control imposed in military kingdom formations. It is never easy to disentangle in such formations the well-meaning action, resulting in 'progress' for the subjected, from the 'basest' motivation that powers it – which is, as Marx would have it, economic. She despairingly saw herself as a cog in that wheel, inextricably caught in the casuistry that legitimates life on this model of dissembling about the 'base' 'truth'. Otherwise, if one 'sidesteps' it and hears from some forbidden angle the contradictory 'thoughts that thronged its house' to render its justifications a mere mirage or a house of cards ('The Blood Flows Back', 85), the soul might suddenly find such fraudulent existence intolerable. Instead, one must play this very long, controlled game at every level – 'in private as in public life', as Pompey goes on to tell us in the next paragraph. One must ride on, on this dissembling plain of language – or 'drown' (in the blood of it), say her conflicting metaphors, revealing themselves as such. Both movements are powered by the same knowledge whether 'hidden' (85) or revealed – whether one is waving, or drowning.

Perhaps one of the reasons that Smith was quite famously and generally unhappy about the way her single poems would be placed in magazines or read on radio or read by critics was that each work requires its fellows for balance and contextualised reading – contextualised not only in terms of cultural reference but also in terms of her own quite complicated sociolinguistic vision displayed best *between* the poems, as it is displayed between passages in the novels. As one perceptive and unnamed reviewer for *Granta* put it,

> the tone of each individual poem ... is subject to the further control of a reserve tone which forms the unifying background of reference for this book.... [T]he use of a characteristic thought-structure which expresses only prominent ideas clearly and the rest implicitly, allows Miss Smith to deliver her intensities – however slight – without change of voice, and in the manner of public utterance. The result is a seemingly careless verse whose impact is both immediate and personal.[10]

Though certainly not always 'careless', Smith's verse is exactly this: intimate stuff that is also and disturbingly 'public utterance' – that is, ourselves as readers shot through with the same. Her collections require reading as a whole – which will make addressing each one here in this chapter exceedingly difficult if I wish to do them anything like proper justice. This first one houses a number of shorter pieces that fit, in almost painfully beautiful ways, into the larger vision that the collection offers and which I have done my best to describe. For example, and in conclusion to this section of my chapter, there is 'Alfred the Great', a four-liner whose tone and register issue from the 1662 Prayer Book, *Te Deum*, *not* to be entirely 'deflated' (*SS: AB* 124) as Spalding suggests, but rather to tenderly explicate the absurdities in the existence of other 'cogs' in the social 'weal':

> Honour and magnify this man of men
> Who keeps a wife and seven children on £ 2 10
> Paid weekly in an envelope
> And yet he never has abandoned hope. (19)

Churchill would famously describe Alfred the Great, England's ruler in the ninth century, as 'the greatest Englishman that ever lived' (Churchill Ch. 7, Vol. 1) in part because he defended England from the Viking raids and also because he encouraged religious rebirth. An enlightened figure, he equally famously was the first translator of Boethius's *The Consolation of Philosophy*, a text that as we know from our reading of *The Holiday* figured centrally in Smith's thought. Her use of *The Consolation* as a frame for that narrative, articulating a kind of heroism in the midst of imprisonment which her speaker Celia felt was no longer possible in her own time, is perhaps glossed here as being exhibited, if in 'deflated' circumstances, by this 'man of men': a working-class figure who, in his tight space of possibilities, his position near the 'base' of that cruel economic pyramid, has not 'abandoned hope' with Dante's hell-dwellers (Dante 47). Some kind of philosophy must sustain him, she seems to suggest, in that prison which she draws, in its straightforwardly illustrative accompanying sketch, as a wall of bricks hemming him in his tidy jacket and bowler into his mid-picture space, beyond which on his left hang clothes on a line, drying, and a fence with a flower or two, or perhaps the heads of children and dogs peeping up from under his legs. Smith is often capable of celebrating the staying-power of such inhabitants of her cultural arena. But again the poem is complicated by others in the collection, like 'Road Up' which depicts a working man lying in the middle of Euston Road in protest against the world which 'split his dreams asunder' (78). In its company, and upon second look, 'Alfred the Great' also implies with its title that the complex empire which has been built upon the confinement of the working man depends on his thorough and perhaps unthinking interpolation within the same vision that comes, top-down, from his rulers, and from the text of history which 'names' him. Tender and cruel at once, Smith's treatment of the figures she depicts in her poems is based upon her understanding that she and they together take part in something much larger, which neither could possibly be clever enough to put into words.

II

The middle (war) years: Smith's poems, drawings and stories

The next two collections Smith published, *Tender Only to One* (1938) and *Mother, What is Man?* (1942), seem to play out the possibilities that her earlier poems set up, while *Harold's Leap* (1950) marks a new departure into the plentiful rewritings of fairytale many have discussed in recent criticism. During the decades that followed, these would then make room for her increasingly substantial poetic interactions with the Church, the past and the body politic that were perhaps directed into the poetry following the cessation of her prose writing in the late 1940s. Certainly *Tender Only to One* seems to give over much of its overtly topical and politicised vision to her novel *Over the Frontier*, which Smith was composing at the same time; and certainly *Mother, What Is Man?* seems far more dedicated than *The Holiday* to the silence or 'dumbness' that Celia hopes to reject (53), its poems being on the whole short, often epigrammatic, and tense – even terse with a kind of amputated effect. In this second, very substantial section of the chapter I will try to offer a sense of how these generally less-discussed collections interact with the novels and the stories, as well as how the poems demonstrate their already well-developed relationship with her drawings. With the help of her generically hybrid radio play, *A Turn Outside*, broadcast on the BBC's Third Programme in 1959, I will then move in my final section to consideration of the last twenty years of Smith's better-known writing, including her fairytale revision and her performance of her (always already performative) poems.

Cases in point: re-reading feminist re-readings of the poems and drawings

While a number of the poems in *Tender Only to One* continue to exist in direct dialogue with the novels, such as 'To a Dead Vole', and 'Dear Karl' (*Over the Frontier*),[11] there is also a slightly greater percentage that, like the two stories published a year later, 'Surrounded by Children' and 'The Herriots' (1939), seem to be focussed on the bleeding of external turmoil and cultural changes back into the domestic space. Of course the first collection also included many such as these, and those I have already discussed above often engage the same concerns. But I have been careful in this chapter, as I was in Chapter 3, to first outline the larger galaxy of Smith's discursive influences and entrapments before moving to the domestic arena, because it is key that we understand that the same larger issues crowd into these seemingly localised poems as well. The 'private life', as we know, is no way separate from the public, inter-war and wartime domain in her work. Smith's interest in understanding how individuals become interpolated into culture at large, and her desire to probe familiar utterance – whether by one person or between those in relationship – caused her to dedicate a number of poems to female voices, and a number, too, to male voices. More are female perhaps because, as we know from the novels, her own best patient for analysis was herself, as Joyce was for Joyce. But as I encounter recent commentary about the poetry and its drawings – routinely read as importing an unequivocally feminist project into the texts because 'making a statement on femininity was...the *primary* focus' of Smith's art (Severin 51–52) – I find myself feeling very uncomfortable, because if we read the whole of the work, not just the very few poems that might fit such arguments, we know that it simply is not true that Smith 'depict[s] single women as adventurers and creators...deal[ing] a blow to the patriarchal society of her time' (Severin 57); she far more often leaves them in the same 'muddle of Europe's dreaming' in which she found herself. Such projects preclude delivery of the kind of complex, close-cultural reading of texts that current theory should require – even when the latter is clearly invoked, as in Kristin Bluemel's potentially ground-breaking argument about the aesthetics of 'violence' in Smith's poems that, she suggests, cause their verbal/visual mixtures to clash in a meeting of codes. Her set-up for the argument displays symptoms of the jump-to-conclusions that will pre-empt, in her close-readings, the multivalent nature of the effects of those aesthetics:

> [I]t is necessary to remember that in the decades when Smith was actively producing and publishing her poem-doodles, T.S. Eliot and W.H. Auden dominated English poetry, war and cold war determined English politics, and an idealized domestic sphere supposedly devoid of poetry or politics defined the lives of most English women. If we agree with [Jack] Barbera

that '[it] would have been as unlikely for [Eliot] to decorate his serious poems with doodles as it would have been for him to sing them', it can be assumed that 'Stevie Smith's decoration of her text was a subversive act' (236). [Alison] Light's attention to the related issue of women's writers' subversion of canonical literary history suggests that we need to prioritize questions of gender as we look more closely at relations between specific words and images in Smith's texts. (116)

But I want to ask: Why? Where was that crucial step in logic that took Bluemel from Barbera's suggestion that Smith's undermining of the seriousness of her work might be seen as being 'subversive' to the assumption that such subversiveness *must* have 'questions of gender' as its 'priority'? Why might Smith not be interrupting the bellicose rhetoric of 'war and cold war' as supported by both genders? A gendered perspective might indeed inform critique of all manner of cultural phenomena, yet the same problems that have historically arisen in re-readings of modernist women poets are again showcased in this argument, which ultimately suggests, through its choice of poems to read and its readings of those poems, that feminine disruption is sequestered to issues *about* women or women's experiences, specifically and exclusively. The argument therefore dismisses once again from the female poet's repertoire every other kind of subversive project, such as the sociolinguistic and simultaneously political and cultural one that I describe in this book; it also disallows the self-implosive, self-critical perspective on her own gender *as it takes part in larger cultural relations* that Smith most often displayed. Such arguments are not making the poststructuralist one that women cannot wield patriarchal language given their subjection by it, unless it be to cause a 'revolution' from within it.[12] Dynamics such as these could easily be discovered within the vast range of Smith's poems that deal widely with cultural issues beyond those that prioritise women's concerns. But the result of such derailed theorising is that it is only those poems and drawings – the ones that can be read as sporting a triumphalist feminist viewpoint – that have surfaced for attention in recent Smith studies, giving readers the impression that this was the central priority *and extent* of her writerly project. Yet even in such poems about domestic gender relations, she *most* often probes the far larger conditions that are complexly determining them, and usually indicts both sexes for maintaining the structures that destroy them, as we will see. Bluemel's initial insights are deflected by the imperative to read these poems and drawings as Smith's feminist scoring, her attempt to 'win over her audience through comedy' (123), when Smith's project had little to do with 'a side' 'over' to which she hoped to cajole her readers – and as we saw in Chapter 1, she insisted that her poems were not 'only funny'. A poem from her uncollected grouping in *Me Again* comes immediately to mind:

> Via Media Via Dolorosa
> There's so much to be said on either side,
> I'll be dumb.
> There's so much to be said on either side,
> I'll hold my tongue.
> For years and years I never said a word,
> Now I have lost the art: my voice is never heard,
> For my apprehension
> Snaps beneath the tension
> Of what is to be said on either side. (213)

'Now I have lost the art' hits us with its initial inversion's awkwardness and sudden prosaic sidestep out of the poem. Though the line reverts to iambic pattern, as does the first, part-trochaic and part-iambic, 'either side' repeating line of the poem, it gives way to sadly trochaic (or comically funny, limerick-like?) lines in the penultimate rhyme. The full effect is to clash metrical movements but precariously right itself in iambs in the end, in perhaps clown-like fashion. But what kind of 'end' is it? The rhyme is recalled from the first quatrain – a bit too little too late, a kind of repetition of the same dully repeating rhyme in the first lines, as if to indicate the resignation of the imagination. Perhaps too simple for her to wish it published, this poem like so many others very potently gives us Smith's speaker in 'the middle of the road', and in the 'dolorous' or sad position of *losing her voice* to 'either side'. Such wonderful play on a determiner that is referentially indeterminate suggests discomfiting disagreement without placement or 'side', despite the fact that such formal poetic 'resolution' sounds like a satisfactory end. It is another bit of waving that is managed *via* drowning.

The drawings effect the same displacement that the determiner does above, ensuring that we do not situate 'the poet's voice' anywhere *but* 'via media', between the lines. Yet Laura Severin was quite right to suggest that my earliest work on Smith's poetry did not deal sufficiently with them as representative of a separate art form appearing alongside the poems (Severin 1997, 49). However, her statement that I treated them as 'extensions of the text' is less true; I have always discussed them in much the same way that she does: as 'extradiscursive' complements or coda, whose force is identified with the kind of difference that resides in space as opposed to language (Huk 1993, 249 and *passim*). Indeed, although Severin does, following this critique, offer a section at the start of her chapter on 'Poems and Drawings 1937–66' which discusses the relation of the drawings to other drawings – such as those of Edward Lear, obviously (and more dubiously William Blake, given the brevity of the explained connection) – her attempt to place the drawings within another art form's tradition does nothing discernible to change her *own* readings of them as 'extensions of [Smith's] texts', which in her view deliver feminist suggestions with their thematic (or narrativised) rather than formal help. It is certainly very difficult to avoid such narrativisation, and nearly impossible to attend to *all* of the ways that composite art can 'mean'. But I shall try to illustrate my points above by first discussing some of the Thirties poems that my colleagues have also attempted to read, working as I do towards constructing an approach to the poems that will help me discuss her last and final phase of fully mature poetic work with the *whole* of her cultural project in view.

For an example, we might consider 'Mrs Simpkins', a poem from Smith's first collection. Severin suggests that it offers a more 'complex relation' of text and illustration than those she has thus far discussed (and it is telling that by this mid-point in her treatment the drawings are referred to as 'illustrations' for the texts rather than formal counterpoint). This poem, she argues, 'require[s] the reader/viewer's attention to go back and forth multiple times between text and illustration' (66). This is of course what, in her argument about the text's linearity existing separately from the drawing's spatiality, ought to have been required all along. But in practice, as she writes here by way of summary of her readings thus far, the drawings have simply 'undermine[d] or undercut the overly sweet optimism of the poetry'. In other words, once her reading arrived at the drawing for each of her chosen poems – which are offered, in keeping with her overarching thesis, as examples of 'poems and drawings working together to stop the romance plot' (67) – she found in them the 'truth' of the matter. Either the often mysteriously smiling female figures in the drawings 'know better' than the deluded text or, if they appear abject, they deliver us into the pitiable space of women's objectified status, and *thus* into Smith's real meaning for the poem. Attention to complications *within the text* in both Bluemel's and Severin's readings is either abbreviated or absent, while the drawings provoke imaginations of the 'real narrative' rather than operate in any differing way as drawings. Here in this poem we are asked by Severin to do something more complex, though it is difficult to understand what she means by this. Her reading seems to follow the footprints of her earlier ones, but perhaps such complication arises for her because the drawing actually interrupts the text on the page:

Mrs Simpkins never had very much to do
So it occurred to her one day that the Trinity wasn't true
Or at least but a garbled version of the truth
And that things had moved very far since the days of her youth.

So she became a spiritualist and at her very first party
Just to give her a feeling of confidence the spirit spoke up hearty:
'Since I crossed over dear friends 'it said' I'm no different to what I was before
Death's not a separation or alteration of parting it's just a one-handled door
We spirits can come back to you if your seance is orthodox
But you can't come over to us till your body's shut in a box
And this is the great thought I want to leave with you today
You've heard it before but in case you forgot death isn't a passing away
It's just a carrying on with friends relations and brightness

> Only you don't have to both with sickness and there's no financial tightness.'
> Mrs Simpkins went home and told her husband he was a weak pated fellow
> And when he heard the news he turned a daffodil shade of yellow
> 'What do you mean, Maria?' he cried, 'it can't be true there's no rest
> From one's uncles and brothers and sisters nor even the wife of one's breast?'
> 'It's the truth,' Mrs Simpkins affirmed, 'there is no separation
> There's a great reunion coming for which this life's but a preparation.'
> This worked him to such a pitch that he shot himself through the head
> And now she has to polish the floors of Westminster County Hall for her daily bread. (21–22)

Severin first begins to summarise the poem:

> The poem begins by narrating the fairly ordinary life of Mrs. Simpkins, a middle-class married woman who 'never ha[s] very much to do.' Able to amuse herself as she wishes, she spends her time pondering the truth of the Trinity, which she has begun to doubt. Thus far, Smith's portrait of Mrs. Simpkins is largely descriptive: she is an unremarkable person of a particular class and time.

This will be the last mention of religion or 'spiritism' (as it will be referred to, using a term familiar to modern readers, in other poems in the collection) that Severin will make, despite the fact that the poem has more to do with what we know was one of Smith's greatest concerns – religion, and the way people were making use of it at the time – than it does with Simpkins' gender. Above, Severin sets up her argument that this poem is about women's issues in general by stating that this woman is 'ordinary' given these lines. But the first rhyme of the piece, if we attend to it *as* a poem, should alert us to a deeply comic deflation of Simpkins' manner of 'pondering the truth of the Trinity'; it is obviously *this* that we first focus upon, not her representative status or 'ordinariness'. '[N]ot having much to do' leads to deciding 'the Trinity wasn't true'; the former is the causal phrase, and it is due to such vacuousness, *not* to what Severin suggests would be her more laudable 'pondering', that such truth simply '*occurred* to her'. However harsh this may sound, we must acknowledge that throughout her work Smith *is* harsh with the bored unthinking person, male *or* female, having developed little patience with others of her gender and class who opted not to read anything aside from the most superficial and fashionable books and magazines.[13] Severin herself makes this point in the most valuable sections of her book, which document the nature of a number of those magazines; she even very provocatively connects Smith's line drawings to the drawings in them (53). But that connection is left unelaborated here as she moves into discussion of the drawings – except in the sense that she recovers the fashion-speak of the times:

> However, only four lines into the poem, the poem is disrupted by the drawing of an older, wrinkled woman, surprisingly dressed as a 1920s flapper, complete with dropped waist and short skirt. The drawing would seem to be connected to the poem's previous line: 'And that things had moved very far since the days of her youth.' At first, the drawing merely suggests, like the poem, that Mrs. Simpkins' beliefs are outdated. Yet the flapper costume also insinuates a connection between Mrs. Simpkins and the culture that produced her. Is her silliness at least partially the result of a culture that assigned the role of pleasure seeking and romance to the young women of her day? (67)

It is difficult for me to understand this reading of the drawing. Part of the problem is that Severin seems to have assumed that this poem, because it was included in the first, 1937 collection, was written at that time and thus *after* the flapper era, and that its speaker must also be speaking to us from that moment of the late 1930s. But as we know, Smith wrote many of the poems in her first collection during the 1920s, so the idea that she is an 'older woman' still dressing as the 'young women of her day' is unfounded. She does not appear to be 30 years old, or even 40, as she would *have* to be to have been of age in the 1920s; she is obviously quite an old woman who is most probably dressing, rather foolishly, like the much younger women of her current day in the 1920s. In any case, it is also difficult to understand how her beliefs can be 'outdated' if the poem is about her adoption of iconoclastic notions concerning the Trinity and a fashionable 'spiritism' (much like her garb). Severin's conflicted narrativisation of the drawing ends with the assumption that the bad influences of both 'pleasure seeking and romance' go with the flapper era, and that this accounts for Mrs Simpkins's silliness – yet 'pleasure seeking' was frequently depicted as a breakthrough for women in the era of sexual 'awakening' and of the vote. Moreover, one is left wondering: how does seeking spiritism fit in this category? Severin's form of 'cultural reading' as she defines it in her book's introductory pages contrives here to excuse Mrs Simpkins's foolishness as being wholly culturally induced, but it offers neither a thorough reading of what is actually happening in the poem/drawing, nor even an *explained* reading of the cultural context it seems to rely upon. The rest of this reading, which I have quoted in full, runs like this:

> The rest of the poem, like the drawing, questions the culture's education of women, particularly in married life, as Mrs. Simpkins is left impoverished because she fails to understand the ways in which she is dependent

on her husband. Having been told by Mrs. Simpkins that eternal life will keep them together forever, her husband shoots himself to escape her at least temporarily, leaving Mrs. Simpkins to 'polish the floors of Westminster County Hall for her daily bread.' Though Mrs. Simpkins is foolish, Mark Storey rightly claims that she has gotten 'a raw deal' [*ISOSS* 191], since she has not been in a position to understand hard economic realities. The flat effect of the poem's last line holds out little sympathy to Mrs. Simpkins, yet the drawing of the aging flapper that is associated with Mrs. Simpkins is pitiable. (67)

Severin's recourse to the drawing as holding what we 'should' think of Mrs Simpkins is given as illustration of how we are to conduct the complex 'reading back and forth' between text and sketch. But no line in the drawing or poem justifies the summary statement that Mrs Simpkins is 'left impoverished because she fails to understand the ways in which she is dependent on her husband'. If she did understand that, we are forced to ask, would she not have told him what the spirit said because she would have been afraid he would die and leave her to fend for herself? Is that all that this poem is really about?

So many *other* important things are happening in this poem, if with a studious ambiguity. Some of those things do indeed have to do with marital relations. Yet if one clarifies the message as a gendered one with a 'moral to its story' by narrativising in a way that Smith never did – not even in her novels – and by leaving out all the other competing languages that the piece harbours in its very leaky boat, the whole will be lost. Mark Storey, whom Severin brings into her argument to confirm it above, also simplifies things in his half-page treatment of this poem; it is not at all clear that Mrs Simpkins 'attend[s] spiritualist sessions where she is assured death is not the end'. This takes her role in acquiring such knowledge and the knowledge itself far more seriously than the poem's conflicting descriptions allow. She picks up the spirit's voice at her very first 'party', we are told. We might question the seriousness of her view of her new hobby, given the incongruous choice of words here to describe such a session. It is difficult to know, given Smith's choice of veiling syntax, but it seems only *she*, Mrs Simpkins, supposedly hears the spirit – or rather it speaks up, 'just to give her a feeling of confidence'. That phrase suggests that all of the following revelation is '*just* to give her *a feeling* of confidence' – is it 'real', or even thought by Mrs Simpkins to be real? Of course we suspect that this person who is capable of having conclusions about the Trinity simply 'occur' to her out of boredom – or perhaps out of the desire to have opinions to offer at 'parties' – is also capable of having voices so appear, despite her lack of acquaintance with or knowledge of the workings of such things (the emphasis here being on the fact that this is 'her *very first* party'). Leaving aside what we know about Smith's classical impatience with religious 'mystery' (as we have seen it treated in other poems in the collection), as well as righteous assumptions about the unknowable afterlife, this bit of wisdom that arrives strikes me as highly suspect. Although it concludes with, in the familiar and cringe-provoking fashion of a populist sermon or political speech, 'And this is the great thought I want to leave with you today', all it has produced is a mundane vision – 'You've heard it before but in case you forgot' – of afterlife as the 'everyday', but with the very practical and distinctly *un*-other-worldly appendix of good financial portfolios for all. We are, it seems, to hear the limits of Mrs Simpkins's – whose name conjures the word 'simple' – reach of imagination and discursive repertoire in this report. And in its more startling revelation about the comical 'one-handled door' for spirits' returns to earth, one is stopped on the oxymoronic caveat that it only works if one conducts an 'orthodox seance'. Not only does this sound like someone importing the language of an earlier dogmatism into a supposedly new-found and liberating mode of discovery, but given that Mrs Simpkins next goes home to literally brow-beat her husband for his ignorance of the goings-on at such enlightening and fashionable parties (to which he obviously does not accompany her), this becomes yet another instance in Smith's work of spurious religious righteousness and false knowledge-acquisition, as well as the hypocrisy of wielding the new with the violence of the old – or the 'orthodox', which is never a positive word in Smith's vocabulary. I think of Celia's early line in *The Holiday*: 'Can resistance pass to government and not take to itself the violence of its oppressors, the absolutism and the torture?' (9).

Mrs Simpkins without question participates in her own form of learned violence; Smith makes this clear through the comic consequences of her actions. She *has* undoubtedly been oppressed into her version of 'spuriousness of spirit' by culture, as 'The Failed Spirit' had it at the start of this chapter. Mrs Simpkins has become as a result what Smith often refers to, in her poems about domestic situations as well as in her novels' portrayal of Pompey's frustrated relations, the one who 'bites' – the one who looks to oppress her husband in return. She is perhaps more 'pitiable' only because she, quite inadvertently, and therefore with supreme irony, threatens him with the very thing he helped to create: herself, his biting company for all eternity. She is the 'wife of one's breast', the one most intimately formed with him and made part of him (the phrase perhaps even alluding to the infamous rib of creation). They are, in other words, co-conspirators in their various miseries – though I would argue that he seems even more miserable, given that she is quite sanguine about the prophecy of eternal togetherness whereas the same makes him desperate. In this hilarious locution which leaves its crucial qualifier on the previous line – 'no rest/*From*' all of these relatives – her mention is, in its position of sonic emphasis at the end of the line, *not* of the most loved as the structure leads us to expect, but of the one he most wants *rest from*. She does not seem to register this, but goes on regardless, as though such conventional language of endearment tripping from his mouth has been enough in their relationship. Men are also (if not as singularly or pre-emptively) seduced into suburban homes and their remotely controlled responses in Smith's view, as we recall from Pompey's sympathetic depiction of Freddy's very conventional desires in *Novel on Yellow Paper*. And certainly Smith in the prose and poems continually comes back to Hamlet's dilemma: suicide might be the best option, but what if it is not the end? The poem seems a study of two unlike figures soldered together: one so deeply engrossed by the superficialities that compose her life that even the afterlife is envisioned as a (marginally improved) set of them; the other so firmly 'married to death' that he cannot live without the idea. Yet his choice to kill himself is as highly ironic as her destruction of him, because presumably he does so given his worry that death only brings on more of the same. The continually sub-involuting despair of both figures in the poem – their situation of 'no exit' from the life they have been enculturated to make – seems to be of deepest issue in it, though the ambiguous last lines return us again to the central question of what 'feeds' the spirit. With him gone, she must earn her keep, yes; but given the other valences emanating from these lines it also suggests that she may have 'fed' on browbeating him, and must now find sustenance elsewhere. As Bluemel argues, many of Smith's poems deal with the violent 'eating' of one another that humans do, but we must realise that women eat men *as* problematically as men eat women in these collections, if more helplessly. The far less frivolous nature of that last line's depiction of her mode of sustaining herself (as opposed to engaging in spurious spiritism) suggests, quite equivocally, punishment *and* pitiable fate *as well as*, perhaps cruelly, a possible improvement. This person who has had nothing to do but accumulate fashionable, insubstantial opinions and esoteric wisdom with which she beats her frustrating/frustrated husband has taken a more down-to-earth position of getting one *real* thing in exchange for another 'occupation' less 'silly', anyway, than those she has taken on to date. Or, should one want to whitewash what I do think should be acknowledged as Smith's often hard-edged if multivalent critiques, there is always the possibility of turning to what another poem in the collection, 'From the County Lunatic Asylum', says about the matter:

> The people say that spiritism is a joke and a swizz,
> The Church that it is dangerous – not half it is. (38)

With this poem in view, 'Mrs Simpkins' may be the story of victimisation – since this epigram on the surface suggests that the Church is right, spiritism is 'completely' dangerous (which is what we arrive at if we read the Britishism 'not half it is' or 'not by half' as it normally is read). Certainly Smith at times suggested she felt this way; it is at least as dangerous as any other belief that makes oneself right and anyone else certifiable. But then the Church, as numerous bits of her writing remind us, has historically been far more dangerous than such occult groups have ever managed to be. This poem's drawing of a terrified naked man looking mad in his attempt to escape his cage, or attempting to shout to others outside his cell, makes the statement potentially ludicrous: though we cannot know what he is 'in for', the Church and those who find him dangerous have been far more frightening to the likes of him. 'Not half it is' might be heard as 'not half as dangerous as the Church', or even an emphatic restatement: spiritism certainly *is* dangerous, if one can be incarcerated for it. The drawing here functions as a disturbingly cartoon-like opposition of abject disempowerment – of *experience*, a figure occupying a space that we can only access through his barred window – to the *text* which gives us what 'people say' about a seemingly theoretical matter. The word 'dangerous' becomes refracted as a result, its moral high ground in Church judgement becoming annexed in not wholly clear ways to judicially sanctioned physical consequences for what are supposedly only abstract theories held. We have a seemingly detached caption versus a picture of the extra-textual experience, but there *is* a relation – one of complicity – and a complex causal chain articulated between abstract sign and physical consequence in this composite work.

Smith's drawings are indeed always about the difference between word and world, or between language and visually rendered incarnation or action, though more importantly and complexly about the commerce between them. Therein lie both the humour and politicised subversion as they work in Smith's poem/drawings. Their obvious desire to be *in part* funny – Smith having repeatedly insisted that they were 'not *only* comical' (*MA* 298) – is certainly evinced by their much-noted allusion to comic drawings like Edward Lear's. But as I began to suggest in my introduction to this book, they are also *unlike* Lear's – something Severin has argued as well, though by dismissing the latter via a quote from Lisa Ede who writes that his drawings are 'slavish visual imitations or recreations of a literary event', which is at best a reductive assessment (51, Ede 104). Lear's highly mobile, exaggerated satires or fully reversed, situational ironies are simpler than Smith's, less troubling than her often frozen, usually opaque and multiply-readable drawings are. But she deliberately desired reference to this very popular and well-known Victorian's work, as we know from her naming of him first in her list of obvious if 'deceitful echoes' to be found in her work when she wrote the blurb for the American edition of her *Selected Poems* (*SS: AB* 259). As with *Hymns Ancient and Modern*, another item in her list for that blurb, Smith's purpose in such allusion is to track back 'impurities' in ways of thinking and responding that continue to both inform and entrap her. She *liked* Lear's particular form of impurity, both in terms of his similarly composite poetic responses and his quickness in sketching, which she felt allowed him to get some of 'true cathood' into his drawings of his pet Foss, for example – 'though much, too, of course, of Mr Lear, so "pleasant to know"' (*MA* 141). Again, engaging as Smith does in self-analysis as well as cultural analysis in her work, she would enjoy such a 'Freudian slip' in drawing, the revelation of more than one expected to show, and this comment reveals much about her own work. But Lear's work on domestic situations, for another example, also constituted a deeply critical intervention into the ostensibly clear Victorian code of morality, as well as into its self-congratulatory tradition of empirical thought, and no doubt Smith allied her own comic project to his for that reason, too. One need only look at Lear's last book, his posthumously published limericks and drawings in *Bosh and Nonsense*, to see the haunting similarities between these two poets in rendering horrifying domestic situations in 'not only funny' light.[14] In other words, Smith's composite works did indeed exist in subversive relation to the 'serious poems' of Eliot, as Bluemel argues (116); though as I suggested in Chapter 1, with the help of work on the function of 'nonsense' by Jacques Derrida and Jean-Jacques Lecercle, the tradition destabilised in Smith's work is more largely and importantly the long-lived British *empirical* one. As Lecercle writes, such nonsense is a 'true product of that venerable tradition' (200) and, as Derrida likewise suggests, it recognises that tradition 'as its norm' at the same time it departs from it, often to a 'troubling extreme' (1981, 85). Just so, Smith's composite work handles the pictorial 'extreme' of nonsense in a way similar to the one by which she works existing texts and their relations to the world into her collages of speech.[15] Though travelling close to the edge of extremity, she avoids subverting tradition by *inverse* relation – that is, by allowing empirical text to become 'wrong' or totally non-referential with regard to reality in the drawing, which would simply mean another dip into empiricism with the suggestion that accurate statement *does* exist. Rather, and unlike Lear, she twists both with caricature-like distortion *only so far*, until the causal chain between representation of extra-textual experience and the text's production of it becomes opaquely visible. It is the inextricability of one from the other that seems to matter to Smith in these works, just as the inability to draw the 'other' (as in Lear drawing Foss) without informing the drawing with *self* matters to her.

This takes us back to the drawing for 'Mrs Simpkins'. This portrait's function is not only illustrative – in other words, not only a matter of offering Mrs Simpkins, stuffed as an old woman into the era's fashionable clothing, as a model for the ludicrousness of maturity's surrender of itself to the same superficialities that youth tries on in its search for identity. Smith does offer it in part as such, along with other manifestations of the same: flapper garb worn as a mirror to theological debates made party talk, which in turn mirrors spiritism made occupation for empty minds struggling with modern *ennui*. But the interruptive presence of this drawing after the opening of the poem, and just after we hear that 'things had moved very far since her youth', suspends her *and us* on that line of uncertainty for a moment – in space, even in time. It is as though her unreadable outline – given to us as a line drawing representing what can no more be caught by it than words might catch 'being' – *must* appear just here, as we hear about her qualification of her opinion of the Trinity: her reneging on the initial articulation of a seemingly clear judgement to suggest that the Trinity must be 'at least but a garbled version of the truth'. As her thought loses clarity and singleness, becomes lost in the interference of possible truths, what we suddenly get is the body which is different from but – as the poem's end will make cruelly clear – annexed by physical consequence to the garbled and confused 'thoughts' that surround figures like this, just as they do in the novels. Text does not recede when line drawings appear alongside the poems; its linear language is caught or thrown into deadly comic relief in all its superficiality or conventionality when juxtaposed with equally deadly comic figures whose medium fails also and absolutely to represent actual being. Representations, in other words, abound and collide in these composite works; the representation of utterance is augmented by the generic language of representation in the *depiction* of life: stick figures or line drawings that depend on stereotypes or already-'foreseen' languages of identification. These do sometimes echo, as Severin helpfully argues with the help of Janice Winship, women's magazines' representations through their sketches of 'fantasy or ideal aspects of womanhood'.[16] Indeed, even this drawing does so: this woman is obviously clothed inappropriately in 1920s high-fashion for young women. But *as drawing*, does it do more than narrate further information? The 'complex relation' between drawing and poem does, I think, have to be 'read back and forth multiple times' as Severin suggests – particularly because here, at the start of the poem, the contradiction between representational lines appearing in the drawing mirrors in its different medium the contradictions that appear between the 'lines' or discursive vectors in the text. The disconnection between assertive thoughts on the Trinity and a familiar line from the elderly – 'Things had moved very far from the days of her youth' – is effected by a line that backsteps into admission of confusion and then takes its theological vector and disappears from the poem. In effect, *the poem* disappears for a moment, or must; all lines are suddenly caught between possible ways forward. Next, she will again 'choose a line', another very clear one that she will not, this time, qualify; the resumption of movement is as lame as the original one, though, as is signalled by the fully arbitrary connective 'so': 'So she became a spiritualist.' Here is the causal connection and the inexpressible reason for all the pain to follow. Much of what we are to 'see' next is a struggle for dominance via spurious certainties – one could substitute, perhaps, other revolutionary new ways of thinking like fascism or communism for spiritism – that disallow inquiry into their 'garbled versions of truth' that allow no such second thoughts to derail them. But second, third and fourth thinking is what Smith's poems always do, in company with the drawings' expansion of the dimensions of representation crowding about and shaping the being which remains forever locked between their disjointed 'lines'.

Kristin Bluemel begins her thoughts on the drawings by helpfully describing this complicit relation. Incisively quoting Foucault, she writes:

> [Michel] Foucault... mark[s] out a more dangerous territory in the margins of the text – in the regions beyond word *or* image. Foucault describes the 'few millimeters of white, the calm sand of the page' between word and image as a 'frontier' and claims that there exists 'between the figure and the text a whole series of intersections... enterprises of subversion and destruction, lance blows and wounds, a battle.' Unlike traditional literary critics, Mitchell and Foucault do not believe that images alone threaten the coherence of words in a violent, predatory way, but rather that image and word each pose a fundamental threat to one another at the site of their meeting.
>
> There seems to be no escaping such a threat, for once we have acknowledged what Foucault describes as the 'battle' between line or print across the unclassifiable space that separates them, it is no longer possible to believe in the promise of meaning offered by 'discourse alone' or 'pure drawing'. (114–15; Mitchell 28, 26)

This seems a perfect way to approach Smith's only *false* opposition of word and picture; her 'impure' poetry does exactly this: presents the intersections of representation with the caption, 'no escaping such a threat'. The problem here is that Bluemel loses her theoretical ground as she moves into description of Smith's feminist escapes and triumphs. In, for example, her reading of 'The Wedding Photograph', a poem from Smith's *Selected Poems* (1962) she, like Severin (who of course also focusses on it), leaves much of the text unread. Leaving aside the 'site of their meeting', text's and drawing's, Bluemel speculates about the narrative behind the latter in order to offer its 'secret smile' as an indication of female ascendancy (120). But the poem, though one of Smith's that intriguingly offers a drawing wholly (or nearly) incompatible with the text, does something far more complicated.[17] It is indeed a violent and predatory poem, one of Smith's most provocative:

> Goodbye Harry I must have you by me for a time
> But once in the jungle you must go off to a higher clime
> The old lion on his slow toe
> Will eat you up, that is the way you will go.
>
> Oh how I shall like to be alone on the jungle path
> But you are all right now for the photograph
> So smile Harry smile and I will smile too
> Thinking what is going to happen to you,
> It is the death wish lights my beautiful eyes
> But people think you are lucky to go off with such a pretty prize.

Figure 5.1 The accompanying drawing for 'The Wedding Photograph'. In *Collected Poems* it appears at the lower right-hand side of the page, below the text.

> Ah feeble me that only wished alone to roam
> Yet dared not without marrying leave home
> Ah woe, burn fire, burn in eyes' sheathing
> Fan bright fear, fan fire in Harry's breathing. (425)

Bluemel suggests that this poem 'disguises reality', because '[o]nly the bride and her confidants (the poem's readers) realise that the wedding photograph is really a picture of a femme fatale and her hapless victim':

> The speaker of the poem plans to reverse the processes of objectification guaranteed by her society's gendered double standard. She will use Harry as an object, a prize, that will insure her the freedom to roam before she feeds him to the lions. Like the parents in 'The Photograph,' Harry will pay a tremendous price simply for playing by his society's rules. To the extent that Smith's readers recognize the misogynistic assumptions underlying those rules and can identify with the speaker's desire to make someone else feel their dangerous effects, they will enjoy all the more thoroughly the humor of the poem. (120)

The assumption here is that Smith of course celebrated 'reverse discrimination' or, more worryingly, even beyond 'reverse battering', reverse murder. But none of her other poems or stories or novels suggest that she did; even when such destruction is contemplated metaphorically, as it is by Pompey in her relationship with suburban Freddy, it comes with such remorse and self-loathing that it results, as we know, in Pompey's *own* metaphorical death in the image of 'Flo', the tigress, who dies at the end of *Novel on Yellow Paper*. Bluemel's reading of the text above elides the last stanza to effect a fully vengeful, feminist reading of the situation. But it becomes clear here, before the tone takes a sudden dip into its final and desperate ambiguity, that the girl is not feeling triumphant at all, is in fact disgusted with her own 'feeble[ness]', and indeed may wish to kill *herself* off as well – but I shall return to this in a moment. Bluemel's reading of the drawing:

> The only suggestion that the figure could function as more than a random decoration lies in the girl's raised hand. The motion, the familiar feminine disguise of laughter that admits laughter's impropriety, connects the seemingly innocent doodle with the evil glee of the poem. Reading poem and doodle together, the ideological meanings of the joke in the poem deepen precisely because it is so easy to overlook the implications of the girl's raised hand. Are we privy to the source of the girl's secret smile? or are we ready, like Harry, to dismiss it as part of the standard scenery of a wedding photograph? (120)

Thus the opposition, the 'battle' between text and picture as Foucault put it above, takes place here *not* between a reading of what is in this text and what is in the drawing, but between 'man and woman' in Bluemel's reading – or between her *imagined* narrative of Harry's take on the situation versus the 'source' of the truth of it in the drawing's take. But both text and drawing are 'impure', unclear representations of 'the truth', as Bluemel's set-up to this reading suggested; all kinds of ambiguities arise as one contemplates either one. In the drawing, the figure does *not* seem to be laughing, only smiling, which is wholly appropriate under the circumstances if we are reading the poem narratively. Why indeed should this figure, assuming as Bluemel seems to do that it is the speaker, cover that smile when the text says clearly that 'Harry [must] smile and I will smile too'? Moreover, this girl could be raising her hand to dry a happy tear or to hide the ambiguous 'death wish' (for Harry or herself?) in her eyes, or even to tweak her nose witch-style as easily as to disguise her laugh. Indeed, Severin calls hers 'a witch's attempt to influence the future' (though she admits that 'how the woman is going to get the lion to cooperate with her is unclear') (1997, 68). Severin's reading of this as yet another poem in which poem and drawing work together to stop the romance plot (67) engages in the same background narrativising that Bluemel's does, except at greater length; she considers how to read the drawing with every possible cast member in – child-dressed-for-a-party, speaker-as-child, attendant-at-the-wedding. But the 'open-endedness' she wishes to demonstrate by asking many questions and creating many 'alternative stories' is, like Bluemel's, actually open only to the idea that 'nature is woman's ally in securing freedom from her married state' (69, 68). These are readings *not* of the work, but of narratives behind it and the critics' own foregoing conclusions.

Any reading of the drawing's relationship to the text must be dependent on the text's own discrepancies and lack of coherence. Throughout the poem, and beginning in the first line, the speech has conflicting trajectories; Harry is first dismissed and then, without caesura, kept for the speaker's needs – the line striking a desperate and irreconcilable balance that informs the discrepant nature of the last stanza's content and form. Far more lyrical than the prosaic cruelty of the first two stanzas, which culminates in the second's final and deliberately long, sentence-like, satirical 'bite', this one's introverted sadness complicates the pivotal, multivalent term in the second stanza: death-wish. We know Smith enjoyed deploying Freudian concepts; this one does not refer to one's wish for death for *other* people, unless such is due to the death-drive being perverted or diverted away from self to another. Who does it apply to here? Certainly the vengeful anger of our speaker at her situation suggests that in the first two stanzas it does indeed apply to her woefully fated mate, presented to us by her like a preying mantis's victim. We *do* understand this, as Bluemel suggests; there *is* anger played out in this sadistic *cri de coeur* but it is against, ultimately, not Harry so much as her own weakness. Because she '*dared not* without marrying leave home' – phrasing that suggests she *might* have, *if* she had dared, *if* she had had the courage to break out on her own, left home without enacting this cruel game by its rules. Instead she does play by those rules, and finds herself corrupted by the social sport that normally designates her the prey, the prize. She is, like all of Smith's speakers, caught – and, we might say, most appealing in her intelligence; she knows it. The 'Ah feeble me' is not qualified in any feminist sense; she is indeed condemning herself. Even more importantly, its rhyme with 'Ah woe' suggests, poetically rather than fully securely, that the woe *also* applies to herself, that the 'death wish' is now fully and properly her own. The injunction to 'burn fire, burn fire in eyes' sheathing' is difficult to read, which is perhaps why her critics refrain from trying; but its difficulty *is* the point of the poem. *Her* eyes are the only ones referred to above this line – *they* sheath that (self-directed?) death wish; this may be what will happen to Harry. If the burning is conjured up in the field of that act, *in her* eyes, then the 'bright fear fanned' is a fanning of her own fire within and her own fear as a result – fear of herself, perhaps. And of a fire in Harry's breathing, which could be the desire to be burned by him. Of course the other reading is also very delicately made available here; she is simultaneously fanning the fire in her own eyes that will burn him – that will fan the fear in him, and turn his life's breath into death's fire. These readings are made to coexist, just as the irreconcilable first line suggests they must. And the drawing? Its transfer of subjects I find deeply disturbing. I agree with Severin; this is quite objectively not a wedding dress, thus this is not the speaker (unless recalled from some other time). This figure, whether made 'other' by identity or temporal displacement, effects an interruption of the speaker's subjective drama at the same time that she seems so deeply implicated in it that subjectivity itself is externalised and unowned. I will not narrativise beyond that; it is a female caught in an indefinable gesture and a strange splayed stance that may suggest a kind of awkward pivotal identity with the speaker, though this is debatable. The hand up to her face, the small smile and the eye with brow slightly drawn all suggest a range of possible responses, a volatility in circumscription that our agonised speaker also demonstrates. Perhaps it is indeed the undecidability or volatility of character that Smith probes in this poem – or rather the ways in which youth, if this female in the drawing is as young as she looks, is destined to be caught between the same culturally determined conduits of possibility. Like 'Mrs Simpkins', this poem is not about any one right prevailing through might; its web is entangled and entangling. The drawing once again delivers unknowable being into the circumstance of its unknowableness: the webs of inscribed power relations that will overwhelm it and define even any rebellion against them, dividing self from self and ultimately obviating the very possibility of innocent response.

The idea that 'wish[ing] alone to roam' is in itself a good or strong thing for a woman to do is one that Smith's critics do not question though Smith *does*, in her work as a whole – though her style is to defer judgement by playing out the full range of desires in their available languages. A look at her much discussed poem 'My Hat' (*CP* 315), for example, reveals this. Laura Severin suggests that 'Hats in Smith's poems often represent women's freedom', quoting Smith herself who once noted that 'There are a great many hats in my poems. They represent going away and also running away' (65–66). But Severin's assumption that going or running away equals 'freedom' in the quote represents another leap to conclusions which this poem – like Smith's *oeuvre* as a whole – does not support. The hat flies this female speaker away to a 'peculiar' *'desert* island' (my emphasis) upon which she reflects, much as the boy in 'Little Boy Lost' did, upon the strangeness of not really missing home, though she is not really happy either: 'Am I glad I am here? Yes, well, I am,/It's nice to be rid of Father, Mother and the young man', her former suitor. Obviously the liberation here from strictures suggests its partly feminist content, though the fact that she is wearing the hat on her mother's advice that it 'would help her get off with the right sort of chap' gives us pause; it is her 'Mother' she wishes escape from but also her mother's advice she follows, as Smith's little boy lost followed his father into the woods. Like that other poem, this one also ends with no positive input about her present state of supposed freedom. Indeed, the island is most reminiscent of Tennyson's 'The Lotos Eaters'; it seems bewitched, a place where it is 'always early morning' and 'the green grass grows into the sea on the dipping land'. Smith's figures are often wearing such hats in the poems/drawings, are poised for flight – but flight, again, as we know from the novels, is a dangerous option too. When we hear that 'this hat being so strong has completely run away with [our speaker]', we fear that she is not so much 'in control' as *controlled* by a desire for escape that cuts all human ties, and that we know leaves Smith's speakers, in the poems as in the novels, enthralled in the wish for inertia or psychological death.

If we take ourselves back to Smith's second collection, where I began this section, we find that poems often used to illustrate Smith's desire for 'freedom' in the form of riding away are situated in the novels in ways that again illuminate the highly compromised nature of such escape. For an example, I should offer a poem I have myself misread in the past. 'In My Dreams' (129) – in which Smith's speaker famously tells us 'In my dreams I am always saying good-bye and riding away' – is wholly spliced into *Over the Frontier* at perhaps its most frightening juncture of all: the point at which Pompey decides she has suddenly moved beyond her former muddled state of 'coming to terms with a life-in-death existence' and will instead embrace her uniform. For, as she says, 'since I am thus desperately out of love with life, in war shall I not do well?' (222–24). In my earliest work on Smith's poetry I read this piece as an evocation of her *own* desire to exist beyond the edge of social influence, because I wished to portray her as a female agent in control. But this placement of it in the novel, as well as the image's greater treatment throughout Smith's work, certainly should complicate that reading.

This might better be described as the 'failed spirit' speaking – a speaker whom as we saw earlier Smith described as not herself, but representative of her moment's movement towards war. So many of the poems in this collection are actually against 'flying away', though its title poem, 'Tender Only to One', would on its surface suggest a lyrical love poem to death. The image of the 'petals swing[ing] / to [the speaker's] fingering' in a 'He loves, he loves me not' game might apply to many of the speakers in this collection, swinging as they do in various ways on the brink of ambiguously valued extinction, or the illusion that their pasts or present lives or the world itself can be left behind. The figure of such 'flying away' is sometimes interpreted literally as flying towards disconnection from the world ('Look, Look', 152) or away from the influences of childhood ('Fuite de'Enfance', 158); or less literally flying towards war ('Bye Baby Bother', 144; 'The Lads of the Village', 142); or sometimes as irresponsible flight away from pain and reality ('Nobel and Ethereal', 129). I shall read several of these more closely below, but perhaps 'Look, Look' makes the best transition, given its literal dealing with the metaphor and its oddly gendered drawing.

Indeed, another of the very unique aspects of Smith's work that her critics rarely explore is that, in the poems/drawings as in the novels, male names and references are often annexed to female bodies or experiences and *vice versa*, whether in the texts or in the drawings. Her best-known poem 'Not Waving But Drowning' most famously shows us a female survivor for a drowning male voice in the text (often read, as we might expect, as feminine triumph), but many of her other poems do as well. 'The River Deben', for example, despite its being described as generated by Pompey's rowing experience in *Over the Frontier*, pictures a male rower; and here, alongside this short lyric 'Look, Look', the 'He [that] flies so high' is depicted as a male-faced figure swinging from an acrobat's trapeze in female skirts – far too female in their wide petticoats to be mistaken for male acrobatic garb. He is flung high into the sky, above mountains and even 'over the moon' – an old phrase suggesting transported delight. It is 'too high for you', suggests our speaker, narrating his story in second-person and ending it with the snide comment: 'Is / Not the world / A good sty for you?' Obviously this figure is being equated, given its description as a 'winged piggywig' (perhaps out of Edward Lear's 'The Owl and the Pussycat'), with a 'flying pig' – another old phrase, this one a joke which refers to any impossible or unlikely proposition. The unlikely escape from or transcendence of one's sty of a world, in other words, effects nothing in terms of transformed piggy-ness. It is tempting to think of this poem as a parody of Auden in his poetry collection *Look, Stranger!* (1936); certainly we know from the novels that the utopian 'pinkness' of writers in the Auden circle, and Auden's own depiction of such 'orators' flying above the world on suicide missions to purge themselves of bourgeois tendencies gathered only Smith's scorn. But more clearly here the unisexual valence of this figure swinging between life and total disconnection renders the desire for flight ungendered and gathers *both* sympathy and scorn. Even the speaker's text seems to swing in potential sonic imitation as well as snideness; the end-rhyme displaced by 'is' effects an enjambing swing from the second to third line above – taking us up in the air too, male and female readers alike.

Smith's assessment of the human condition as one of subjection forever to the bullying representations of culture cast both females and males into similar states of desire for flight. In other words, all rhyme in the suspicion that 'Here is no home' (*The Holiday*, 163). This might be viewed as a modernist, essentialising assessment, though she also attends to the differences in the situations of her female figures, often touching feelingly on their specific sorts of entrapment 'on that [Shakespearean] bier, between two men' where we at times found her speakers in the novels. I quote from *The Holiday* above because in this collection is a poem that will be wholly reproduced there, with only slight revision, and its 'Fuite d'Enfance', its flight of/from childhood, takes us back to Shakespeare for both her gendered *and* non-gendered consideration of such entrapment. In the novel, the poem's appearance intersects the main conversation between Caz and Celia on the nature of her longings for death. She cannot be clear about it, and admits that the part that wants to die and the part that does not, that feels it 'has something valuable' to warrant it 'an excuse from death', are constantly 'crying out against each other' (159). It is important to recall that at the end of this passage Celia dreams she will be 'shifted', like imperial England; therefore these desires and discussion of death have many dimensions to them. And indeed, just after she quotes the poem, she has the overwhelming sense that its 'terrible picture of a terrible state of mind' applies to *everybody* in her current wartime and post-wartime context: 'yes, nobody at all at this moment does not seem to me to be in this state' (162). It begins, importantly, with a near-quotation from Shakespeare's Sonnet 144, 'Two loves I have of comfort and despair':

> I have two loves,
> There are two loves of mine,
> One is my father
> And one my Divine.
> My father stands on my right hand,
> He has an abstracted look.
> Over my left shoulder
> My Divine reads me like a book.
> Which shall I follow...
> And following die?
> No longer count on me
> But to say goodbye.

Figure 5.2 The accompanying drawing for 'Fuite d'Enfance'.

> A leur insu
> Je suis venue
> Faire mes adieux.
> Adieu, adieu, adieu. (158)

The poem is offered by Celia as a 'farewell present' to Casmilus and to Heber; in the novel its first lines change objects from 'loves' to 'friends'. Unlike Shakespeare's sonnet, the good and bad influences which are also depicted here on either shoulder are not gendered male and female, respectively – the 'better angel' being a 'man right fair', and the 'worser spirit' a 'woman colour'd ill' (Shakespeare 1775). As the drawing also suggests, Smith's speaker has subverted that sexual dichotomy, with its traditional identification of sinful influence as female, by suspending her figure of childhood between two uncertainly qualified, male powers, a 'father' and a 'Divine'. The girl-figure looks as though she has already begun her 'flight', as her knees have approached her guardians' hips in height and she seems propelled into space. Nothing in the *text* suggests the speaker's gender; though Celia's authorship in the novel might direct us, and the final lines might take us back to another, female voice in Shakespeare's writing: Thisbe's, speaking her very theatrical final words in *A Midsummer Night's Dream*: 'Thus Thisbe dies:/Adieu, adieu, adieu!' (Shakespeare 245). If we read it as Celia's poem, the male influence that is too 'abstracted' from her, too caught up perhaps in the thoughts thronging the constructed world – which in Smith's vocabulary also means flown away from things actual into things dangerously 'mysterious' or metaphysical – must be Heber. The other male influence that is too close, too able to read every dark and condemning thought, is no doubt Casmilus, her inner-daemon/alter-ego, who moves in and out of the 'hell' of human existence and understands the death at the heart of her own. There is no in-between them available to her; she will 'die in following' either, whether it be into abstraction or into self-scrutiny and despair. 'Unknown to them', she suggests, 'I have come to bid my farewells', to make her flight. French is perhaps used because, in the novel, Caz has just been teasingly singing what Celia refers to as nonsense from a French grammar book; but I would argue that it is more importantly used for the same reason that bits of German will also appear in several paragraphs: all of Europe is caught in the same cultural impasse between the 'father's' (or fatherland's, or patriarchy's) 'righteous' abstractions on their 'right' and the inner eye on the 'left' or nether-side, whose knowledge of hellish thought beyond abstraction is 'Divine' and disruptive.

But does she escape? The poem is full of questions, as is the title. Is this an escape or flight *of* childhood, as Hermione Lee translates it (195), in which case it is destined to be superseded or even caught up with, given that the word 'fuite' has, like her earlier poem's title, 'The Fugitive', an element of such connotations in its usage? Or is it a flight *from* childhood, which would mean a leaving of it behind? In Smith's novels, the latter is not possible; neither

Smith's Pompey nor her Celia ever escape the imprint of both empire and parental 'codes' (such as both their fathers encountered in military service) upon their early lives. Nor is it possible in Shakespeare's sonnet, where we are told 'the two spirits do suggest me still':

> And whether that my angel be turn'd fiend
> Suspect I may, yet not directly tell;
> But being both from me, both to each friend,
> I guess one angel in another's hell:
> Yet this shall I ne'er know, but live in doubt,
> Till my bad angel fire my good one out.

Similarly, both Smith's novel and poem deliberately refuse to identify which is which, angel and fiend, much as Shakespeare's speaker too only 'guesses' that 'one [is in] another's hell' – that both are 'from me', and that he/she is 'both to each friend'. '[L]iv[ing] in doubt' is the fate of the sonnet's speaker; we know that it is Celia's fate as well. And though I am tempted to suggest that this figure escapes from *between* the father's 'abstraction' in patriarchal language and the 'Divine's' inability to read her as anything but 'a book' (which may account for why the latter could possibly not know about her coming to make her farewell, if he can read her mind), I find too many textual suggestions that this is too simple a conclusion, however clearly it might reside as one of this poem's desires unmet. Stuck between Shakespeare's agonised sonnet speaker on the one hand and Thisbe's suicide, this desire to fly is uttered, suddenly, in the language of childhood, if we can assume that the title and the subject in the drawing suggest its site. Yet 'Fuite d'Enfance' resides sonically very near 'Fuite à France', intriguingly.

And as always in Smith's poems about possible flight, the frightening question of whether death is a true end or escape erupts within the text or drawing, as it does here beyond this poem in the novel. Though Celia offers it at a strong moment for her in the discussion, when she asserts that death 'is nothing at all': 'For if death is what we are not, how can we have a part in it?' (161), she recognises directly after reciting her poem 'the contradictory nature' of her desires, for in next telling Caz 'he will never forget [her]', she admits the desire to remain. Caz will respond to her self-derisory laugh with his own chilling and 'nasty laugh', locating what she 'is frightened of' in both her thought 'that death might not be the end' (163) and, as she herself locates it, in the idea that 'she flees, but none pursues'. Very few quotes are more self-deflating than this one; perhaps originating in the old aphorism, 'Guilt flees when none pursues', it suggests not only her complicity with all that she would escape but also the ludicrousness, or childishness, of such self-importance, for none will bother to follow though that is what she in part desires. Her fleeing amounts to no triumph in this context. 'You are afraid of the torturers of this world', he says; 'you wish to be on the edge, to stay a little and then go, but in this going there is this hope that something may come up that is beautiful scenery and a country day.' She flees, like Thisbe, both 'the torturers' and a Lion – the lions of childhood, the Lion Aunt, the British Lion of an inescapable national past with its fate to come; yet even in her imaginings of a happy afterlife, the same scenery and countryside that her lifetime's imaginings have produced in context cannot be transcended. She is caught, like Mrs Simpkins, in a situation that even suicide cannot remedy. Perhaps the poem's drawing, then, is the most terrifying in Smith's *Collected Poems*; perhaps this child is not flying out of the picture but is forever caught between these frighteningly large-headed male influences, with only the unsupportable, textually-inherited hope that 'bad angel will fire good one out'. Smith's work often evokes the pictorial rather than the poetic, as her novels' use of painting imagery might suggest, in that both offer more in the way of disturbing collage and unresolved tension than the sort of narrative statement that her critics have assumed may be read within them.

In dialogue: the short stories, the novels, and *Tender Only to One* (1938)

The torturers are not only oversized males or phallic forces, however clearly Smith suggests the imprisoning existence of such for their female progeny. As I began to explain at the outset of this section, Smith's second collection of poems returns again and again to images of childhood and the family – never to celebrate childhood, as Martin Pumphrey suggests, but to consider (quite provocatively, in 1938) the development of children, male *and* female, into 'the torturers'. In many ways, her short stories of the period, particularly 'Surrounded by Children', illuminate her vision of how the very differently stratified levels of social and gendered experience become united in cultural bellicosity or cultural cruelty.[18] This two-page piece, published in 1939, begins with a poetically rendered social breakdown of the figures to be seen on 'a pleasant English summer's day in [Kensington] Gardens and [Hyde] Park' (*MA* 26). Although Jan Montefiore argues that 'as a storyteller [Smith] seems... at her best' in the narrative poems (43), it seems to me that this piece in all its truncated experimentalism could be offered in counter-argument. Montefiore attributes the poems' success to their Benjaminian 'simplicity and strangeness', and the fact that their narrator who is positioned inside the story forces readers to decide the moral (44, 45). This seems quite right, though in my reading the short stories are additionally remarkable for their strange *Steinian* simplicity and strangeness – meaning their repetition, and on-the-spot, participial arrangements of themselves by which elemental building blocks of sense are gradually soldered together by commas (often with the result of sounding painfully contrived and artificial) in order to get at the structural disaster that is social experience, both in terms of her subjects' expression and their behaviour. The beginning of this story is a good example of how they sound. In the park, the poor are separated from the rich and, within their circles, the little girls are 'caring for the brothers' in a way that leaves them more like mothers than children, filled with anxiety rather than the happy and ambiguously termed 'carelessness' that will mark the boys:

> Under the shadow of the trees in Hyde Park the mothers are nursing the babies, and in the long grass of Kensington Gardens and on the banks of the Serpentine the sisters are caring for the brothers, under the trees the aunt walks. What is the aunt doing, under the trees walking? She is thinking of the young man who has the ice-cream vendor's cart; the cart of the ice-cream vendor is upon the road, he is peddling briskly away from the walking aunt.
> The Brothers of the sisters and the babies of the mothers have no care at all; theirs is a careless fate, to be pampered and cared for, no matter if there is no money the brothers will have the sisters to jump around after them, the babies will have the mothers to nurse them, the aunt will have the pleasure of sweet dreams under the tree and the ice-cream vendor will have his escape upon the saddle of his bicycle cart.

The cycle of subordination, exploitation, dreaming and escape continues with a twist in Smith's other short story of the period, 'The Herriots'; a brief look at this piece before continuing might illuminate the potential consequences of the above.

In it she imagines *another* kind of female, symbolically named 'Peg Lawless', whose upbringing by two women – one of whom would teach her housekeeping by whipping her for her 'absent-mindedness', the other being 'affectionate and impatient, preferred to do it herself' – causes her to fit the above mould only imperfectly. Smith's main character therefore becomes an interestingly handicapped figure; her 'queer way' is characterised by not being able to manage signs and their referents: 'She said lobster and saw bloater', therefore managing only to bring home the wrong things from the market. Such lopsided vision, seemingly the result of two discrepant female influences, leaves her confused and likewise unable to manage the structural chain that defines her socially. She 'had been brought up to think that men were to fetch and carry' and cannot negotiate with new female in-laws who 'unquestioningly put the wishes of the men first' – a situation that prompts her to feel that she had 'married into an Indian or Turkish family' (which might reveal Smith's prejudices, or her subversion of the idea that western social structures are somehow more 'modern' than the east's). But she also reproduces gendered structures of behaviour, in our very first introduction to her relations with Coke, by calling upon him to 'fight that boy' who pulled her hair. The interdependent and cyclic deployments of social power and pain in the story are further layered by economic change and suburban developments. Peg becomes a battered wife in a story which begins by examining the tightening economic boxes of the Thirties, linking that baseline of culture in suffocating 'Bottle Green' to almost inevitable violence. It happens when absent-minded (rather than endlessly caring) women like Peg end up with 'quick-tempered' husbands like Coke, who is perhaps symbolically connected by name to the capitalist enterprise described as quickly transforming what was once his neighbourhood's 'wicked old spacious days of King Edward' into 'rows of small houses' (*MA* 74). Although he 'would have made a career in the army – if there had been a war' (75), Coke is still like the small boys in the park: though 'warm-hearted and affectionate', he is untrained to 'care' for his family, full of hatred for his jobs and desperate because 'he could do nothing else'. The hopelessness that accompanies the arrival of a baby and the continuing loss of jobs on Coke's part causes the story to lean into the surreal, and Peg to lean metaphorically towards death. In her dreams she sees herself knocking on a door which will, in yet another one of Smith's inimitably palimpsestic interfaces between dream and reality, come to be opened by an old woman who employs Peg (to take her daily to the cemetery), who falls 'in love' with her, and who of course represents death (78). Her advice to Peg is that 'It is very vulgar to think in the absurd terms "you can get away". There is only one way in which you can get away, in the lofty and ethereal conception of the aristocrat, and that is to die and be buried' (79). Equating the desire to 'get away' through death with aristocratic vanity, 'etherealness' (always charged negatively in Smith's work) and self-importance, the story resolves in much the same way that 'Surrounded by Children' will – in a collage of jammed discursive directives, because Coke will, with good news of (another) new job, find them in the cemetery just as the old woman proposes her 'ending' to the story. He is 'lit up like a flame' with joy, but as always the image of fire suggests in Smith's work that he is *also* death to Peg, yet another mandate over her shoulder whom she can, 'following die' ('Fuite d'Enfance', *CP* 158). The piece ends with Peg and Coke sitting on either side of the old woman on the symbolic 'seat beneath the yew tree' which, ever since Hardy's plentiful renderings of the image, has poetically called up death. Though the old woman explains her tears as being due to her happiness for the young couple, we are left with uncertainty that the stated is not its opposite in every corner of this picture. The last sentence's description of Coke giving 'her' – Peg? the old woman? – a piece of chocolate that he had bought for the baby turns the screw again; Peg and the possibly inconsolable death-figure become one in this 'picture' of indecorous desires and desperation placated like a baby by forces that must school it to take its 'rightful' place.[19]

Returning to the next paragraphs of 'Surrounded by Children' and the same processes at work there, we move to the problematic inheritances that differ for the 'high-class' children. Their introduction to the recyclable violence in culture is of another order but no less transformable into that of the common lot. These with the 'baby accents of the ruling classes' are watched by hired servants in the Park and Gardens; and although its little girls are not careworn, they like their brothers are nevertheless locked into cages/roles with the help of their 'ferocious nannies'. Even their voices are constrained by their placement in this part of the scene, for '...the clichés too, already they are there, a little affected is it not? and sad, too, that already the children are so self-aware almost already at a caricature of themselves – "we are having fun"' (26). Such supposed 'expression' of experience, learned as all these behaviours are learned – from their parents – is spoken 'with tight lips above baby teeth' in a kind of potentially violent snarl behind the smiling.

Although the experiences between classes seem divergent, they are nonetheless able to be drawn into 'unison' – by, in part, hatred for the commonly persecuted. As Pompey put it when caught in her affiliation of self with country before concern for the rights of the oppressed, the Jews: 'Do we not always hate the persecuted?' (*OTF* 158). Here, the figure to be persecuted comes on the scene as a 'famously ugly old girl' who 'as she walks she talks' (27). Her kind are familiar sights in urban London, where the madness and solitude of the 'one of many', as Smith puts it in a poem in *Tender Only to One*, renders the 'walking dream' of such a worthless female, neither child-caring anymore or rich, 'very different...from the walking dream of the love of the ice-cream vendor' (26–27) which powers the aunt in this story, though we cannot help but feel that the two are placed on a continuum of possibility. 'Ah, upon the old girl is no eligible imagination for the nurture of a love-life of entertainment value' (27); instead, her hands like 'delicate long birds' claws, clasp the air about her', looking for some foothold. She finds it in a 'deserted perambulator' intended for 'a grand infant of immensely rich parentage'. We cannot help but, in this tiny story, relate back the perambulator to the other vehicle repeatedly placed in our focus, the vendor's cart upon which the boy was able to escape earlier, though this figure's current desire seems also complexly related to the fact that our narrator keeps calling her an '*old girl*'. Her regressive and transgressive need to, 'come what may', get into that pram may be related to the fact that, like the young 'sisters' of prioritised brothers in the park, who 'anxiously comb back from [their] brow[s] with [similarly] long soiled finger[s] the lank lock[s]' (26), she has been long-neglected and needs to be at last prioritised, loved; as Celia puts it in the discussion I just examined above, 'It is love that everybody is after, make no mistake' (*TH* 163). But what she gets instead, for exhibiting what many feel and should pity, is a surrounding by children – all of them suddenly mobilised, suddenly 'woken' like Pompey out of their varying roles in the dream of culture, to 'close in upon her fast', as Smith puts it in deeply predatory terms. They are suddenly 'united in a childish laughter', as if cast in one of the period's Hitchcock films where the innocent become the diabolical. And, suddenly, 'the sisters of the brothers have forgotten their care', as every child gathers to witness what becomes a 'grotesque crucifixion':

'Ah,' cries the sad beldame, transfixed in grotesque crucifixion upon the perambulator, stabbing at herself with a hatpin of the old fashion so that a little antique blood may fall upon the frilly pillow of the immaculate vehicle, 'what fate is this, what nightmare more *agaçant* so to lie and so to die, in great pain, surrounded by children.'

Such is Smith's revision of familiar phrases signalling domestic scenes of comfort, of being 'surrounded by children'. Here at the end of the story, she is a 'beldame' sans merci *from others*, in Smith's demystification of lovelorn, balladic death-figures. Translated in her suffering into a heroic sacrifice, she is also a comical one, filled with 'annoyance' at her fate, given Smith's inimitably prismatic approach to the utterly mundane and therefore most potently socially tragic. But she causes her 'antique blood' to fall 'upon the frilly pillow of the immaculate vehicle' like an ancient shadow upon cultural 'scripture', its dream; and indeed, the dreams of the aunt too might end in such 'nightmares' because children, like the adults whom they mirror, require delivery from 'care', from their sense of entrapment. In Smith's work the latter too often comes in the form of mobilisation into cruel collectives, into league with 'the common lot', as one poem from Smith's wartime collection will put it, echoing 'The Failed Spirit' with which I began this chapter:

> There is a fearful solitude
> Within the careless multitude,
> And in the open country too,
>
> He mused, and then it seemed to him
> The solitude lay all within;
> He longed for some interior din:
>
> Some echo from the worldly rout,
> To indicate a common lot,
> Some charge that he might be about,
> But oh he felt that he was quite forgot. ('Forgot!', 201)

In Smith's translation of the collective 'death drive', which we saw her elaborate in the trilogy, the isolated in their social cages wish for escape and dissolution in the crowd – 'to run mad' as Germany was described as doing in *Over the Frontier*. In this story published the following year, even the girls join in, happy to 'forget their care', to victimise the oppressed from within an illusion of unity. It seems her second poetry collection's analysis of cultural violence sprung out of such comprehensive enfolding of social actors in numerous levels of dreaming and 'forgetting' developed directly alongside her prose explorations of the same.

Therefore one finds in the collection many poems that in one way or another interrogate the instances of inculcated fierceness. 'The Photograph'

(145), for example, ostensibly about a baby boy photographed on a tiger-skin rug, depicts in its drawing a crying infant struggling between its innocent, frilly baby's clothing and what looks like its alter-ego: the 'second head' of the tiger rearing angrily over its shoulder. The explicitly British setting of this poem and its reference to the tiger rug – a familiar relic of imperial 'tourism' and domination – demand a cultural reading that extends far beyond the familial drama at hand.[20] The admonition, 'Parents of England, not in smug / Fashion fancy set on a rug / Of animal fur the darling you would hug', lest it 'scent the savage he sits upon' and 'tiger-possessed abandon all things human', once again links Smith's old themes of inadequate love at home availing itself of identification with that other 'kingdom' to which English children belong: the one presided over by the 'British Lion', which might be said to 'abandon all things human' in its mode of 'colonising animal'. The poem is preceded in the collection by one of the more alarming ones addressing the coming war, 'Bye Baby Bother', and therefore its troubling valence trades on an increasing tension in the volume. Initiated in the repetitive question-and-answer form of an old English ballad, it breaks off in characteristic Smithian fashion into prosaic military speak in the fourth stanza, and ends with a truncation that viciously mimics the 'tearing' (always glossed as lionish in Smith's work) forecast for the male speaker's 'bothered' generation:

> Bye Baby Bother
> Where is your brother?
>
> They so-and-so and so-and-so
> And twisted his guts
> In a nasty way
> Because he said they were nuts.
>
> Bye Baby Bother
> How shall I keep them from your pother?
>
> I will be quiet now, Mother, but when there is a general mobilization
> Dozens of chaps like me will know what to do with our ammunition.
>
> Dozens by hundreds will be taken and torn,
> Oh would the day had died first when you were born. (144)

The origin of the current 'bother' for this son whom we might assume is often in this state, being so named by his mother, catches us off guard in the second-stanza with its sudden, graphic description of torture applied to a brother simply because a suggestion was made that someone's – 'their' – ideas were 'nuts'. The remainder of the lines and their final Sophoclean suggestion are pure prophecy as well as typical Smithian philosophy.

We recognise above the learned response of a particular kind of violence for males that Smith explores in the stories; she signals it sonically here with the near equivalence of 'brother' and 'bother' and then 'pother' (or trouble). In this collection several startling poems treat male subjects who seem to helplessly then *re-deploy* hate and physical one-upmanship in frustrating romantic or domestic situations with 'cold' or 'diffident' women ('I HATE THIS GIRL', 106; 'The Murderer', 117). It seems very possible that in 'Lads of the Village', too, Smith was commenting on the building tradition of post-Great War songs combining violence and sex that, in the hands of an entertainer like George Formby, were reaching many listeners; his 'When the Lads of the Village Get Cracking' may have even been in her mind as she composed her poem. Formby's rather horrifying lyrics describing 'every mother's son, shouldering a gun', 'just like proper soldiers all in a row', require less than a quote of a couple of stanzas to reveal the general thrust of their connection between warring, winning and women:

> Now a girl on the land was waving her hand as friendly as can be.
> Talk of invasion, she wasn't afraid
>
> She winked her eye at me and murmured 'Come on invade'.
> When the lads of the village get cracking down the road to victory.
>
> Now we ran a dance it was full of romance, and did we have fun o gee.
>
> We looked for the Colonel and found the old chap
> Practising manoeuvres with a girl on his lap.
> When the lads of the village ... [etc.].[21]

The small-boyishness of the 'o gee' is perhaps in fine keeping with the muddle of early and later 'training' these troops (and Formby's audience) seem to be getting. Smith's poem by similar title is far less comic than we would expect, if it *is* actually a commentary on this particular song. In any case, its far more sober and general commentary on poets' songs in response to war may help explain why, in the next collection, she will suggest like Adorno that it might be better if 'The Poets are Silent'. Her 'Lads of the Village' reads thus:

> The lads of the village, we read in the lay,
> By medalled commanders are muddled away,
> And the picture that the poet makes is not very gay.
>
> Poet, let the red blood flow, it makes the pattern better,
> And let the tears flow, too, and grief stand that is their begetter,
> And let man have his self-forged chain and hug every fetter.
>
> For without the juxtaposition of muddles, medals and clay,
> Would the picture be so very much more gay,

> Would it not be a frivolous dance upon a summer's day?
>
> Oh sing no more: Away with the folly of commanders.
> This will not make a better song upon the field of Flanders,
> Or upon any field of experience where pain makes patterns the poet
>   slanders. (142)

A comparison of this with Jon Silkin's or Geoffrey Hill's poems about war and the immorality of poetic responses to atrocity two decades later would not go amiss here.[22] But if in the interest of space we simply attend to the above condemnation of the clash of 'patterns' – the actual pain of battlefield experience that most cannot know, and the 'slander', as her speaker viciously calls it, of poems or songs that, like Formby's, translate such experience back into obscene or 'frivolous dances' for the public – we have an example of Smith's clearest offering of moral judgement on the role of art in war. The repeated use of the word 'pattern' is intriguing; we know that, as I explained in Chapter 1, she referred to things like morality and religion as 'human patterns', as though she were discussing sewing patterns. The 'fabrication', if I may be forgiven the pun, of verbal patterns like writing, speaking and singing as opposed to non-verbal patterns that 'pain makes' on other 'field[s] of experience' comes into issue here as it does in all of her poems, if more simply and angrily; the poet's words are 'slander' – lies, misrepresentations – of those fields, like the too-neatly-rhyming 'Flanders' battlefield of the Great War. The foregrounding of language's artifice, its propensity to clarify, equalise and translate highly discrepant realities is embodied in the medal/muddle wordplay, by which the 'muddle of Europe's thinking', the great wound of unclear boundaries that is world war, is clarified in the heroism and 'medals' that come to symbolise and represent it for the people. She makes up a verb, to suggest the lack of an accurate one in language's repertoire for war; her lads are 'muddled away' in stark contrast to the more familiar kinds of comforting, ordered phrases in Formby's song where '[they] go, rain or snow, just like proper soldiers all in a row'. And here, of course, her debt to Blake's anger is also clearest; those 'self-forged chains' make no effort to distort either Blake's image or his rage in his poem 'London' against the 'mind-forged manacles' that cage the human soul.

Yet the volume will end with 'The Violent Hand', whose speaker is female, and whose dangerous, 'dangling' fate may be to 'clutch / With violent hand the rosary' proffered by a military 'angel most cynical... With a smile of brass' (160). Many other things go on in this typically complex piece that, with its drawing's background references to a church interior's depictions of Virgin and child on one side of the altar and the crucifixion on the other, again ponders the iconography of necessary pain that, for Smith, inscrutably accompanies Christianity's analogy of domestic and holy 'family' experience. The female role in this poem of supporting with unquestioning faith 'her own side' in the midst of the violence of the world's movements around her is opposed elsewhere in the collection with the potential choice of rejecting faith, and choosing to see death as the only 'divine' state in such a place. In what I consider the collection's most successful poem, 'Mother, among the Dustbins', the titular figure is, by making such a decision, once again thrust between two men – God or dominant culture on the one side and, in this case, her own son on the other. Yet it is not wholly clear which interlocutor speaks the fourth and fifth stanzas of the poem, which leaves its meaning once again caught between lines of thought. The 'thought that informs the hope of our kind' that is accused of being an 'empty thing' could be *either* the hope of death *or* the hope of God below – and thus the accusation one made by either against the other:

> Mother, among the dustbins and the manure
> I feel the measure of my humanity, an allure
> As of the presence of God, I am sure
>
> In the dustbins, in the manure, in the cat at play,
> Is the presence of God, in a sure way
> He moves there. Mother, what do you say?
>
> I too have felt the presence of God in the broom
> I hold, in the cobwebs in the room,
> But most of all in the silence of the tomb.
>
> Ah! but that thought that informs the hope of our kind
> Is but an empty thing, what lies behind? –
> Naught but the vanity of a protesting mind
>
> That would not die. This is the thought that bounces
> Within the conceited head and trounces
> Inquiry. Man is most frivolous when he pronounces.
>
> Well Mother, I shall continue to feel as I do,
> And I think you would be wise to do so too,
> Can you question the folly of man in the creation of God?
>   Who are you? (118)

(One imagines Smith photographed alongside dustbins, as Samuel Beckett has famously been photographed.) Smith articulates more clearly here than perhaps anywhere else her sense that 'positive thought' emerges as a necessity in the face of its absence, as perhaps the thought of heavenly God emerges from humanity's situation in an absolutely opposite domain. Her sense is indeed not unlike Derrida's articulated thirty years later, in 'Violence and Metaphysics', where such 'desire' gives ironic grounding to language's structures built on absent centres and proliferating fabrications,

Figure 5.3 The accompanying drawing for 'Mother, among the Dustbins'.

'patterns' produced *mise-en-abîme*. Because 'inaccessible, the invisible is the most high' (1978, 93); but since the 'violence' of self-imposition on the world as 'egoity is the absolute form of experience', God can only be 'for me what he is by my own conscious production' (132, 133). Even the mother's *non*-positive location of God in death rather than life requires such a process; 'before all atheism or all faith, ... before all language about God or with God, God's divinity... must have a meaning for an ego in general'

(132). Therefore religion – or atheism, Derrida suggests – by its very ontology will always be synonymous with a war of egos, a violence effected here in this poem by son against mother as the result of her production of a differing model of self. Suddenly her meaning in his life is violently erased in order to impose his own: 'Who are you?' That question, taken in its typically Smithian, multiply-readable way, can suggest everything from the most superficial dismissal of her as 'anyone' important enough to question traditional 'wisdom', to his questioning of her female ability to question 'man's' ironic 'creation of God' to, indeed, his questioning of her very presence anymore, should she become invisible 'among the dustbins' given his newly imposed 'reality' inscribed upon them: one that sees what she will not see, 'the presence of God...mov[ing] there', and therefore one that finds her presence incompatible, by necessity erasable. The drawing also suggests the unclean and complicit lines of reality and identity, as well as the 'overwritten' nature of both the text and the desires it describes. In the text, manure, the dustbins and the 'real' produce God, abstractions and language; in the drawing, the street runs through the very head of the small, haughty-looking and 'protesting' boy, and the cat's tail becomes his weaponry – what looks like a knife pointed at his mother from within his aggressively crossed arms. This cat is a key link to the novels; it is without question the same 'cat on the cradle' from the initial image of *Novel on Yellow Paper* which, as we know, supports the whole of the trilogy through to its transformation in the last pages of *The Holiday*. Here that cat is also doing its balancing act, though on what looks like a precariously angled wheelbarrow of some kind; the bundle under its feet which should be trash, like the trash in the further dustbin, looks more nearly like a human form, a baby, in swaddling. And is the eye of that baby angled oddly, evilly? In any case, this 'sick cat' explicates the boy's behaviour, because as we saw in the last two chapters, its role is to 'trounce inquiry'; it annuls innocent existence and replaces it with the kind of dominating, self-imposing, violent presence that the boy is also attempting as he moves to the centre of the drawing. But whose is the 'vanity of a protesting mind / That would not die'? Could the boy be responding with the interjection 'Ah!' to her 'pronounced' vanity in entombing God? We have seen the way that Smith will indict her speaker Celia in *The Holiday* for seeming to wish to die but feeling that something of value in her excuses her, ultimately, from it. This poem also resolves in some space between the arguments offered, though we cannot help but note that it is 'Mother' who will be left among the dustbins; the boy is ascendant, the cat is a fearful prophecy.

Further dialogue: *Mother, What is Man?* (1942) and *The Holiday*

And that prophecy, we might say, came true. *Mother, What is Man?* (1942), her wartime collection, will harshly answer its titular question; it is the most unremittingly dark of Smith's collections. It takes its title from Francis Thompson's 'An Anthem of Earth', as Frances Spalding helpfully locates it, reminding us that the latter was also quoted in *The Holiday* at just that moment that Celia and Caz are discussing man's disingenuous desire for peace. As we saw in Chapter 4, Caz has accused men of praying for peace but remaining 'like rabbits that foul their pasture'; Celia at first laughingly objects then quotes:

> Ay, Mother, mother, what is this Man, thy Darling kissed and cuffed, thou lustingly engenderst, to sweat and make his brag and rot, crowned with all honour and shamefulness. (183)

Then, as though the quoted text changes her mind, Celia 'shifts' in Caz's arms, suddenly scowls and says: 'It was better...in the war.... You know, Caz, there is something devilish about war, devilish exciting I mean. "Earth hath not anything to show more fair", ahem, it is different now, is it not?' (183–4). She means 'it is different in the post-war', but of course her use of the well-known quote from Wordsworth's sonnet 'Composed upon Westminster Bridge, September 3, 1802' leads us to also ask whether she means that things have changed in England since Wordsworth lovingly addressed 'The City' of London as the sight most 'fair', most 'touching in its majesty' (Wordsworth 107). This volume, housing 'The Failed Spirit' and a dozen other poems that directly reference the war, would suggest so. Particularly as we get to the poem that Celia quoted in full *against herself* as she tried desperately to argue the fairness of England's policy on India:

> Voices Against England in the Night
>
> 'England, you had better go,
> There is nothing else that you ought to do,
> You lump of survival value, you are too slow.
>
> England, you have been here too long,
> And the songs you sing are the songs you sung
> On a braver day. Now they are wrong.
>
> And as you sing the sliver slips from your lips,
> And the governing garment sits ridiculously on your hips.
> It is a pity that you are still too cunning to make slips.'
>
> Dr Goebbels, that is the point,
> You are a few years too soon with your jaunt,
> Time and the moment is not yet England's daunt.
>
> Yes, dreaming Germany with your Urge and Night,
> You must go down before English and American might.
> It is well, it is well, cries the peace kite.
>
> Perhaps England our darling will recover her lost thought
> We must think sensibly about our victory and not be distraught,

Perhaps American will have an idea, and perhaps not.

But they cried: Could not England, once the world's best,
Put off her governing garment and be better dressed
In a shroud, a shroud? Oh history turn thy pages fast! (216)

The poem enacts the conflict between these 'voices' – the one that mimics Caz's thoughts earlier in the novel about England's being a mere 'survival lump' that needs 'shifting', like Celia (*TH* 125), and Celia's 'distraught' and defensive responses consisting alternately of visions of herself *as* 'shifty' England and superlative descriptions of England's justice and goodness. The line above in which one voice addresses England as its 'darling' reflects this latter, over-the-top patriotic come-back; but even as such, it wavers in the poem's penultimate stanza full of 'perhapses' about England's 'recovery of lost thought'. Hermione Lee's decision is that the first three stanzas are certainly spoken by Goebbels, Germany's Nazi Minister of Propaganda until 1945, and that the stanzas that follow are clear-cut: 'Stevie Smith opposes the pacifists and those who say that the Empire is outworn' (Lee 200). I might agree that the first stanzas mock-quote Goebbels speaking, though this voice also directly quotes Smith's own characters' in *The Holiday*. But I cannot agree with Lee's latter assessment, which depends upon not only assuming that what follows is *Smith* speaking sincerely – a common problem, as we have seen, in Smith criticism – but also depends on not actually reading the rest of the poem, or its other 'voices against England in the night'. The responding voice makes only the weakest of cases against the first stanzas' indictments; it suggests only that Germany is 'a few years too soon' in assuming that England is to go, and then reveals itself ironically distraught in victory, afraid that England has no direction and no future, her 'thought' being 'lost'. The voices that finish the poem are a 'they', not Dr Goebbels, but they are saying the same things he does: England must go. Who are 'they'? I would myself not rule out the possibility that the first stanzas are also 'they' speaking, though that matters less; more importantly, given the popular usage of the idea of 'voices in the night' disturbing one's sleep, my assumption is that 'they' are internal voices. The passage in which this poem arises in *The Holiday* suggests the same. Celia is being overridden by 'voices against England', like her alter ego Caz's as well as her own at crucial moments; this 'muddle of dreaming' leaves her exhausted and distraught as our representative of declining England itself.

Other poems in the volume also suggest that Smith hardly envisioned America as the right 'might' to rescue England or Europe from its fate. In 'The Little Daughters of America' – with its epigraph, *'Pearl Harbor 1941'* – the effect of the interrupted rhyme is part comic and part destructive of the epic (if trochaic) impulse that the second line sets up:

> Admirals Curse-You and No-More
> Set their compasses and sailed for war.
>
> I am sorry that all the little daughters of America
> Should be involved in a thing like this; upon my word. (182)

The two daughters depicted in the drawing look anxious in one case and angry, brows drawn, in the other; the undecidability of their 'innocence' appropriately accompanies this truncated, enigmatic poem. But I am most interested in the obvious symmetry between the poem's beginning and end – the Admiral's names being utterances, words: 'Curse-You' and 'No-More', and the final words of the poem a familiar ejaculation expressing surprise or shock, 'upon my word'. The latter phrase, actually meaning 'upon my honour', is offered in its current, 'colloquial' form; but still, as in all Smith's poems, words however abstracted from history have their larger effects. *Very* large, here, if we hear the very names of the actors in the battle as representatives of language appearing in its performative function; *upon these words* the war begins. And may we read the last line as an expression of sadness that little daughters *are* involved in things like this? Perhaps they must be, due to the power of those words to mobilise the sentiments required from women and children in order for the revenge – the 'cursing' – to work and win.

The poem is preceded in the collection by perhaps the most troubling of them all – though others giving us timely if anachronistic encounters with figures like Torquemada might rival it – in which a 'Le Majeur Ydow' in an equally short and enigmatic piece sends off figures to a fate we can only imagine. The allusion is to Jules Barbey d'Aurevilly's 1874 novel *Les Diaboliques*, in which certain 'hardened celibates' like Major Ydow are discussed during a dinner attended by a number of atheists. We know from *Novel on Yellow Paper* that Smith linked celibacy to what she coined the disease of 'cenobites' – those 'forestallers' who in disciplining or denying their own desires seek to destroy the pleasure or well-being of others. Here in this poem, spoken in French by a Major in what by 1940 was a Vichy Government (and Smith's knife-edged references to 'Pétainismus' in the novels suggest her feelings about right-wing France), we get what is perhaps an appropriately vague fit of anger and destruction from a figure whose inability to understand his own frustrations makes them doubly dangerous:

> 'E bien! Marche!', fit le Majeur Ydow,
> 'Any more gentlemen like that? *I'll see them off!*'
>
> But there were no gentlemen really, only the phantoms
> He warred with in his perpetual tantrums. (181)

As in 'The Little Daughters of America', the power of words to *become* people, at least in terms of their real effect on the world, seems suggested here with the odd usage of the verb 'to be' in the French. We seem to hear that Ydow 'fit', or *was*, the words 'Eh bien! Marche!'; his whole being, in other words, seems translated into 'see[ing] off' the phantoms he exorcises from himself (given the potentially first-person form of the verb 'marcher') and 'phantom' others. The drawing for this poem is of a distracted, mad person dressed neatly in a fully buttoned suit jacket and necktie. The fact that we cannot know what he means by gentlemen 'like that', who get seen off, is immaterial; such a force in the world, given power to do so, will not choose victims logically or understandably. Our inability to know who is right – Major Ydow or the speaker of the second stanza – about whether or not any gentlemen are actually there mirrors such a figure's own solipsism in warfare. Smith may be wondering whether solipsism and the rendering of the rest of the world *as self* – the violence of 'egoity', as Derrida refers to it – is the necessary prerequisite for reducing others to single definitions, things 'like that', and actually 'see[ing] them off'.

Among other poems in the collection that swing on either similar desires to dominate – to 'drop...bomb[s] upon...church steeple[s]' ('No More People', 213) – or desires to remember times when speakers 'did not care for war or death' ('My Heart was Full', 195) or when they *did* ('The Failed Spirit', 218; 'Dirge', 186; 'Death in the Rose Garden', 212), there are numerous equally short pieces about unhappy or violent domestic and personal lives. Even the first poem in the collection, 'Human Affection', a simple four-line poem about the love between mother and child, is accompanied by a drawing that disturbingly depicts the mother as an explosive – quite literally. Her tensed arms and diabolically drawn brows are topped by fire-like hair, in the midst of which what looks like an enormous candle or bomb is planted, its wick aflame. The innocent voice of the little girl speaks the poem's text (while in the drawing, the unisexual child-figure is trying unsuccessfully to hold the mother's spiky fingers):

> Mother, I love you so.
> Said the child, I love you more than I know.
> She laid her head on her mother's arm,
> And the love between them kept them warm. (163)

The poem makes clear through redundant explanation that so 'said the child', *not* the mother; the mother's point of view we cannot know. In her 1969 essay 'What Poems are Made of', Smith quotes this poem as she thinks about people who make a success of the 'difficult' 'husband-wives-children and pet animals situation' (*MA* 129, 128), which packed into such a phrase becomes itself an explosive. Such situations – even between females, perhaps *particularly* between females in Smith's work – are so dangerous in her eyes that just after quoting this 'warm' poem (minus its drawing) she moves, in this coyly written essay, to say 'But love is sometimes demanded'

Figure 5.4 Accompanying drawing for 'Human Affection'.

in which case children can be 'turned to stone'. The statement is followed by the strikingly sharp couplet entitled 'I'll have your heart' from *Tender Only to One* (whose drawing depicts a stern-looking woman holding an all-but full-grown daughter on her knee): 'I'll have your heart, if not by gift my knife/Shall carve it out. I'll have your heart, your life' (148). '[I]f mother-love enclosure be', as another poem in *Mother, What is Man?* wonders, 'It were enough, my dear, not quite to hate me' (217); but we also see poems in this collection in which mothers wish to be free of the demands of children, to 'tumble the baby in' the pool to 'sink or swim' on their own ('She said...', 182). 'Love Me!' cries one poem, but love in Smith's collection is the always-desired but rarely delivered thing that, ironically, along with greed and 'cenobitism', constitutes the root of much of the world's evil. 'Half Japan!' will not be injured by 'love' itself, as Donald Davie suggests (see pp. 65–66 above), but by *lack of it* in Smith's view – and by what such lack drives people to do in order to inscribe themselves *somewhere*, have some sense that they exist and not only 'spuriously'.

We have seen her propose, in 'The Failed Spirit' and 'Forgot!', that human isolation or alienation rejoices in war – or that at least it 'seems to be up to the moment the most successful endeavour' against the fear of it, offering as it does collective 'din' (201) and identity. Smith's analysis of love gone wrong at every level of family existence examines the results of both abjection and 'demand' – what Bluemel referred to as 'violent consumption', the need to 'eat' others (123 and *passim*), though in this collection both 'Mother has been had' ('Mother', 195) *and* father, too. Poems about females consumed by men and life are balanced by others like 'The Sliding Mountain', in which the metaphorical 'black rocks of the sliding mountain' hover darkly over a man named 'Domesticity' and his wife, 'an ivy tree'; she clings to him with evil eyes in the drawing while 'the little children laugh and scream,/For they do not know what these things mean' (219). His hands are being pulled in different directions by his kids, and he and his wife are stood in a line-drawn crossroads; he is, in other words, dragged apart by the family 'unit', is again in danger of exploding. The hunger to *have* love, rather than give it, and control *through* it Smith always relates back to the larger problem of disturbed egoity conducting the drive towards either domination or suicide or, more often, a complex mixture of the two. Such drives, as we know from the novels, underlie not only the 'disease of dictators' but the subscription to it by constituents longing to find an '-ism' to make their own as well as be owned by. The hunger for the same was indeed dangerous and violent in Smith's view, as she wrote in one of her letters to Naomi Mitchison,

> You are in the world, & so am I – & at the moment the world is a great deal too articulate! (You will agree!!).... If you knew the letters I still get. The ones from the women – all so hungry & worrying. Hunger for a nostrum, a Saviour, a Leader, anything but to face up to themselves & a suspension

of belief.... It is like a baby cutting its teeth –& fighting against it all the time: 'Oh what is to happen to me now, oh these teeth. The future is nothing but one large tooth, oh is there no Saviour to save me from my tooth?' Yes, our times are difficult but our weapon is not argument I think but silence & a sort of self-interest, observation and documentation (I was going to say 'not for publication' but I am hardly in a position to say that!). (*MA* 257–8)

Because, as we know, this was exactly what she was publishing – observation and documentation drawn from her own cultural as well as self-analysis. In this collection's second poem, 'A King in Funeral Procession', the love of an 'affectionate people' (we read, the 'Human Affection' of the first poem still in our ears) cries out 'Give us the body' of the King; they would 'eat' him as their own identity, 'lifting up the[ir] bab[ies]' to do the same, while he dies crying out 'De Profundis...Clamavi a toto corde meo Domine' (From the depths of my heart I have cried unto thee, oh Lord): 'Not one proud look they have left me' (164). Smith's double-edged use of this familiar lament from Psalm 129, where a voice cries out to God for the people, to give them eternal rest, depends upon her calling up Baudelaire's *Les Fleurs du Mal* as well. Baudelaire's version of the lament, 'De Profundis Clamavi', subtitled 'From the depths, a scream', features a cry coming from the 'heart's tomb' which is surrounded by a sombre universe where fear and curses make the day seem night (Baudelaire 63). Smith's King is also drained of his 'high minded[ness]', is 'ill' and eaten up by the people's hunger for him. Leaders/abstractions can be loved dearly, *as oneself*, while day-to-day relations with others are, as Smith writes, 'difficult' in this collection. Perhaps this is why Smith includes a parody of Robert Herrick's poem of obsessive love, 'Upon Julia's Clothes' in which, instead of a tercet commanding us to watch as 'Julia goes' and attend to 'the liquefaction of her clothes', we have yet another mother commanding 'My child, my child, watch how he goes, / The man in Party coloured clothes' (214). Its German title, 'Hast Du dich verirrt?' ('Are you mistaken?'), leads us to wonder whether the 'Party' is capitalised because it represents 'political party' and the mistaken attraction to the disease of dictators in Smith's mid-war landscape. As she suggested earlier in the letter quoted above, she worried that Mitchison's inner panic was translating her own egoist trauma into the death drive: 'I think at the present moment you are in a state of mind that hungers for the disaster it fears' (*MA* 257).

This collection *as* war collection wars with itself, as is clear from her unusual choice of addressing the poetry of her time directly in two diametrically-opposed poems to 'Poets' – one of which, 'The Poets are Silent', congratulates poets for 'be[ing] silent about the war' (208). Neil Corcoran reads this as evidence of Smith's 'spirited decidedness' and the poem's 'refusal to defend its point of view' (70), but he leaves out consideration of the first two lines of the poem in order to do so:

> There's no new spirit abroad,
> As I looked, I saw;
> And I say that it is to the poets' merit
> To be silent about the war.

As we know, Smith's poems go in fear of 'new spirits' – be they spiritisms or ideological 'abstractions'. The 'silence' she refers to, as she also refers to it in the letter to Mitchison above, is made up of a 'suspension of belief' in rhetorical attempts to find a 'nostrum or Saviour or Leader'. She was not alone, as we have seen, in doing so; camps of poets as diverse as the writers of the New Apocalypse and the Movement writers in their nascence would do the same. Given the stripped landscape of the early 1940s, when Hitler and even Stalin were also being slowly unmasked, Smith may in that second line be celebrating the ability to look and simply *see* – not find excess and atrocity covered by either political rhetoric *or* poetic rhetoric. This poem helps us read the irony of the particularly subtle 'Study to Deserve Death', which on the surface seems a celebration of brave 'warrior soul[s]' (185) but is also and more potently a Falstaffian send-up of poetic sermons about honourable death.[23] But where does that leave *her* in writing about war? Her speaker mourns, in a four-line *cri de coeur* entitled 'Poet!' (170), that 'Poet, thou art dead and damned, / Thou speakst upon no moral text'. The archaic diction in this piece offsets the uncertain seriousness of its call for moralising; yet the next lines – 'I bury one that babbled but; – / Thou art the next. Thou art the next' – leaves wide open the critique of all writing at her wartime moment, including her own. Does *she* 'babble' – should she be buried for her playful pieces in this collection, however 'moral' and engaged? What does the 'Thou' do; what crime by poetic standards will make her/him, or their 'art', be 'next' for burial? This gnomic little piece stands, with its partner piece above, alongside Geoffrey Hill's 'September Song' in my reading – not because her temptation is to 'write an elegy for herself', but because its self-consciousness throws all poetic response into question at the same time that it demands response from poets. *Smith's* response in this volume was to be 'silent' by being self-observant, by documenting what she saw around her in her most intimate relations with the 'too articulate world'. Yet we recall that in response to Professor Dryasdust's question in *Over the Frontier* about whether she was interested in politics and the 'fight against fascism', Pompey jump[s] to [her] feet and cr[ies] aloud '*C'est la vie entière que c'est mon métier*' with such great self-importance that she must instantly deflate it, claiming just after this cry that it 'out-herod[ed] the Herod of all their childish theories' (256–57). Smith's extraordinary contribution to mid-century poetics involves not only her suggestion that writing about politics meant writing about 'all of life' in culture but also her self-reflexive knowledge that to think one can do that, caught up in it as one is, is perhaps the greatest hubris of all. Her work would for the rest of her life catch within it the multiplicities as well as complicities of such a self-assigned task.

III

Smith's poetry of the 1950s and 1960s

Smith's two collections of the 1950s, despite the difficulties she had in getting them into print – as she had in publishing *any* of her poems until late in the decade – nonetheless demonstrate the start of a more voluble, narrative tendency that would characterise her work through to her final volumes. The short-story writing would flower in the publication of several pieces deeply related to the novels – 'Is There a Life Beyond the Gravy?' (1947), for example, a dreamier rendition of *The Holiday* formed in brief – and then cease altogether with two published in 1955. However, it is arguable that poems like 'Angel Boley' and 'The House of Over-Dew' – the latter an interpolated story near the end of *The Holiday*, where it suggested that segregationist religious fantasies result in 'European war[s] and personal defeat' (*CP* 554) – are really short stories that are lineated, allowing for greater rhetorical and sonic variation stanza to stanza. Smith seemed to be moving into a phase concentrated on playing out her characters, her 'voices in the night', in narrative poetry that, particularly with the start of her currency on the performance circuits of the 1960s, was reaching larger audiences. In a sense, what these poems do is draw together the complex workings of *all* of her generic tendencies, adding a particular speciality in replaying the vague outlines of fairy tales in ways that combine her salient interests in demonstrating her speakers' entrapment in earlier, half-forgotten stories of culture with her interests in examining how adult confusions and cruelty are cultivated in the young. As I suggested in Chapter 2, some of her popularity on the reading circuit was due to a reductive reading of what she was – and *was always* – attempting to present; and recent re-readings of her performances are equally misleading in their translation of her triumph as a performer into a gendered one in the era of cultural revolution. In my own understanding of that triumph – which it surely was – Smith's performance of her work instructed listeners in the reading act they ought to have been able to conduct for themselves all along, performative as the poems are and always have been in nature. As Frances Spalding notes in a quote, Smith was surprised that her performances were so revelatory: 'Sometimes quite intelligent people come up to me afterwards and say: It puts new meaning into it when you read it. And I say: You are simply telling me you cannot read' (*SS: AB* 266). Smith *had* always tried to clarify, in essays and other writings about her practice, the necessary dissonance that her poems must be heard to present in order for them to work. In a moment I will turn to close-reading a short selection of the more familiar pieces from her 1950s as well as 1960s collections, but first a consideration (and *re*-consideration of others' considerations) of what her reciting and singing of them might lend to such reading is in order.

Smith as performance poet and playwright

What Smith's performances always did was present discord, whether between text and tone or between one generic or rhetorical persuasion and another – 'the tension', as we heard it in 'Via Media Via Dolorosa', 'of what is to be said on either side'. Yet they have been read as developing a music hall approach to performance in order to 'maximize the power of her poetry's satiric comments on love and marriage' and 'mock tradition with poems that encourage escape and resistance' (Severin 123, 128). But Laura Severin's chapter on Smith's 'Sung Poems' at the end of her book is built on a series of mistaken facts and contextualisations for the work, which again signals the difficulty of effecting what she calls an 'historical and cultural reading' (3) with other kinds of ruling motives in mind. The main problem in the chapter arises from Severin's construction of a Victorian music hall tradition for Smith's poetry which then takes on various sub-theses about its subversions of gender and class stereotypes.[24] This seems generated by a remark Smith made, in a mid-career letter to a publisher, about the possibility that her work might be 'looked upon' as having an 'intimate revue' effect, having just seen an audience react to Hedli Anderson's singing of Elizabeth Lutyens' settings of some of her poems. But 'intimate revue' has no connection to music hall, and especially not to the Victorian music hall tradition. The term was used after 1929 and referred to a much later and distinctly less 'popular' form of entertainment, often practised in universities in Britain (and outside them in France), based on 'smart, topical revue in small, intimate theatres'. The *OED* will further explain, with a wonderful quote, that it was 'a quiet British archness which put the phrase "Intimate Revue" into the language'. However much we might like to think of her 'goals as a performer' including taking on a massively popular form in order to overturn the 'hierarchical structure, which perpetuated notions of "good art"' (Severin 119–20), Smith was simply not envisioning with this remark any fully 'low-brow', popular space for her poetry (which, like her novels, did require as she herself suggested a 'quite intelligent' listener). Moreover, Severin's suggestion that Smith did not make use of the possibilities she envisioned for 'mixed media composition' until 'late in life', and that, '[a]s in her illustrated poems, Smith was beginning to reject "pure poems," or formalist art, in favor of an art form driven by consideration of its audience and a desire to collapse boundaries between "high" and "low"' (119) makes little sense, since the poems had been written to tunes and were 'impure' from the beginning of her career in the 1920s. Indeed, almost all of the poems that Severin discusses in this chapter are from the 1942 collection and earlier, which makes even less sense; obviously they were written to their tunes long before Smith ever made the above statement in her letter or performed them. But in order to make her argument, Severin assumes that if an earlier poem does not have a title that explicitly states it is to a tune – such as 'To the Tune of the Coventry Carol', which she asserts is the *only* one in Smith's first collection to be written with a tune in mind – then it must not be. But as Smith's persona puts it in her 1959 radio play, 'A Turn Outside', 'nearly all the poems do have some tune' (*MA* 335), and indeed *have* had them, from the very start.

Re-thinking about the place of such tunes and tonalities in Smith's work might start with the hints offered in the radio play, given its transitional moment in her *oeuvre* and its interest in articulating the long relation of sound and music to the texts. It was broadcast in May 1959, about a year after Smith had begun reading her poems at the Gaberbocchus Commonroom in Kensington (organised by PEN), and just a month before her first reading in association with Michael Horovitz's *New Departures* magazine and his nascent series of 'Live New Departures' arts circuses and jazz events through which her new fame as a performer would largely be won. The play's premise is simple but effective. The 'interview' that constitutes its action is one of *and* by herself, it seems (though her persona from the start opts to be called 'dear', because it 'is less personal' (*MA* 335). It becomes, quite interestingly, a 'meta-interview' as well as meta-theatrical, a send-up of the genre on radio as well as a drama with one character – that is, yet another form of Smithian 'psychomachia'. For her interviewer turns out to be her own desire for the end, waiting to take her for 'a turn outside' – a phrase familiar to Smith's readers as one that suggests 'a nice change', a 'shifting', a 'holiday' that becomes permanent: death. In this Beckettian space, talk *equals* existence, as well as the desire to be identified, heard; and Smith's persona's desperation in the matter is very clear. Even her 'stammering' 'I I I I I' (347, 349) when asked why she is frightened seems key. The loss of identity becomes contingent upon losing articulacy, and the danger of getting as a response her interviewer's 'Now don't stammer. It always comes out so badly on air' (347), suggests the performative nature of existing in the world 'upon my word'. No doubt the choice of radio play is crucial here; 'no sound' equals 'no existence' in this purely aural medium. Yet in the end, it is also clear that talking has simply postponed the satisfaction of her equally strong, underlying drive towards extinction, which wins in the end with her sudden cry against what once again sounds like a Freudian construction of death for 'having taken so long over it, hanging about here, ... so utterly *inactive*' all along (357; Smith's emphasis). In the meantime, within this frame, Smith reveals quite a lot about not only current views on culture and language but about her own particular methods of writing.

Most importantly for my present purposes, her interviewer at the play's beginning asks several questions about the tunes for her work, quoting a poem from *Harold's Leap* (1950), 'Behind the Knight', as being one of his favourites:

> Behind the Knight sits hooded Care,
> And as he rides she speaks him fair,

> She lays her hand in his sable muff,
> Ride he never so fast he'll not cast her off. (*CP* 231)

After it is sung, the interviewer asks whether she made up the tune (which remains unidentified). Her response:

> SS: Well yes, or is it something ancestral, like that poor Knight on his old horse; yes, in a way I have made it up.
>
> INTERLOCUTOR: You try one.
>
> SS: Well, it is difficult you know, because of often having come some way off from, so to say, the original tune.... (335)

Smith's singing of her poems far less often relied on a particular traditional tune to be deconstructed than on, as her poems' shapes and diction often do, a 'something ancestral' that sounds familiar but cannot usually be remembered except with 'difficulty' – suggesting, therefore, the deep-rooted, nearly unconscious, formative familiarity of these ways of intoning and expressing ideas. She often 'makes it up' but only 'in a way'. Very economically, Smith suggests with this that 'originality' is only 'so to say' – for it is never so; every aspect of her work is aware of being formerly inscribed within indelible influences. Her suggestion here that her 'poor Knight' suffers the same is helpful; *something* mysterious and hooded (not easily identified) riding behind him, annexed to him, called 'Care', 'speaks him fair'. In other words, *words*, voices in the night, former inscriptions of 'care', literally speak him into being. The multivalent word 'care' connotes duty, beauty and even sexual desire – the erotic impulse driving him forward into life itself, if we read this 'complex' in Freudian fashion as Smith's set-up here seems to ask us to do. All have their hold over him, drive him forward into capitalised Knightly duty, have their hand in his 'sable muff'. The latter is an old image for pubic hair, and the drawing for the poem makes clear that this is where her hand has indeed been placed. The drawing also suggests that he is a puppet; he looks terribly stuck, like a ventriloquist's doll on the neck of the horse, his face entirely devoid of affect, 'Care's' hands in his vitals, seemingly manipulating him in every sense. The fact that, as Frances Spalding helpfully notes, this poem was connected to a ballad by Kipling –

> What's that that hirples at my side?
> The foe that you must fight, my lord.
> That rides as fast as I can ride?
> The shadow of your might, my lord. (*SS: AB* 90)

– makes these points clearer, even if we would not have ourselves located the source of her ballad quatrain's sound. Kipling's famously Ango-Saxon

Figure 5.5 Accompanying drawing for 'Behind the Knight'.

timbre and feel in his poems are intact here, and their familiarity causes audiences to recognise them as their own if not their exact 'origin', as products of the way their culture has also enculturated them to conduct internal battles, to obey 'hooded Care'.

And the fact that she goes on to suggest that the next example she offers might be sung to either 'Greenland's Icy Mountains' or to 'Jerusalem the Golden' clarifies her at times arbitrary but never ineffective connections and allusions. Much of the work was, of course, like Celia's badly bifurcated memory of 'From Greenland's Icy Mountains' at the start of *The Holiday*, arranged *between* bits of remembered texts and tunes, giving the singing or recitation its disturbing sliding quality given that, as we know from the novels, half-forgetting of influences suggests full digestion of them and acceptance of their collusion. Much of Smith's mature work read on the circuit was *not* sung, of course, or even chanted in plainsong. Many poems recited in the radio play must *not* be sung, as we are told by our speaker, and later anecdotes about Smith's readings suggest that connecting them to a recognisable tune might, in some cases, simplify an effect that was meant to be quite complex and discordant. Frances Spalding quotes at length Norman Bryson's exquisitely written and wonderfully helpful account of Smith's reading at King's College in Cambridge in the later 1960s, when apparently Smith had some conversation with him and students before beginning her reading to a small undergraduate audience.[25] I quote at length, because the following explains much of what I have tried to suggest throughout my readings of Smith's work in this book:

> She recited her poems in an extraordinary declamatory style, almost singing them, quite high pitched. It was not an easy style to understand. It wasn't a church voice, and it wasn't incantation like Yeats, and it wasn't the alarming voice that might come from behind a mask of Greek tragedy, like Sylvia Plath. There seemed elements of all these in the voice she used, but the dominant tone was of cheerfulness exaggerated, as if the rise and fall of a cheery, vernacular voice were pushed higher and lower and became a stylized sing-song that wasn't cheerfulness but had an alienated relation to cheerfulness....
> It became tremendous, quite amazing, when she recited not her own poems but border ballads.... She introduced into her performance of ['Twa Corbies'] extraordinary and inappropriate tones, of sheer disgust – through the clotted words, but it felt almost like disgust *at* the words – and of enormous disappointment.... It was rather alarming that our conversation about middle English, which had been somewhat polite... suddenly produced this drama, this explosion in which the implications of the words grew out of words, then became stronger and almost crushed the words.... The voices were polyphonic in the sense that they didn't combine – one couldn't see what the cheeriness had to do with the disappointment or the disgust.
> The performance was unnerving because it was so excessive.... The meaning of the words was set aside in the performance. And the *motives* for this were entirely unrevealed: this seemed almost the main point. It was as though what was being dramatized was a state of being so pent up, so much without outlet, that emotions couldn't have, any longer, appropriate objects. Without appropriate objects they went to live in an abstracted world of their own, where they further split up amongst themselves (the

polyphony). Nothing in the world could focus them or make them cohere, or earn them or deserve them. (*SS: AB* 267–68)

Bryson captures about as well as can be done what we already have seen in the novels, poems and stories: Smith's 'excessive' disgust with the cage of language, that Wittgensteinian world of words she was created by, felt exiled from and was forced to inhabit in order to exist before extinction. As she put it in the irreverently named poem, 'The Word' (her revision of Romantic, Wordsworthian, 'My Heart Leaps Up' convictions about the mirroring of divinity in the self and natural world),

> My heart leaps up with streams of joy,
> My lips tell of drouth;
> Why should my heart be full of joy
> And not my mouth?
>
> I fear the word, to speak or write it down,
> I fear all that is brought to birth and born;
> That fear has turned my joy into a frown. (*Scorpion and Other Poems, CP* 542)

'The implications of words [grow] out of words', just as Bryson put it, except that Smith would have meant even more by the phrase. Words in the above poem take over one's innocent 'joy'; they resolve the speaker's voice into mechanical iambic pentameter in the final tercet, symbolically bringing something 'fearful' out of their own past back to be 'born' in one's personal speech – something made to sound like a Yeatsian rough beast slouching up once again. No wonder Smith in the reading 'inappropriately' signed her 'frown' at language, twisting words into unnatural speech-sounds, or attempting to 'crush' them by allowing their own etymologies and implications to rise up against them. Both her singing of words within old, perhaps not nameable but recognisable rhythms *and* her 'stylization' of natural speech, her foregrounding of an inability to 'speak from the heart', explains her lack of '*motive* revealed'; it is, as Bryson understood through careful listening, the 'main point' – because her motives are arranged by the texts she helplessly ventriloquises. One might say that the appearance of her 'inappropriately' clad body – dressed as she always seemed to be, in innocent-looking pinafores and white stockings – produced in company with the discordant sound of her physical voice alerted at least some in her audience to the deeper discrepancies at the very heart of her project. Her sounded 'disgust *at* the words' in company with her discrepant 'cheerfulness' sounding in 'alienated relation' to them should have alerted audiences to her commentary on her culture's hold on her through *language itself*, though her listeners may have produced a simpler kind of reading when left alone with the poems on the page.

Smith's fairytale mode

Smith's last collections written in the 1950s and 1960s – *Harold's Leap* (1950), *Not Waving but Drowning* (1957), *Selected Poems* (1962), *The Frog Prince* (1966) and the posthumously published *Scorpion and Other Poems* (1972) – hold the poems we know best, among them most of the ones she famously wrote in mock-fairytale mode. Which is not to say that each collection is not also (if slightly less so) topical and political. *Harold's Leap* holds, for example, 'The Leader' (289), her chilling poem about Hitler, and the human moral cowardice that refuses to bring down 'leaders'; *Not Waving but Drowning* holds '"Come on, Come back": Incident in a future war' (333), which menacingly deploys images from the 'Memel Conference' as well as *Over the Frontier* launched into future mode, its focus on a female subject 'left just alive' in once-more-war-torn Austerlitz but with 'memory... dead forevermore'[26]; *Selected Poems/The Frog Prince* (grouped together in *CP*) holds 'Under Wrong Trees... Freeing the Colonial Peoples' (420), which satirises the necessary and cyclic infantilisation of colonial 'subjects' to the British throne; *Scorpion and Other Poems* holds 'How Do You See?' (516–21), a frank dialogue with the Vatican as well as theologians and scholars about the smoke-and-mirrors nature of doctrinal decision-making. These poems are rarely anthologised; only the last one named above appears, for example, in Lee's best-known *Stevie Smith: A Selection*. But having discussed how poems in Smith's earlier collections depend on such accompanying works to give them all their full polyphony and contextualised reference, I will leave most of the poems mentioned above to my readers to 're-read' for themselves while I, in the space that remains, address the growing number of fairytale works that appear in these volumes.

When our thoughts turn specifically to women's reinterpretations of fairytales, most of us find it difficult not to think simultaneously of Sandra Gilbert, Susan Gubar, and their now famous and illuminating re-reading of 'Snow White' as patriarchy's story of how 'woman has internalized the King's rules' (38). Critical studies since theirs have offered readings of contemporary women writers/poets 're-view[ing], revis[ing], and reinvent[ing fairytales] "in the service of women"', even 'find[ing] true images of [them]selves' (Rose 211) and 'telling their own authentic stories' (Montefiore 42). Accordingly, Jan Montefiore attempts to read Smith's 'The Frog Prince' and 'I rode with my darling...' as examples of how 'women poets invoke the fairy tale in order to counter its proverbial "experience" with their own axioms... [yet] avoid those "explanations" which kill the memorable simplicity and wisdom of true storytelling' (43). By thus implying that there has been some kind of 'axiomatic' feminist revision in Smith's fairytale poems buttressed by such 'wisdom' this kind of analysis links, whether it wishes to or not, her very different use of ambiguity and treatment of the genre with traditional manipulations of it. But Smith is writing *against*, quite precisely, the 'simplicity' and 'strangeness' of stories that gesture mysteriously towards their own wise, underlying 'counsel'. Her speakers locate themselves instead through their inflections of the discourses that arise in the narratives. In other words, they situate themselves among the violent clashes of cultural-textual trajectories that contribute to a fairytale's notorious ambiguity and lurking strains of cruelty. We find them 'lost' in that nexus, itself a mirror of subjects struggling into being in the 'muddle of Europe's dreaming' where, it might be said, socialising genres like this one are bound *en face* to the 'self'.

In 'The Frog Prince' Smith does, of course, as Montefiore points out, retell part of this apparently simple tale of love's transformation of life from a view 'inside the story' – and even from inside an actor not usually developed in the tale: the frog. But this leads to no specifically feminist commentary, particularly as the (of course male) frog represents no gendered prejudices offered for subversion. Nor does the fact that 'it is up to the reader or listener to decide what the moral is' provide subversion – and tellingly, Montefiore does offer here what the new 'axiom' we are to retrieve from the poem might be (44). What *is* remarkable and revealing in this poem is its clash of internalised languages, which conflict without finally jeopardising the frog's decision to act exactly as he is 'fated' to in the story. This clash causes us to imagine how, as my quotes from Felicity Nussbaum's work put it in my first chapter, incongruous discourses can fuse coercively in order to construct seemingly our *own* 'natural' or 'right' decisions which are actually culturally framed and mandated. They also construct gender and gendered expectations in Smith's tale (out of froggish ambiguity or 'amphibiousness'), which then influence arguments between discourses caught in the act of misdefining present situations and future scenarios. There is nothing mysterious about what Smith called the 'very English mixture' of them that entraps this frog in his destiny (*SS: AB* 260); each one is specific to Smith's own linguistic horizon – from the child-like rhythm, rhyme and diction of the fairytale genre to the repertoire of her own unmistakably English suburbanite complacency; from the heroic and gradually all but evangelistic rhetoric of politicised persuasion with its incitative repetition to what finally pales into echoes of idle if effusive social chatter in the repeated (and emptied) adjective '*heavenly*'. We hear their contradictory but ultimately collusive interplay as the frog squats at his crossroads, considering his own attitude towards his apparent options: continued froghood or 'disenchantment' – a state extolled by fairytale tradition but rendered suspect in the course of his internal dialogue:

> I am a frog
> I live under a spell
> I live at the bottom
> Of a green well

And here I must wait
Until a maiden places me
On her royal pillow
And kisses me
In her father's palace.

The story is familiar
Everybody knows it well
But do other enchanted people feel as nervous
As I do? The stories do not tell,

Ask if they will be happier
When the changes come
As already they are fairly happy
In a frog's doom?

I have been a frog now
For a hundred years
And in all this time
I have not shed many tears,

I am happy, I like the life,
Can swim for many a mile
(When I have hopped to the river)
And am for ever agile.

And the quietness,
Yes, I like to be quiet
I am habituated
To a quiet life,

But always when I think these thoughts
As I sit in my well
Another thought comes to me and says:
It is part of the spell

To be happy
To work up contentment
To make much of being a frog
To fear disenchantment

Says, It will be heavenly
To be set free,
Cries, Heavenly the girl who disenchants
And the royal times, heavenly,
And I think it will be.

> Come then, royal girl and royal times,
> Come quickly,
> I can be happy until you come
> But I cannot be heavenly,
> Only disenchanted people
> Can be heavenly. (407)

The poem immediately and comically (and, in Smith's poetry, typically) falls out of balladic fairytale rhythm by its second stanza, as our speaker leaves off the mysterious hocus-pocus and cuts to the chase in non-rhyming and prosaic summary of his lot. As her drawing of an unbalanced-looking frog suggests, our speaker steps momentarily out of the story to question how he feels about all this while reeling between *several* enchanting discourses – including the one about disenchantment. First there is 'habituat[ion]/To a quiet life', in the 'green well' of London's suburbs, perhaps, which we get the feeling does not *often* involve 'hopp[ing] to the river' or stepping out of frame. Intimately connected with such ordinary settings, however contradictorily, are the influential ones of fairytale's ubiquitous but misleading dreamlands, described as 'freedom in her father's palace'. Through such description, the poem forecasts for unwitting frogs (culture's 'toadies') another kind of circumscription within another kind of spellbinding – but this time human and thus patriarchally ruled – domestic text. He in the end affirms the latter enthusiastically through an internalised, rhetorical, coercive voice that first pummels his 'false consciousness' – his being 'happy', 'content[ed]' in frogdom – with the instigatory rhythms of revolutionary propaganda that then suspiciously modulate into an unlikely blend with feudal and salvational tones in order to celebrate 'royal girl and royal times' located in fairytale's 'ever after'. As in the trilogy, radical revolt and cries for freedom are easily co-opted here by other kinds of dreams and unrealistic visions that culture, always conservative, propagates to 'save' itself.

Smith's biographers as they analyse this poem take at face value Smith's own brief introduction to it at her readings in the 1960s, when she described it as 'a religious poem' because the too-contented frog 'nearly missed the chance at that great happiness, but, as you will see, he grew strong in time' (S 267; SS: AB 273). Ironically, they must momentarily forget a crucial bit of biography to do so – the fact that Smith, like Celia on the last page of *The Holiday*, feared the cultural consequences of Christian mystifications, particularly of heaven and hell. Here at the end of the poem, the refraction of the emphasised word *'heavenly'* alone should undo her biographers' reading; it resonates precariously in the final stanzas in each of its fairytale, moral/spiritual and superficially social modes ('such a *heavenly* party'), scattering and problematising the frog's most powerful internal voice, demonstrating the latter's construction by contradictory discourses infiltrating both fact and fantasy. The voice, as in so many of Smith's poems, *'says* it will be heavenly', repeatedly, before our speaker 'thinks so'; cultural scripts spoken by internal actors precede the 'belief' that Smith feared in its simple forms. All of these discourses are found here to collude in the propagation of inherited (English) social patterns: marriage, domestication and 'royal', filial obeisance to centralised standards and values; even radical break-out is always already inscribed within the *telos* of the dominant cultural myth. As a consequence, verbal irony gathers in Smith's potential prince's joyful use of the word 'disenchanted', whose most familiar denotative synonym is, of course, 'disillusioned' – which is indeed what the frog may become if his union resembles what his equally idealistic younger readers will experience in the tougher, 'real-life' institution of marriage. Yet the ironies in this poem obtain from such complex sets of slippages between signs and intended or imminent meanings that no simple reassignments of value are possible; there is no positive relocation of that heavenly state. Rather than espousing either the 'heavenliness' beyond or the frog's 'quiet life', Smith leaves us, too, reeling drunkenly between discourses and desires; but unlike the frog we are cognisant of being 'under the influence' of words, images, dreams and rhetoric. With inverse irony, we might say that perhaps the only surely valuable experience awaiting our frog prince is a necessary and painful disenchantment which, as he cannot yet realise, *will* mean 'freedom' but by another definition: in the form of being, as we are, aware of his own entrapment. It will be, in other words, the erotic 'coming' he and so many of Smith's characters long for as they lust after transcendence of themselves – but only in that it will provide a glimpse of himself caught between discourses: metaphorical 'death' achieved momentarily through exile from the symbolic order that fetched him there.

Such disenchantment often gives way to the desire for escape or even death, for the dream-outcome of reaching a 'beyond' through flight – though we know that Smith's suspicions about such desires weigh them down heavily in such poems. The characters who, unlike the frog prince, go knowingly and willingly into the disenchanting darkness of blankness are most often women – not because they enjoy special powers but rather because they *don't*. Their experience is of an even more oppressive entrapment within dominating discursivity than their male counterparts come to know. And yet their chosen fates never contrast in any simple way with, or manage to transcend, their alternatives; theirs never become 'new stories' assigned greater value in relative terms.

For example, in 'I rode with my darling...' from *Harold's Leap* (260), one such woman, heading off towards the fulfilment of her dreams with her potential male hero, parts ways with him in order to stay in the forest with a Blakean 'angel burning bright'. Somewhere between fairytale tradition and old English balladry, this poem collapses a number of storytelling and poetic modes into its Dantesque 'dark wood' of textual directions. Like Blake's 'tyger' of experience, this herald signals potential if ambiguous disaster for what is left of her innocence (though the value of the latter becomes destabilised by the poem's end):

> I rode with my darling in the dark wood at night
> And suddenly there was an angel burning bright
> Come with me or go far away he said
> But do not stay alone in the dark wood at night.
>
> My darling grew pale he was responsible
> He said we should go back it was reasonable
> But I wished to stay with the angel in the dark wood at night.
>
> My darling said goodbye and rode off angrily
> And suddenly I rode after him and came to a cornfield
> Where had my darling gone and where was the angel now?
> The wind bent the corn and drew it along the ground
> And the corn said, Do not go alone in the dark wood.
>
> Then the wind drew more strongly and the black clouds covered the moon
> And I rode into the dark wood at night.

Here in the first part of the poem, the speaker's departure from her conventional role and initial, somewhat innocent self – she did after all ride out, like Young Goodman Brown, into the night, *and* with her 'darling' – is accomplished through conventional disobedience; her darling is the one who obviously assumes himself 'responsible' for both their actions and for deciding what is 'reasonable'. His diction slips humorously out of fairytale mode into the recognisable tones of male dominance in everyday life; such slippage calls attention to the reinforcement of culture's power structures and values in even the most fantastic and anarchic of narrative genres. Smith might be seen to revise such familiar fictional events to the extent that she focusses them upon the female figure, who decides not once but twice in the poem to do the 'unreasonable', breaking the form and rhythm of the poem as well as its expected directions first in the seventh line and, more emphatically, in the fourth stanza above (if with one setback in line 9).

But the second half of the poem becomes more difficult to read because it bears no clear evaluation or judgement of her actions or their outcome. It even seems to elicit from our speaker a dismissal of the women as well as the men in her life, a dismissal that has presented a formidable stumbling block to feminist critics:

> There was a light burning in the trees but it was not the angel
> And in the pale light stood a tall tower without windows
> And a mean rain fell and the voice of the tower spoke,
> Do not stay alone in the dark wood at night.
>
> The walls of the pale tower were heavy, in a heavy mood
> The great stones stood as if resisting without belief.
> Oh how sad sighed the wind, how disconsolately,

> Do not ride alone in the dark wood at night.
> Loved I once my darling? I love him not now.
> Had I a mother beloved? She lies far away.
> A sister, a loving heart? My aunt a noble lady?
> All all is silent in the dark wood at night.

Smith's speaker finds herself in a situation that, on the surface, is like that of her less adventurous 'Little Boy Lost'. But it more deeply and importantly resembles that of Robert Browning's hero in 'Childe Roland to the Dark Tower Came', a work whose images often surface beneath the experience of characters in her poems and novels. She once explained her admiration for Browning's particular version of Roland's story – for the latter's bleak last stand at the desolate dark tower against all those who had come before him, all those lost 'adventurers [his] peers' (Buckler 288) – by writing, as we saw in Chapter 2, that 'that whole poem is so full of the feeling of courage without hope and resistance without belief' (*SS: AB* 61). The key phrase, 'resistance without belief', reproduced in the second line of the penultimate stanza above, helps us to re-read not only this poem's 'resolution' but Smith's general strategies as they take form in all of her work. They involve, first of all, bringing her speakers into disenchanting confrontation, like Roland's, with 'all all' that have gone before them or have had a dominant hand in constructing their 'stories' – including sympathetic but deeply complicit, instructing figures like mothers and sisters and aunts. However much recent critics have wished to celebrate the 'house of female habitation'[27] that Smith knew as a child, and whose characters – like her 'Lion Aunt' – come up repeatedly in her trilogy and poems, this poem confirms a reading of the novels in which Smith *critiques* them, along with all other female as well as male influences. Even the ideal of 'resisting without believing' is brought into jeopardy by the fact that the tower's voice, too, tells her not to ride in the dark wood at night – though the result of that ideal being jeopardised paradoxically also suggests possible confirmation of it, since belief even in such disbelief is thrown into question. In the same way, Smith's poems resist simple resistance in order to better attend to all the voices that come into play without believing in the rightness of their stories or any others that might be constructed. It is certainly a bleak but courageous strategy of living and writing, and the end of this poem conveys it along with the repeated presence of its counter-option in the Dylan Thomasesque line: 'Do not go / stay / ride alone in the dark wood at night.' If one does not venture at all, then one does not (as our speaker *does*) approach that strange periphery of disenchantment, where all those many voices of one's cultural text become distant, are perceived to 'lie', by *double entendre*, 'far away', as well as problematically 'fall silent'. This poem arguably ends in metaphorical death at the cessation of discourse – our speaker's patterns, as in 'The Donkey'

(535), 'broken all up'; whether or not it *should* end so is the 'argument' of the poem, which might mean 'internal fight' by redefinition of that poetic convention in Smith's hands. Should the speaker put herself beyond all those sympathetic influences, however defamiliarised they may seem when one confronts the thought of them in spaces outside the conventions that relations with them perpetuate? Though figurative death in Smith's hands is not quite like that state that Thomas's speaker urges his father to 'rage against' in 'Do Not Go Gentle into That Good Night', it *is* one almost as desperately and universally avoided. Certainly one can say that the poem's interactions with Dante, Blake, Browning, Thomas and other masculine voices resident within it introduce another gendered, post-'linguistic turn' perspective into their precincts, in order to hybridise the connotative definitions of the 'dark wood'. But the final interrogatives – each one difficult and by no means rhetorical – produce no new feminist axiom to follow; they only leave us with a speaker in dialogue with herself, at an estranging intersection of discourses and with no arrows home.

And that is where I must leave Stevie Smith. Though I do so hoping that my readings have amply demonstrated Smithian strategies that my readers may for themselves detect at work in her voluminous *Collected Poems*. She would use them to take on the biggest players in her context, such as the Church, enacting an approach that was not one but revealed the inconsistencies in others. As an *envoi*, rather than turning to one of her many and famous poems awaiting the coming of death – like 'Come Death (2)' (571) and 'Black March' (567) – I think a quick return to a late, lengthy and prophetic poem I began to discuss in Chapter 1, 'How do you see?', will connect what I have just been discussing in the fairytale poems to her interventions in culture in general. Commissioned by the *Guardian* in 1964, and published at Whitsun, it aroused such controversy between angry Christians and others who congratulated her that the following Saturday an entire letter page was given over to it (*SS: AB* 240). Though it also addresses current social issues, like the Vatican's 'shifty theology of birth control', it begins by asking the impossible question, 'How do you see the Holy Spirit of God?' (516). In other words, it questions *as* representations the 'fairy stories' that accompany every exercise of trying to comfort or shield oneself before the unknowable, as well as justify ruling the world through such abstractions:

> Yes, it is a beautiful idea, one of the most
> Beautiful ideas Christianity has ever had, ...
> He is so beautifully inhuman, he is like the fresh air.
> They represent him as a bird, I dislike that,
> A bird is parochial to our world, rooted as we are
> In pain and cruelty. Better the fresh air.
>
> But before we take a Christian idea and alter it

We should look at what the idea is, we should read in their books
Of holy instruction what the Christians say
Of the beautiful Holy Ghost? They say

That the beautiful Holy Ghost brooded on chaos
And chaos gave birth to form. As this we cannot know
It can only be beautiful if told as a fairy story
Told as a fact it is harmful, for it is not a fact.

But it is a beautiful fairy story. I feel so much
The pleasure of the bird on the dark and powerful waters,
And here I like to think of him as a bird, I like to feel
The masterful bird's great pleasure in his breast
Touching the water. Like! Like! What else do they say?

Oh I know we must put away the beautiful fairy stories
And learn to be good in a dull way without enchantment,
Yes, we must. What else do they say? They say

That the beautiful Holy Spirit burning intensely,
Alight as never was anything in this world alight,
Inspired the scriptures. But they are wrong.
Often the scriptures are wrong. For I see the Pope
Has forbidden the verse in Mark ever to be discussed again
And I see a doctor of Catholic divinity saying
That some verses in the New Testament are pious forgeries
Interpolated by eager clerks avid for good.

Ah good, what is good, is it good
To leave in scripture the spurious verses and not print
A footnote to say they are spurious, an erratum slip?
. . . .

Yes, nowadays certainly it is very necessary before we take
The ideas of Christianity, the words of our Lord,
To make them good, when often they are not very good,
To see what the ideas are and the words; to look at them.

Does the beautiful Holy Ghost endorse the doctrine of eternal hell?
Love cruelty, enjoin the sweet comforts of religion?
Oh yes, Christianity, yes, he must do this
For he is your God, and in your books

You say he informs, gives form, gives life, instructs. (516–17)

Comically drawn back and forth throughout the poem, in love with the 'beauty' of the 'fairy story' as the early stanzas above make clear, Smith's speaker – like Smith herself – is a 'backslider as a non-believer'. More subtly, this seeming quibbling about the 'representation' of the Holy Ghost as a bird reveals the bait of metaphor – of 'Like! Like!' – which punningly means both that the imaging forth of the bird gives her 'pleasure', and that she 'likes' it, but that she worries too about such enchantment's spuriousness, for it cannot be 'fact', as God is not 'parochial to our world'. Having worried over the fictionality of scripture, which she then is able to treat as *text* sadly missing its 'erratum slips', the real assault begins. It focusses on manipulations by Catholic figures like the Pope – believed infallible and directly inspired by the Holy Spirit – who have the power even to contradict the *basis* of their own power by disallowing certain biblical passages to be discussed freely while doctrinal reverence for the inspired scriptures remains intact. In the stanzas that follow she again questions, as she did in *The Holiday*, the Christian Church's 'expedient' focus on the crucifixion, which links it to the Romans whose use of the same as 'the best remedy for Jewish obstinacy we seem to have heard echoes of…in our own times' of war (*TH* 129–30). Smith's genuine attraction to and confusion by the idea of Christ – exemplified in poems like 'Christmas' (222) – plays its part here but is overwhelmed by the contradictions created by Church 'hierarchy' in the governance of its people which, as the poem ends, her speaker compares to the end of 'the colonial system'. Though the verse was struck from conversation Smith suggests that 'the blood' *is* there – here – on the 'child of Europe', as she puts it (twice) in this poem, reminding us of her speaker Celia's identification of herself with not only Christianity but with the fate of post-war Britain:

> It was a child of Europe who cried this cry,
> Oh Holy Ghost what do you mean as to Christ?
> I heard him cry. Ah me, the poor child,
> Tearing away his heart to be good
> Without enchantment. I heard him cry:
>
> Oh Christianity, Christianity,
> Why do you not answer our difficulties?
> If He was God He was not like us
> He could not lose.
> . . . .
>
> Oh what do you mean, what do you mean?
> You never answer our difficulties.
> . . . . . .
>
> Oh how sad it is to give up the Holy Ghost
> He is so beautiful but not when you look close,
> And the consolations of religion are so beautiful,
> But not when you look close.
> Is it beautiful, for instance, is it productive of good

> That the Roman Catholic hierarchy should be endlessly
>   discussing at this moment
> Their shifty theology of birth control, the Vatican
> Claiming the inspiration of the Holy Spirit? No, it is not good,
> Or productive of good. It is productive
> Of contempt and disgust. Yet
> On the whole Christianity I suppose is kinder than it was,
> Helped to it, I fear, by the power of the Civil Arm.
> . . . .
> Oh Christianity, Christianity,
> That has grown kinder now, as in the political world
> The colonial system grows kinder before it vanishes, are you
>   vanishing?
> Is it not time for you to vanish? (518, 520–521)

The 'child' pays dearly, must rip out its 'heart' – that is, the beautiful images that lie at the very centre of spiritual existence – for this disenchantment, from which it will in these stanzas 'go away bleeding'. The poem leaves us on this unresolved battlefield created, she makes clear, by *textual* equivocation on the part of worldly authority: a theme that resounds in all of her work when speaking about leaders, cultural mystifications and mind control. These themes situate her directly within her mid-century moment in time; there is even a reference to the arms race below, at the end of the poem. And yet, writing as she did in the wake of two world wars that she did not believe signalled the end of twentieth-century violence, her subtle psychosocial analysis of the long-term effects of culture's immersion in the contrivances of linked churches-and-states allowed her, in this late poem, a harsh prophecy that seems from my perspective rather unnervingly current as I finish this book.

> I think if we do not learn quickly, and learn to teach children,
> To be good without enchantment, without the help
> Of beautiful painted fairy stories pretending to be true,
> Then I think it will be too much for us, the dishonesty,
> And, armed as we are now, we shall kill everybody,
> It will be too much for us, we shall kill everybody.

Notes

1 Introduction: between the lines; re-reading Stevie Smith and literary modernism

1. Muriel Spark, 'Melancholy Humor' (*ISOSS* 73); originally published in the *Observer* (3 November 1957): 16. Philip Larkin, 'Frivolous and Vulnerable' (*ISOSS* 79); originally published as a review of Smith's *Selected Poems* in the *New Statesman* in 1962, and later reprinted in *Required Writing: Miscellaneous Pieces 1955–82* (London: Faber, 1983). Seamus Heaney, 'A Remarkable Voice' (*ISOSS* 213); reprinted from *Preoccupations: Selected Prose 1968–1978* (London: Faber, 1980).
2. Philip Larkin, from his review for the *New Statesman* (see note 1). Spalding notes that this review was 'the one that changed people's attitudes towards Stevie', dissuading them that hers was 'dangerously close to light verse' by suggesting that her work was serious and bore 'the authority of sadness' (257). Especially key for my point here is Spalding's lovely recovery of Smith's own response to the review: 'I got the impression that P. Larkin, though placing us much in his debt, was uneasy, hence shifting around a bit and coming out with the old charge of *fausse-naivete*!' (letter to John Guest, 3 October 1962; *SS: AB* 257; note 46, p. 317).
3. In 'Tradition and the Individual Talent', T.S. Eliot offers his famous image of tradition as a row of 'existing monuments' which 'form an ideal order among themselves' until the new work arrives to readjust it 'ever so slightly' – 'and this is conformity between the old and the new' (*Selected Essays of T.S. Eliot*, New York: Harcourt, 1950, p. 5).
4. Figures like H.D., Kathleen Raine, Denise Levertov and others have found genuinely inspirational connections in the work of classical figures beyond the fragmentary Sappho, but their work often rewrites such texts or merges their heroes and gods with powerful goddesses from the *Hermetica* and matriarchal lore.
5. Several important examples of such arguments: Arthur Rankin devotes his book-length study to describing Smith as a direct descendant of the Romantic spiritual visionaries, particularly Blake (*The Poetry of Stevie Smith: 'Little Girl Lost'*, Gerrards Cross, Buckinghamshire: Colin Smythe, 1985); Hermione Lee in her influential introduction to *SS: AS* writes that 'Arnold's *Culture and Anarchy* loom[s] behind her' and illuminates her political attitudes'; Sanford Sternlicht in *SS* asserts that Smith 'was...as much a Tory as any stuffy club man' (1); Frances Spalding in *SS: AB* writes that Smith was sympathetic to Orwellian politics (159), and to Eliot's poetics of impersonality (197–98); Jan Montefiore discusses Smith's 'easy relation to tradition' and subversive use of popular forms (43), and Laura Severin gives us Smith as a proto-poststructuralist feminist engaged in wholly 'resistant antics'.
6. I refer here obliquely to Severin's book. For a fuller critique of current methods used for reading Smith, see Huk (1999).
7. Implicitly important to the re-reading of Smith, and indeed to a good many branches of postmodernist theory, were Bakhtin's visions of 'the dialogic imagination' (the title of a key collection of his essays; see *Works Cited*). In his work, which, very broadly speaking, interprets identity and social formation as interactive and constructed through the medium of language, 'dialogue' occurs either between people

or internally and reflects the 'relativisation' of culture: its 'awareness of competing definitions for the same things. Undialogised language is authoritative or absolute' (427). Feminists have for almost twenty years been revising Bakhtinian models of social inter-animation by re-envisioning the nature of feminine input, which is disadvantaged along with other social 'others' in ways that Bakhtin's largely class-oriented construct does not take into account (see Thomson for one early analysis of these revisions).

8. Review by Bernard Bergonzi entitled 'Tones of Voice' which appeared in the *Guardian*, 16 December 1966, p. 7; Barbera and McBrien report that his review 'angered her' (265).
9. Mark Storey, 'Why Stevie Smith Matters'. *Critical Quarterly* 21: 2 (Summer 1979): 41–55; reprinted in Sternlicht, where the quote appears on p. 176.
10. See, for example, books like John L. Mahoney's (1998), a collection of essays in which his own refers to Smith as 'Stevie', or the chapter focussing on her and R.S. Thomas in Neil Corcoran's fine survey, in which Smith is consistently referred to as 'Stevie Smith' rather than simply by surname as is Thomas.
11. Chapter on 'Jean Rhys' by Coral Ann Howells, p. 376 in Bonnie Kime Scott (1990).
12. This extended quote from Light (1994) is an amalgamation from pp. 241–42, 244 and 246.
13. Light quotes from Rose's line about poetry being 'among other things, one of the places where what has not been lived can be explored' from *The Haunting of Sylvia Plath* (Virago, 1991) but without providing a page number. Were this to suggest an Adornoesque picture of 'The Lyric and Society', I might find it useful (see Works Cited).
14. The portmanteau image is from Spalding (*SS: AB* 175). The de-emphasis of Smith's work as a novelist has been perpetuated by nearly all of her critics, although Catherine A. Civello, Laura Severin and Gill Plain have recently begun to turn things around by including substantial readings of the novels in their books on her work, and several very fine theoretical readings have been done in article-form by writers like Richard Nemesvari and Phyllis Lassner. Sanford Sternlicht, for example, in his own book-length study, calls her prose 'plotless', and notes that Smith will be remembered for her poems, not her novels (17, vii).
15. I refer especially to the extended treatments it has received in the book-length studies by Civello and Severin (as well as Plain, in the chapter she devotes to primarily *Over the Frontier*).
16. For my own reading of this passage, see Chapter 3, p. 119.
17. My greatest difficulty with Plain's reading is that binaries are created that are scantily analysed. Pompey undergoes a 'loss of innocence' (75) according to Plain, and finds within herself 'the capacity for Fascism' (76). Not only is Fascism left undefined as a historical phenomenon, equated with religion and treated as a metaphysical evil responsible for the full range of Pompey's ills, but all of the other discursive phenomena that pollute Pompey's monologue are left unconsidered.
18. 'Family Affair'. *Books of the Month* 72: 3 (March 1957): 9; quoted in Severin (6).
19. See Symons, Chapter 6, 'The Heart of a Dream', pp. 48–62.
20. 'Metacommentary' is a term most notably used by Fredric Jameson to describe the 'postmodern' critical act, which 'now takes in its own mental processes as well as the object of those processes', recognising 'in this heightened and self-conscious' space one's own struggles and limitations as interpreter (4).
21. *SS: AB* 54. Osbert Burdett's quote comes from *The Beardsley Period: An Essay in Perspective* (London: John Lane, 1925), pp. 267–68.

22. See Civello's Chapters 6 and 7, which are devoted to a reading of the novels.
23. See Yeats (338–39).
24. Quote from Smith. See S 283 for Barbera and McBrien's biographical explanation of this poem, in which they recall her suggestion that 'The Donkey' is a celebration of age, the end of being in the 'shafts' of employment.
25. See Easthope, 'Donald Davie and the Failure of Englishness' in Acheson and Huk (17–33).
26. See 'Dear Karl', CP 125, in which Smith's speaker exhorts her friend, with the gift of a selection of Whitman's poetry, to 'Fare out on a strange road' for once, see beyond his own entrapped point of view.
27. SS: AB 260. Spalding tells us that when *Selected Poems* seemed to be selling poorly in the States, despite the efforts of their American publisher, Smith admitted that it was a very English mixture and possibly not right for an American audience.
28. Smith mistrusted what she called 'international art', asserting that writers must work from the materials at hand – which of course constitutes an implicit criticism of the transcendental perspective. It is also important to remember – and this will come to bear importantly on my readings of her first novel in Chapter 3 – that Smith came to consciousness in, and in some ways never grew beyond, a Great Britain that referred to itself synecdochically as 'England', and demonstrated all the attendant centrist thinking that we have since decried as 'colonial' in relation to the devolved 'Kingdom'.
29. Roy Fuller, *The London Magazine*, 5 January 1958: 64.
30. See, for example, Betjeman. I find Betjeman's reductive reading of Smith's work particularly interesting as he is often categorised with her as a poet engaged in satirising suburban life (see Peter Childs 107).
31. Peter Marks, 'Illusion and Reality: the Spectre of Socialist Realism in Thirties Literature' in Williams/Matthews, p. 29; the quote is drawn from the Writers' International Statement issued in 1934 (p. 38).
32. *The Poet's Garden* is the American title for Smith's *The Batsford Book of Children's Verse* (London: Batsford, 1970), reissued as *Favourite Verse* by the Chancellor Press in 1984. It is ambiguously identified no doubt because it seems to be an adult's rather than a child's selection as intended.
33. See Corcoran's second chapter for a fine introductory discussion of MacNeice's use of parable. There are several versions of the name I give here for the Auden generation; 'MacSpaunday' incorporates MacNeice, Stephen Spender, W.H. Auden, and C. Day Lewis.
34. This quote is used by Spalding to illustrate quite the opposite: that Smith valued fairy tales for their promotion of 'virtues she admired: faithfulness, wiliness and courage' (90).
35. Smith tells the story of being shouted after by children while out riding on horseback; apparently she looked to them like the well-known jockey of the time (the 1920s), Steve Donoghue. More about Smith's choice of this sobriquet as a pen-name will be said in Chapter 2; see Spalding, 3, for reference to the story.
36. I refer to a lecture on 23 March 2003 at the University of Notre Dame by Stephen Prickett. Its title was 'Purging Christianity of its Semitic Origins: Arnold, Kingsley, and The Bible'; it represented his most recent work on the connections that were then developing between English and German Protestant anti-Semitism across a range of textual discourses.
37. This poem is quoted at length at the very end of this book.

38. 'The Necessity of Not Believing' was actually published, but in an undergraduate journal, *Gemini*, by the Indian poet Dom Moraes who was then a student at Oxford (*S* 212).
39. *SS: AB* 61. Smith's quote comes from a broadcast she made on the programme 'World of Books', transmitted 23 December 1961: BBC WA.

2 'The times are the times of a black split heart': Stevie Smith's life and work in context

1. Smith in interview with John Horder, *Guardian* (7 June 1965).
2. For a differing view of the Thirties see Light (1991, p. 7ff), who argues that the male 'modernist prophets and minor *cognoscenti* lament[ed] both the proletarianisation and the domestication of national life' during peacetime, which they saw as a 'lower-class and effeminate' period to follow the heroic battles of the Great War.
3. See Severin 5–6 for a short discussion of Smith's possible 'ambivalen[ce] towards "old" feminism, and its class allegiances...'.
4. See, for example, *SS: AB*, 14; *S*, 141; *SS* 1. Barbera and McBrien demonstrate how such misperceptions occur by basing theirs on (1) an excerpt from *The Holiday*, reading the speaker's (Celia's) thoughts as though they were Smith's own, and (2) an excerpt from Smith's review of William Plomer's autobiography throughout which Smith is being highly ironic about 'middle-class virtues'.
5. Donald Davie would within five years of this broadcast produce his famous Movement-heralding book, *Purity of Diction in English Verse*, which would advocate a 'bridging' of Augustan and contemporary poetry by way of excision of those bad principles (i.e., unclear usage due to imagistic logic and abandonment of proper syntax) accumulated through 'Romantic poetry' (within which he includes everything from the symbolists through to the work of Pound and Eliot) (79). The Movement would be accused of 'Little Englandism' by unsympathetic critics and social historians (see Chapter 3, note 40).
6. Severin's article (1998) works on the thesis that '[f]rom Victorian discourse Smith inherited a concept of girlhood as a time somewhat "outside" the responsibilities of the adult woman' (24) and relatively undifferentiated from boyhood. Though this is perhaps true, she then uses this thesis to explain why, in her view, Smith at 50 years old and in the 1950s (a retrogressively domestic era) suddenly looked to recreate herself in the image of a child in order to tap into this pre-gendered sensibility, though this claim seems to be based solely on Spalding's report that Smith's new hair-cut with a fringe 'made more pronounced the childlike aspect of her nature' (*SS: AB* 208). Yet Smith did not, as Severin suggests (31), *suddenly* begin to draw on 1920s writers like Loos and Parker in the 1950s; she was drawing very heavily on both writers since the beginning of her career, and is even famously quoted as saying that her first novel was far too Parkeresque. Severin's readings of the later poems themselves are often misrepresentative as a result, perhaps, of her thesis. For example, poems like 'The Lady of the Well-Spring' do not offer the child's choice of retreat from adult spaces to the Lady's mythic bower as anything but a very questionable one – here, one that bloodies her feet as she runs towards it, and holds her 'captive' by this 'rich fat lady' whose body is 'shadowed with grass-green streaks' to mirror the French-drawing room from which the little girl escaped, which was also 'barred by the balcony shadows', like a prison.
7. That Smith may have demonstrated such prejudice at times does seem likely since she viewed most sexual passions – and particularly 'revolutionary' ones – with a wary

eye. Yet evidence like Spalding's – a retrieved line from her reading notebooks which refers to 'the sins of Sodom and Lesbos' (*SS: AB* 184) – seems especially unconvincing, as Smith rarely used the word 'sin' outside her critiques of Christianity, and her references to the Old Testament are more often irreverent than respectful. Some of Smith's drawings suggest the range, at any rate, of her sexual imagination; see, for example, the deeply sensual one that accompanies her short poem 'The Pleasures of Friendship' (*CP* 208), in which two attractive women chat as they walk in rhythm along a sunny lakeside, the further figure's arm draped so fully over her mate's shoulder that her open hand seems to be caressing the latter's breast.
8. Review of Mary Renault's novel *The Charioteer* in the *Spectator* (16 October 1953).
9. I think of a passage edited out of *The Holiday*'s typescript: 'I love my aunt I love her, as I do not love men, as I do not love parties, but I can get by with men and I can get by with parties' (*SS: AB* 182). Celia's sentiment may be a permutation of Smith's own 'fear' of loving men, as she put it (meaning perhaps her fear of the role it, like parties, forced her to play).
10. Spalding tells one story of a lesbian love Smith experienced after the war; no origin for the story or name for the lover is disclosed (*SS: AB* 183).
11. From the back cover of *CP*, 1985.
12. For two recent examples of correctives to these trends see Dowson and Joannou.
13. As Nemesvari writes, Douglas West in a review in the *Daily Mail* (17 September 1936) 'suggests [that *Novel on Yellow Paper* is] what would have happened if Miss Gertrude Stein had written *Gentlemen Prefer Blondes*' (Nemesvari 35).
14. See Chapter 6 of *A Room of One's Own* for Woolf's contemplation of how such a sentence might develop. See my own Chapter 3 for discussion of how differently from Woolf Smith conceived of language that might be freed from conventional constraints (pp. 128–29).
15. For a swift introduction to the kind of images and rhetoric concerning 'significant form' that I describe here as 'mystical', see the first chapter of Bell.
16. Letter dated 11 September 1936; discovered by Spalding in the Palmers Green Papers – those that were in the possession of Smith at the time of her death.
17. *S* 85; this echo of Garnett's assessment is from the novelist Pail Bailey.
18. Spalding reports on Smith's correspondence with Jameson, whose blurb for Smith's first novel's dust jacket proclaimed it a work of genius. Jameson apparently wrote to Cape's editor, Ruth Atkinson, that *Over the Frontier* had 'the poetry, the malice, the sadness of a mind peculiarly sensitive to something which is happening in the world, which perhaps only a poet can deeply feel' (147).
19. *S* 89; from a review by Marie Scott-James.
20. Martin was a journalist and editor of the *New Statesman* from 1930–60.
21. *S* 107. The exact quote is: 'All my rich friends are communists, they have the cosmic conscience, you know, they have it rather badly' (from 'Mosaic', *Eve's Journal* (April 1939): 107).
22. *S* 139. This comes from Smith's review of 'Books' in *Other Voices*, 28 January 1955, in which she is commenting on *Nineteen Eighty-Four* and once again deriding this kind of 'black heart' despair that leads, as with Eliot, to 'sick-man fancy of a pool of self-abasement for all the world to dip in, and his sick man's lust for extreme future cruelty' when, in Smith's view, nothing more was likely to happen in 1984 than a 'Bank Rate at four per cent and Mr. Priestley's successors still whining cheerfully about nothing worse than currency restrictions and passports.' I will return to the significance of this vision of despair linked to cruelty when discussing the novels in Chapter 4.

23. The one member of the Thirties literary insiders who supported Smith at almost every opportunity was Cecil Day Lewis, whose ideas Smith loathed (*MA* 270). Nonetheless, he published several of her works in *Orion* while he was editor, and recommended her for the Queen's Gold Medal while he was himself the country's Poet Laureate.
24. Inez Holden, 'Some Women Writers'. *The Nineteenth Century and After*, vol. 146 (1949): 130.
25. See, for example, *TLS* (4 October 1957): '... her verse offers somewhat informal commemorations of markedly feminine yieldings....'
26. Although my reading of both Smith and Beckett differs from his, I am indebted here to Christopher Ricks for his thoughts on their strikingly similar relationship to language (Ricks 202–04; Horovitz 158).
27. See Spalding (140) for a different view of this changed activity. She writes that '[d]espite... complaints about the task of reviewing it became a major outlet for her intellectual energies, perhaps using more than was wise: as she became increasingly eminent as a reviewer, her novel-writing slackened and eventually ceased'.
28. If one counts 'Over-Dew', incorporated into *The Holiday*, there are eleven short stories by Smith. (The other ten are all reprinted in *MA*.)
29. Dick 44. And it may also have been that Smith was forced to write only poetry, which can be 'carr[ied]... round while you're doing the housework', after her retirement, when her aunt's needs turned her into cook, housekeeper and nurse.
30. *SS: AB* 176. Polly Hill was one of those Smith helped when it came to publishing poems.
31. See Morrison. One woman poet was accepted as being part of the Movement – Elizabeth Jennings. Her early work demonstrates the process of its own 'chastisement' (see note 5) in order to comply with the emerging 1950s aesthetic.
32. *SS: AB* 213. This is 'one story that reached Kay Dick' but is not substantiated in any other way by Spalding.
33. *The Faber Book of Twentieth Century Verse*, John Heath-Stubbs and David Wright, eds (London: Faber, 1953).
34. See Horovitz (1969). *The Children of Albion* is an anthology of 'revivalist' poets – named, obviously, in honour of Blake.
35. See Shakinovsky.
36. Emily Dickinson's famous rubric for recognising good poetry was: 'If I feel physically as if the top of my head were taken off, I know *that* is poetry.'
37. From Plath's poem, 'Lady Lazarus'; 'Nazi lampshade' is a reference to a product made out of Jewish victims of the Nazi genocide.
38. See Sarfatti, 250.
39. I quote here from Mengham's essay in Mengham and Howlett, 34.
40. See David Midgely's essay, 'The ecstasy of battle: some German perspectives on warfare between modernism and reaction' in Mengham and Howlett, 114.
41. The fragment of a quote here recollects the first version of Auden's poem 'Spain', which notoriously called for 'the conscious acceptance of guilt in the necessary murder' of those whom '[h]istory cannot help nor pardon' in order for a better time of 'perfect communion' to come. Auden in partnership with his editor Edward Mendelson would later subtly change these lines to rid them of their communistic flavour (*Selected Poems* 54).
42. The first two quotes are from Smith's friend Anthony Thwaite's two literary histories (see *Works Cited*), and the last the only line about Smith to appear in Davie (1989, p. 233). For more generous histories see Corcoran and Peter Childs.
43. Stevie Smith, as quoted in the *Observer* (9 November 1969).

3 The trilogy's take-off in the Thirties: A close-cultural reading of *Novel on Yellow Paper*

1. See Chapter 2, p. 47 (*MA* 300), for this comment on reviews of her work.
2. I allude here to MacNeice's well-known poem, 'Sunlight on the Garden'. MacNeice quotes from Shakespeare's *The Tragedy of Antony and Cleopatra* the repeating line with which Antony begins his final addresses to Cleopatra: 'I am dying, Egypt [Cleopatra], dying' (Act IV, xv) – signalling the end of an era for Rome due to his self-indulgence, his 'decadence'.
3. Smith's first novel was written on the yellow office paper used for making carbon copies, as was explained in Chapter 2. 'Yellow book' calls up images of tabloid news-reporting as well as avant-garde experiments from the turn of the century.
4. Quoted in Becker and Caiger-Smith (unpaginated). Auden's statement was made in 1936.
5. See Mellor, pp. 133–42.
6. See Conrad (66): 'All Europe contributed to the making of Kurtz...'.
7. *Heart of Darkness* by Joseph Conrad was published serially in *Blackwood's Magazine* in 1899, but not reviewed until reprinted in its first hardcover volume with *Youth* and *The End of the Tether* (whose overall title was *Youth*) in 1902.
8. See Jameson (1979).
9. See Chapter 2, p. 46.
10. I refer here to the famous definition of 'the image' that Ezra Pound makes in his essay 'A Retrospect': it is that which 'presents an intellectual and emotional complex in an instant of time' in order to achieve 'that sudden sense of liberation', as one does when working through repressed knowledge in psychotherapy. Pound refers to Hart rather than Freud, which demonstrates the currency of such new thought even more clearly. Smith's less optimistic view of modernist practices as providers of this liberation becomes clear in my reading. See Faulkner, 60.
11. See for example David Bradshaw's essay, 'Hyam's Place: *The Years*, the Jews and the British Union of Fascists' in Joannou, pp. 179–91.
12. Kurtz's composition – his benevolent western cultural report on the rationale for 'Suppression of Savage Customs' with its implosive postscript, 'Exterminate all the brutes!' (66) – also reflects, as does the speech of Smith's speaker, his rhetorical world of justifications, which covers for atrocities such as were beginning to be glimpsed as well in Hitler's Germany and Stalin's Russia of the Thirties.
13. Edith Sitwell, 'Some Notes on My Own Poetry' in Sitwell (1949), pp. xiv–xv.
14. See 'Looking Back on the Spanish War' in Orwell 2000, p. 225.
15. See note 2.
16. See the end of Act 4, scene iii, line 291 (Baker *et al.*, p. 1174). The line is spoken by the servant boy, Lucius, as he awakes from slumbering over the instrument he was playing in order to comfort the increasingly agitated Brutus – whose own end, following his assassination of Caesar, is very near. Smith will draw heavily on references to *Julius Caesar* in the last novel of her trilogy.
17. Eliot identifies his speaker (via his epigraph to the poem) as one akin to Guido da Montefeltro, one of the false counsellors in the eighth circle of *The Inferno*, who believes he may confide in Dante given that he knows none can leave once they enter the circles of hell. See Dante, p. 461 (Canto XXVII).
18. Lassner does not deal with the specifically mythological half of the speaker's name, however; she only briefly explicates Smith's use of the historical Pompey.
19. See note 36 in Chapter 1.

20. As the *Norton Anthology* refers to them. See p. 2585 of Volume 1 of the seventh edition of *The Norton Anthology of English Literature*, Stephen Greenblatt, Associate General Ed. (New York and London: W.W. Norton & Co., 2000).
21. See Carroll, pp. 37–39.
22. Famously, and throughout *Heart of Darkness*, Conrad's narrator Marlow interrupts the flow of his tale by turning on his fictional audience and demanding 'Do you see?' in a many-sided, metafictional joke on the transparency of text. Her extended commentary on Marlow's statement that '[w]e live, as we dream – alone...' (43) will receive more treatment in Chapter 4.
23. See Smith on her Aunt, Madge Spear ('the Lion of Hull') in Chapter 2, pp. 45–46, and in *SS: AB* 8–9.
24. Woolf's *Mrs Dalloway* might be read, from one angle, as a gentle revision of Eliot's poem, which she of course admired as one of its publishers. But in her novel, images from 'The Waste Land', such as the central one in Part IV of the drowned sailor, reappear in mournfully comic fashion in shell-shocked Septimus's visions of himself as the lonely prophet, a 'drowned sailor' on the rocks (102–4): that is, the Ezekiel figure from Eliot's poem, it seems, come to tell the world that 'trees are alive' and 'dogs will become men' and such already-said things like Keats's 'beauty, that was the truth now' (105). His sense that 'the millions' need his vision to change their lives is directly countered by the vision of Clarissa, because she sees the unruly and often lovely particulars as well as people all around her; she is not, like Eliot, immersed in the classical text of his western culture which appears to hold all the (old) answers as well as implicit condemnations of the present. Of course the poem offers far more than this, but Woolf's critique of Eliot, like Smith's, is provoked by his writing of his own despair large over the whole of the world that he presumed, in typical modernist fashion, to know in all its unsavoury essence. The assumptions made in many modernist texts about which elements of culture were central, and which not, may be said to have coincided with their leanings towards fascist visions and prophecies about the future of 'kultur'. Eliot's lectures, which hold the highly xenophobic and anti-Semitic materials I refer to, were republished (Eliot, 1968).
25. My partial disagreement with Lassner's conclusions are evident here. Smith *did* seem, at least at times, to envision history as working in large cycles, as did Woolf; she is also, at times, capable of 'collaps[ing] distinct events into an epic battle with the barbarians within and at the gates' (Lassner 138). Her tendency to translate such forces into what she herself identified as quasi-Freudian ones both furthers and complicates such transhistorical visions when they arise in her work. This in no way eviscerates her deeply historical commentary, as I suggested above; it simply exists in inevitable contradiction.
26. See the last stanza of Wilfred Owen's poem, 'Apologia Pro Poemate Meo' (Owen, 39–40), where the poet tells his audience on the home front that they are not worth the soldier's 'mirth' – a hilarity gained from a kind of intelligence about the nature of the new high-tech slaughter that no patriotic on-looker could possibly fathom.
27. See Sherry; quoted here from the typescript Prologue of the forthcoming manuscript.
28. Ivan Hewett, 'Anxiety and Escapism' in the South Bank Centre's programme (1994) to accompany its year's worth of events examining the 1930s: 'The Thirties: Anxiety and Escapism'.
29. Apter, Introduction to the 'Criticism in Translation' section of *PMLA* 117: 1 (January 2002): 70. Apter quotes from Auerbach's 1937 letter to Benjamin in which he

laments similar developments in Turkey and underlines Benjamin's own fears about 'monoculturalism', as Apter refers to it, joining forces with ' "primal" identity politics'.
30. The dangers of this kind of reading are especially evident in the details of Severin's commentary on the novels. For example, she asserts that Pompey sees the face of Freddy in her flu-inspired hallucination of the fiend in the street; on the basis of this she brings in Rosalind Coward's ideas about feminine distraction from independence (see *Female Desire*). But the text gives us no indication at all that the fiend looks like Freddy, and the fiend is not, as her argument about his offering of pleasure demands, 'holding a carton of ice cream' but standing amid empty ones. Pompey's vision is consistent with her immediately previous, darkly building feelings about 'the world of ignoble animals' she lives in, and of the 'black night of foreboding' that her 'black heart' understands.
31. See Smith's poem 'Freddy' (*CP* 65), in which she uses this word in a send-up of the ironically frenchified snobbery of the suburban middle class.
32. The false memoirs of August Kubizek, a childhood friend of Hitler's, recount a story that may be in part, at least, true, given what Hitler told his architect Albert Speer in 1938 at the Nuremberg party rallies: that listening to Wagner's *Rienzi* as a young man had inspired in him the vision of succeeding in uniting the German Empire and making it great once more. Rienzi was the fourteenth-century popular leader of Rome who, due in great part to his reading of the classics, felt it was his destiny to restore Rome to its former glory as Italy's central city. He is considered a forerunner of twentieth-century Italian nationalism.
33. See note 28, Chapter 1. Alfred Austin, Poet Laureate from 1896 to 1913, offers an explanation of his own sweeping use of the designation in his *Songs of England* (1898):

> [B]y 'England' for which no other appellation equally comprehensive and convenient has yet been discovered, it is intended to indicate not only Great Britain and Ireland, but Canada, Australia, South Africa, India, and every spot on earth where men feel an instantaneous thrill of imperial kinship at the very sound of the Name [Victoria] (quoted in K. Millard, 28; I am indebted to Peter Childs who returned my attention to this passage on his pp. 15–16).

34. Severin reads these images slightly differently. She argues that 'Smith also disrupted the linearity of the romance narrative through the insertion of brief fantasies, always escapes from culture into a nature landscape. These fantasies tie Pompey to her matrilineage, since her aunt, a mother figure, is called Auntie Lion . . .' (32). Pompey's 'haystack' longings are read accordingly. Her reading ironically re-connects feminine power to nature in a very traditional way even though these novels do not engage that traditional imagery.
35. From Cathryn Vasseleu's surprisingly titled essay (which has nothing to do with Smith, but seems to allude to her poem, 'Not Waving but Drowning'), 'Not Drowning, Sailing: Women and the Artist's Craft in Nietzsche' in Patton, p. 77. I am indebted to Vasseleu for the quotes from Nietzsche himself that I use here.
36. I refer to Ezra Pound's use of the 'numen' or numinous in his writings; and indeed, the Pound poem I quote from, his well-known sequence 'Hugh Selwyn Mauberley' (Pound 61–77), swings on the re-occurrence of the numinous in the form of Aphrodite's eyes flashing out from contemporary artworks. Smith herself focusses on Venus and love/desire as the betrayed but still powerful force at work in the modern century, as we shall see later on in this chapter. Pound relegated

Nietzsche to the realm of thought versus action (see *Selected Prose*, Faber, 1973, p. 391) and, as Hugh Kenner puts it, Pound was unwilling 'to perfect his insight and let the world go as it would (that way lay Nietzsche)' (377). Smith, in contrast to Pound, seems to suggest that thought *is* action, taking part as she did in a new stage of modernist writing slowly losing hold of the idea of the essential 'real' so crucial to initial modernist aesthetics.

37. In her retelling of the story of *The Bacchae*, Pompey remembers Dionysus saying to Pentheus, when he was cross-dressed, 'you look just like...my old aunt I'll tell you about next time' (134) – which seems in direct imitation of her own dwellings on her Aunt Lion. The easily unveiled joke here is that Dionysus's aunt is Agave, Pentheus's mother, who is fated to tear her own son apart on the mountain.

38. I phrase this in deliberately objectionable terms to draw our attention to what I think may be images of Smith's inadvertent perpetuation of the use of residual binaries like 'western culture' and its opposition in 'the Turk' – an opposition reminiscent of those in *Othello* and other earlier English texts. There is always an argument that might suggest she uses this binary in order to overturn it; here, as I suggested at the outset of the chapter, I do think Smith's construction of 'fate' as the Turkish *kismet* suggests the inevitable downfall of Europe as Smith knew it, and her model of narration for that downfall – *psychomachia* – may also suggest that 'the Turk' is, in her view, deeply central, an internalised actor in her vision of western culture's vulnerability to its own ills.

39. This word arises on p. 209, when it is spelled 'womblandish' and describes the 'so warm, so close' atmosphere on a walk in the non-specific countryside; but then on the next page we are 'now in imagination' in the parkland in her own suburb, Scapelands, where the word takes the pseudo-German spelling I use in this passage and suggests the drive towards death that she resists in this scene. She uses the same description on p. 234 – 'too warm and too close' – to describe the suburban homes she must visit.

40. See Chapter 4, pp. 187–89. Donald Davie's *Purity of Diction in English Verse* represents a view of the desirability of purging English poetry of foreign as well as obfuscatory elements – a view not unrelated to those articulated in Eliot's *Christianity and Culture* in the same era (see note 24).

41. See P. Childs, 46. 'The representation of soldiering had shifted [by the beginning of the First World War] from images of mercenaries to ordinary "Tommies", made popular after Kipling's Tommy Atkins in the *Barrack-Room Ballads*. Many soldier's songs were published in *Tommy's Tunes* (1917) and *More Tommy's Tunes* (1918).'

42. Smith's work was also surrounded by other critical films and texts, such as Alfred Hitchcock's *The Thirty-Nine Steps* (1935), made from John Buchan's novel that portrays suburban respectability as hiding deep levels of villany, as well as detective fictions from the decade such as Agatha Christie's, which often set out to undermine romantic conceptions of the English family home.

43. On page 200 Pompey tells us, in a commentary on Racine's play that extends to the next page as well, that her longest poem took for its title his line, *La Fille de Minos et de Pasiphaë* – something that, significantly, is not true for Smith herself (as far as we know; no such poem has yet been located in her unpublished work).

44. The injunction to do so happens several times in this novel and even in *Over the Frontier* ('Dear Reader, work this out for yourself', p. 119).

45. A harlequin is a traditional theatrical figure whose many-coloured or parti-coloured clothing connotes relationship with all players on stage as well as the audience. Conrad refers to his Russian sailor as, specifically, a harlequin (69).

306   Notes

46. Christopher Ricks begins his book *Beckett's Dying Words* with two comparisons between Smith and the early Beckett (2, 8), suggesting that both longed for a loss of consciousness, only hinting at the far more profound cultural commentary that their figurative death-wishes delivered, respectively. See also Ricks' 1981 essay in the opening issue of *Grand Street* (vol. 1, no. 1, pp. 147–57: 'Stevie Smith') as well as his better known short chapter on Smith in *The Force of Poetry* (see Works Cited) in which he also draws similar comparisons between Smith and Beckett.
47. This image will also reappear in startling and disturbing new form at the end of the trilogy – see Chapter 4, pp. 206–07.

4   Framing the war: the second two novels of the trilogy

1. Not only does Celia Phoze (sonically similar to 'froze') feel continually cold (*TH* 7 and *passim*), but Smith's reference through her name back to Pompey's riff about Jonathan Swift's mistress-figure Celia at the beginning of *Novel* clarifies the significance of such freezing in narrational terms. In Chapter 3 (see pp. 85–86), we saw that Pompey presents this figure as the antithesis of decorous reserve; the fact that 'Celia shits', which so disgusts her lover, is offered as the flip side to comely constipation, and as an analogue for Pompey's 'running on'. Smith connects this novel's frozen Celia to Ben Jonson's translation of Catullus's song to Lesbia (Carmen V), which becomes Jonson's 'Song to Celia' – an ominous development, as we will see at the end of this chapter.
2. Rudyard Kipling, epigraph to one of his *Plain Tales from the Hills* (1890), 'Pig'. This one, fictionally attributed to 'The Old Shikarri', reads: 'Go, stalk the red deer o'er the heather,/Ride, follow the fox if you can!/But, for pleasure and profit together,/Allow me the hunting of Man –/The chase of the Human, the search for the Soul/To its ruin – the hunting of Man.' This story is about the revenge of one man upon another for having sold him a vicious horse that nearly slays him. Since both work in the government, revenge is achieved by inventing a spurious plan to feed the British army on pig meat, which then allows the buyer to commission endless researching and reporting from the horse-seller. All of which will come to no good end – he will be humiliated for not producing the right text, and will be 'shown up in print'. Perhaps Smith was interested in warfare that begins at the most concrete and famously dubious of exchanges – horse-selling – and escalates along the level of manipulation of the governmental machinery of information and textual production. Certainly she seems interested in ironically deploying Kiplingesque Raj stories to gloss the allegory of postcolonial payback that lurks at the heart of her use of this story.
3. See Jacques Lacan's explanation of the imaginary as elusive self-identification in *Écrits* (1–7, 42).
4. In Shakespeare's play, the lines as spoken by Brutus in the famous tent scene read: 'There is a tide in the affairs of men/Which, taken at the flood, leads on to fortune' (IV. ii. lines 270–71). All the leaders in the play are caught in a cycle of unmeasured public adoration followed by deadly condemnation, as Murellus's castigation of townspeople for forgetting their allegiance to Pompey in their celebration of Caesar makes clear at the outset: 'You blocks, you stones, you worse than senseless things!/O, you hard hearts, you cruel men of Rome,/Knew you not Pompey?' (I. i. lines 35–37). Throughout this chapter I will be concerned with Smith's commentary via this most political of Shakespeare's plays and other

sources on not only corruption in leadership but also the 'senselessness' of interwar public opinion and responses in the arts.
5. It is tempting to also regard Smith's picture of the economy of power in European affairs as a cynical re-write of Machiavellian diagrams of the cyclical nature of war. Machiavelli's thesis was that valour brings peace, peace brings idleness, idleness disorder, disorder ruin, ruin good order, good order valour, etc. See Hayley in *Works Cited* for further description of the sixteenth century as precursor to twentieth-century arms races and fascination with warfare.
6. Mitchison quoted in Plain (6); from *Among You Taking Notes... The Wartime Diary of Naomi Mitchison*. Dorothy Sheridan, ed. (Oxford: Oxford University Press, 1986), p. 61. In this quote, Mitchison is explaining the change of mood in the Carradale Labour Party.
7. Laval was of Pétain's Vichy Government – and was one of Germany's best tools within it.
8. See my discussion of this phenomenon in Chapter 1, p. 27. As Smith writes in her essay 'Some Impediments to Christian Commitment', she saw the flocking towards Papacy following the Great War – the 'stampede of the sensitive and the intellectual person away from the vulgarities of the secular world into the Catholic Church' (*MA* 157) – as constituting a kind of escapism she found dangerous, given the requisite faith one must then have in the Church's bloody judgements as executed in its 'shady past'.
9. Belloc and Chesterton were so entangled in their development of a literary relationship between art and the political possibilities of 'distributism' (a medieval, hierarchical, anti-capitalist, anti-Fabian socialist philosophy) that they were often jointly referred to as 'Chesterbelloc'. The overt anti-Semitism of the poems published in *New Witness* and the quintessentially modernist propensity of both Belloc and Chesterton to rehabilitate tyrants like Napoleon (Chesterton's *The Napoleon of Notting Hill* (1904) was dedicated to Belloc) make the mix of contradictory politics and utopian religious visions in the publication volatile and potentially dangerous. Wyndham Lewis, in a timely addition to his early and well-known fascistic leanings, felt drawn to Roman Catholicism as well; he called it the only 'real religion', presumably because of its hierarchical absolutisms, mystical symbology and ritual forms. As early as 1916, he wrote in a letter to Pound from his army station: 'I have adopted the Roman Catholic category in my siege battery' (Meyers 277–78), despite the fact that he was a non-believer.
10. See my preliminary discussion of these allusions in the previous chapter, p. 105.
11. See *OTF* 52 for one example of Pompey's attacks on the radio as new medium.
12. Ivan Petrovich Pavlov, the Russian physiologist and experimental psychologist, had become well established as an explorer in the realm of conditioned (gastric and neural) responses by the time Smith wrote the first novel of her trilogy; in 1935 the Russian government, pleased with his theories about the mechanistic and 'trainable' nature of human reflexes, built him his own laboratory, a year after which he died. And there are of course countless moments in Beckett's later plays, such as *Happy Days*, when even the most seemingly ordinary and 'natural' human response turns out to be prompted – by either the oppressive sound of bells or, more subtly, the sudden awareness of being watched.
13. Kay Dick adds to this conversation by recalling that Smith had at one point intended to call *The Holiday* 'Death and the Girl' (59).

14. I am indebted to Gill Plain for reminding me of this passage in Kristeva's essay 'About Chinese Women' (1986, p. 153). See Plain's discussion of war and social organisation (18–19), in the course of which she explains how 'war' functions in the economy of the symbolic order.
15. Continuing with the metaphor she summons, Smith's Pompey thinks here of 'the torture of the rack', 'whose succeeding torment of the nerves newly released from physical reality...continue[s] that torment unpressed and undesired, for the undoing of their victim'.
16. Laura Severin's reading asserts that '[t]he shift in the middle of *Frontier*...marks a move from the "feminine" genre of the romance plot to the "masculine" genre of the adventure story' in order to save her speaker from 'the romance plot's dysphoric ending, death' (37). The idea that the 'adventure story' template marks the novel generically is also put forward by Janet Watts in the Introduction to the Virago edition of *Over the Frontier*, which may have influenced readings such as Severin's.
17. Jan Montefiore very rightly suggested early on that this novel, in its deployment of 'that myth of frontiers and borderlines' that characterise the 'Audenesque parable', should be read against the work of its male contemporaries (23–24), though sadly she did not herself go on to do so.
18. For an alternative reading of Grosz's career as continuingly engaged, see Flavell.
19. It is difficult to understand, in Lassner's otherwise fine if brief reading of Pompey's engagement with Grosz's painting, why she perceives the work to offer Pompey a 'military icon' (Lassner 143). There is no indication in Lassner's article that she (unlike myself) has seen this obscure painting, if it exists, and Pompey's description offers no suggestion that this rider is anything but what I describe here, unless his effeminate pose suggests connection with the 'Generalissimo' at the end of the novel and therefore prefaces Smith's argument about the psychosexual politics of war (see below, p. 174).
20. In other passages of *OTF* Pompey connects Pater with Professor Dryasdust, suggesting that like him the work seems *jejeune* and ineffectual – except, as she suggests wickedly, with the help of Juvenal's *Satires*, 'To win the applause of schoolboys and furnish matter for a prize essay' (93–94). Such comments about schoolboys may well constitute commentary on the Auden group's games, too, with their mythologisations of schoolboy experience.
21. I have in mind the many representations in modernist texts of 'the elusive desired' as the figure of Venus or Aphrodite, the return of whom would signal cultural rejuvenation. Perhaps the most disturbing of them can be found in Ezra Pound's work – from 'Hugh Selwyn Mauberley' onward through the *Cantos* – given the 'flip side' vision of dictatorship and cultural fascism he would come to espouse during the war.
22. George Grosz, from the catalogue *Prints and Drawings of the Weimar Republic* (translated by Eileen Martin; Stuttgart, 1985), p. 61; quoted in Harrison and Wood, p. 393.
23. See, for example, Smith's review, 'Poets Among the Beasts'. *Daily Telegraph and Morning Post* (3 April 1958).
24. In the first paragraph of Robert Graves' classic autobiography, *Good-bye to All That* (London: Jonathan Cape, 1929), which 'is one of the finest and most vivid records of the trench warfare of the 1914–1918 war' (R.P. Graves 102), Graves writes that his objectives in writing it are simple and threefold: 'an opportunity for a formal good-bye to you and to you and to me and to all that; forgetfulness,

because once this has been settled in my mind and written down it need never be thought about again; money' (101). Smith might have been directly parodying this book's famous first paragraph, given its perfect description of Pompey's attitude in Smith's own first two books of her trilogy. (Smith's novels were first published by the same publisher, Jonathan Cape, and only seven and nine years later, respectively.)

25. Although other forms of surreal response, such as those of *The New Apocalypse* poets who would anthologise themselves by 1939 (see Hendry and Treece 1939 and 1941), were equally interested in what J.F. Hendry describes as a 'Social Pathology that would be the extension of psycho-analysis to society' (158), their tendency to mystify potential remedies, be they political or spiritual, and promote the re-mythologisation of culture would have cast them in Smith's view into the same realm of evasion, 'dream' and vulnerability that she assigned to the Auden group *and* her speaker Pompey.

26. On page 241 of the novel, Pompey suggests that it is a 'blurred film sequence' that she is in throughout this 'Life of Pompey'.

27. See Jane Dowson's chapter, 'Women Poets and the Political Voice' in Joannou (46–62), in which she suggests that the novels 'deal with war but [Smith] tends to focus on cosmic evils as a microcosm of an individual's social identity' (55; see also Dowson's introduction to Smith's poems in her anthology *Women's Poetry of the 1930s*). The fact that Smith was deeply uncertain about what has been traditionally described as 'cosmic evil', and that she constantly rewrites the 'Satanic' as a function of human vice is made evident not only in her poetry and prose but in her essays as well; see, for example, 'Some Impediments to Christian Commitment' as well as her poem, 'Satan Speaks' (*MA* 153, 244).

28. See Jean Baudrillard's now classic description of the effects of an accelerated pace in consumption of images in his essay 'Fatal Strategies', pp. 185–206.

29. Raymond Williams later explicates the trajectory of one strand of post-Brechtian work in ways that gloss Smith's concerns here. 'This is the conversion of shock, loss and disturbance to conscious insult and a deliberately perverse exposure. Of course much of this belongs directly to the old order, which can both use degradation as a means of adaptation and control – if we are as filthy as this ("and we are") there is no point in anything else – and, more publicly, in the mode of spectacle, use degradation as diversion, the pastime of calloused nerves. But there is also something not too easily separable from this in some radical work, and this at its best – for the worst is merely ephemeral – is the old twist: "a raw chaotic resentment, a hurt so deep that it requires new hurting, a sense of outrage which demands that people be outraged". There have indeed been some dangerous moments of this kind, as in the radical or pseudo-radical "theatre of cruelty" ' (100). He writes from a vantage point a bit later than Smith's, but his thoughts mirror hers rather well.

30. Pompey continually notes that the dealer is 'short-of-breath' (12), though when she stands 'laughing and laughing' with him in front of fleshy drawings like 'On the Beach', she further qualifies that observation by saying he 'is perhaps only rather short of breath' – suggesting, perhaps, his lascivious approach to the Grosz drawings that he finds most clever and enjoyable.

31. Kurtz's report is a text that becomes, finally, the 'text within the text' for Conrad's novel – meaning that, as in Smith's work, it functions like a poetic pivot. In it, his expected 'White Man's Burden' rhetoric about his anticipated mission in the Congo – much like that one would find about 'ethical imperialism' anywhere else

in the nineteenth century – is blown apart by his hand-scrawled epilogue that we assume was added after rhetorical dream hit upon experience: 'Exterminate all the brutes!' (66).
32. *The Relief of Chitral* (1895), one of the grander military epics of the nineteenth century, is yet another story of a colonial 'hunt' and victory (see my opening discussion of *The Holiday*). Set in South Asia, this one is co-written by G.J. Younghusband and Sir Francis Edward Younghusband, the far-ranging explorer of Manchuria, China and India and commander of military expeditions like the one that forced a treaty upon the Dalai Lama, opening up Tibet to western trade.
33. The translation for this line, now considered a proverbial expression, is 'an immense, misshapen, marvellous monster whose eye is out', or 'whose only eye is out'; in one French translation I found the alternative is 'privé de la lumière'.
34. See Orwell's 'Antisemitism in Britain' for a dissertation on the mid-century tendency to protest as Pompey does here but 'privately' express 'very different sentiments' (2000, 282).
35. Shakespeare I. ii. lines 282–83: 'But for mine own part, it was Greek to me.' Pompey's lack of comprehension is likened through Smith's allusion to Casca's supposed 'not marking' of what all the events surrounding Caesar's rise to power really mean. However, though Brutus remarks that Casca has become a 'blunt fellow', Cassius cautions him that he is as quick as ever he was, and that 'This rudeness is a sauce to his good wit,/Which gives men stomach to digest his words/With better appetite' (lines 300–03). So too it would seem to be with Pompey.
36. Dr Gluck is the powerful Jewish villain – also a diplomatic representative of the German Empire – in Chesterton's novel *The Flying Inn* (1914) as well as the song 'The Logical Vegetarian' published in *New Witness*. For an argument that Chesterton's treatment of Jews changed in his work after 1933, see Stephen Medcalf's introduction to the selected poems (Chesterton 7).
37. Auden's much discussed epigraph to *The Orators: An English Study* reads: 'Private faces in public places/Are wiser and nicer/Than public faces in private places'.
38. Pages 202–03. Although Pompey protests that she and Tom 'shan't forget' Aaronsen's goodness to them, and that they will 'countersign [his] papers and [he] can leave when [he] like[s]', his 'tired expression of good-humoured doubt' meets 'these rather official pompous words of [hers]' which, as she puts it, 'are something that I daresay he has heard before'.
39. I refer to the first version of Auden's poem 'Spain' (see Chapter 2, note 41).
40. On p. 251 Pompey tells us that her 'darling Beau Minon' has again recovered '*her* former good spirits' (my emphasis). And on p. 222 of the novel, she marvels that the strange recognition of death that came over her parrot Joey (a childhood memory she mysteriously shares with Tom) no longer moves her now, 'or touch[es] my withers, however wrung and wrung again are the Beau-Minon withers, to be set at late night upon such unfathomably motived departure', over the frontier. This mixed image of being flung into death/darkness with anxiety displayed in wrung hands and withers suggests identification of rider and horse, and perhaps through the blending we are to also understand that the animal flung out of stable, neither governed nor 'darling' anymore, is a figure for the uncontrolled release of the aggressive death instinct that, as it is exposed in *Hamlet*, absorbs all supposedly 'free souls' in its 'Knavish' business.
41. 'Generalissimo' is the term Winston Churchill uses to refer to the supreme commander of the French forces in his speech in the House of Commons on 4 June 1940 (Dettmar and Wicke 2702).

42. Sigmund Freud, *Beyond the Pleasure Principle*; see note 47 for more detail on the death drive, which Smith would invoke by name to underwrite even more deeply the third novel of the trilogy.
43. Long yellow teeth are also characteristic of the British in general in the trilogy; this might have something to do with the 'decayed' image that Smith creates of her own countrymen in her connection of them to the etiolated state of the twentieth-century United Kingdom with that of Pompey's Rome (see, for example, *NOYP* 20).
44. Smith quotes this poem in her story 'Syler's Green: a return journey', which was broadcast on the BBC's Third Programme on 5 August 1947 (Morris 83; *MA* 91).
45. See Chapter 1, p. 150.
46. And indeed, Freud's view is tangentially in keeping here, since he continually asserted that it is 'instinctual repression upon which is based all that is most precious in human civilization' (315).
47. Freud began to develop his theory concerning the Eros/Thanatos dynamic in the 1919 paper 'The Uncanny', in which he probed the desire to repeat and decided that its instinctive power could override that of the pleasure principle. In *Beyond the Pleasure Principle* (1920), which given her obvious interest in Freud's new theory Smith would seem to have had to have read, he ultimately links such compulsions to the *'urge inherent in organic life to restore an earlier state of things'* (308). It may be that, given his definition of sadism as 'a death instinct which, under the influence of the narcissistic libido, has been forced away from the ego and ... only emerged in relation to the object', in *The Holiday* the disintegration of Pompey's increasingly sadistic, warring ego has resulted in the return of the death-drive proper for one half of its protagonist, Celia. Smith's coupling of the death drive in her novel with the sexual one is key; as Freud writes in his conclusion, drawing perhaps inadvertently on centuries of poetry that have equated orgasm with metaphorical death, 'We have all experienced how the greatest pleasure attainable by us, that of the sexual act, is associated with a momentary extinction of a highly intensified excitation. The binding of an instinctual impulse would be a preliminary function designed to prepare the excitation for its final elimination in the pleasure of discharge' (336–37). The 'degenerate' nature of our speakers' love affairs in the trilogy is often inflected by sadistic and/or masochistic elements that help explicate larger cultural imbalances that Smith viewed as both generative and reflective of private ones.
48. For a very different reading of desire in the novel, see Severin 42–47. The continuous references to death are bypassed in her reading in order to argue that the work's main concern is the overcoming of relations based on 'sameness and difference' and the establishment of a 'rhythm of friendship' instead of romance in human relations – something she believes Celia fruitfully manages with Caz. Her conclusions are based on reading the book's dark and indeed nearly hopeless 'rhythms' and ending as happy ones.
49. *Molloy*, *Malone Dies*, and *The Unnameable* were first published in French in 1953 (Paris: Editions de Minuit) and translated by Beckett for publication by Grove Press in 1958. The resonances between Beckett's and Smith's production of immediately unpublishable work during the war is intriguing (*Watt*, which was written between 1942 and 1945, languished until 1953; *Malone Dies*, finished in 1948, could not be published until 1951, producing in Beckett the same kind of despair that in Smith led, in part, to her suicide attempt in 1953). The similarities between their experiments with formal choices no doubt connect their publishing

histories; both explore extreme forms of first-person monologue in which the speaker is imprisoned by structures of logic or traces of past writing as it underwrites speech.
50. Many have speculated about the possibility that Edward de Vere, 17th Earl of Oxford (1550–1604), actually wrote Shakespeare's plays.
51. In *The Tragedy of King Lear*, as readers will recall, Edmund as the illegitimate son of Gloucester drives his half-brother Edward out of his father's favour through subterfuge. Following this betrayal, Edward adopts the desperate disguise of abject poverty, clothing himself in rags and retreating to the cave where he dwells under the pseudonym, 'mad Tom'.
52. Smith's analysis of herself as template for her diagnosis of European culture is made evident here, because these lines come *verbatim* from her essay 'Some Impediments to Christian Commitment', which details her own angst in being such a 'child of Europe' (see *MA* 156).
53. Smith suggests in this paragraph that though American ideology previously forced it into singing a 'fine free song' for India, self-interest could breed a hypocritical turn-about post-war. That the USSR is also presented as a probable predator suggests, again, Smith's lack of sympathy with her leftist friends. But most interesting to me here is her indictment of 'the democracies' and particularly the UK itself. We recall here, with the help of Smith's allusions to pre-war Indian declarations of independence (1930) and her characters' damning assertions that the Indian 'Congress don't look so good now', that Britain had stifled the Indian press and political activities for years, imprisoning Congress members throughout the Thirties and outlawing Congress altogether in 1942 when India refused to contribute to the war effort without clear indication that independence would immediately follow.
54. For my fuller quote from this crucial poem, see p. 65.
55. Though Adorno's call has been over-simplified, a scholarly sin I participate in here; what he really called for was a new kind of lyric response. See my extended discussion of the resonance between Adorno's ideas and mid-century changes in poetic form in 'Poetry of the Committed Individual: Jon Silkin, Tony Harrison, Geoffrey Hill and the Poets of Postwar Leeds', Acheson and Huk, pp. 175–220.
56. The quote is from Donald Davie's 'Ars Poetica' (Davie 1983; 58); the stanza before this line suggests famously that the Movement's return to traditional forms in poems – safe and quieter spaces, like that of Celia's railway carriage – 'Guarantees that the space has / Boundaries, and beyond them / The turbulence it was cleared from.' Though this poem was published in the 1970s, it was still very much in keeping with his thoughts on the need for 'chastity' in English diction as articulated in his essays that began to appear as early as the late 1940s and in his 1952 book which he himself alluded to as the Movement's manifesto, *Purity of Diction in English Verse* (see Morrison, 38; also pp. 35–37 for his argument that the Movement was well under way in Oxbridge by the late 1940s).
57. Thompson *et al.*, 153.
58. I allude to the now-infamous book by that name on the 'postcolonial' situation of the Commonwealth, with its playful reference to Star Wars and popular film: *The Empire Writes Back* (see Ashcroft in *Works Cited*).
59. That invincible image may also be remembered from its use by Aulus in Macaulay's 'The Battle of Lake Regillus' to symbolise the absurdity of the Thirty Cities ('jays and carrion-kites') in challenging the 'eagle's nest' (Rome) (Macaulay 442).

60. Americans find it confusing, but the term 'public schools' has traditionally been associated with the most elite establishments and the most difficult to enter, such as Eton and so on.
61. There are many passages in which the novel offers overt connections between our speaker and England. For example, on p. 92 Celia says upon reaching her holiday and stopping for a moment's reflection: 'I am a middle-class girl, conditioned by middle-class thoughts, when I think of England, my dear country, I think with pride, aggression and complacency. I tie up my own pride and advantage with England's. I have no integrity, no honesty, no generous idea of a better way of life than that way which gives cream to England' (once more playing on the image of England as lion or cat). But Celia's self-hating reflexivity causes her to add: 'But where can one get this idea of a new world, and how can one believe in it? The people are like me, they are awful; they are not like me, they are awful.'
62. The quote is from Gibbon's *History of the Decline and Fall of the Roman Empire*; Smith was known to use it in prefaces to recorded readings of her poetry.
63. Sitwell's suite of poems, *Façade* (nine of which were published in 1922, the year of Eliot's 'The Waste Land'; others were added, and a number were set to music by William Walton). 'Hornpipe' is set to the music of the hornpipe, and depicts an aquatic encounter between Lady Venus and Queen Victoria (with laureate Tennyson in tow). It is in part a send up of the Victorian queen, who is pictured as not only repressed and defensive but racist as well, since she dismisses Venus as a 'hottentot, without remorse' given that she has received gifts from the African emperor and others who worship her. See Sitwell (1987, 20).
64. Smith refers several times to the book *The Fairchild Family* in the novel; various characters are seen reading it and Celia connects Heber here with its purposes as a 'Child's manual: being a collection of stories calculated to shew the importance and effects of a religious education' (description in the British Library catalogue for the version entitled *The History of the Fairchild Family* (London, 1818–47). It was published in several versions, one of them by A. & C. Black in London in 1913.

5 Between waving and drowning: Stevie Smith's poems, stories and radio play

1. Barbera and McBrien 'cannot help but feel that against a background of war and cruelty Stevie is examining at close range in her third book of poems terrifying questions about evil and the human heart' (142). Smith suggests this herself when, for example, she tells us in her essay 'What Poems Are Made Of' that this piece is spoken by a 'he' who does not realise the benefits of solitude and instead 'tried to do some war work' (*MA* 128). The need to re-examine Smith as a 'war poet' is even more pronounced than it is for Emily Dickinson; see Wolosky's *Emily Dickinson: A Voice of War* (1984), which begins with the consequential acknowledgement that a number of Dickinson's poems were written with an eye to or actually during the American Civil War.
2. In Smith's later poem 'Childe Rolandine', 'This cropping One is our immortality' (*CP* 331), and in others it seems made in 'God's image' as Smith translates what she sees as problematic Christian dogma focussed on the sacrifice and consumption of Christ into her image of 'God The Eater' (*CP* 339). The other potential reference here, given the word 'adamantine', is to Milton's *Paradise Lost*, Book I, where Satan and his fate are described in marshal terms: 'Him the Almighty

Power / Hurld headlong flaming from th' Ethereal skie / With hideous ruine and combustion down / To bottomless perdition, there to dwell / In Adamantine Chains and penal Fire, / Who durst defie th' Omnipotent to Arms' (lines 44–52). Though if these lines from *Paradise Lost* are really meant to be recalled to our memory, added irony may be gained from noting Milton's assumption that God too wields might by virtue of his own store of 'Arms'.

3. See Geoffrey Hill's first book, *For the Unfallen* (1952), a shrewd and devastating distortion of the usual tribute to 'the fallen'. Its grave and graceful, metrically intricate address is *not* to the ennobled dead but rather to us who simply go on in the ignoble but continuing present. Hill's self-castigating black comedy and self-reflexive use of 'grace' in his prosody both connects him to and distinguishes him from Smith.
4. '*For the Unfallen*: A Sounding' in Robinson, 20.
5. Though as she says to Jonathan Williams in an interview, she does find it easier to 'get out of the way' in the poems. Reversing the going wisdom about genres, she says: 'In a poem you can turn the emotions and feelings onto someone else, onto different characters. You can invent stories. You'd think you could do that in a novel. Other people obviously can, and have. But I can't' (*ISOSS* 46). It is difficult to know whether Williams' inability to appreciate the novels did not cause her to downplay them in the interview. I interpret her statement to mean that while the poems are often snapshot speeches or momentary intersections of discourses, the novels' extended, 'blurry film'-like historical horizon and texture as well as deep study of their 'subjects' led her into the kind of sustained investigation of self that prevents 'invention', demands complex exposition or analysis in order to get it right. Perhaps this explains her sense that when she was happy she lived and despised writing, her avoidance of it constituting 'a fear of life' (40).
6. The play enjoyed full houses at the Vaudeville Theatre in London. Clifford Williams directed it, Mona Washbourne played Smith's Lion Aunt and Peter Eyre was the narrator.
7. All further page numbers associated with poems in this chapter will appear without reference to the *Collected Poems* from which they are quoted.
8. Sternlicht rather improbably suggests that the child in this poem is 'rewarded by Fate' with survival – that is, with being led away from the sight at the back of the shop (1990, 38).
9. See p. 177 in Chapter 4.
10. I am indebted to Frances Spalding for reproducing this in her biography (*SS: AB* 125; from *Granta* 5 May 1937).
11. See pp. 99–100 in Chapter 3.
12. See Kristeva (1984); she often applied her thinking to male texts.
13. It is important to note that Smith rarely judged working-class figures in the same way; her impatience was largely with those who 'never had very much to do' and opted to collude in culture's plan to keep them ignorant.
14. For example, on p. 9 of the book is this (see Figure 5.6). Its accompanying text reads:

> There was an old man on some rocks – Who shut up his wife in a box –
> When she cried – 'let me go!' – He merely said – 'No! – Don't make such a noise in that box!'

The quickly and sharply rendered hands (Smith lamented her lack of skill on this score), the mobility oddly stopped by contradictory elements (the man's facial

Figure 5.6

cast versus his body's movement), the ambivalence of the female's expression – as well as the overall effect connect these two artists' work.
15. See *SS: AB* 123–24 for a description of how even Chesterton's drawings for Belloc's novels echo in Smith's own.
16. Severin 53; she quotes from Winship, p. 140.
17. Both Severin and Bluemel responsibly explain that Smith was known to annex poems and drawings somewhat arbitrarily, as well as change them in some cases over time. James MacGibbon in *The Collected Poems* makes this bibliographical problem clear as well (9). I deal with the issue in an endnote because I assume that whether a drawing is actually drawn for a poem or whether it is placed there afterwards, it still produces the same kinds of complicating and expansive effects I describe above. As we know from Smith's letters, by the middle of the 1950s she was producing poems 'all with several drawings *each*' (*MA* 299); her work was always about multiplication and not singular lines of resistance.
18. There is little evidence to support Severin's suggestion, however, that the stories are 'far more savage in tone than her novels, reviews and many of her poems', and that they therefore must be 'read as a response to continuing waves of conservatism' (96). The stories are, in fact, often direct extensions of the novels and poems; if their tone is harsher than the novels' that is due to the compression of the generic form. Severin's definition of the word 'conservatism' has little to do with the larger political climate; she narrows the word and her reading of Smith's responses in reference to 'social disorder due to the same problem: changing gender roles' (100).

19. In Severin's reading of this story, it is actually 'resolved' (111); Mrs Barlow becomes the female saviour of Peg and the final scene depicts a 'peaceful threesome' (115).
20. Bluemel's reading is misled, in part, in her misidentification of the baby boy's clothing, which she does not seem to realise are not 'concretely...[a] little girl['s]' (117) but rather the standard garb for a baby that age in the early part of the century.
21. I drew these lyrics from the largest website devoted to Formby on the internet: www.georgeformby.co.uk/lyrics/g_h.htm ('Songs 1921–61'). Formby was apparently, if we can believe this site's sources, the most popular and highest paid entertainer by 1939, earning over £100,000 per year. According to these sources, he went on to entertain an estimated 3,000,000 servicemen during the Second World War and took part in two Royal Command Performances.
22. See my chapter in Acheson and Huk: 'Poetry of the Committed Individual: Jon Silkin, Tony Harrison, Geoffrey Hill and the Poets of Post-War Leeds', pp. 175–219.
23. This poem's final stanza, following three tercets in which conventional patriotic rhetoric dominates, and in which only those who fought well and never 'sheathed their swords' merit congratulation in death – a terribly unSmithian theme – suddenly changes tone: 'Prate not to me of suicide, / Faint heart in battle, not for pride / I say Endure, but that such end denied / Makes welcomer yet the death that's to be died.' The 'Prate not' helps me to understand this tongue-in-cheek poem in the best tradition of Falstaff's speeches on 'Honour' in *I Henry IV*, which actually make clear that war is in no one's interest other than those who make interest on it – 'Profit and Batten', as Smith puts it in another poem in this collection ('Villains', 181).
24. Smith brought a South Kensington accent to her radio readings – something that, as Francis Spalding writes, put speech delivery coach Rachel Marshall 'in advance of her time in not trying to impose upon others a BBC pronunciation' (*SS: AB* 231). Severin translates this as a suggestion that it effected specific subversion of 'classist' attitudes at the BBC (121), but there is no class ramification for that particular accent – it could, in fact, be quite high class indeed. Smith's voice was simply 'idiosyncratic' in its South Kensington pronunciation of 's's, as Spalding explains. As Seamus Heaney heard it, it had 'the longueurs and acerbities, the nuanced understatements and tactical intonations of educated middle-class English speech' ('A Memorable Voice: Stevie Smith', *ISOSS* 212).
25. Spalding does not date this performance, and the text is from a letter written to her by Bryson in 1984. But Bryson would not have gone up to Cambridge until the latter end of the 1960s, so I assume the approximate date from that.
26. Austerlitz was fought over by the three empires in the nineteenth century and left, like Memel in the twentieth, a fractured community. The Treaty of Versailles in 1919 took Memel out of German rule; its variegated, largely Lithuanian and German population was then annexed again by Hitler in the era of the appeasements. Smith's 'girl soldier Vaudevue', who strips off her uniform to drown herself in the icy lake, seems to escape her enemy but is actually the victim of herself and her own name. The latter means a light song of vaudeville status; many were produced during the war, such as 'The Lads of the Village', and they take centre stage in this poem. For her favourite song, '[f]avourite of all the troops of all the armies', which she had 'sung too', '[m]arching to Austerlitz', was 'Come on, Come back'; its title not only becomes the title of this poem but more importantly what her enemy waiting for her to return sings. And most importantly, it represents what she ultimately *does* – goes back to her Freudian, elemental state,

through the waters that are 'as black as her mind': 'Vaudevue / In the swift and subtle current's close embrace / Sleeps on, stirs not, hears not the familiar tune' (334).
27. See 'A House of Mercy', *CP* 410–11.

Works Cited

Acheson, James and Romana Huk, eds. *Contemporary British Poetry: Essays in Theory and Criticism* (Albany: State University of New York Press, 1996).
Adams, Bronte and Trudi Tate, eds. *That Kind of Woman: Rebellious Stories by Colette, H.D., Anaïs Nin, Virginia Woolf and Others* (London: Virago, 1991).
Adorno, Theodor. 'Lyric Poetry and Society', Bruce Mayo, trans., in *Telos* 20 (1974): 56–71.
Alvarez, A. 'Deadly Funny' (a review of *CP*). *Observer* (3 August 1975).
Ashcroft, Bill, Gareth Griffiths and Helen Tiffin, eds. *The Empire Writes Back: Theory and Practice in Post-Colonial Literatures* (New York and London: Routledge, 1989).
Auden, W.H. Introduction to *Tales of Grimm and Andersen*, selected by Frederick Jacobi, Jr (New York: Random House; The Modern Library, 1952).
———. *The Orators: An English Study* (New York: Random House, 1967; Modern Library, 1934).
———. *Selected Poems* (New Edition). Edward Mendelson, ed. (New York: Vintage Books, 1979).
Bakhtin, M.M. *The Dialogic Imagination: Four Essays by M.M. Bakhtin.* Michael Holquist, ed., Caryl Emerson and Michael Holquist, trans. (Austin: University of Texas Press, 1981).
Barbera, Jack. 'The Relevance of Stevie Smith's Drawings' in *Journal of Modern Literature* 12 (July 1985): 221–36.
Barbera, Jack and William McBrien. *Stevie: A Biography of Stevie Smith* (Oxford and New York: Oxford University Press, 1985).
Baudelaire, Charles. *Les Fleurs du Mal* [The Flowers of Evil]. James McGowen, trans. and notes, Jonathan Culler introd. (Oxford and New York: Oxford University Press, 1998).
Baudrillard, Jean. *Selected Writings.* Mark Porter, ed. (Stanford: Stanford University Press, 1988).
Becker, Lutz and Martin Caiger-Smith, eds. *Art and Power: Images of the 1930s* (South Bank Centre: catalogue for an exhibition at the Hayward Gallery, 'Art and Power: Europe under the dictators 1930–45', 1995).
Beckett, Samuel. *Murphy* (New York: Grove, 1957).
Bell, Clive. *Art* (London: Chatto & Windus, 1927).
Benstock, Shari. 'Expatriate Modernism: Writing on the Cultural Rim' in Broe and Ingram, pp. 18–40.
Bergonzi, Bernard. 'Tones of Voice' (a review of *The Frog Prince and Other Poems*). *The Guardian* (16 December 1966): 7.
Betjeman, John. 'Something Funny' (a review of *SAMHTO*). *Daily Telegraph* (12 December 1958).
Blake, William. *The Poems of William Blake.* W.H. Stevenson, ed. (with text by David V. Erdman) (London: Longman Annotated English Poets series, 1971).
Bluemel, Kristin. 'The Dangers of Eccentricity: Stevie Smith's Doodles and Poetry' in *Mosaic* 31: 3 (September 1998): 111–32.
Boothby, Richard. *Death and Desire: Psychoanalytic Theory in Lacan's Return to Freud* (New York: Routledge, 1991).

Broe, Mary Lynn and Angela Ingram, eds. *Women's Writing in Exile* (Chapel Hill and London: The University of North Carolina Press, 1989).
Brothers, Barbara. 'Writing against the Grain: Sylvia Townsend Warner and the Spanish Civil War' in Broe and Ingram, pp. 349–68.
Browning, Robert. *Robert Browning's Poetry: Authoritative Texts and Criticism*. James F. Loucks, ed. (New York: Norton & Co., 1979).
Buckler, William Earl. *The major Victorian Poets: Tennyson, Browning, Arnold* (Boston: Houghton Mifflin, 1973).
Calder, Angus. *The Myth of the Blitz* (London: Jonathan Cape, 1991).
Carr, Helen. 'Poetic Licence' in *From My Guy to Sci-Fi: Genre and Women's Writing in the Postmodern World*. Helen Carr, ed. (London: Pandora, 1989), pp. 135–62.
Carroll, Lewis. *The Annotated Alice: Alice's Adventures in Wonderland* and *Through the Looking Glass*. Martin Gardner, ed. (Harmondsworth: Penguin Books, 1970).
Chadwick, Whitney. *Women Artists and the Surrealist Movement* (London: Thames and Hudson, Ltd, 1985).
Chesterton, G.K. *Poems for All Purposes: The Selected Poems of G.K. Chesterton*. Stephen Medcalf, ed. (London: Pimlico, 1994).
Childs, David. *Britain Since 1945: A Political History*. Third Edition (London: Routledge, 1992).
Childs, Peter. *The Twentieth Century in Poetry: A Critical Survey* (London: Routledge, 1999).
Churchill, Winston. *History of the English-Speaking Peoples*, Vol. 1 (London: Cassell and Company, Ltd, 1956–58).
Civello, Catherine A. *Patterns of Ambivalence: The Fiction and Poetry of Stevie Smith* (Columbia, SC (U.S.A.): Camden House, 1997).
Cixous, Hélène. 'The Laugh of the Medusa', Keith Cohen and Paula Cohen, trans. *Signs* 1: 4 (Summer 1976).
Conrad, Joseph. *Heart of Darkness*. Second Edition, Case Studies in Contemporary Criticism Series, Ross C. Murfin, ed. (Boston and New York: Bedford Books/St Martin's Press, 1996).
Corcoran, Neil. *English Poetry since 1940* (Harlow, Essex: Longman, 1993).
Couzyn, Jeni, ed. *The Bloodaxe Book of Contemporary Women Poets: Eleven British Writers* (Newcastle upon Tyne: Bloodaxe Books, 1985).
Davie, Donald. *Selected Poems* (Manchester: Carcanet Press, 1985).
——. *Under Briggflatts: A History of Poetry in Great Britain 1960–1988* (Chicago: University of Chicago Press, 1989).
——. *Purity of Diction in English Verse* (1952) and *Articulate Energy* (1955) (Harmondsworth, Middlesex: Penguin Books, 1992).
Davies, Alistair and Alan Sinfield. *British Culture of the Postwar: An Introduction to Literature and Society 1945–1999* (London and New York: Routledge, 2000).
Derrida, Jacques. *Writing and Difference*. Alan Bass, trans. (Chicago: University of Chicago Press, 1978).
——. *Dissemination*. Barbara Johnson, trans. (London: Athalone Press, 1981).
Dettmar, Kevin and Jennifer Wicke. *The Longman Anthology of British Literature; Volume 2C: The Twentieth Century*. (London and New York: Longman, 2002).
Dick, Kay. *Ivy and Stevie* (London: Allison & Busby, 1983).
Dickinson, Emily. *The Complete Poems of Emily Dickinson*. Thomas H. Johnson, ed. (London: Faber & Faber Ltd, 1975).
Dostoyevsky, Fyodor. *The Brothers Karamazov* (New York: Bantam Classics, 1981).

———. *Notes from the Underground.* Constance Garnett, trans. (New York: Dover Publications, Inc., 1992).
Dowson, Jane, ed. *Women's Poetry of the 1930s: A Critical Anthology* (London and New York: Routledge, 1996).
DuPlessis, Rachel Blau. *Genders, Races and Religious Cultures in Modern American Poetry, 1908–1934* (Cambridge: Cambridge University Press, 2001).
———. *Writing Beyond the Ending: Narrative Strategies of Twentieth-Century Women Writers* (Bloomington: Indiana University Press, 1985).
Eagleton, Terry. 'New Poetry' in *ISOSS*, pp. 82–83.
Easthope, Antony. *Englishness and National Culture* (London and New York: Routledge, 1999).
Ede, Lisa. 'Edward Lear's Limericks and their Illustrations' in *Explorations in the Field of Nonsense.* Wim Tigges, ed. (Amsterdam: Rodopi, 1987).
Eliot, T.S. *Christianity and Culture* (including *The Idea of a Christian Society* and *Notes Towards the Definition of Culture*) (New York and London: Harcourt Brace Jovanovich, 1968).
Faulkner, Peter, ed. *A Modernist Reader: Modernism in England 1910–1930* (London: Batsford, 1986).
Flavell, M. Kay. *George Grosz: A Biography* (New Haven and London: Yale University Press, 1988).
Forgacs, David. 'Fascism, Violence and Modernity' in Mengham and Howlett, pp. 5–21.
Freud, Sigmund. *Beyond the Pleasure Principle* (1920) in *On Metapsychology: The Theory of Psychoanalysis*; The Pelican Freud Library, Vol. 11, James Strachey, general ed., Angela Richards, volume ed. (Harmondsworth: Penguin Books, 1984).
Gilbert, Sandra M. and Susan Gubar. *The Madwoman in the Attic: The Woman Writer and the Nineteenth-Century Literary Imagination* (New Haven: Yale University Press, 1979).
Giles, Judy and Tim Middleton, eds. *Writing Englishness: 1900–1950* (London and New York: Routledge, 1995).
Glazener, Nancy. 'Dialogic Subversion: Bakhtin, the Novel, and Gertrude Stein' in Hirschkop and Shepherd, pp. 109–29.
Graves, Richard Percival. *Robert Graves: The Years with Laura Riding 1926–1940* (London: Weidenfield & Nicolson, 1990).
Greenhalgh, Peter. *Pompey: The Republican Prince* (London: Weidenfeld and Nicholson, 1981).
Hanscombe, Gillian and Virginia L. Smyers. *Writing for their Lives: The Modernist Woman 1910–1940* (Boston: Northeastern University Press, 1987).
Harding, Sandra. *The Science Question in Feminism* (Ithaca: Cornell University Press, 1986).
Hardy, Thomas. *The Complete Poems of Thomas Hardy.* James Gibson, ed. (London: Macmillan, 1976).
Harrison, Charles and Paul Wood, eds. *Art in Theory: 1900–1990* (Oxford: Blackwell, 1992).
Hayley, J.R. *Renaissance War Studies* (London: Humbledon, 1983).
Hendry, J.F. 'Myth and Social Integration' in *The White Horseman: Prose and Verse of the New Apocalypse*, J.F. Hendry and Henry Treece, eds (London: Routledge, 1941), pp. 153–79.
———. and Henry Treece, eds. *The New Apocalypse* (London: Fortune Press, 1939).
Herrmann, Anne. *The Dialogic and Difference* (New York: Columbia University Press, 1989).
Hill, Geoffrey. *For the Unfallen* (London: Faber & Faber, 1956).

Hirschkop, Ken and David Shepherd, eds. *Bakhtin and Cultural Theory* (Manchester and New York: Manchester University Press, 1989).
Hirsh, Elizabeth. *Modernism Revised: Formalism and the Feminine (Irigaray, H.D., Barnes)* (Ann Arbor: UMI Dissertation Information Service, 1989).
Hobsbawm, Eric. *Age of Extremes: The Short Twentieth Century 1914–1991* (London: Abacus, 1994).
Holden, Inez. 'Some Women Writers'. *The Nineteenth Century* 146 (August 1949): 130–36.
Hollander, Robert and Jean, trans./eds. *The Inferno*, by Dante Alighieri (New York: Anchor Books, 2002).
Horovitz, Michael, ed. *Children of Albion* (Harmondsworth, Middlesex: Penguin Books, 1969).
——. 'Of Absent Friends' in *ISOSS*, pp. 147–65.
Huk, Romana. 'Eccentric Concentrism: Traditional Poetic Forms and Refracted Discourse in Stevie Smith's Poetry'. *Contemporary Literature* 34: 2 (1993): 240–65.
——. 'Poetic Subject and Voice as Sites of Struggle: Toward a "Postrevisionist" Reading of Stevie Smith's Fairy Tale Poems' in *Dwelling in Possibility: Women Poets and Critics on Poetry*, Yopie Prins and Maeera Shreiber, eds (Ithaca and London: Cornell University Press, 1997).
——. 'Feminist Radicalism in (Relatively) Traditional Forms: An American's Investigations of British Poetics' in *Kicking Daffodils: Twentieth-Century Women Poets*, Vicki Bertram, ed. (Edinburgh: Edinburgh University Press, 1997).
——. 'Misplacing Stevie Smith'. *Contemporary Literature* 40: 3 (1999): 507–23.
Isherwood, Christopher and Edward Upward. *The Mortmere Stories* (London: Enitharmon Press, 1994).
Jameson, Fredric. *Fables of Aggression* (Berkeley: University of California Press, 1979).
——. *The Ideologies of Theory (Essays 1971–1986)*, Vol. I: *Situations of Theory* (Minneapolis: University of Minnesota Press, 1988).
Joannou, Maroula, ed. *Women Writers of the 1930s: Gender Politics and History* (Edinburgh: Edinburgh University Press, 1999).
Jones, David. *Selected Works of David Jones*. John Matthias, ed. (Orono, Maine and Cardiff: National Poetry Foundation and University of Wales Press, 1992).
Jones, Edwin. *The English Nation: The Great Myth* (Gloucestershire: Sutton Publishing Ltd, 1998).
Joyce, James. *A Portrait of the Artist as a Young Man: Text, Criticism, and Notes*. Chester G. Anderson, ed. (Viking Critical Library Series; Harmondsworth, Middlesex: Penguin Books, 1977).
Kafka, Franz. *The Castle*. Willa and Edwin Muir, trans. (Harmondsworth, Middlesex: Penguin Books, 1979).
Kenner, Hugh. *The Pound Era* (Berkeley and Los Angeles: University of California Press, 1971).
Kristeva, Julia. *The Kristeva Reader*. Toril Moi, ed. (Oxford: Blackwell, 1986).
——. *The Revolution in Poetic Language* (New York: Columbia University Press, 1984).
Lacan, Jacques. *Écrits: A Selection*. Alan Sheridan, trans. (New York and London: W.W. Norton & Co., 1977).
Larkin, Philip. 'Frivolous and Vulnerable' in *ISOSS*, pp. 75–81.
——. 'Stevie, Good-bye' in *ISOSS*, pp. 114–16.
——. *The Less Deceived* (London: The Marvell Press, 1955).
Lassner, Phyllis. '"The Milk of Our Mother's Kindness Has Ceased to Flow": Virginia Woolf, Stevie Smith, and the Representation of the Jew' in *Between 'Race' and Culture: Representations of 'the Jew' in English and American Literature*, Bryan Cheyette, ed. (Stanford: Stanford University Press, 1996), pp. 129–44.

Lear, Edward. *Bosh and Nonsense* (London: Allen lane, 1982).
Lecercle, Jean-Jacques. *Philosophy of Nonsense* (London: Routledge, 1994).
Lee, Hermione, ed. Introduction. *Stevie Smith: A Selection* (London: Faber, 1983).
'Les Années 30', an issue of *Beaux Arts Magazine*. Charles-Henri Fammarion, ed. (Paris: January 1997).
Lewis, Wyndham. *The Art of Being Ruled* (Corte Madera, CA: Ginko Press, 1979).
Light, Alison. *Forever England: Femininity, Literature and Conservatism between the Wars* (London and New York: Routledge, 1991).
——. 'Outside History? Stevie Smith, Women Poets and the National Voice' in *English: The Journal of the English Association* 43: 177 (Autumn 1994): 237–59.
Macaulay, Lord Thomas Babington. *The Lays of Ancient Rome & Miscellaneous Essays and Poems* (with and introduction by G.M. Trevelyan) (London and New York: J.M. Dent & Sons and E.P. Dutton & Co., 1958).
MacNeice, Louis. *The Strings are False: An Unfinished Autobiography*. E.R. Dodds, ed. (London: Faber & Faber, 1965).
Mahoney, John L. *Seeing into the Life of Things: Essays in Literature and Religious Experience* (New York: Fordham University Press, 1998).
Maslen, Elizabeth. *Political and Social Issues in British Women's Fiction, 1928–1968* (Houndmills, Basingstoke, Hampshire: Palgrave Books, 2001).
Mayer, A.J. *Why Did the Heavens Not Darken? The 'Final Solution' in History* (New York: Pantheon Books, 1988).
Mellor, David Alan. 'Mass Observation: The Intellectual Climate' in *The Camerawork Essays* (London: Rivers Oram, 1997).
Mengham, Rod and Jana Howlett, eds. *The Violent Muse: Violence and the Artistic Imagination in Europe, 1910–1939* (Manchester: Manchester University Press, 1994).
Meyers, Jeffrey. *The Enemy: A Biography of Wyndham Lewis* (London: Routledge & Kegan Paul, 1980).
Millard, Elaine. 'Frames of References: The Reception of, and Response to, Three Woman Poets' in *Literary Theory and Poetry: Extending the Canon*, David Murray, ed. (London: Batsford, 1989), pp. 62–84.
Millard, Kenneth. *Edwardian Poetry* (Oxford: Clarendon Press, 1991).
Milton, John. *Complete Shorter Poems*. John Carey, ed. (London: Longman, Annotated English Poets Series, 1968).
Mitchell, W.J.T. *Picture Theory: Essays on Verbal and Visual Representation* (Chicago: University of Chicago press, 1995).
Mitchison, Naomi. *Among You Taking Notes . . . The Wartime Diary of Naomi Mitchison*. Dorothy Sheridan, ed. (Oxford: Oxford University Press, 1986).
Montefiore, Jan. *Feminism and Poetry: Language, Experience, Identity in Women's Writing* (London and New York: Pandora, 1987).
Morris, John, ed. *From the Third Programme: A Ten-Year's Anthology* (London: Nonesuch Press, 1956).
Morrison, Blake. *The Movement: English Poetry and Fiction of the 1950s* (London: Methuen, 1980).
Nussbaum, Felicity A. *The Autobiographical Subject* (Baltimore: John's Hopkins University Press, 1989).
Orwell, George. *Collected Letters, Essays and Journalism by George Orwell: Volume I An Age Like This: 1920–1940* (London: Secker and Warburg, 1968).
——. *Burmese Days* (Harmondsworth: Penguin Books, 1989).
——. *Essays* (Harmondsworth, Middlesex: Penguin Classics, 2000).
Owen, Wilfred. The *Collected Poems of Wilfred Owen* (London: Chatto & Windus, 1963).

Palgrave, F.T., ed. *The Golden Treasury* (London: Macmillan, 1875).
Parker, Dorothy. *The Portable Dorothy Parker*. Brendan Gill, Introduction (Harmondsworth, Middlesex: Penguin, 1976).
Patterson, Annabel. *Fables of Power: Aesopian Writing and Political History* (Durham and London: Duke University Press, 1991).
Patterson, David. 'Laughter and the Alterity of Truth in Bakhtin's Aesthetics' in *Discours social/Social Discourse* III, 1 & 2 (Spring–Summer 1990): 295–309.
Patton, Paul, ed. *Nietzsche, Feminism and Political Theory* (London and New York: Routledge, 1993).
Penguin Modern Poets 8: Edwin Brock, Geoffrey Hill, Stevie Smith (Harmondsworth: Penguin Books, 1966).
Peppis, Paul. *Literature, Politics, and the English Avant-Garde: Nation and Empire, 1901–1918* (Cambridge: Cambridge University Press, 2000).
Plain, Gill. *Women's Fiction of the Second World War: Gender, Power and Resistance* (Edinburgh: Edinburgh University Press, 1996).
Porter, Roy, ed. *Myths of the English* (Cambridge: Polity Press, 1992).
Pound, Ezra. *Selected Poems* (New York: New Directions Books, 1957).
Priestley, J.B. *English Journey* (London: Heineman Ltd in association with V. Gollancz Ltd, 1934).
Pumphrey, Martin. 'Play, Fantasy and Strange Laughter: Stevie Smith's Uncomfortable Poetry' in *ISOSS*, pp. 97–113.
Rankin, Arthur. *The Poetry of Stevie Smith: A Little Girl Lost* (Gerrards Cross: Colin Smythe, 1985).
Ricks, Christopher. *The Force of Poetry* (Oxford: Clarendon Press, 1984).
——. *Beckett's Dying Words* (The Clarendon Lectures 1990; Oxford and New York: Oxford University Press, 1993).
Robinson, Peter, ed. *Geoffrey Hill: Essays on His Work* (Milton Keynes and Philadelphia: OPen University Press, 1985).
Rose, Ellen Cronan. 'Through the Looking Glass: When Women Tell Fairy Tales' in *The Voyage In: Fictions in Female Development*. Elizabeth Abel, Marianne Hirsch and Elizabeth Langland, eds (Hanover, MA: University Press of New England, 1983), pp. 209–27.
Sarfatti, Margherita. *Dux* [a biography of Mussolini] (Milan: 1928); Frederick, Whyte, trans. and condensed, *The Life of Benito Mussolini* [preface by Benito Mussolini] (New York: Frederick A. Stokes Company, 1925).
Sartre, Jean-Paul. *Situations*. Benita Eisler, trans. (New York: George Braziller, 1965).
Schenck, Celeste M. 'Exiled by Genre: Modernism, Canonicity, and the Politics of Exclusion' in Broe and Ingram, pp. 225–50.
Severin, Laura. *Stevie Smith's Resistant Antics* (Madison: University of Wisconsin Press, 1997).
——. 'Becoming and Unbecoming: Stevie Smith as Performer'. *Text and Performance Quarterly* 18: 1 (January 1998): 22–36.
Shakespeare, William. *The Riverside Shakespeare*. Second Edition, Herschel Baker *et al.*, eds (Boston and New York: Houghton Mifflin Co., 1977).
Shakinovsky, Lynn J. 'Hidden Listeners: Dialogism in the Poetry of Emily Dickinson' in *Discours social/Social Discourse* 1 & 2 (Spring–Summer 1990): 199–215.
Sherry, Vincent. *The Great War and the Language of Modernism* (Oxford: Oxford University Press, 2003).
Sitwell, Edith. *Street Songs* (London: Macmillan, 1942).
——. 'Some Notes on My Own Poetry' in *The Canticle of the Rose: Poems 1917–1949* (New York: The Vanguard Press, 1949), pp. xi–xxxviii.

———. *Façade* (with an interpretation by Pamela Hunter) (London: Gerald Duckworth & Co. Ltd, 1987).
Skelton, Robin. *Poetry of the Thirties* (Harmondsworth: Penguin Books, 1964).
———. ed. *Poetry of the Forties* (Harmondsworth: Penguin Books, 1968).
Smith, Stevie. *The Holiday* (London: Virago, 1979).
———. *Novel on Yellow Paper* (London: Virago, 1980).
———. *Over the Frontier* (London: Virago, 1980).
———. *Me Again: Uncollected Writings of Stevie Smith*. Jack Barbera and William McBrien, eds (New York: Farrar Straus Giroux, 1981).
———. *Stevie Smith: A Selection*. Hermione Lee, ed. (London: Faber, 1983).
———. *The Collected Poems of Stevie Smith*. James McGibbon, ed. (Harmondsworth: Penguin Books, 1985; also published in the U.S. by New Directions).
———. *Some Are More Human Than Others: A Sketchbook by Stevie Smith* (New York: New Directions, 1989).
Spalding, Frances. *Stevie Smith: A Biography* (New York and London: Norton, 1989).
Steiner, George. *George Steiner: A Reader* (Harmondsworth, Middlesex: Penguin Books, 1984).
Spender, Stephen. *Forward from Liberalism* (London: Victor Gollancz Ltd (Left Book Club Edition), 1937).
———. 'Introduction'. *Journey to the Border* (London: Enitharmon Press, 1994).
Sternlicht, Sanford. *Stevie Smith* (Boston: Twayne Publishers, 1990).
———. ed. *In Search of Stevie Smith* (Syracuse: Syracuse University Press, 1991).
Stevenson, Sheryl. 'Stevie Smith's Voices'. *Contemporary Literature* 33 (1992): 24–45.
Symons, Julian. *The Thirties and the Nineties* (Manchester: Carcanet Press, 1990).
Tatham, Michael. 'That One Must Speak Lightly' in *ISOSS*, pp. 132–46.
Taylor, Dr Stephen. 'The Suburban Neurosis'. *Lancet* (26 March 1938): 759–61.
Thaddeus, Janice. 'Stevie Smith and the Gleeful Macabre' in *ISOSS*, pp. 84–96.
Thompson, E.P. *et al.*, eds. *Out of Apathy* (London: New Left Books, Stevens & Sons, 1960).
Thomson, Clive. 'Mikhail Bakhtin and Contemporary Anglo-American Feminist Theory' in *Critical Studies: A Journal of Critical Theory, Literature and Culture* 1: 2 (1989): 141–61.
Thwaite, Anthony. *Contemporary English Poetry: An Introduction* (Oxford: Heinemann, 1968).
———. *Twentieth-century English Poetry: An Introduction* (New York: Barnes and Noble Books-Imports, 1978).
———. *Poetry Today: A Critical Guide to British Poetry 1960–1984* (London and New York: Longman, 1985).
Upward, Edward. *Journey to the Border* (London: Enitharmon Press, 1994).
Voris, Renate. 'The Autobiographical Phallacy' in *Communications from the International Brecht Society* (CIBS) 16: 1 (1986): 52–58.
Warner, Marina. 'Speaking with Double Tongue: Mother Goose and the Old Wives' Tale' in Porter, pp. 33–67.
Whitemore, Hugh. *Stevie: A Play by Hugh Whitemore from the Life and Work of Stevie Smith* (Oxford: Amber Lane Press, 1984).
Williams, Jonathan. 'Much Further Out Than You Thought', an interview with Stevie Smith in *ISOSS*, pp. 38–49.
Williams, Keith and Steven Matthews, eds. *Rewriting the Thirties: Modernism and After* (London and New York: Longman, 1997).
Williams, Raymond. *The Politics of Modernism: Against the New Conformists* (London and New York: Verso, 1989).

Wills, Clair. 'Upsetting the Public: Carnival, Hysteria and Women's Texts' in Hirschkop and Shepherd, pp. 130–51.
Wilson, Jean Moorcroft. *Virginia Woolf, Life and London: A Biography of Place* (New York: W.W. Norton, 1988).
Winship, Janice. 'A Woman's World: "Woman" – An Ideology of Femininity' in *Women Take Issue: Aspects of Women's Subordination* (Hutchinson: Women's Studies Group Centre for Contemporary Cultural Studies at the University of Birmingham, 1978).
Wolff, Janet. *Feminine Sentences: Essays on Women and Culture* (Cambridge: Polity Press, 1990).
Wolosky, Shira. *Emily Dickinson: A Voice of War* (New Haven: Yale University Press, 1984).
Woolf, Virginia. *A Room of One's Own* (Harmondsworth: Penguin Books, 1945).
——. *Mrs Dalloway* (New York and London: Harcourt Brace Javanovich, 1953).
——. *A Writer's Diary* (Frogmore, St Albans, Herts: Triad/Panther Books, 1978).
Yaeger, Patricia. *Honey-Mad Women: Emancipatory Strategies in Women's Writing* (New York and Oxford: Columbia University Press, 1988).
Yeats, W.B. *Collected Poems* (London: Macmillan (Papermac), 1982).

Index

Aaron, 167
Acheson, James, 298, 312, 316
Adorno, Theodor, 187, 265, 297, 312
Aikins, Conrad, 58
Albert (Prince Albert), 27
Alfred (the Great; King of Wessex), 233, 234
Alvarez, A., 21
Anand, Mulk Raj, 196–7
Andersen, Hans Christian, 25
Anderson, Hedli, 279
Antony (Marc Antony; *Marcus Antonius*), 80
Apter, Emily, 95, 303–4
Aristotle, 150
Armitage, Eric, 43
Arnold, Matthew, 3, 85, 296, 298
Ashcroft, Bill, *et al.*, 312
Astaire, Fred, 43
Atkinson, Ruth, 300
Atlee, Clement, 56, 134
Auden, W.H., 8, 15, 25, 31, 47, 52, 53, 57, 69, 99, 112, 116, 131, 142, 143, 150, 157, 159, 160, 168, 227, 235, 254, 298, 301, 302, 308, 309, 310
Auerbach, Erich, 95, 303
Austin, Alfred, 304

Bacon, Francis, 183
Bailey, Paul, 300
Bakhtin, M.M. 5, 20, 21, 217–18, 296–97
Barbera, Jack, 20, 42, 51, 236, 297, 298, 299, 313
Baring, Maurice, 41, 154
Barrett, Helen, 212
Barthes, Roland, 49, 125
Baudelaire, Charles, 169, 276
Baudrillard, Jean, 160, 309
Beardsley, Aubrey, 145, 297
Becker, Lutz, 144, 302
Beckett, Samuel, 8, 60, 103, 128, 138, 153, 181, 182, 187, 189, 211, 267, 280, 301, 306, 307, 311
Beethoven, Ludwig van, 152, 153

Bell, Clive, 50, 300
Belloc, Hillaire, 41, 136, 161, 307, 315
Benjamin, Walter, 95, 124, 259, 303–4
Benstock, Shari, 2
Bergonzi, Bernard, 11, 297
Betjeman, John, 298
Blackburn, Thomas, 62
Blake, William, 3, 40, 46, 64, 127, 224, 225–6, 227, 228, 266, 289, 292, 296, 301
Bluemel, Kristin, 20–1, 235–6, 238, 244, 246, 248–51, 275, 315, 316
Boethius (*Anicius Manlius Severinis Boethius*), 181, 212, 233
Boothby, Richard, 15, 23
Bosch, Heironymus, 180
Bowen, Elizabeth, 49
Bradshaw, David, 302
Brecht, Bertolt, 16, 142, 309
Breton, André, 47, 55, 131, 159
Breughel, Pieter, 226
Brittain, Vera, 58, 59
Brothers, Barbara, 57
Browning, Robert, 14, 29, 231, 291, 292
Brutus (*Marcus Junius*), 78
Bryson, Norman, 283–4, 316
Buchan, John, 305
Buckler, William Earl, 291
Bunting, Basil, 17
Burdett, Osbert, 13, 297
Byron (George Gordon, Lord Byron), 19

Caesar, Julius (*Caius Julius Caesar*), 77, 78, 83, 173
Caiger-Smith, Martin, 144, 302
Camus, Albert, 83
Carlyle, Thomas, 136
Carr, Helen, 27, 29
Carrington, Leonora, 55
Carroll, Lewis, 86, 112, 303
Casement, Roger, 137–8, 157, 161, 232
Cato (*Marcus Porcius Cato*), 78
Catullus (*Caius Valerius Catullus*), 186, 209, 306

326

Chadwick, Whitney, 55, 131
Chamberlain, Neville, 56, 134
Chekhov, Anton Pavlovich, 115
Chesterton, G.K., 41, 136, 154, 167, 307, 310, 315
Childs, Peter, 298, 301, 304, 305
Chilver, Sally, 47, 61
Christ, Jesus, 22, 29, 204–5, 313
Christie, Agatha, 41, 305
Churchill, Winston, 56, 134, 135, 181, 233, 310
Cicero (*Marcus Tullius Cicero*), 77, 210
Civello, Catherine, 10, 297, 298
Confucius (*K'ung Fu-tse*), 208
Conrad, Joseph, 41, 69, 80, 86, 105, 120, 126, 128, 137, 151, 156–7, 159, 164, 167, 191, 302, 303, 305, 309
Corbière, Tristan, 27
Corcoran, Neil, 276, 297, 298, 301
Couzyn, Jeni, 1
Coward, Rosalind, 304
Creeley, Robert, 64
Cromwell, Oliver, 210

Dante (*Dante Alighieri*), 82, 180, 224, 233, 289, 292, 302
Danton, Georges Jacques, 127
d'Aurevilly, Jules Barbey, 272
Davie, Donald, 17, 65–6, 187, 275, 299, 301, 305, 312
de Mille, Cecil B., 178
De Vere, Edward, 183, 312
Derrida, Jacques, 10, 11, 21, 129, 246, 267–9, 273
Dettmar, Kevin, 310
Dick, Kay, 20, 31, 40, 44, 45, 47, 51, 301, 307
Dickinson, Emily, 14, 17, 65, 187, 229, 301, 313
Donne, John, 65, 151
Donoghue, Steve, 46, 298
Dostoyevsky, Fyodor, 5, 8, 12, 35, 41, 180, 181, 203, 205, 207, 211–12, 213, 217
Dowson, Jane, 300, 309
DuPlessis, Rachel Blau, 3, 18, 94

Easthope, Antony, 17, 298
Eckinger, Karl, 59, 100–1

Ede, Lisa, 245
Eden, Anthony, 134
Edward VIII, 11
Eliot, T.S., 2, 3, 5, 17, 29, 30, 41, 47, 55, 75, 84, 88, 92, 107, 118, 119, 147, 159, 169, 222, 235–6, 246, 296, 299, 300, 302, 303, 305, 313
Enright, D.J., 27
Euripides, 106, 108, 109
Eyre, Peter, 314

Faulkner, Peter, 302
Flavell, M. Kay, 59, 180, 308
Foote, Samuel, 173
Ford, Ford Madox, 41
Formby, George, 265–6, 316
Foucault, Michel, 26, 248, 250
Fowler, Helen, 47
Franco, Francisco, 98
Franklin, Benjamin, 88–9
Freud, Sigmund, 14, 23, 41, 71, 72, 74, 75, 86, 90, 105, 120, 122, 129, 148, 171–2, 174, 176, 180, 186, 200, 201, 202, 230, 246, 251, 280, 302, 303, 311, 316
Fuller, Roy, 298

Gandhi, Mohandas Karamchand (Mahatma), 205
Garnett, David, 51, 60, 139, 300
George V, 94
Gibbon, Edward, 19, 205, 207, 313
Gibbs, Phillip, 94
Gilbert, Sandra, 285
Gilbert, William (Gilbert and Sullivan), 222
Giles, Judy, 94, 121–22, 131
Ginsberg, Allen, 64
Glazener, Nancy, 13
Goebbels, Paul Joseph, 271
Goethe, Johann Wolfgang von, 103
Golding, William, 178
Goya (y Lucientes), Francisco José de, 160
Graves, Richard Percival, 308
Graves, Robert, 150, 308
Greenblatt, Stephen, 303
Greenhalgh, Peter, 78
Grimm, Jakob and Wilhelm ('the Brothers Grimm'), 19, 25

Grosz, Georg, 59, 140, 143, 145, 146, 147, 148, 149, 150, 152, 153, 157, 159, 160, 161, 169, 174, 178, 180, 183, 229, 308, 309
Gubar, Susan, 285
Guest, John, 296

H.D. (Hilda Doolittle), 17, 107, 296
Hadrian, 119
Haldane, J.B.S., 116
Hall, Radclyffe, 45
Harding, Sandra, 13
Hardy, Thomas, 65, 175
Harrison, Charles, 308
Harrison, Tony, 312, 316
Hartley, L.P., 47
Hawthorne, Nathaniel, 171
Hayley, J.R., 307
Heaney, Seamus, 1, 6, 7, 296, 316
Heath-Stubbs, John, 62, 301
Heber, Reginald, 189–92, 194, 205, 210
Hegel, Georg Wilhelm Friedrich, 129
Heidegger, Martin, 188
Hendry, J.F., 15, 309
Herod, 149, 277
Herrick, Robert, 276
Hewett, Ivan, 303
Hill, Geoffrey, 216, 266, 277, 312, 314, 316
Hill, Polly, 301
Hirsch, Elizabeth, 3
Hitchcock, Alfred, 14, 262, 305
Hitler, Adolf, 59, 79, 92, 98, 100, 101, 103, 106, 133, 135, 143, 146, 155, 204, 277, 285, 302, 304, 316
Hoare, Sir Samuel, 134, 135, 136, 146, 161, 182
Hobsbawm, Eric, 22
Hoggart, Richard, 53
Holden, Inez, 47, 57, 182, 184, 197, 301
Hollo, Anselm, 64
Homer, 41, 201
Hooker, Jeremy, 216
Horder, John, 299
Horovitz, Michael, 18, 27, 63, 64, 280, 301
Houston, Libby, 64
Howard, Ebenezer, 121
Howells, Coral Ann, 297
Howlett, Jana, 301

Huk, Romana, 296, 298, 312, 316
Hulme, T.E., 66

Inge, William Ralph, 41
Iscariot, Judas, 206
Isherwood, Christopher, 25, 52, 53, 116, 142

Jackson, Glenda, 68, 219
James, Henry, 41
Jameson, Fredric, 67, 70, 297, 302
Jameson, Storm, 49, 52, 300
Jennings, Elizabeth, 301
Joannou, Maroula, 70, 300, 302, 309
Johnson, Samuel, 41
Johnston, Denis, 54, 83, 134
Jones, David, 17, 180
Jones, Edwin, 26
Jonson, Ben, 186, 209, 306
Joyce, James, 2, 19, 22, 34, 46, 48, 50, 51, 116, 119, 120, 123, 172, 193
Juvenal (*Decimus Junius Juvenalis*), 308

Kafka, Franz, 41, 61, 152, 164, 182
Kallin, Anna, 61
Kamm, Josephine, 39
Keats, John, 303
Kenner, Hugh, 305
Kingsley, Charles, 298
Kipling, Rudyard, 41, 132, 133, 161, 196, 281–2, 305, 306
Knox, Ronald, 27, 90–1
Korda, Alexander, 10, 82, 178, 179
Kristeva, Julia, 21, 141, 236, 308, 314
Kubizek, August, 304

Lacan, Jacques, 130, 306
Landseer, Edwin Henry, 46
Larkin, Philip, 1, 6, 20, 21, 47, 49, 67, 213, 296
Lassner, Phyllis, 13, 48, 50, 59, 75, 76, 83, 89, 166, 176, 297, 302, 303, 308
Laval, Peter, 134, 307
Lawrence, D.H., 2, 41
Lear, Edward, 19, 20, 21, 46, 237, 245–6, 254, 314–15
Lecercle, Jean-Jacques, 21, 246
Lee, Hermione, 4, 184, 227, 257, 271, 285, 296
Lehmann, Rosamond, 47, 52, 57, 58

Lemprière, John, 81
Lenin, Vladimir Ilyich, 22
Lessing, Gotthold Ephraim, 101
Levertov, Denise, 296
Lewis, Cecil Day, 53, 298, 301
Lewis, Wyndham, 66, 136, 307
Light, Alison, 5, 6–7, 8, 9, 93, 94, 122, 236, 297, 299
Loos, Anita, 41, 46, 48, 49, 299
Lowell, Robert, 67
Lucan (*Marcus, Annaeus Lucanus*), 78
Luther, Martin, 91, 98, 102
Lutyens, Elizabeth, 61, 279

Macaulay, Thomas Babington, 177, 190–1, 193, 195, 226, 312
MacBeth, George, 62, 64
McBrien, William, 42, 51, 297, 298, 299, 313
MacGibbon, James, 61, 315
Machiavelli, Niccolò, 307
MacNeice, Louis, 25, 29, 53, 69, 80–1, 217, 298, 302
Madge, Charles, 47
Mahoney, John L., 28, 297
Mann, Thomas, 100
Manning, Olivia, 47, 57
Marinetti, F.T., 66
Marks, Peter, 298
Marshall, Rachel, 316
Martin, Eileen, 308
Martin, Kingsley, 54, 300
Marx, Karl, 56, 98, 115, 116, 168, 232
Matthews, Steven, 298
Medcalf, Stephen, 310
Mellor, David Alan, 302
Mendelson, Edward, 301
Mengham, Rod, 301
Merleau-Ponty, Maurice, 188
Metellus (*Q. Caecilius Metellus Pius Scipio*), 77
Meyers, Jeffrey, 307
Middleton, Tim, 94, 121–22, 131
Midgely, David, 301
Millard, Elaine, 5
Millard, Kenneth, 304
Milton, John, 9, 92, 119, 210, 313–14
Mitchell, W.J.T., 248
Mitchison, Naomi, 47, 54, 57, 60, 69, 116, 134, 275–6, 277, 307

Montefiore, Jan, 8, 259, 285–6, 296, 308
Moore, George, 41
Moraes, Dom, 299
Morris, John, 311
Morrison, Blake, 301, 312
Moses, 167
Mosley, Oswald, 75
Mottistone, Lord, 135
Muggeridge, Malcolm, 56
Mussolini, Benito, 22, 66, 164–5, 171

Napoleon (Napoleon Bonaparte), 93, 136
Nemesvari, Richard, 10–11, 13, 297, 300
Nichols, Robert, 50
Nietzsche, Friedrich, 21, 22, 66, 105, 106, 108, 228, 304, 305
Nordau, Max, 78
Nussbaum, Felicity, 4, 14, 286

Olson, Charles, 17
Orwell, George, 3, 44, 46, 54, 56, 80, 87, 124, 129, 135, 136, 187, 188, 196, 197, 202, 224, 296, 310
Owen, Wilfred, 90, 303

Parker, Dorothy, 21, 41, 48–9, 299
Parsons, Ian, 48, 50
Pater, Walter, 145, 161, 308
Patten, Brian, 64
Patterson, David, 21
Patton, Paul, 304
Pavlov, Ivan Petrovich, 138, 307
Pearson, Neville, 40, 62
Pétain, Henri Philippe Omer, 272, 307
Pilate, Pontius (*Pontius Pilate*), 80
Pinter, Harold, 201
Plain, Gill, 9–10, 27, 297, 307, 308
Plath, Sylvia, 14, 31, 61, 66, 67, 283, 297, 301
Plomer, William, 299
Poe, Edgar Allan, 19, 41
Pompey the Great (*Cneius Pompeius Magnus*), 71, 76–9, 80, 83, 99, 106, 127, 133, 134, 302, 311
Pope, Alexander, 24
Pound, Ezra, 2, 17, 22, 107, 108, 299, 302, 304–5, 308
Prickett, Stephen, 298
Priestley, J.B., 101, 122, 300
Pumphrey, Martin, 6, 7, 217, 259

Racine, Jean, 41, 123, 124, 146, 305
Raine, Kathleen, 296
Rankin, Arthur, 64, 296
Ransom, John Crowe, 62
Renault, Mary, 300
Rhys, Jean, 6
Richardson, Dorothy, 41, 47, 48, 58, 94
Ricks, Christopher, 218, 221, 301, 306
Rienzi, Cola di, 304
Roberts, Michael, 47
Robinson, Peter, 314
Rose, Ellen Cronan, 285
Rose, Jacqueline, 7, 297

St Anthony, 91, 102
Santayana, George, 46
Sappho, 296
Sarfatti, Margherita, 301
Sartre, Jean-Paul, 141, 187, 188
Schopenhauer, Arthur, 106
Scott-James, Marie, 300
Scott, Bonnie Kime, 297
Scott, Walter, 136
Severin, Laura, 9, 10, 11, 41, 42, 73, 74, 93, 94, 96–7, 115, 129, 176, 217–18, 235, 237–8, 240–2, 245, 247, 248, 251, 252, 253, 279, 296, 297, 299, 304, 308, 311, 315, 316
Shakespeare, William, 16, 19, 28, 41, 64, 78, 80, 97, 98, 100, 102, 123, 124, 133, 170–1, 175, 183, 184, 205–6, 221, 225, 255–8, 302, 306, 310, 312
Shakinovsky, Lynn J., 301
Sheridan, Dorothy, 307
Sherry, Vincent, 91, 303
Showalter, Elaine, 35
Silkin, Jon, 266, 312, 316
Simon, John, 134
Sitwell, Edith, 49, 57, 78, 207, 302, 313
Sitwell, Sacheverell, 78, 81
Skelton, Robin, 53, 54, 56
Smith, Charles (father to Stevie Smith), 32
Smith, Molly (sister to Stevie Smith), 27, 35, 36, 39, 41, 45, 68
Socrates, 208
Sophocles, 126, 219, 228, 264
Sorel, Georg, 66
Spalding, Frances, 22, 35, 39, 42, 43, 49, 56, 60, 77, 100, 101, 180, 195–6, 197, 231, 233, 269, 278, 281, 283, 296, 297, 298, 299, 300, 301, 314, 316
Spark, Muriel, 1, 296
Spear, Ethel (mother to Stevie Smith), 32–6, 39, 46
Spear, Madge (Aunt to Stevie Smith), 27, 33, 35, 36, 45, 68, 196, 303
Speer, Albert, 304
Spender, Stephen, 53, 56, 57, 141–2, 298
Spinoza, Baruch (Benedict), 41
Stalin, Joseph Vissarionovich, 24, 26, 79, 92, 185, 277, 302
Stein, Gertrude, 3, 13, 17–18, 33–4, 44, 49, 57, 73, 95, 127, 128, 259, 300
Steiner, George, 17, 187, 188
Sterne, Laurence, 14, 41, 71, 73
Sternlicht, Sanford, 6, 48 296, 297, 314
Stevenson, Sheryl, 217–18
Storey, Mark, 5, 242, 297
Struthers, Jan, 122
Sullivan, Arthur (Gilbert and Sullivan), 222
Swift, Jonathan, 43, 85–6, 92, 186, 306
Symons, Julian, 297

Tatham, Michael, 26, 28
Taylor, Stephen, 121
Tennyson, Alfred (Lord), 84, 93, 144, 212, 253, 313
Thaddeus, Janice, 5
Thomas, Dylan, 47, 291–2
Thomas, R.S., 297
Thompson, E.P., 188, 312
Thompson, Frances, 41, 269
Thomson, Clive, 297
Thurber, James, 20, 21
Thwaite, Anthony, 68, 301
Tolstoy, Leo, 125
Torquemada, Tomás de, 92, 95–6, 190, 272
Treece, Henry, 309
Troubridge, Lady (Una Vincenzo), 45
Tzara, Tristan, 73

Upward, Edward, 53, 116, 141–2, 159

Vasseleu, Cathryn, 304
Victoria (Queen Victoria), 27, 304, 313

Virgil (*Publius Vergilius Maro*), 162
Voris, Renate, 3, 6

Wagner, Richard, 101, 304
Walton, William, 313
Ward, Mrs. Humphrey, 27, 72
Warner, Marina, 16
Warner, Sylvia Townsend, 57
Washbourne, Mona, 314
Watts, Janet, 45, 104, 308
Waugh, Evelyn, 20
Waugh, Patricia, 2, 3
Wayne, John, 39
West, Douglas, 300
West, Rebecca, 11
Whitemore, Hugh, 68, 219
Whitford, Frank, 143–4, 145
Whitman, Walt, 17, 298
Wicke, Jennifer, 310
Williams, Clifford, 314
Williams, Jonathan, 224, 314

Williams, Keith, 298
Williams, Raymond, 18, 142, 309
Williams, William Carlos, 17, 227
Wilson, Jean Moorcraft, 59
Winship, Janice, 247, 315
Wittgenstein, Ludwig, 284
Wolff, Janet, 2, 12
Wolosky, Shira, 313
Wood, Paul, 308
Woolf, Leonard, 53
Woolf, Virginia, 1, 3, 12, 39, 41,
    44, 48, 50, 53, 59, 75, 80, 89,
    93, 94, 97, 107, 135, 139, 141,
    155, 156, 183, 218, 300, 303
Wordsworth, William, 270, 284
Wright, David, 62, 301

Yeats, W.B., 15, 62, 284, 298
Younghusband, Francis
    Edward, 310
Younghusband, G.J., 310